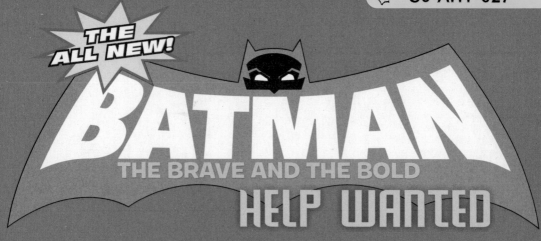

THE ALL NEW!
BATMAN
THE BRAVE AND THE BOLD
HELP WANTED

SHOLLY FISCH Writer
RICK BURCHETT DAN DAVIS DARIO BRIZUELA ETHEN BEAVERS Artists
GABE ELTAEB GUY MAJOR Colorists
DEZI SIENTY SAL CIPRIANO Letterers
RICK BURCHETT, DAN DAVIS & GABE ELTAEB Cover Artists

BATMAN created by BOB KANE

Jim Chadwick Editor – Original Series
Chynna Clugston Flores Assistant Editor – Original Series
Robin Wildman Editor
Robbin Brosterman Design Director – Books

Bob Harras VP – Editor-in-Chief

Diane Nelson President
Dan DiDio and **Jim Lee** Co-Publishers
Geoff Johns Chief Creative Officer
John Rood Executive VP – Sales, Marketing and Business Development
Amy Genkins Senior VP – Business and Legal Affairs
Nairi Gardiner Senior VP – Finance
Jeff Boison VP – Publishing Operations
Mark Chiarello VP – Art Direction and Design
John Cunningham VP – Marketing
Terri Cunningham VP – Talent Relations and Services
Alison Gill Senior VP – Manufacturing and Operations
Hank Kanalz Senior VP – Digital
Jay Kogan VP – Business and Legal Affairs, Publishing
Jack Mahan VP – Business Affairs, Talent
Nick Napolitano VP – Manufacturing Administration
Sue Pohja VP – Book Sales
Courtney Simmons Senior VP – Publicity
Bob Wayne Senior VP – Sales

THE ALL NEW BATMAN – THE BRAVE AND THE BOLD VOLUME 2: HELP WANTED

DC Comics, 1700 Broadway, New York, NY 10019
A Warner Bros. Entertainment Company.
Printed by RR Donnelley, Willard, OH, USA. 7/20/12. First Printing.
ISBN: 978-1-4012-3524-6

Library of Congress Cataloging-in-Publication Data

The all-new Batman : the brave and the bold volume two : help wanted /
Sholly Fisch ... [et al.].
      p. cm.
   "Originally published in single magazine form in ALL-NEW BATMAN: THE BRAVE
AND THE BOLD 7-12."
   ISBN 978-1-4012-3524-6
   1. Graphic novels. I. Fisch, Sholly. II. Title: Brave and the bold volume
two. III. Title: Help wanted.
   PN6728.B36A45 2012
   741.5'973–dc23
                              2012016124

SUSTAINABLE FORESTRY INITIATIVE   Certified Sourcing
www.sfiprogram.org
SFI-01042
APPLIES TO TEXT STOCK ONLY

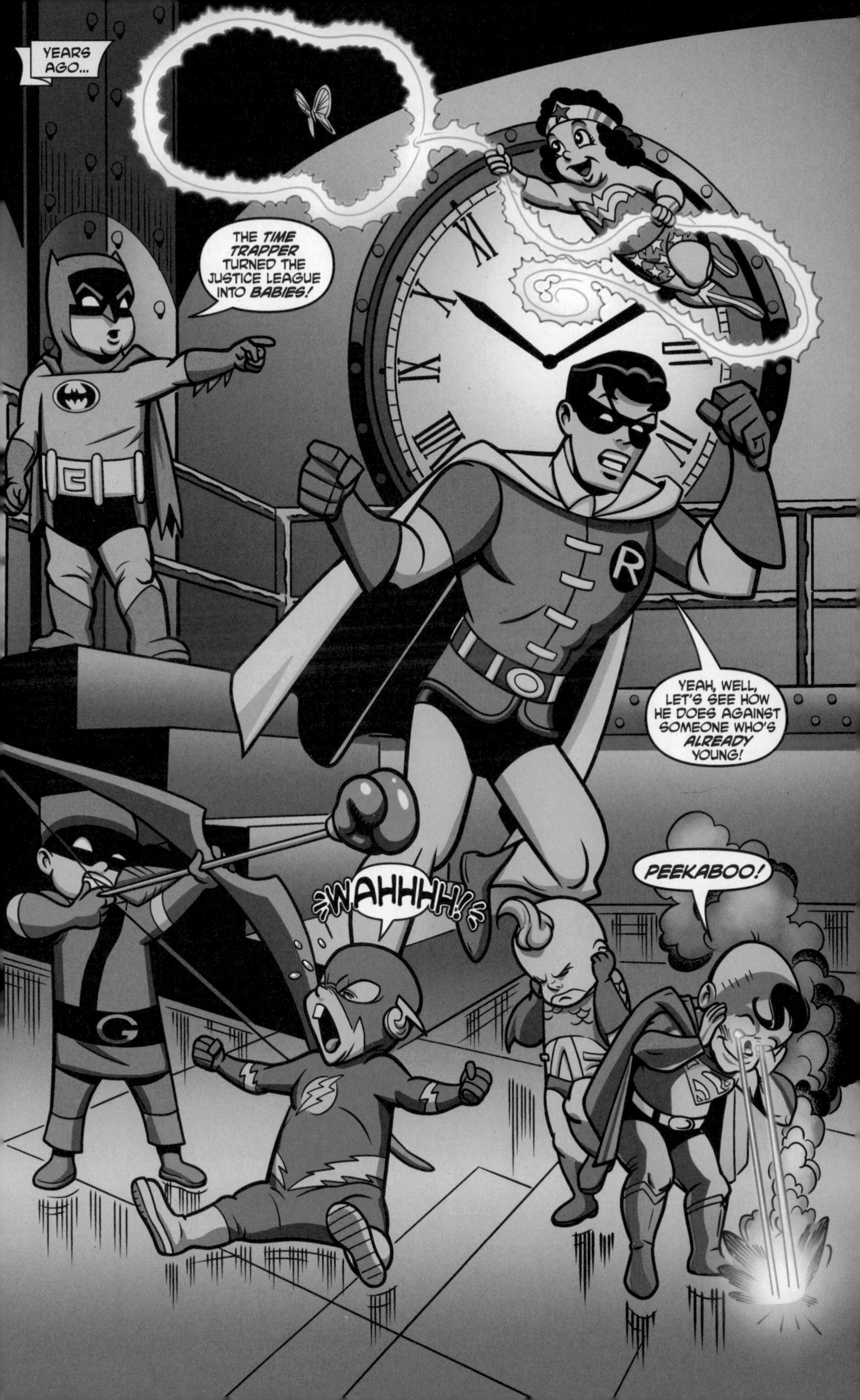
YEARS AGO...
THE TIME TRAPPER TURNED THE JUSTICE LEAGUE INTO BABIES!
YEAH, WELL, LET'S SEE HOW HE DOES AGAINST SOMEONE WHO'S ALREADY YOUNG!
WAHHHH!
PEEKABOO!

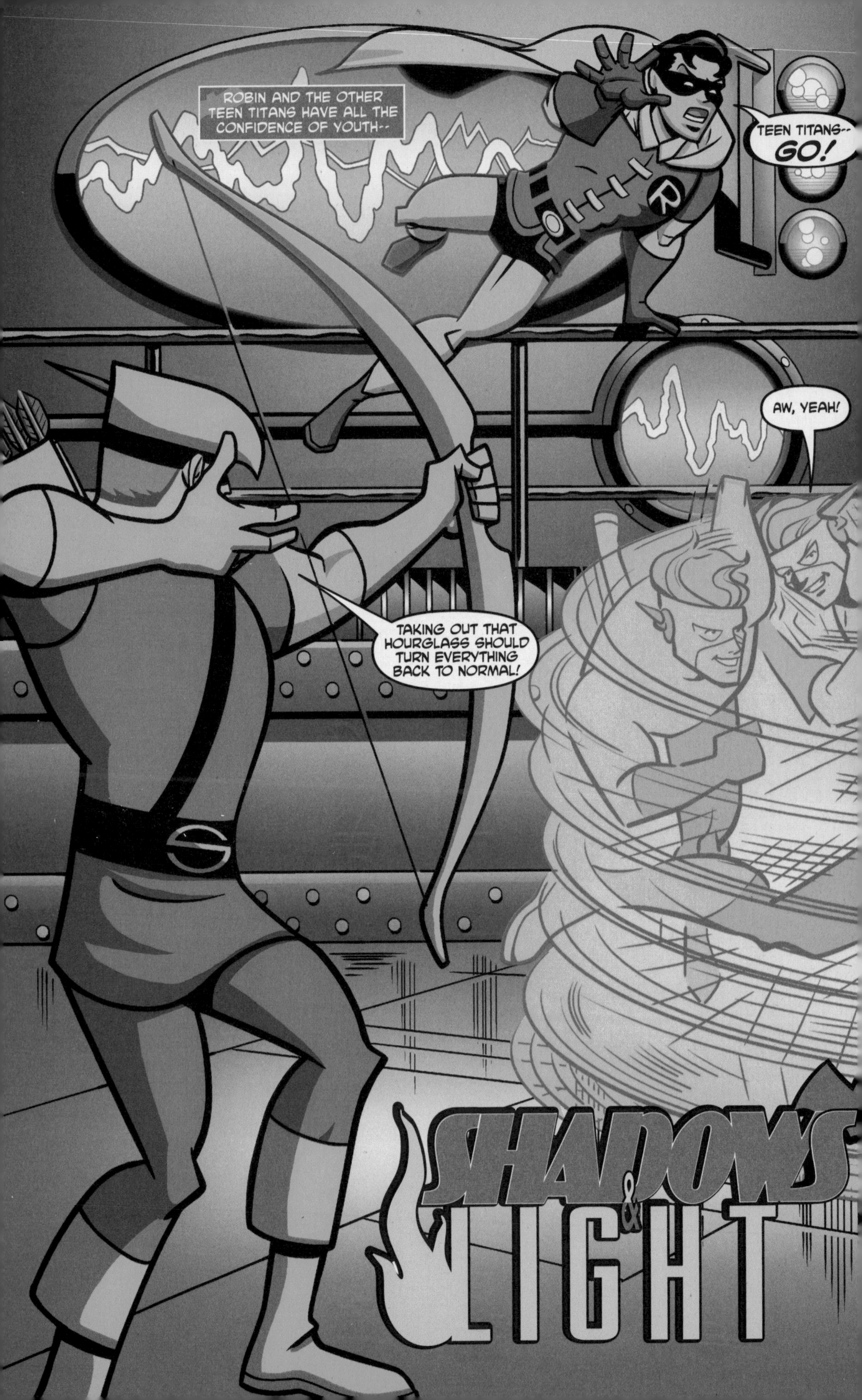
ROBIN AND THE OTHER TEEN TITANS HAVE ALL THE CONFIDENCE OF YOUTH--
TEEN TITANS-- GO!
AW, YEAH!
TAKING OUT THAT HOURGLASS SHOULD TURN EVERYTHING BACK TO NORMAL!
SHADOWS & LIGHT

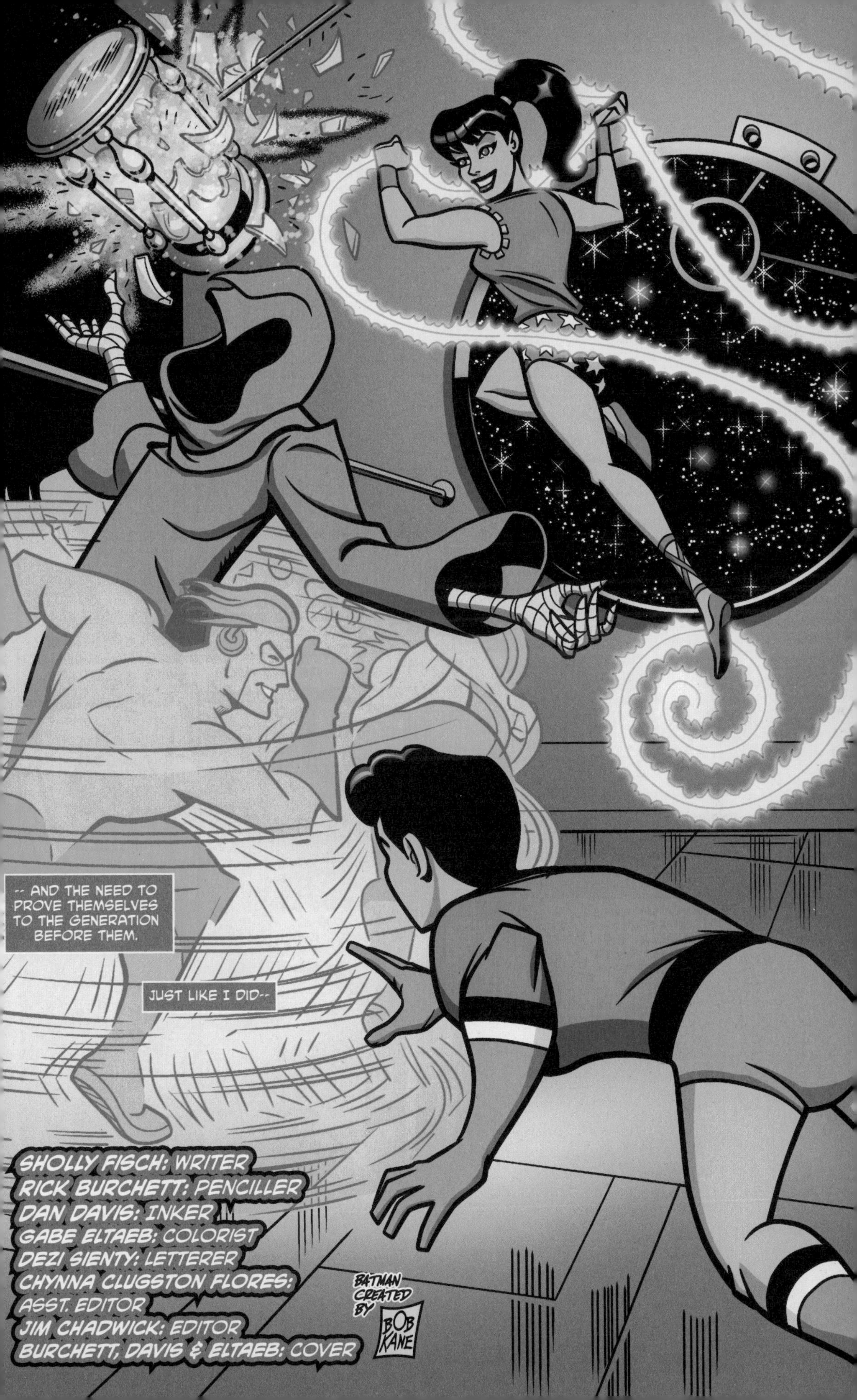
-- AND THE NEED TO PROVE THEMSELVES TO THE GENERATION BEFORE THEM.
JUST LIKE I DID--
SHOLLY FISCH: WRITER
RICK BURCHETT: PENCILLER
DAN DAVIS: INKER
GABE ELTAEB: COLORIST
DEZI SIENTY: LETTERER
CHYNNA CLUGSTON FLORES: ASST. EDITOR
JIM CHADWICK: EDITOR
BURCHETT, DAVIS & ELTAEB: COVER
BATMAN CREATED BY BOB KANE

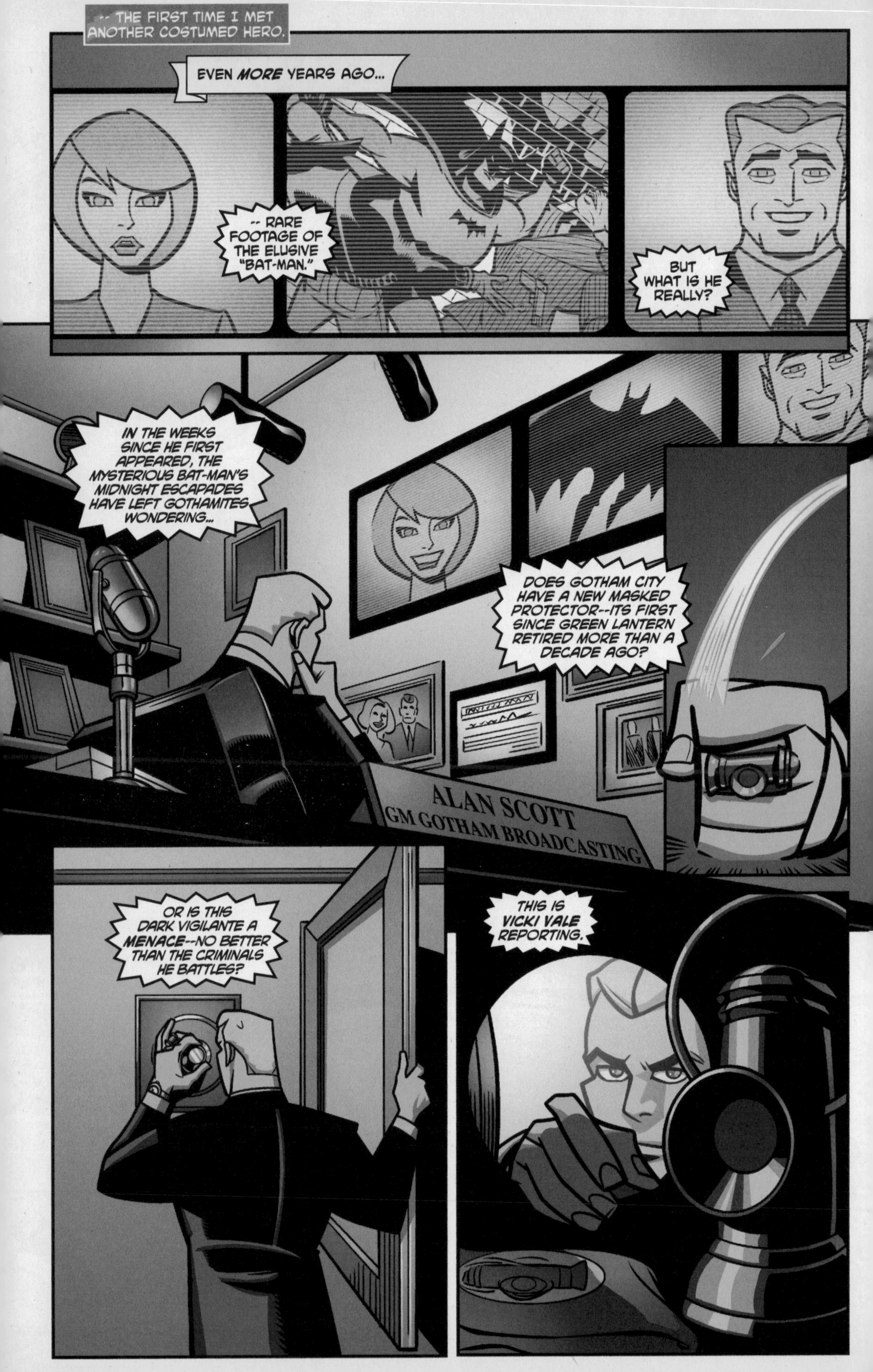
-- THE FIRST TIME I MET ANOTHER COSTUMED HERO.
EVEN *MORE* YEARS AGO...
-- RARE FOOTAGE OF THE ELUSIVE "BAT-MAN."
BUT WHAT IS HE REALLY?
IN THE WEEKS SINCE HE FIRST APPEARED, THE MYSTERIOUS BAT-MAN'S MIDNIGHT ESCAPADES HAVE LEFT GOTHAMITES WONDERING...
DOES GOTHAM CITY HAVE A NEW MASKED PROTECTOR--ITS FIRST SINCE GREEN LANTERN RETIRED MORE THAN A DECADE AGO?
ALAN SCOTT
GM GOTHAM BROADCASTING
OR IS THIS DARK VIGILANTE A *MENACE*--NO BETTER THAN THE CRIMINALS HE BATTLES?
THIS IS *VICKI VALE* REPORTING.

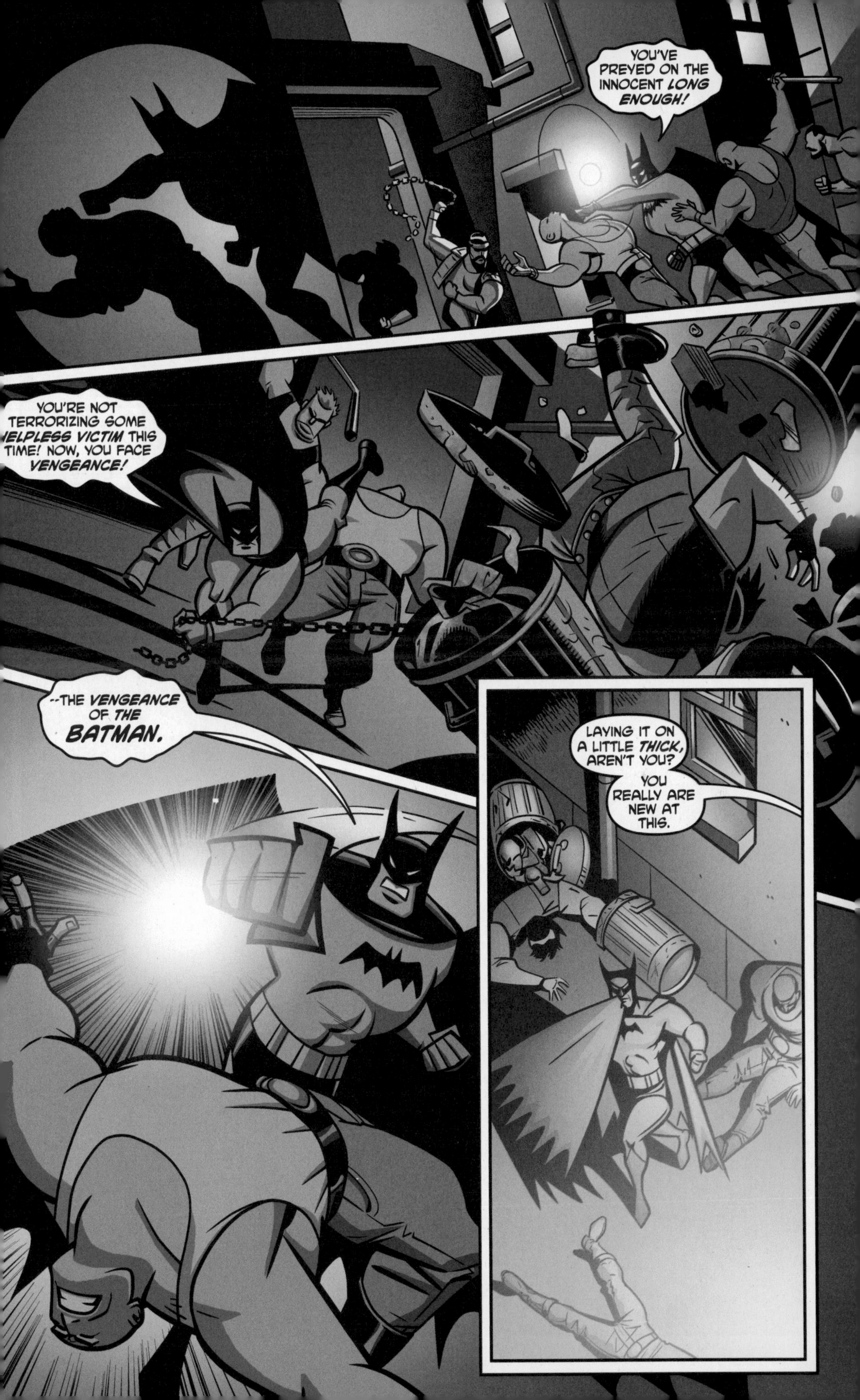

YOU'VE PREYED ON THE INNOCENT LONG ENOUGH!
YOU'RE NOT TERRORIZING SOME HELPLESS VICTIM THIS TIME! NOW, YOU FACE VENGEANCE!
--THE VENGEANCE OF THE BATMAN.
LAYING IT ON A LITTLE THICK, AREN'T YOU?
YOU REALLY ARE NEW AT THIS.

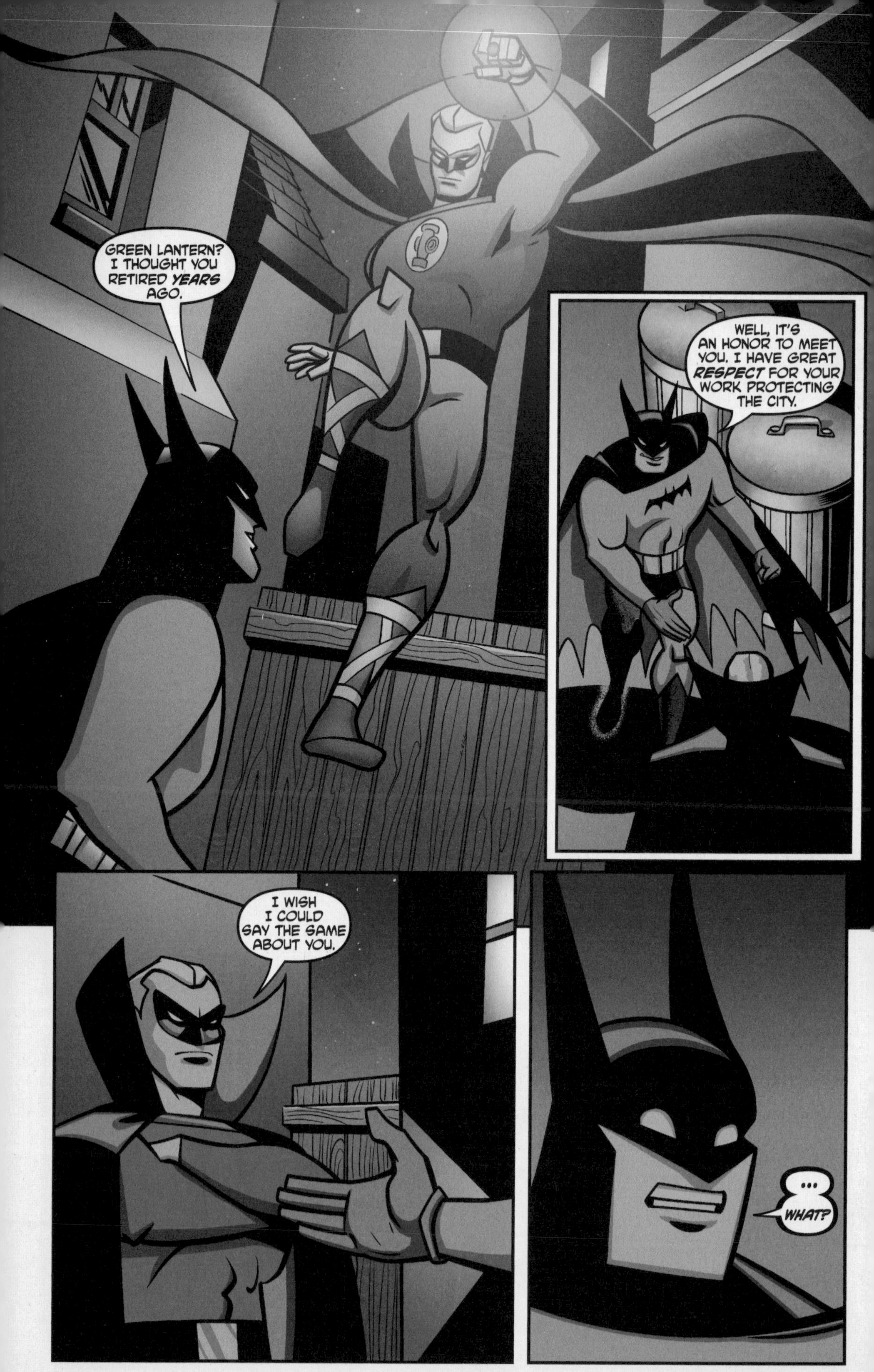
GREEN LANTERN? I THOUGHT YOU RETIRED YEARS AGO.
WELL, IT'S AN HONOR TO MEET YOU. I HAVE GREAT RESPECT FOR YOUR WORK PROTECTING THE CITY.
I WISH I COULD SAY THE SAME ABOUT YOU.
...WHAT?

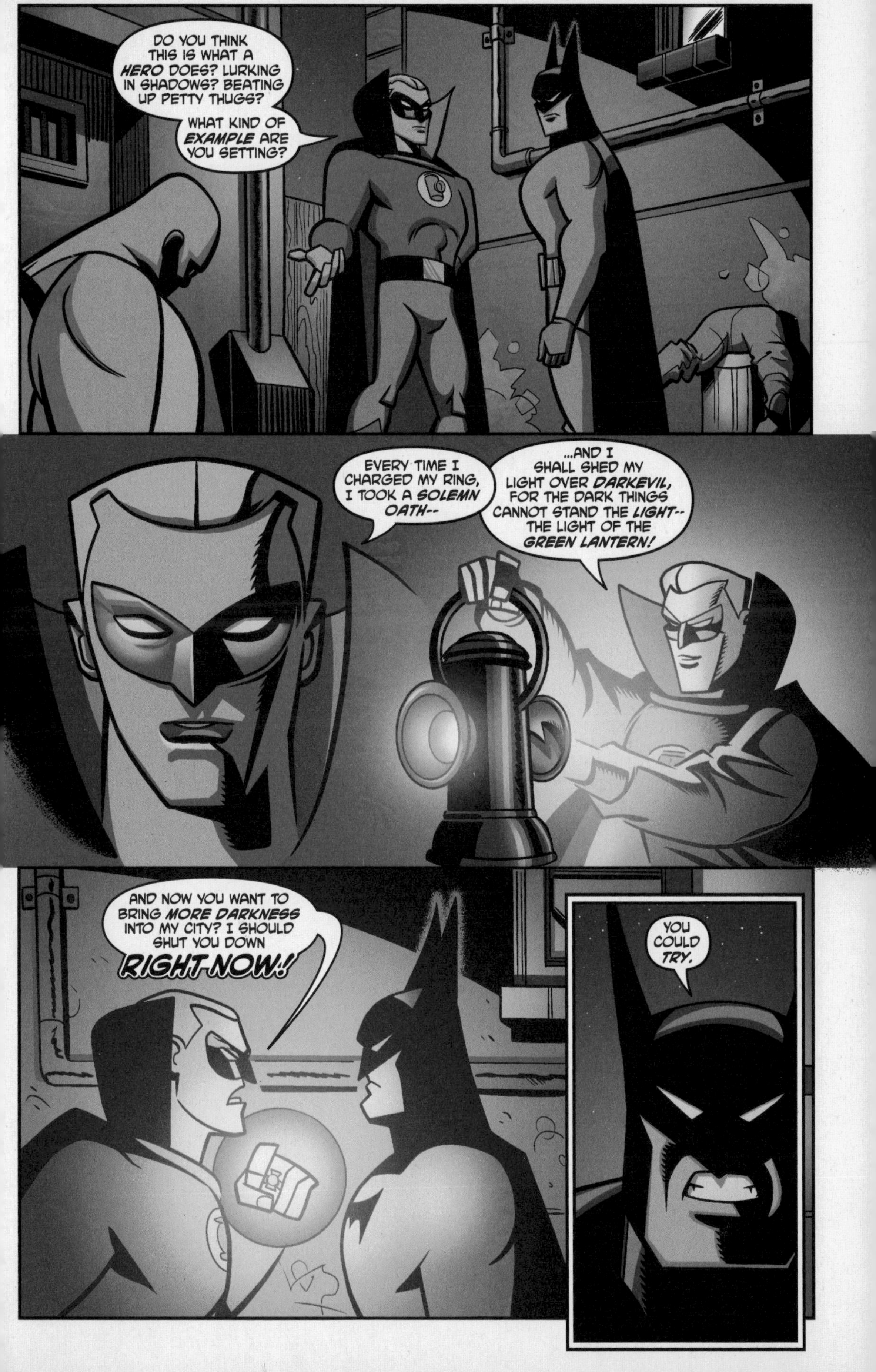
DO YOU THINK THIS IS WHAT A HERO DOES? LURKING IN SHADOWS? BEATING UP PETTY THUGS?
WHAT KIND OF EXAMPLE ARE YOU SETTING?
EVERY TIME I CHARGED MY RING, I TOOK A SOLEMN OATH--
...AND I SHALL SHED MY LIGHT OVER DARKEVIL, FOR THE DARK THINGS CANNOT STAND THE LIGHT-- THE LIGHT OF THE GREEN LANTERN!
AND NOW YOU WANT TO BRING MORE DARKNESS INTO MY CITY? I SHOULD SHUT YOU DOWN
RIGHT NOW!
YOU COULD TRY.

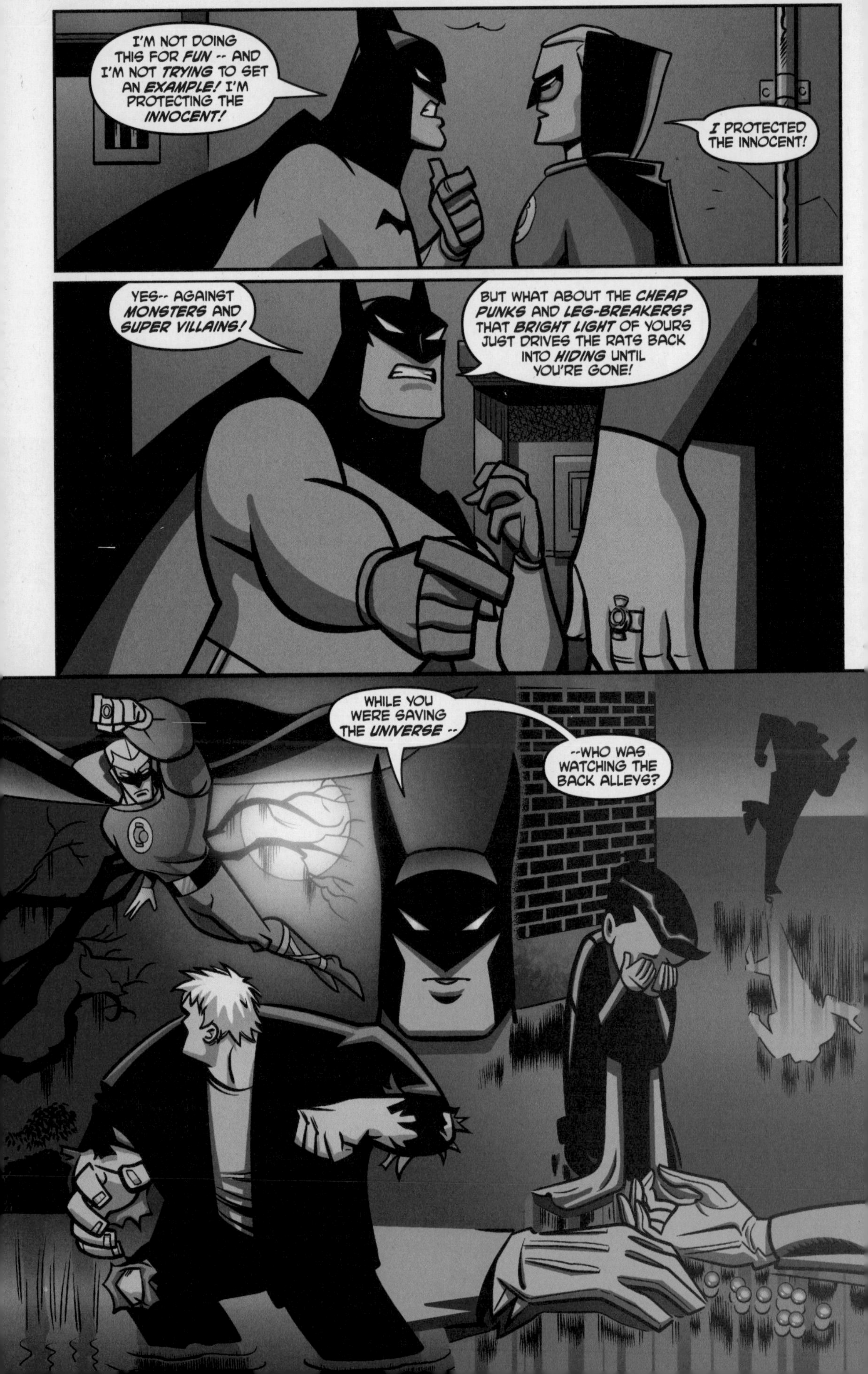
I'M NOT DOING THIS FOR FUN -- AND I'M NOT TRYING TO SET AN EXAMPLE! I'M PROTECTING THE INNOCENT!
I PROTECTED THE INNOCENT!
YES-- AGAINST MONSTERS AND SUPER VILLAINS!
BUT WHAT ABOUT THE CHEAP PUNKS AND LEG-BREAKERS? THAT BRIGHT LIGHT OF YOURS JUST DRIVES THE RATS BACK INTO HIDING UNTIL YOU'RE GONE!
WHILE YOU WERE SAVING THE UNIVERSE --
--WHO WAS WATCHING THE BACK ALLEYS?

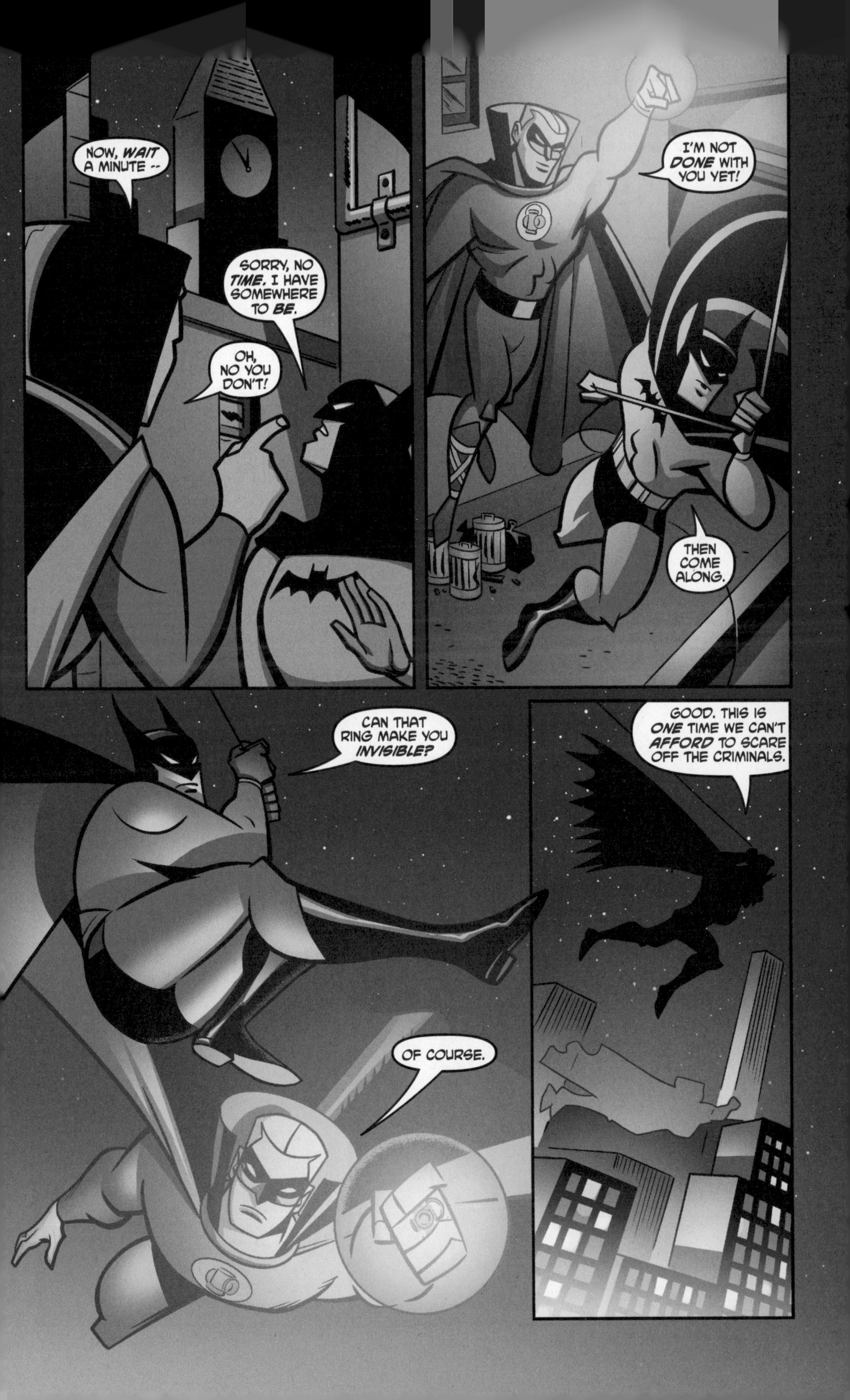
NOW, WAIT A MINUTE --
SORRY, NO TIME. I HAVE SOMEWHERE TO BE.
OH, NO YOU DON'T!
I'M NOT DONE WITH YOU YET!
THEN COME ALONG.
CAN THAT RING MAKE YOU INVISIBLE?
OF COURSE.
GOOD. THIS IS ONE TIME WE CAN'T AFFORD TO SCARE OFF THE CRIMINALS.

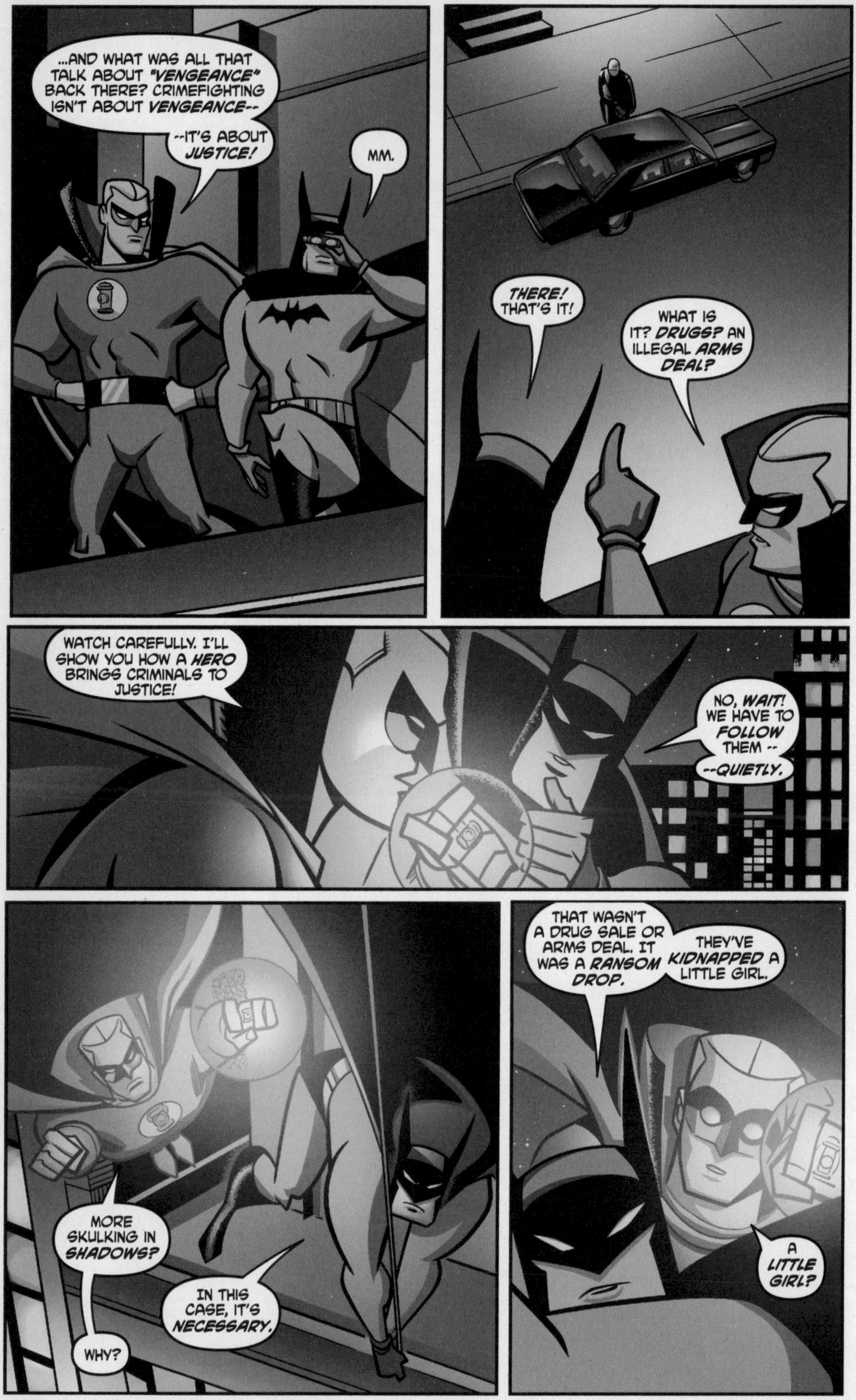

...AND WHAT WAS ALL THAT TALK ABOUT "VENGEANCE" BACK THERE? CRIMEFIGHTING ISN'T ABOUT VENGEANCE--
--IT'S ABOUT JUSTICE!
MM.
THERE! THAT'S IT!
WHAT IS IT? DRUGS? AN ILLEGAL ARMS DEAL?
WATCH CAREFULLY. I'LL SHOW YOU HOW A HERO BRINGS CRIMINALS TO JUSTICE!
NO, WAIT! WE HAVE TO FOLLOW THEM --
--QUIETLY.
MORE SKULKING IN SHADOWS?
IN THIS CASE, IT'S NECESSARY.
WHY?
THAT WASN'T A DRUG SALE OR ARMS DEAL. IT WAS A RANSOM DROP.
THEY'VE KIDNAPPED A LITTLE GIRL.
A LITTLE GIRL?

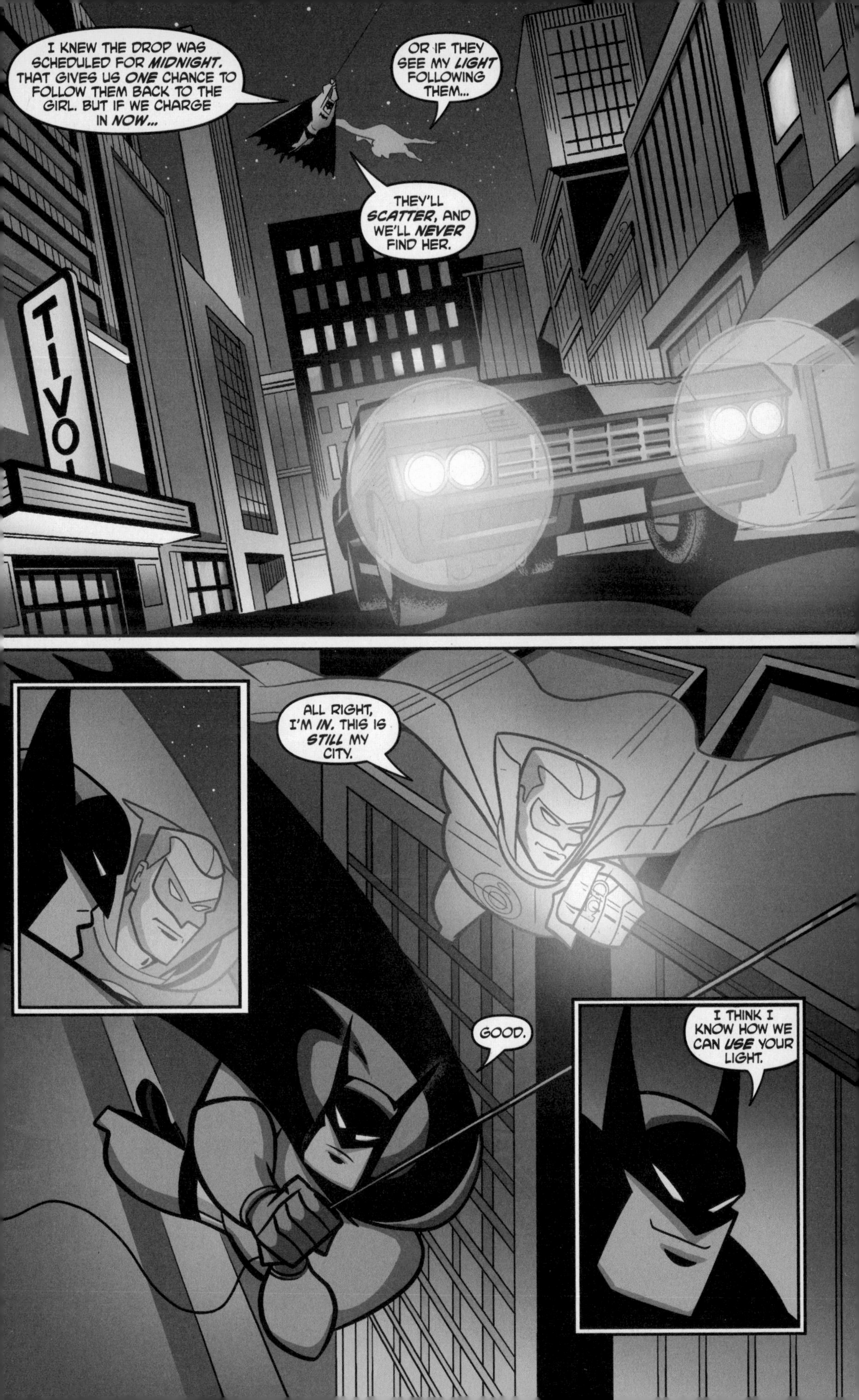
I KNEW THE DROP WAS SCHEDULED FOR MIDNIGHT. THAT GIVES US ONE CHANCE TO FOLLOW THEM BACK TO THE GIRL. BUT IF WE CHARGE IN NOW...
OR IF THEY SEE MY LIGHT FOLLOWING THEM...
THEY'LL SCATTER, AND WE'LL NEVER FIND HER.
TIVOL
ALL RIGHT, I'M IN. THIS IS STILL MY CITY.
GOOD.
I THINK I KNOW HOW WE CAN USE YOUR LIGHT.

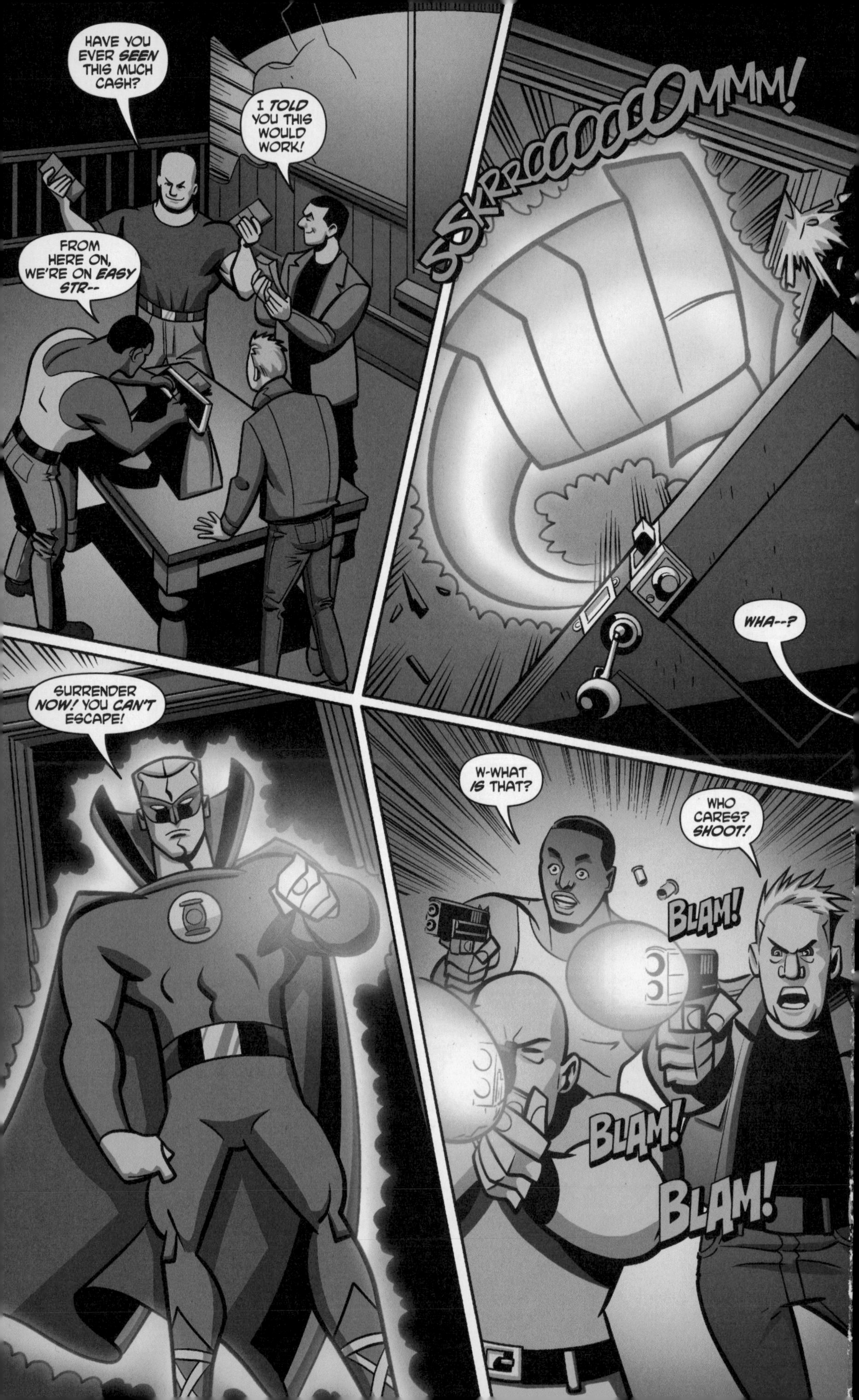
HAVE YOU EVER SEEN THIS MUCH CASH?
I TOLD YOU THIS WOULD WORK!
FROM HERE ON, WE'RE ON EASY STR--
SSKRROOOOOOOMMM!
WHA--?
SURRENDER NOW! YOU CAN'T ESCAPE!
W-WHAT IS THAT?
WHO CARES? SHOOT!
BLAM!
BLAM!
BLAM!

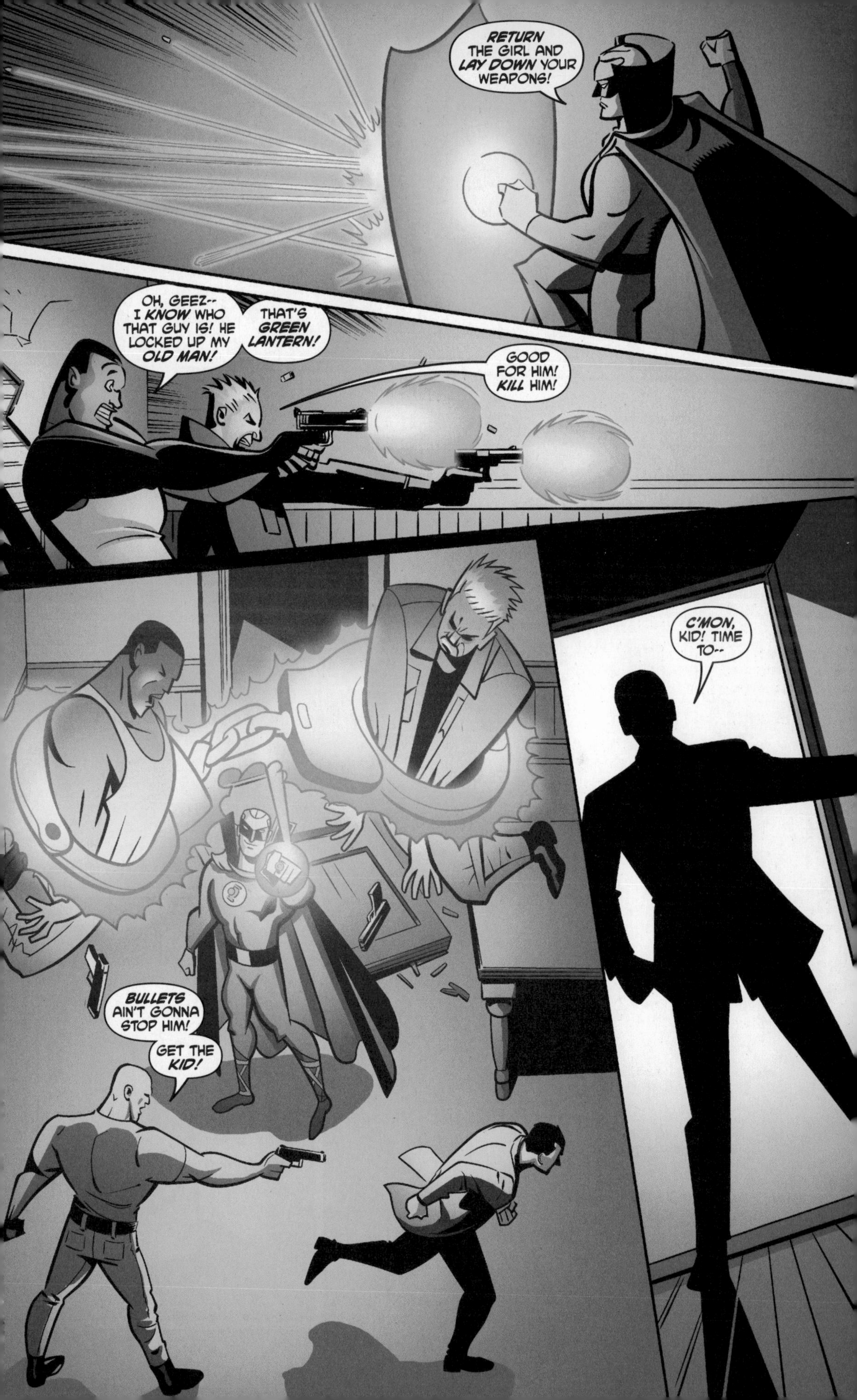

RETURN THE GIRL AND LAY DOWN YOUR WEAPONS!
OH, GEEZ-- I KNOW WHO THAT GUY IS! HE LOCKED UP MY OLD MAN!
THAT'S GREEN LANTERN!
GOOD FOR HIM! KILL HIM!
C'MON, KID! TIME TO--
BULLETS AIN'T GONNA STOP HIM!
GET THE KID!

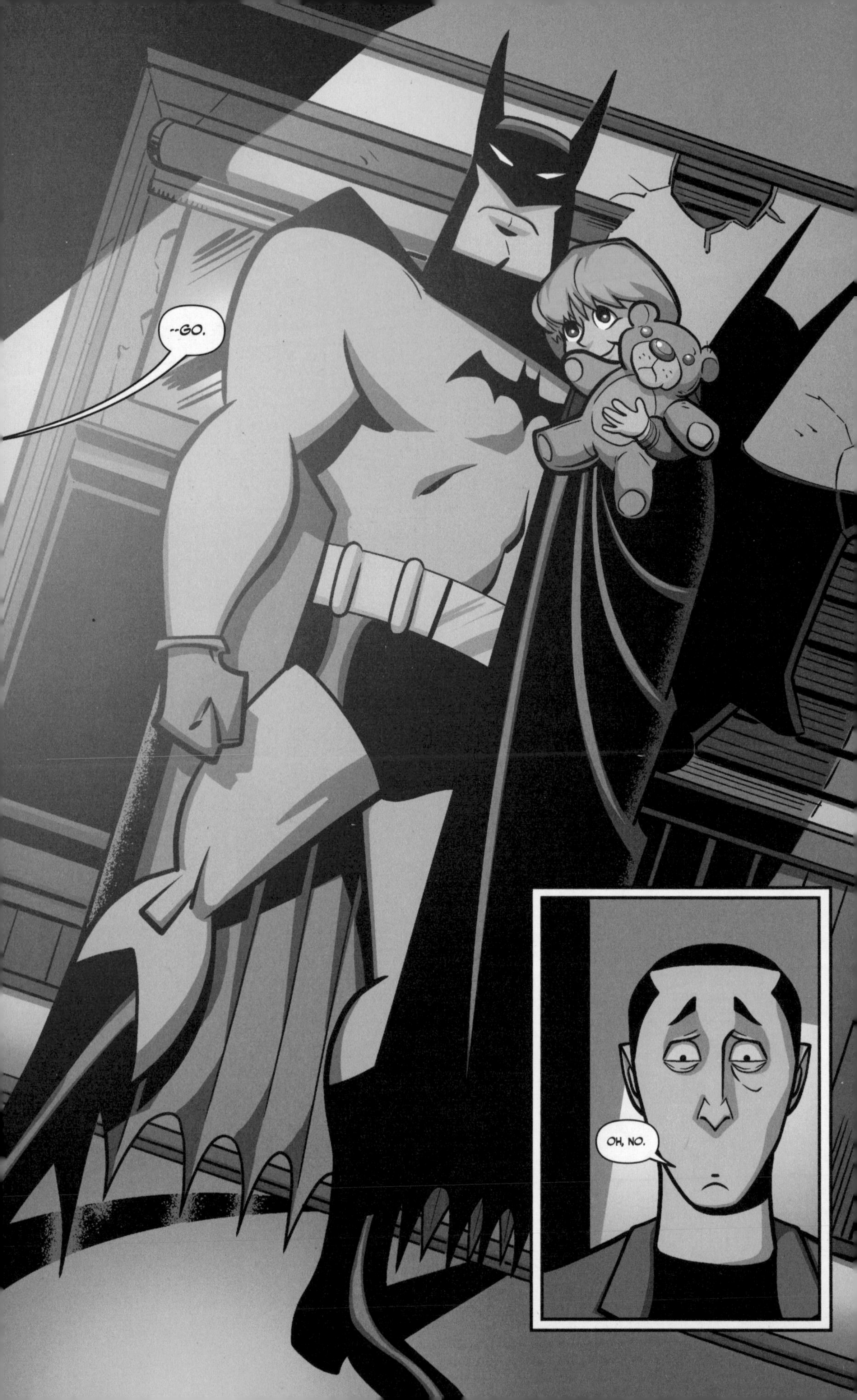
--GO.
OH, NO.

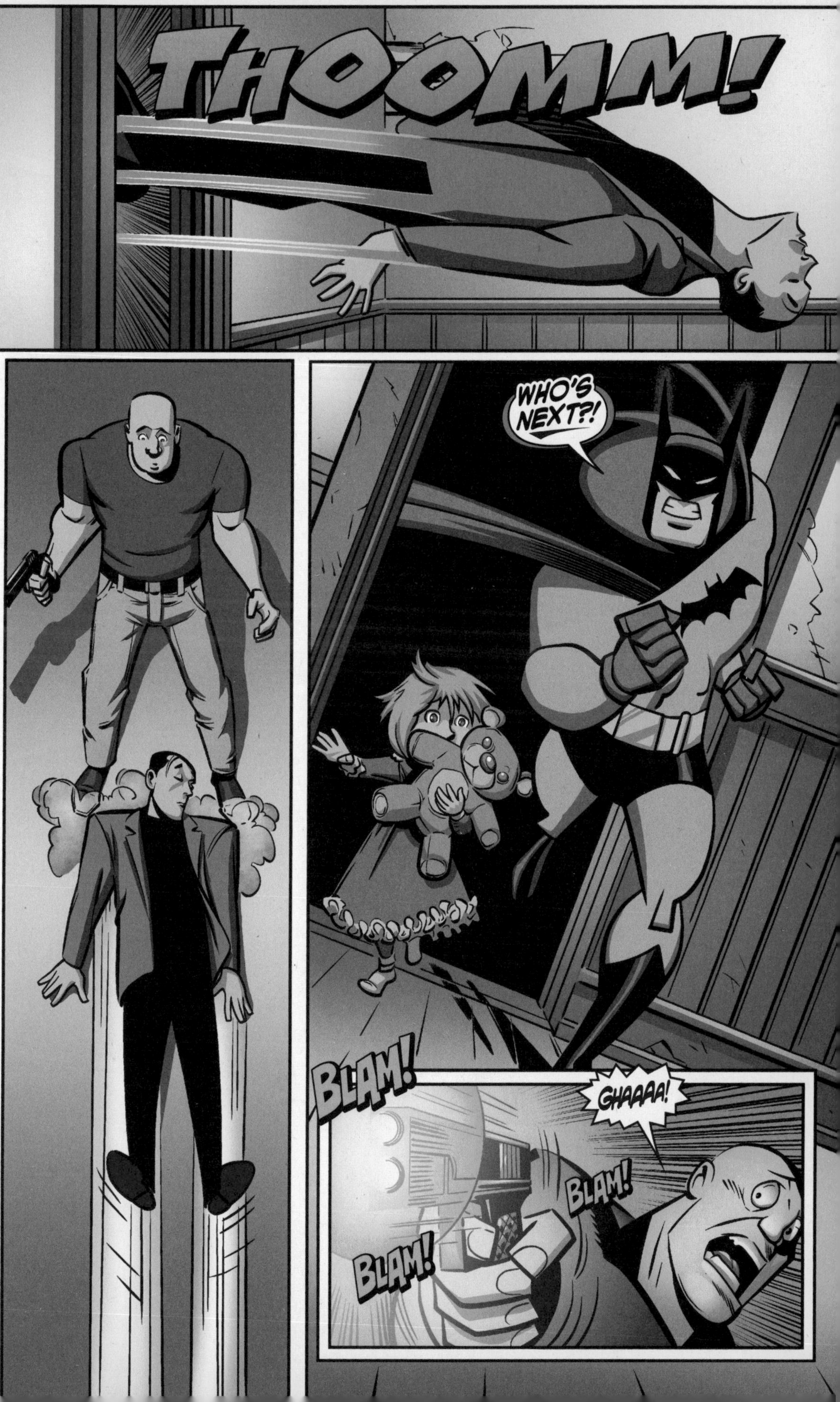
THOOMM!
WHO'S NEXT?!
BLAM!
GHAAAA!
BLAM!
BLAM!

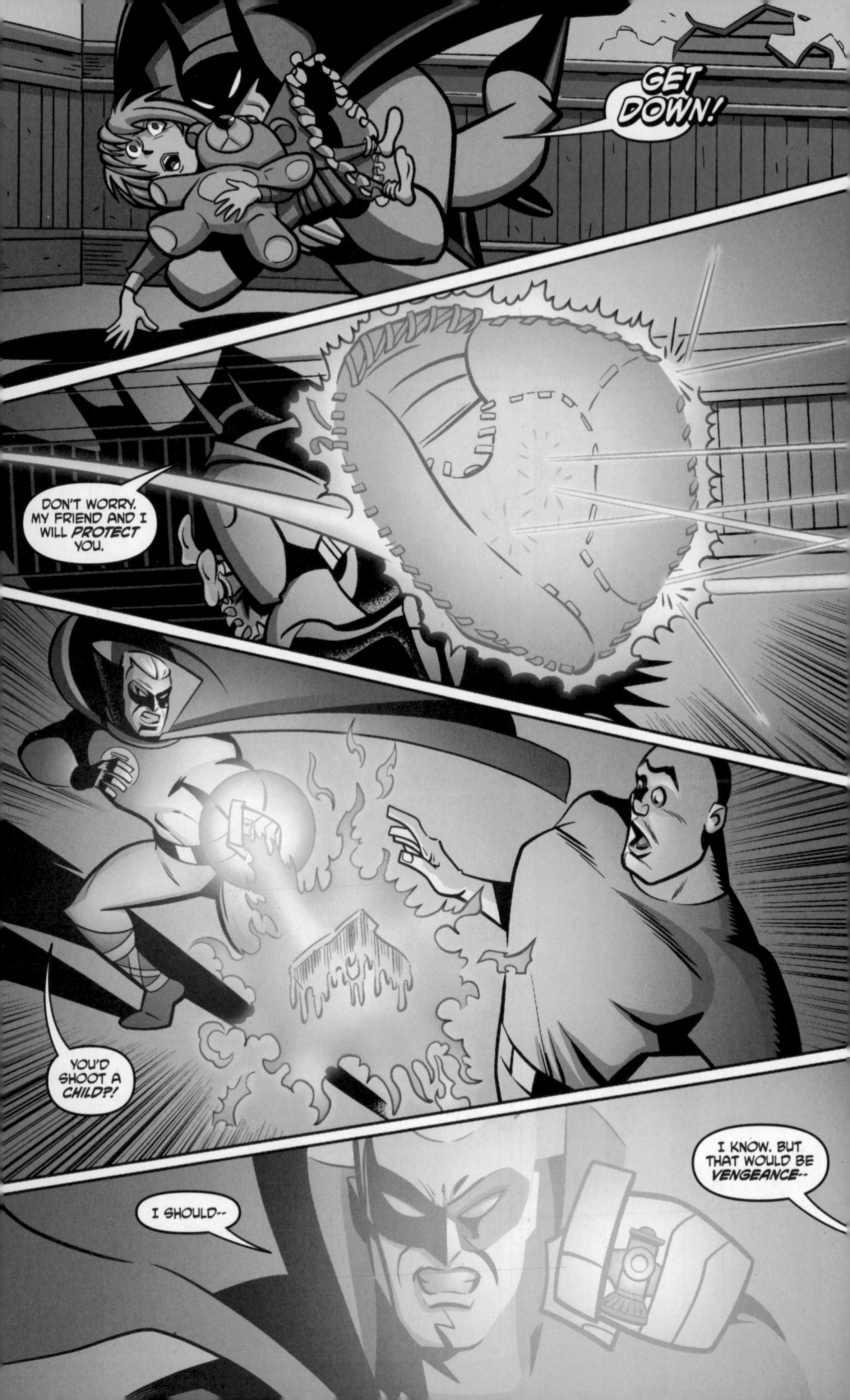
GET DOWN!
DON'T WORRY. MY FRIEND AND I WILL *PROTECT* YOU.
YOU'D SHOOT A *CHILD?!*
I SHOULD--
I KNOW. BUT THAT WOULD BE *VENGEANCE--*

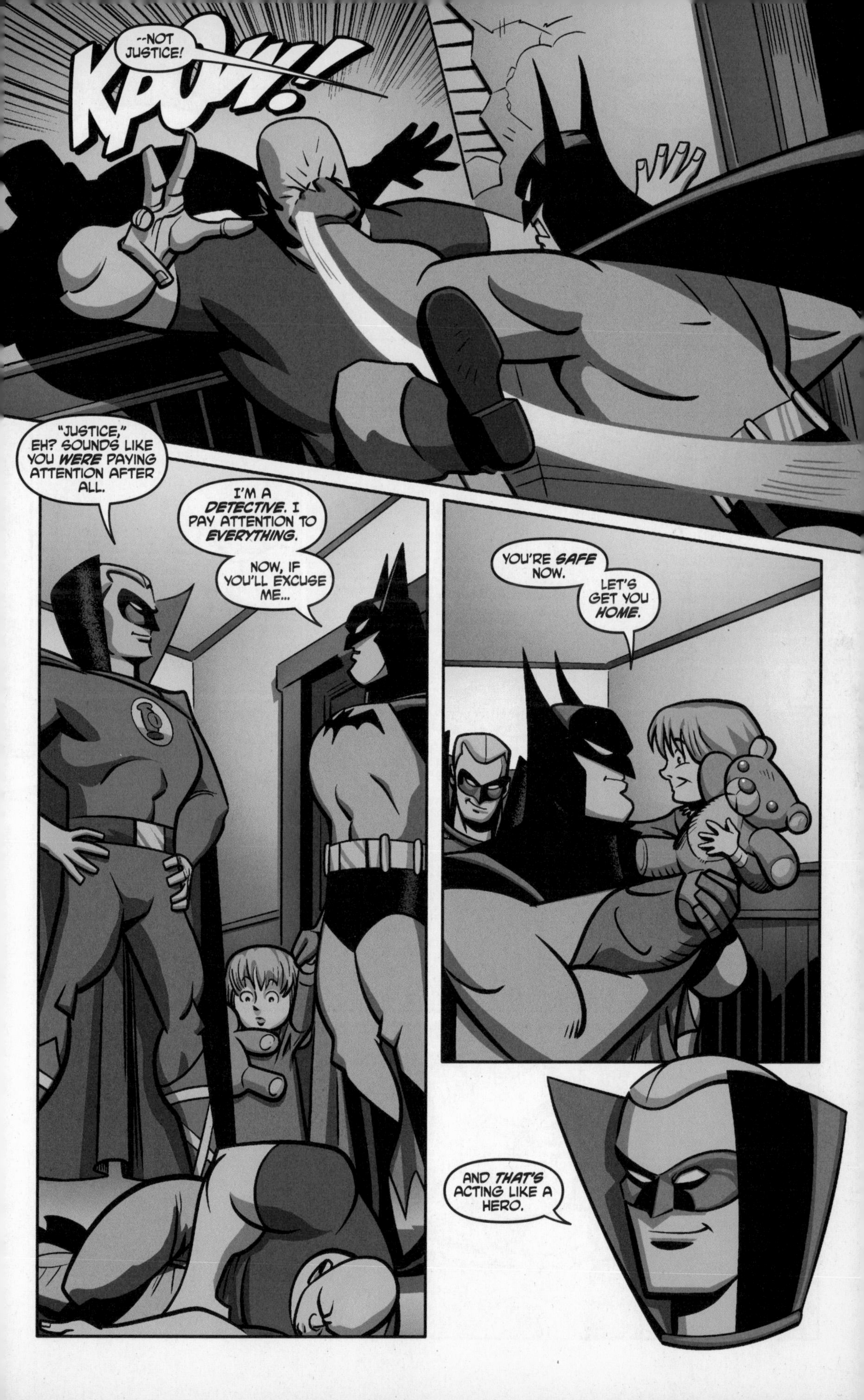
KPOW!!
--NOT JUSTICE!
"JUSTICE," EH? SOUNDS LIKE YOU WERE PAYING ATTENTION AFTER ALL.
I'M A DETECTIVE. I PAY ATTENTION TO EVERYTHING.
NOW, IF YOU'LL EXCUSE ME...
YOU'RE SAFE NOW.
LET'S GET YOU HOME.
AND THAT'S ACTING LIKE A HERO.

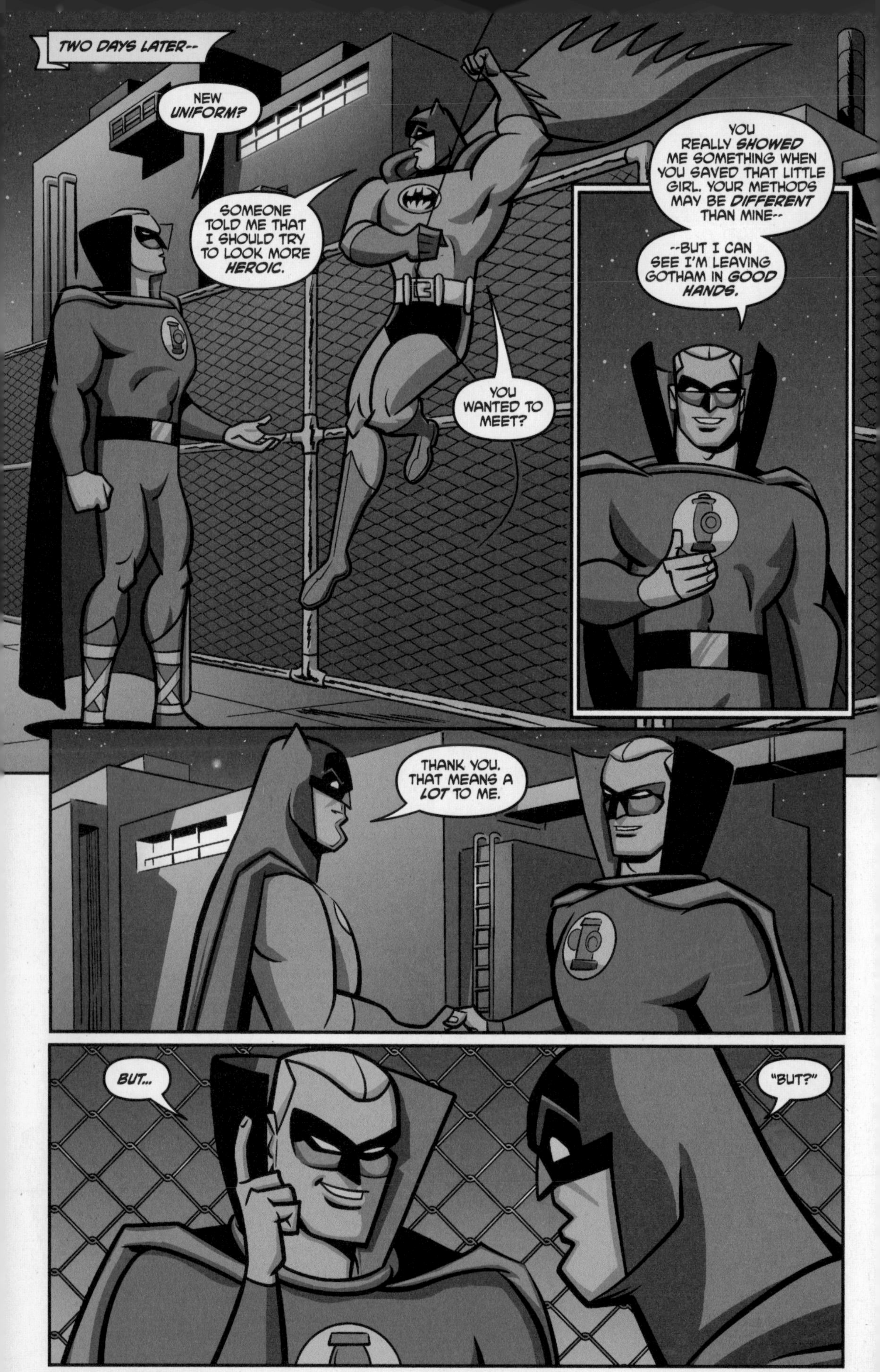
TWO DAYS LATER--
NEW UNIFORM?
SOMEONE TOLD ME THAT I SHOULD TRY TO LOOK MORE HEROIC.
YOU WANTED TO MEET?
YOU REALLY SHOWED ME SOMETHING WHEN YOU SAVED THAT LITTLE GIRL. YOUR METHODS MAY BE DIFFERENT THAN MINE--
--BUT I CAN SEE I'M LEAVING GOTHAM IN GOOD HANDS.
THANK YOU. THAT MEANS A LOT TO ME.
BUT...
"BUT?"

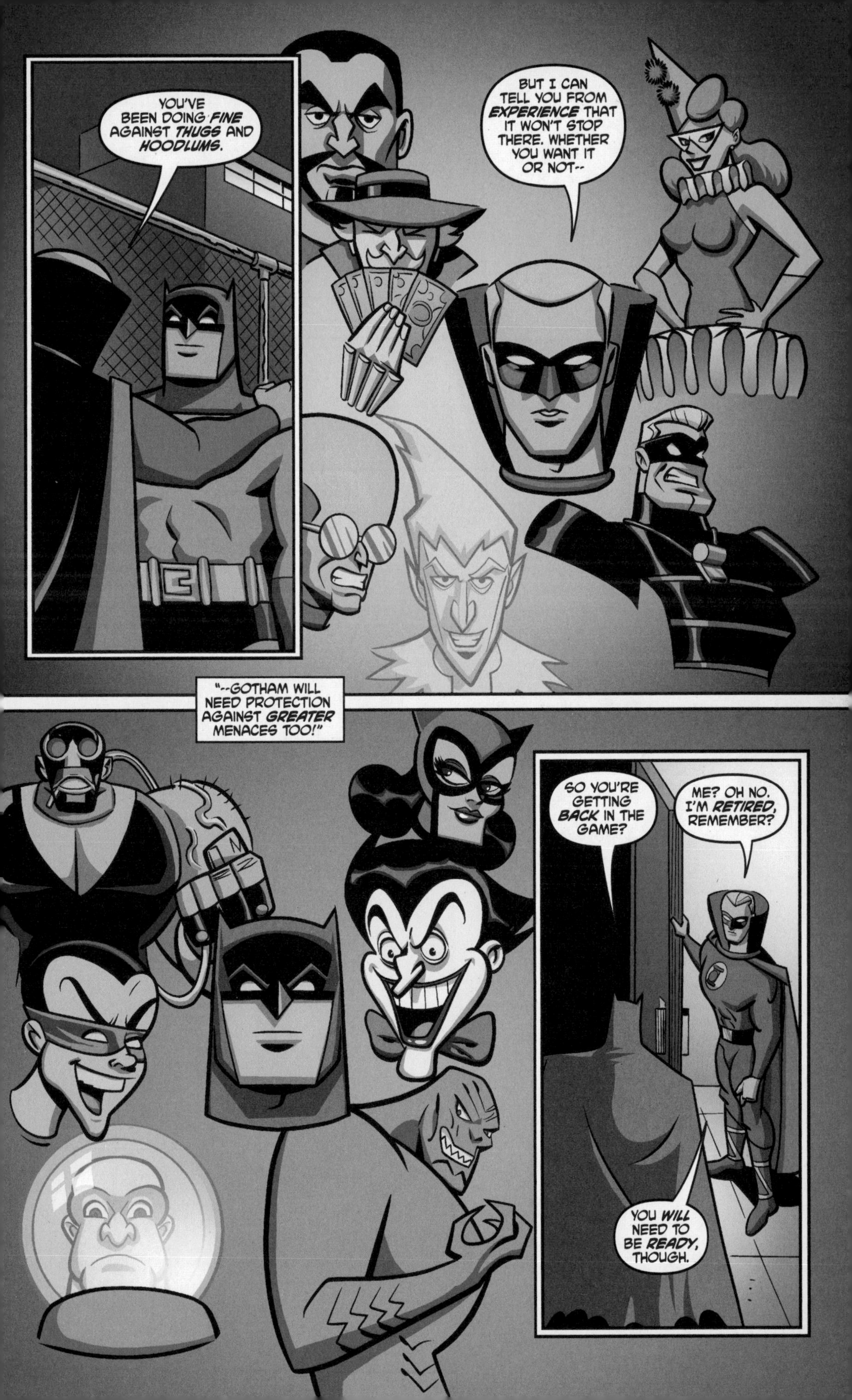

YOU'VE BEEN DOING FINE AGAINST THUGS AND HOODLUMS.
BUT I CAN TELL YOU FROM EXPERIENCE THAT IT WON'T STOP THERE. WHETHER YOU WANT IT OR NOT--
"--GOTHAM WILL NEED PROTECTION AGAINST GREATER MENACES TOO!"
SO YOU'RE GETTING BACK IN THE GAME?
ME? OH NO. I'M RETIRED, REMEMBER?
YOU WILL NEED TO BE READY, THOUGH.

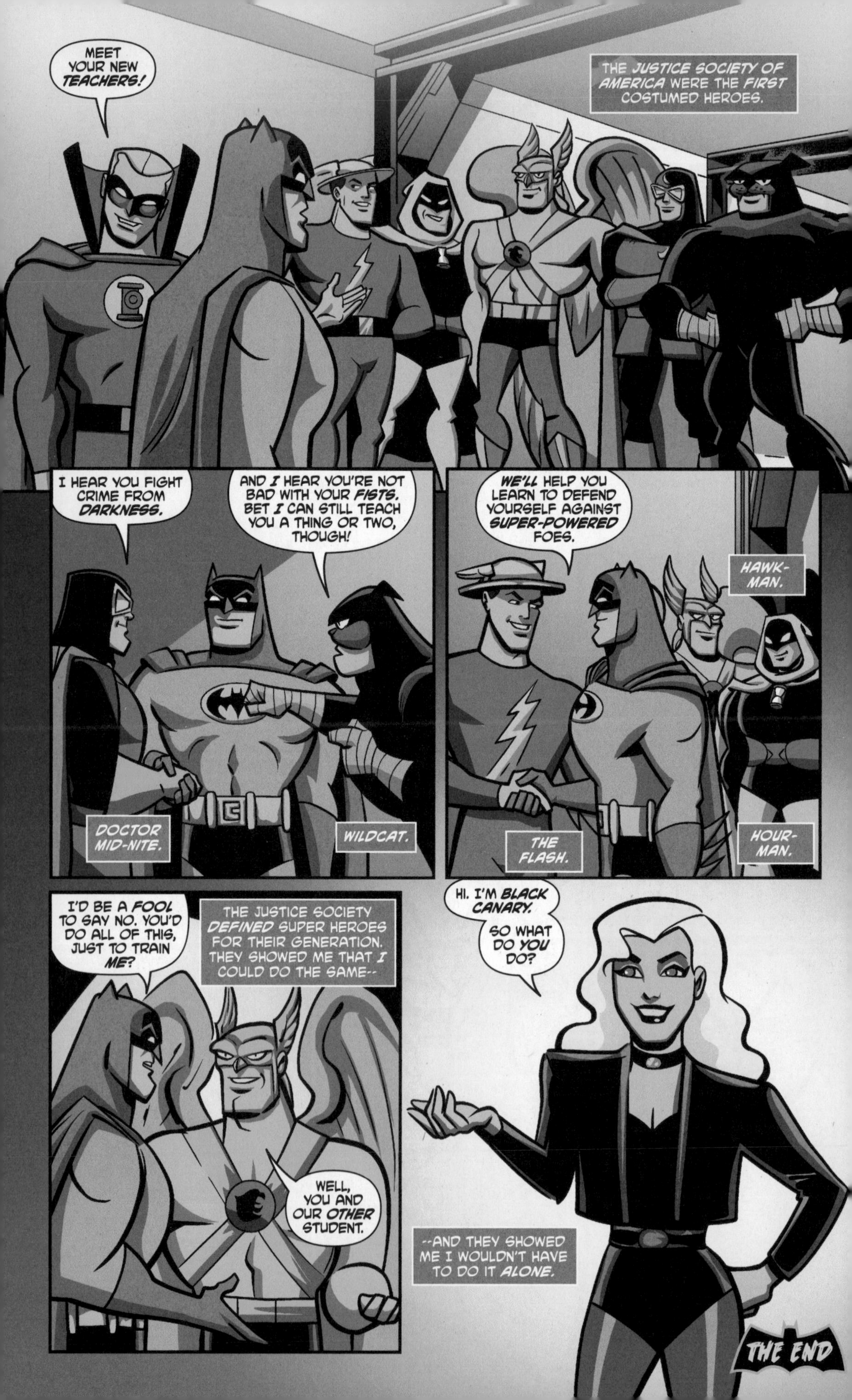
MEET YOUR NEW TEACHERS!
THE JUSTICE SOCIETY OF AMERICA WERE THE FIRST COSTUMED HEROES.
I HEAR YOU FIGHT CRIME FROM DARKNESS.
AND I HEAR YOU'RE NOT BAD WITH YOUR FISTS. BET I CAN STILL TEACH YOU A THING OR TWO, THOUGH!
DOCTOR MID-NITE.
WILDCAT.
WE'LL HELP YOU LEARN TO DEFEND YOURSELF AGAINST SUPER-POWERED FOES.
HAWK-MAN.
THE FLASH.
HOUR-MAN.
I'D BE A FOOL TO SAY NO. YOU'D DO ALL OF THIS, JUST TO TRAIN ME?
THE JUSTICE SOCIETY DEFINED SUPER HEROES FOR THEIR GENERATION. THEY SHOWED ME THAT I COULD DO THE SAME--
WELL, YOU AND OUR OTHER STUDENT.
HI. I'M BLACK CANARY.
SO WHAT DO YOU DO?
--AND THEY SHOWED ME I WOULDN'T HAVE TO DO IT ALONE.
THE END

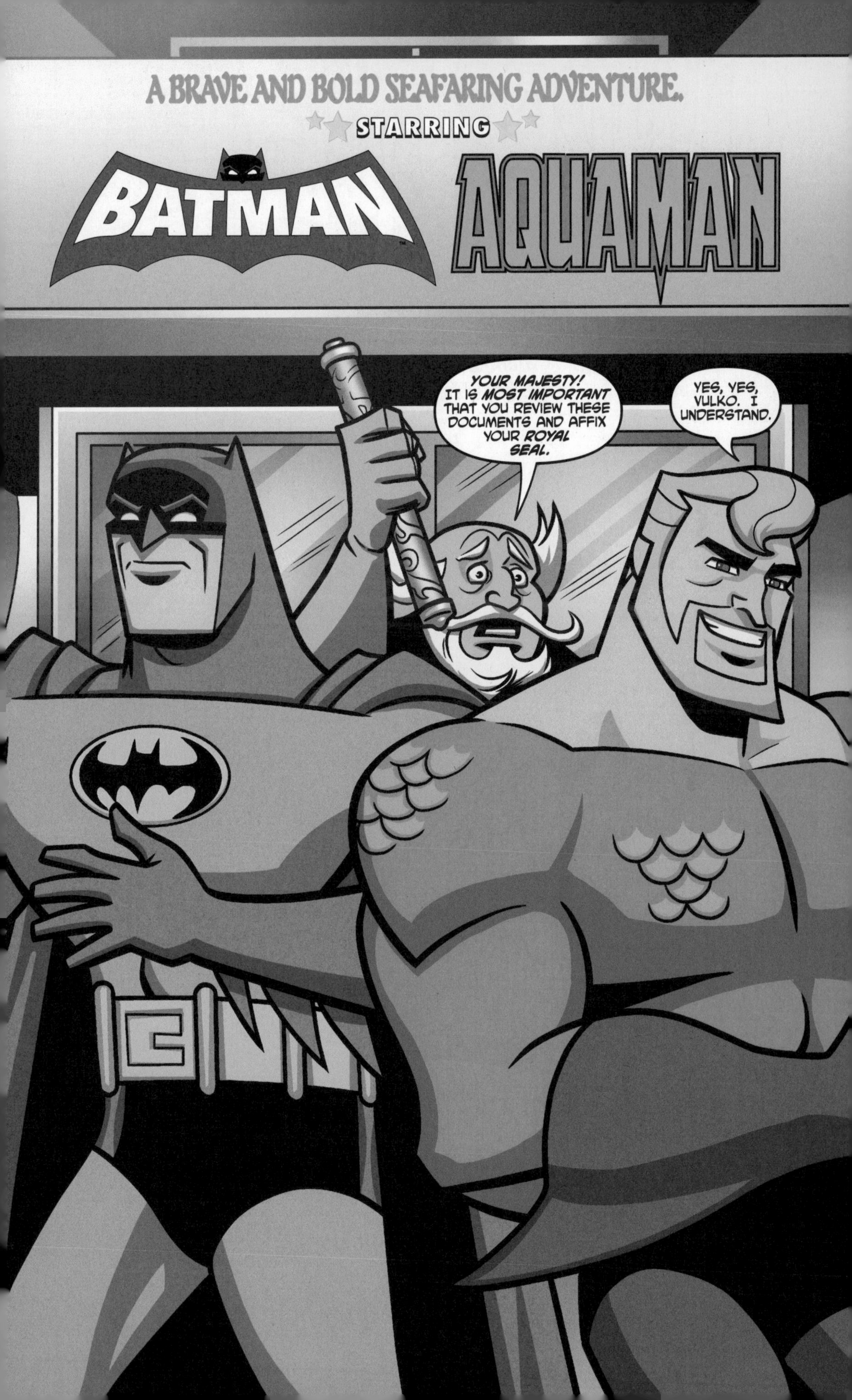
A BRAVE AND BOLD SEAFARING ADVENTURE.
STARRING
BATMAN
AQUAMAN
YOUR MAJESTY! IT IS MOST IMPORTANT THAT YOU REVIEW THESE DOCUMENTS AND AFFIX YOUR ROYAL SEAL.
YES, YES, VULKO. I UNDERSTAND.

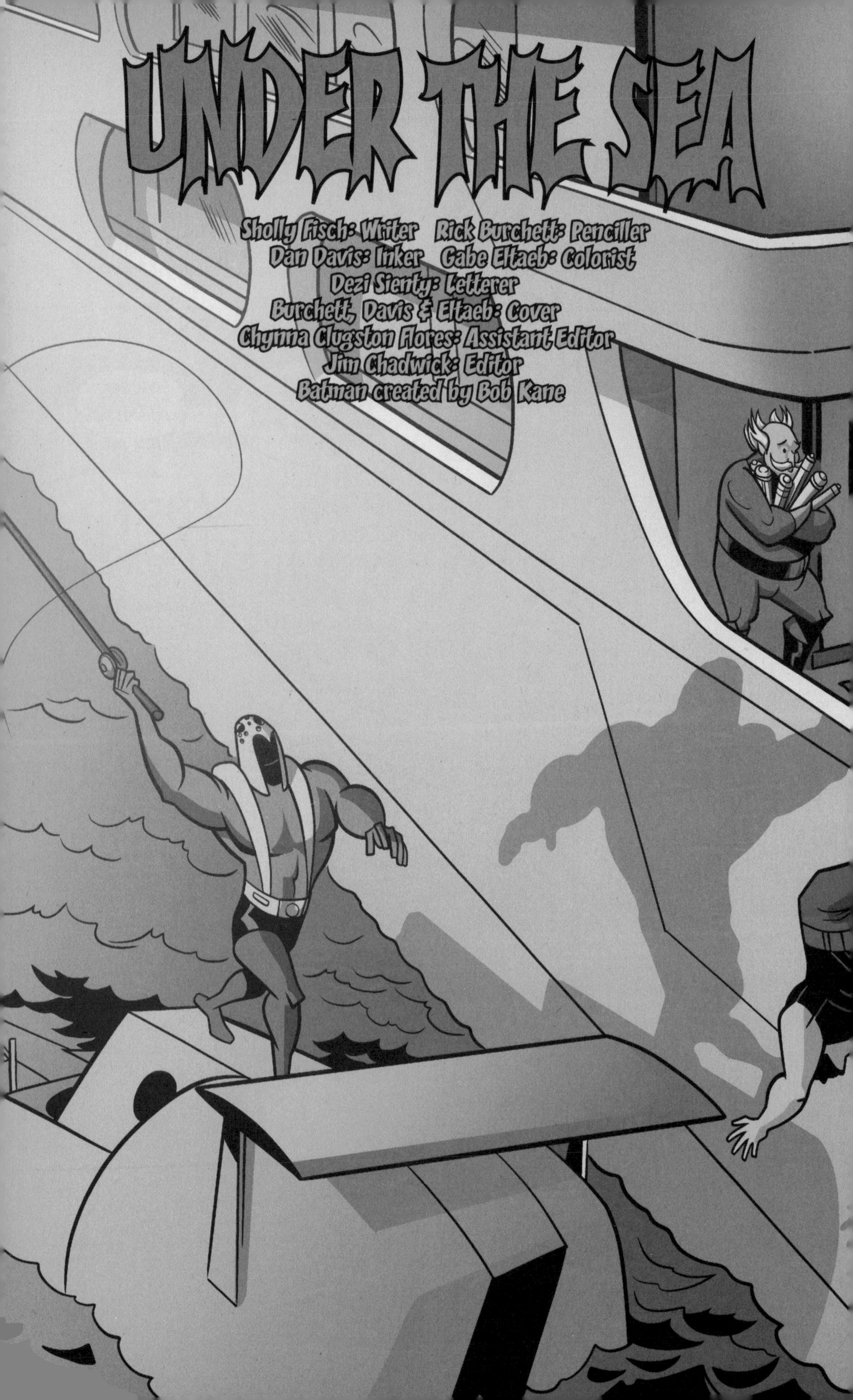
UNDER THE SEA
Sholly Fisch: Writer Rick Burchett: Penciller
Dan Davis: Inker Gabe Eltaeb: Colorist
Dezi Sienty: Letterer
Burchett, Davis & Eltaeb: Cover
Chynna Clugston Flores: Assistant Editor
Jim Chadwick: Editor
Batman created by Bob Kane

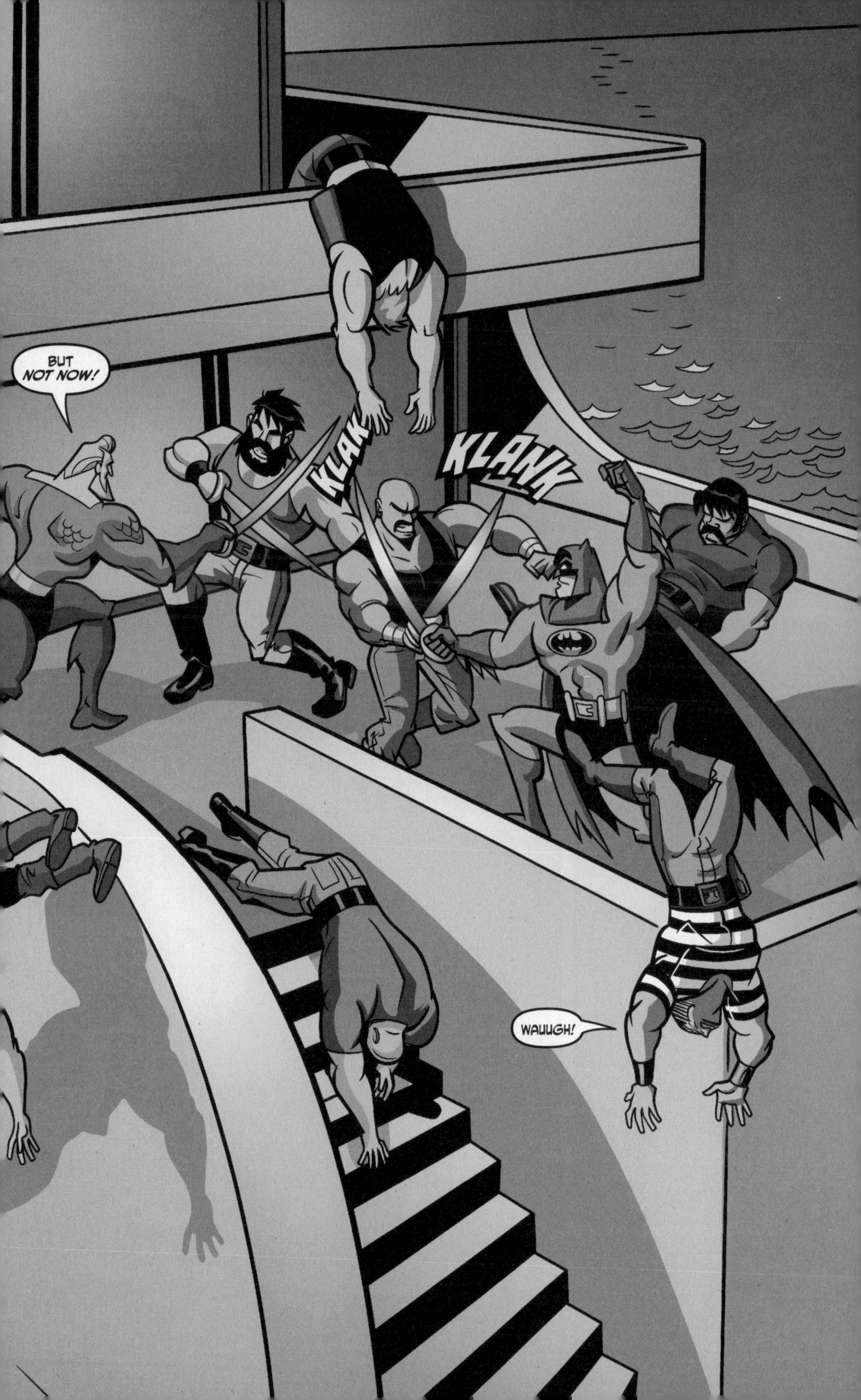
BUT NOT NOW!
KLAK
KLANK
WAUUGH!

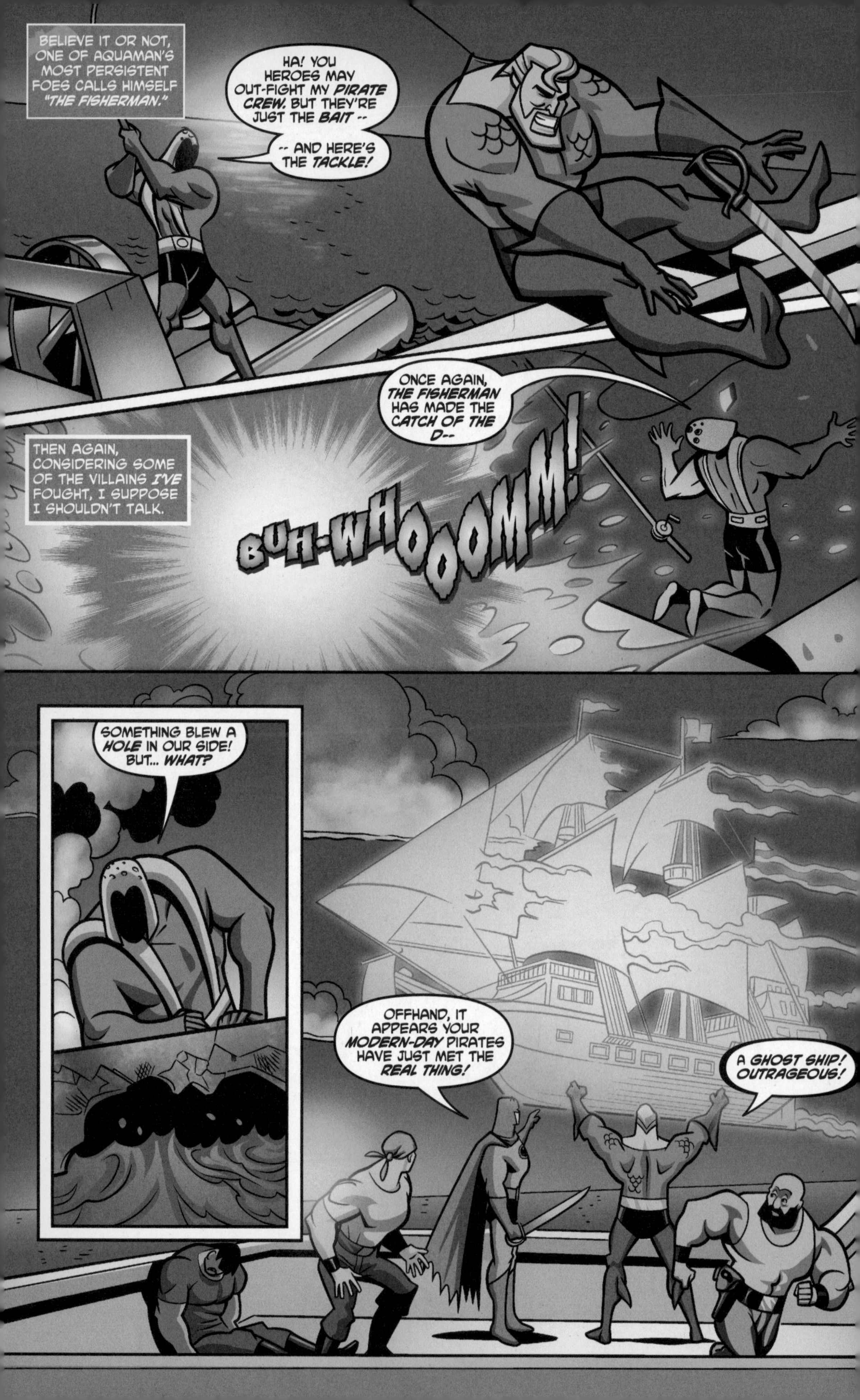
BELIEVE IT OR NOT, ONE OF AQUAMAN'S MOST PERSISTENT FOES CALLS HIMSELF "THE FISHERMAN."
HA! YOU HEROES MAY OUT-FIGHT MY PIRATE CREW. BUT THEY'RE JUST THE BAIT --
-- AND HERE'S THE TACKLE!
THEN AGAIN, CONSIDERING SOME OF THE VILLAINS I'VE FOUGHT, I SUPPOSE I SHOULDN'T TALK.
ONCE AGAIN, THE FISHERMAN HAS MADE THE CATCH OF THE D--
BUH-WHOOOOMM!
SOMETHING BLEW A HOLE IN OUR SIDE! BUT... WHAT?
OFFHAND, IT APPEARS YOUR MODERN-DAY PIRATES HAVE JUST MET THE REAL THING!
A GHOST SHIP! OUTRAGEOUS!

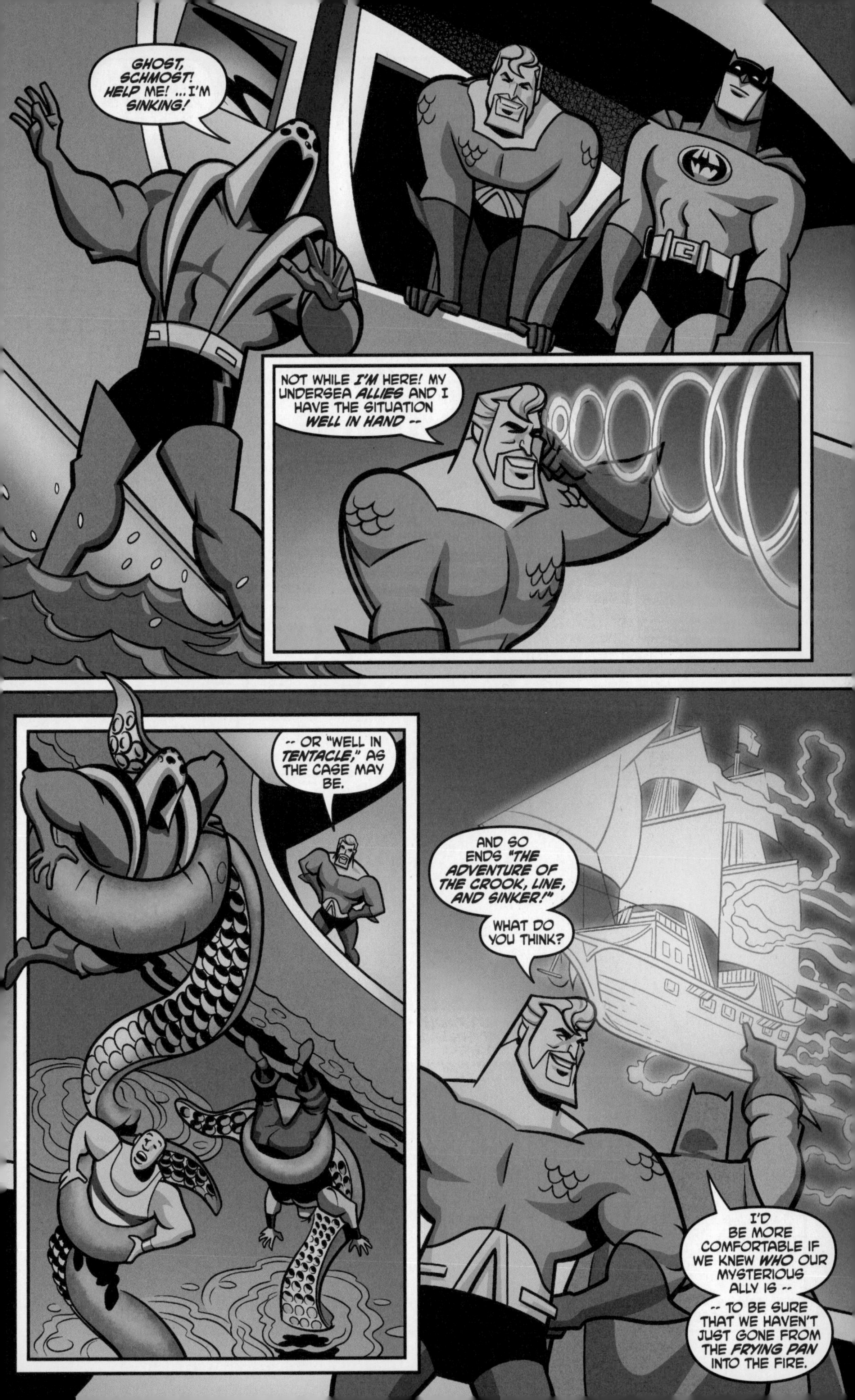
GHOST, SCHMOST! HELP ME! ...I'M SINKING!
NOT WHILE I'M HERE! MY UNDERSEA ALLIES AND I HAVE THE SITUATION WELL IN HAND --
-- OR "WELL IN TENTACLE," AS THE CASE MAY BE.
AND SO ENDS "THE ADVENTURE OF THE CROOK, LINE, AND SINKER!"
WHAT DO YOU THINK?
I'D BE MORE COMFORTABLE IF WE KNEW WHO OUR MYSTERIOUS ALLY IS --
-- TO BE SURE THAT WE HAVEN'T JUST GONE FROM THE FRYING PAN INTO THE FIRE.

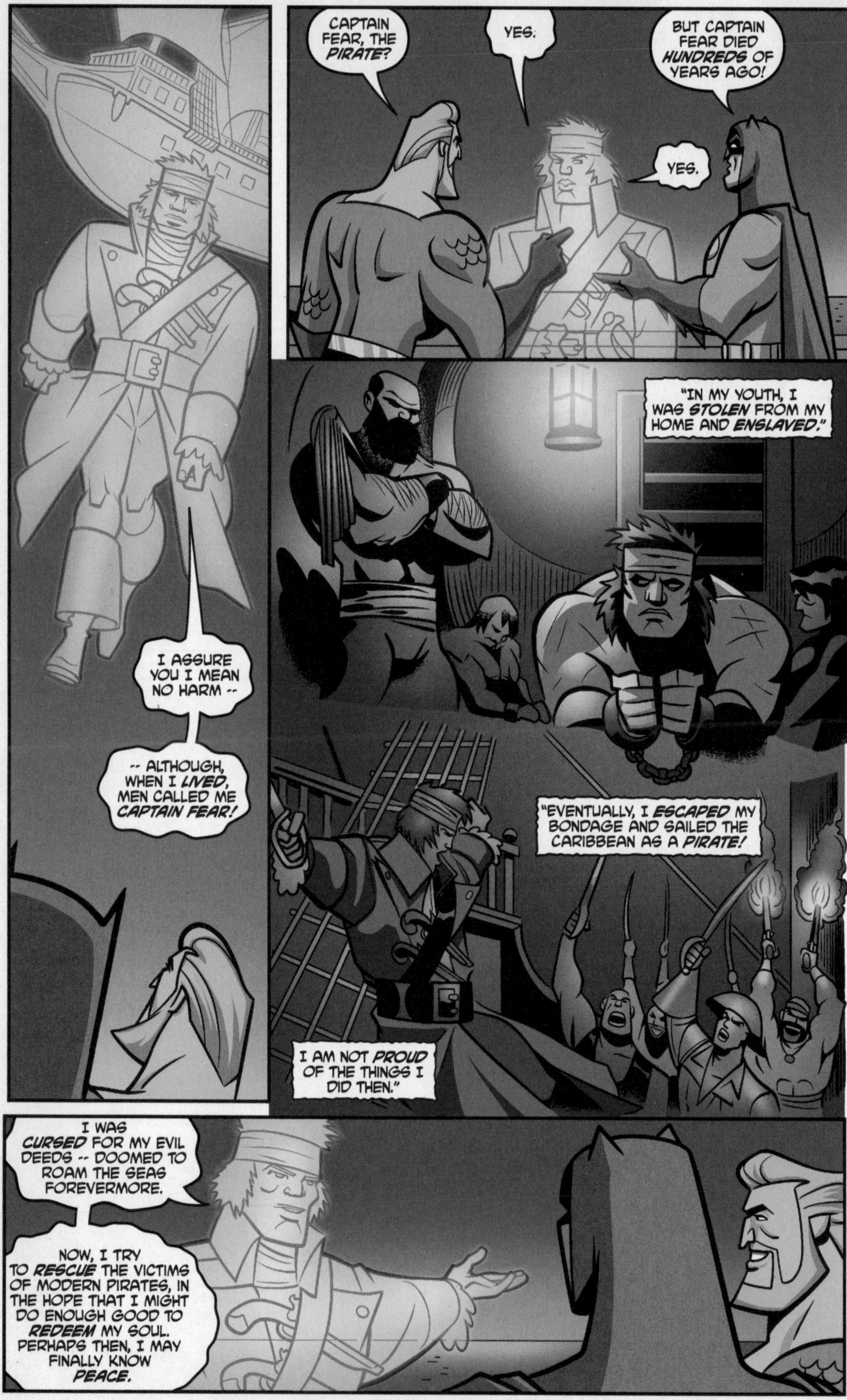
CAPTAIN FEAR, THE PIRATE?
YES.
BUT CAPTAIN FEAR DIED HUNDREDS OF YEARS AGO!
YES.
I ASSURE YOU I MEAN NO HARM --
-- ALTHOUGH, WHEN I LIVED, MEN CALLED ME CAPTAIN FEAR!
"IN MY YOUTH, I WAS STOLEN FROM MY HOME AND ENSLAVED."
"EVENTUALLY, I ESCAPED MY BONDAGE AND SAILED THE CARIBBEAN AS A PIRATE!
I AM NOT PROUD OF THE THINGS I DID THEN."
I WAS CURSED FOR MY EVIL DEEDS -- DOOMED TO ROAM THE SEAS FOREVERMORE.
NOW, I TRY TO RESCUE THE VICTIMS OF MODERN PIRATES, IN THE HOPE THAT I MIGHT DO ENOUGH GOOD TO REDEEM MY SOUL. PERHAPS THEN, I MAY FINALLY KNOW PEACE.

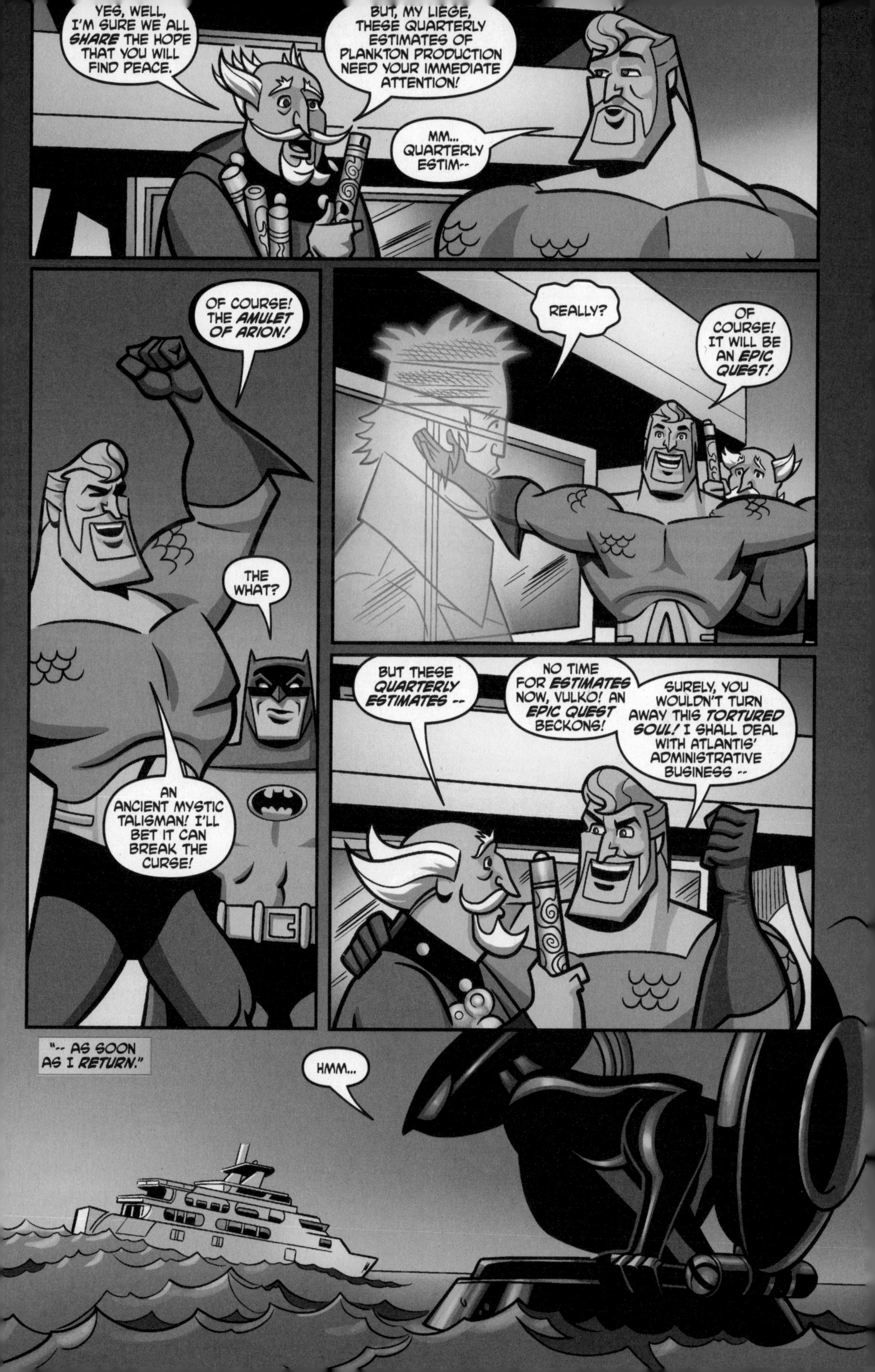
YES, WELL, I'M SURE WE ALL SHARE THE HOPE THAT YOU WILL FIND PEACE.
BUT, MY LIEGE, THESE QUARTERLY ESTIMATES OF PLANKTON PRODUCTION NEED YOUR IMMEDIATE ATTENTION!
MM... QUARTERLY ESTIM--
OF COURSE! THE AMULET OF ARION!
THE WHAT?
AN ANCIENT MYSTIC TALISMAN! I'LL BET IT CAN BREAK THE CURSE!
REALLY?
OF COURSE! IT WILL BE AN EPIC QUEST!
BUT THESE QUARTERLY ESTIMATES --
NO TIME FOR ESTIMATES NOW, VULKO! AN EPIC QUEST BECKONS!
SURELY, YOU WOULDN'T TURN AWAY THIS TORTURED SOUL! I SHALL DEAL WITH ATLANTIS' ADMINISTRATIVE BUSINESS --
"-- AS SOON AS I RETURN."
HMM...

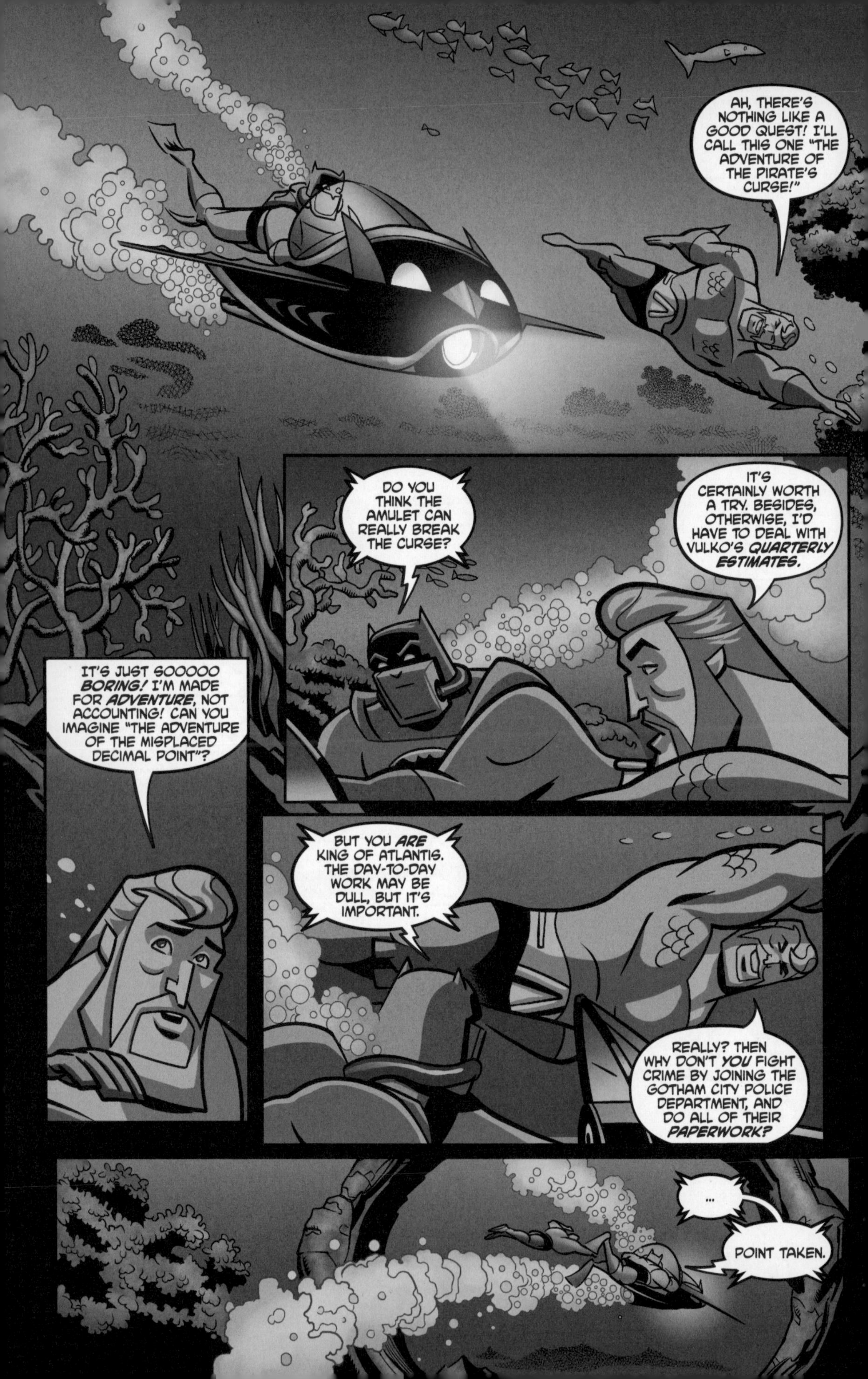

AH, THERE'S NOTHING LIKE A GOOD QUEST! I'LL CALL THIS ONE "THE ADVENTURE OF THE PIRATE'S CURSE!"
DO YOU THINK THE AMULET CAN REALLY BREAK THE CURSE?
IT'S CERTAINLY WORTH A TRY. BESIDES, OTHERWISE, I'D HAVE TO DEAL WITH VULKO'S QUARTERLY ESTIMATES.
IT'S JUST SOOOOO BORING! I'M MADE FOR ADVENTURE, NOT ACCOUNTING! CAN YOU IMAGINE "THE ADVENTURE OF THE MISPLACED DECIMAL POINT"?
BUT YOU ARE KING OF ATLANTIS. THE DAY-TO-DAY WORK MAY BE DULL, BUT IT'S IMPORTANT.
REALLY? THEN WHY DON'T YOU FIGHT CRIME BY JOINING THE GOTHAM CITY POLICE DEPARTMENT, AND DO ALL OF THEIR PAPERWORK?
...
POINT TAKEN.

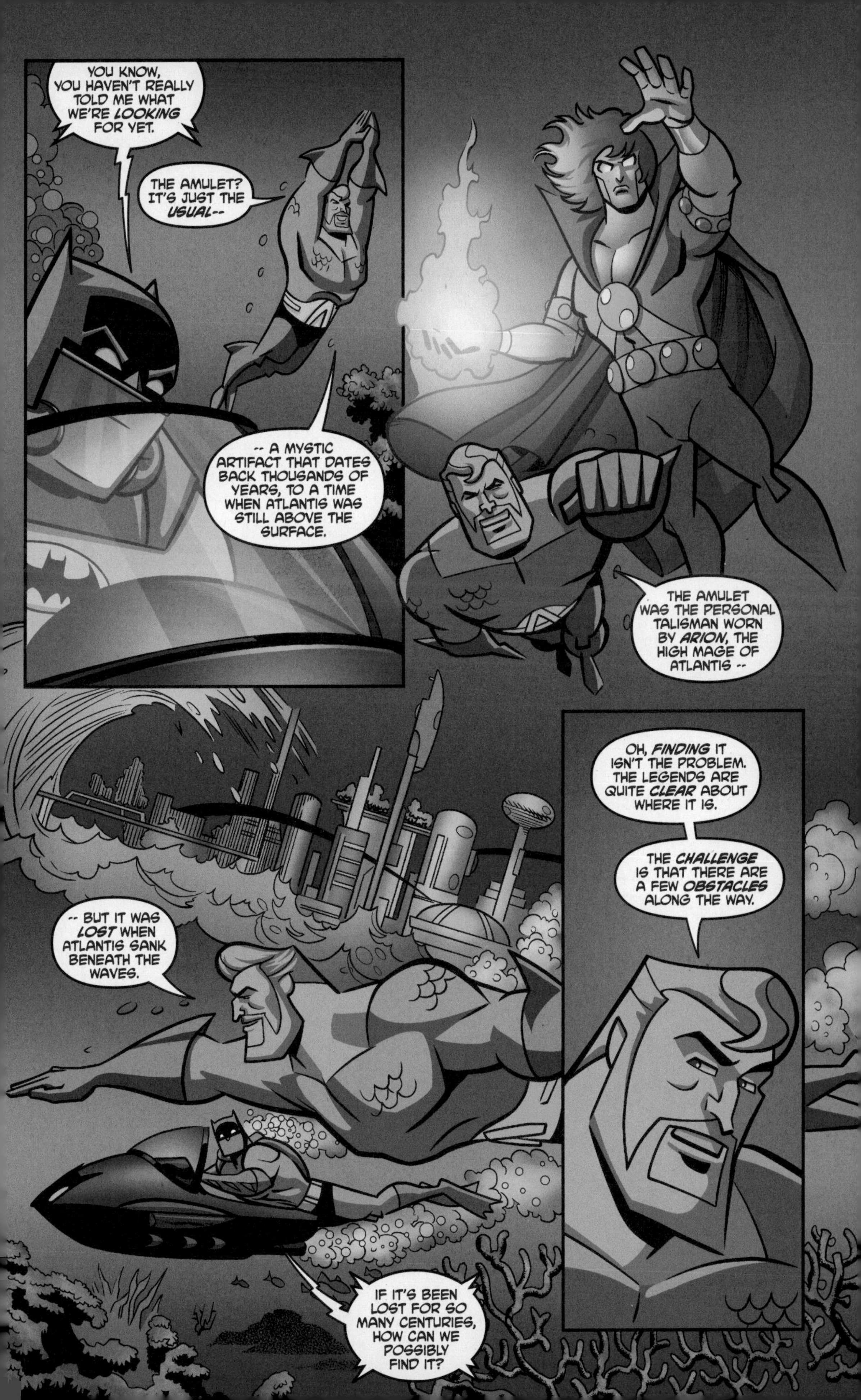
YOU KNOW, YOU HAVEN'T REALLY TOLD ME WHAT WE'RE *LOOKING* FOR YET.
THE AMULET? IT'S JUST THE *USUAL*--
-- A MYSTIC ARTIFACT THAT DATES BACK THOUSANDS OF YEARS, TO A TIME WHEN ATLANTIS WAS STILL ABOVE THE SURFACE.
THE AMULET WAS THE PERSONAL TALISMAN WORN BY *ARION*, THE HIGH MAGE OF ATLANTIS --
-- BUT IT WAS *LOST* WHEN ATLANTIS SANK BENEATH THE WAVES.
IF IT'S BEEN LOST FOR SO MANY CENTURIES, HOW CAN WE POSSIBLY FIND IT?
OH, *FINDING* IT ISN'T THE PROBLEM. THE LEGENDS ARE QUITE *CLEAR* ABOUT WHERE IT IS.
THE *CHALLENGE* IS THAT THERE ARE A FEW *OBSTACLES* ALONG THE WAY.

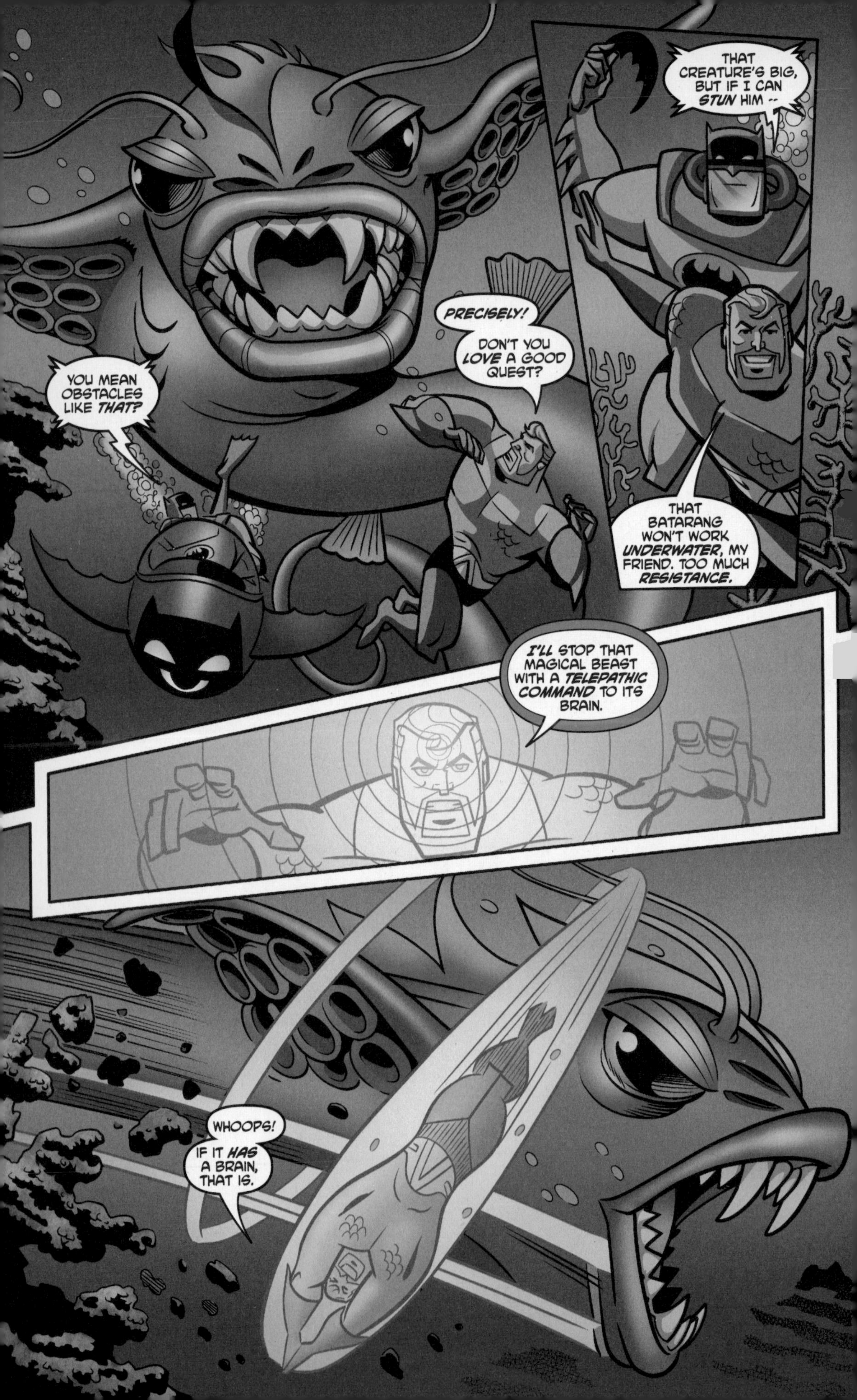

YOU MEAN OBSTACLES LIKE THAT?
PRECISELY!
DON'T YOU LOVE A GOOD QUEST?
THAT CREATURE'S BIG, BUT IF I CAN STUN HIM --
THAT BATARANG WON'T WORK UNDERWATER, MY FRIEND. TOO MUCH RESISTANCE.
I'LL STOP THAT MAGICAL BEAST WITH A TELEPATHIC COMMAND TO ITS BRAIN.
WHOOPS!
IF IT HAS A BRAIN, THAT IS.

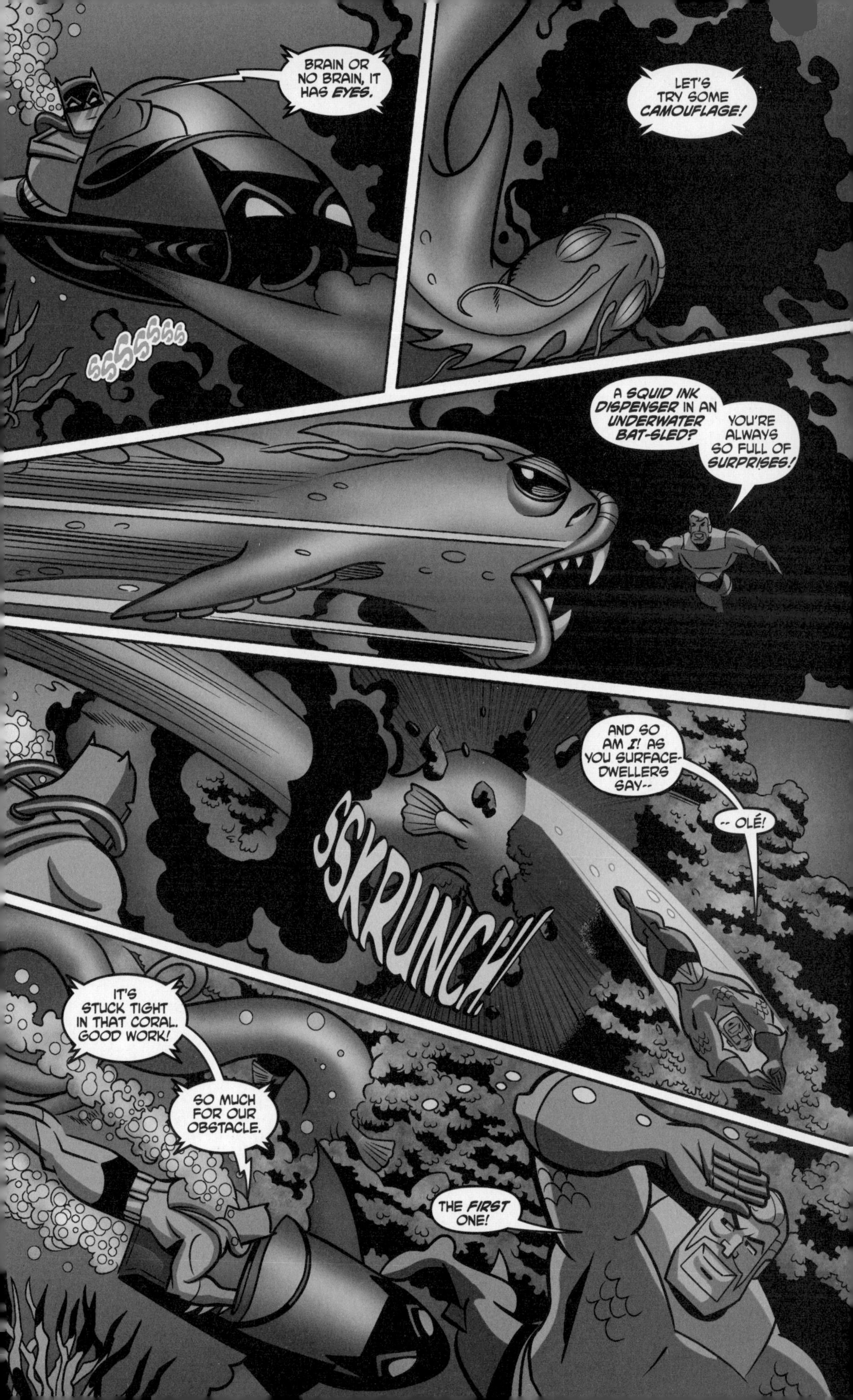
BRAIN OR NO BRAIN, IT HAS EYES.
SSSSSSS
LET'S TRY SOME CAMOUFLAGE!
A SQUID INK DISPENSER IN AN UNDERWATER BAT-SLED?
YOU'RE ALWAYS SO FULL OF SURPRISES!
AND SO AM I! AS YOU SURFACE-DWELLERS SAY--
-- OLÉ!
SSKRUNCH!
IT'S STUCK TIGHT IN THAT CORAL. GOOD WORK!
SO MUCH FOR OUR OBSTACLE.
THE FIRST ONE!

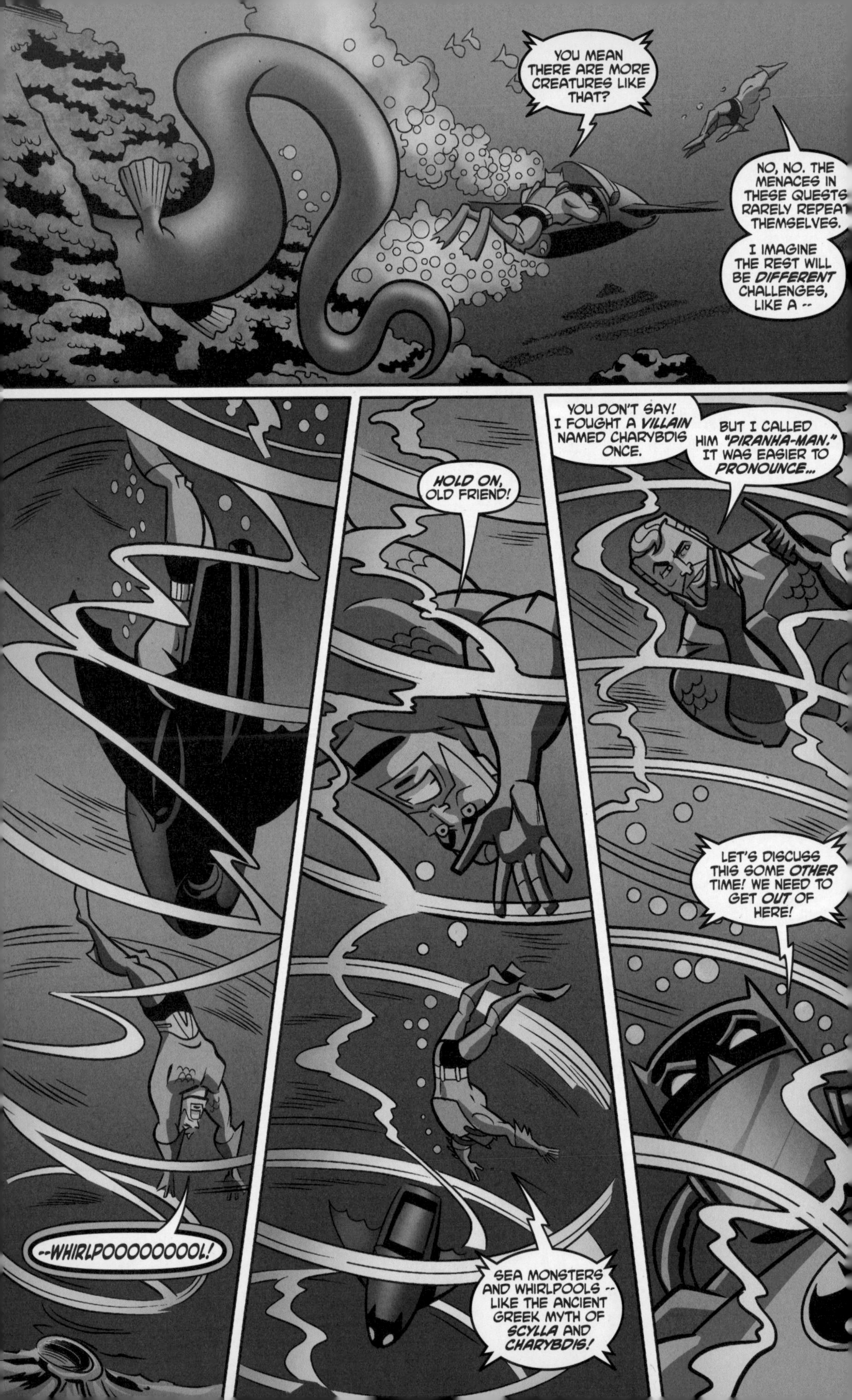
YOU MEAN THERE ARE MORE CREATURES LIKE THAT?
NO, NO. THE MENACES IN THESE QUESTS RARELY REPEAT THEMSELVES.
I IMAGINE THE REST WILL BE *DIFFERENT* CHALLENGES, LIKE A --
--WHIRLPOOOOOOOOL!
HOLD ON, OLD FRIEND!
SEA MONSTERS AND WHIRLPOOLS -- LIKE THE ANCIENT GREEK MYTH OF *SCYLLA* AND *CHARYBDIS!*
YOU DON'T SAY! I FOUGHT A *VILLAIN* NAMED CHARYBDIS ONCE.
BUT I CALLED HIM *"PIRANHA-MAN."* IT WAS EASIER TO *PRONOUNCE...*
LET'S DISCUSS THIS SOME *OTHER* TIME! WE NEED TO GET *OUT* OF HERE!

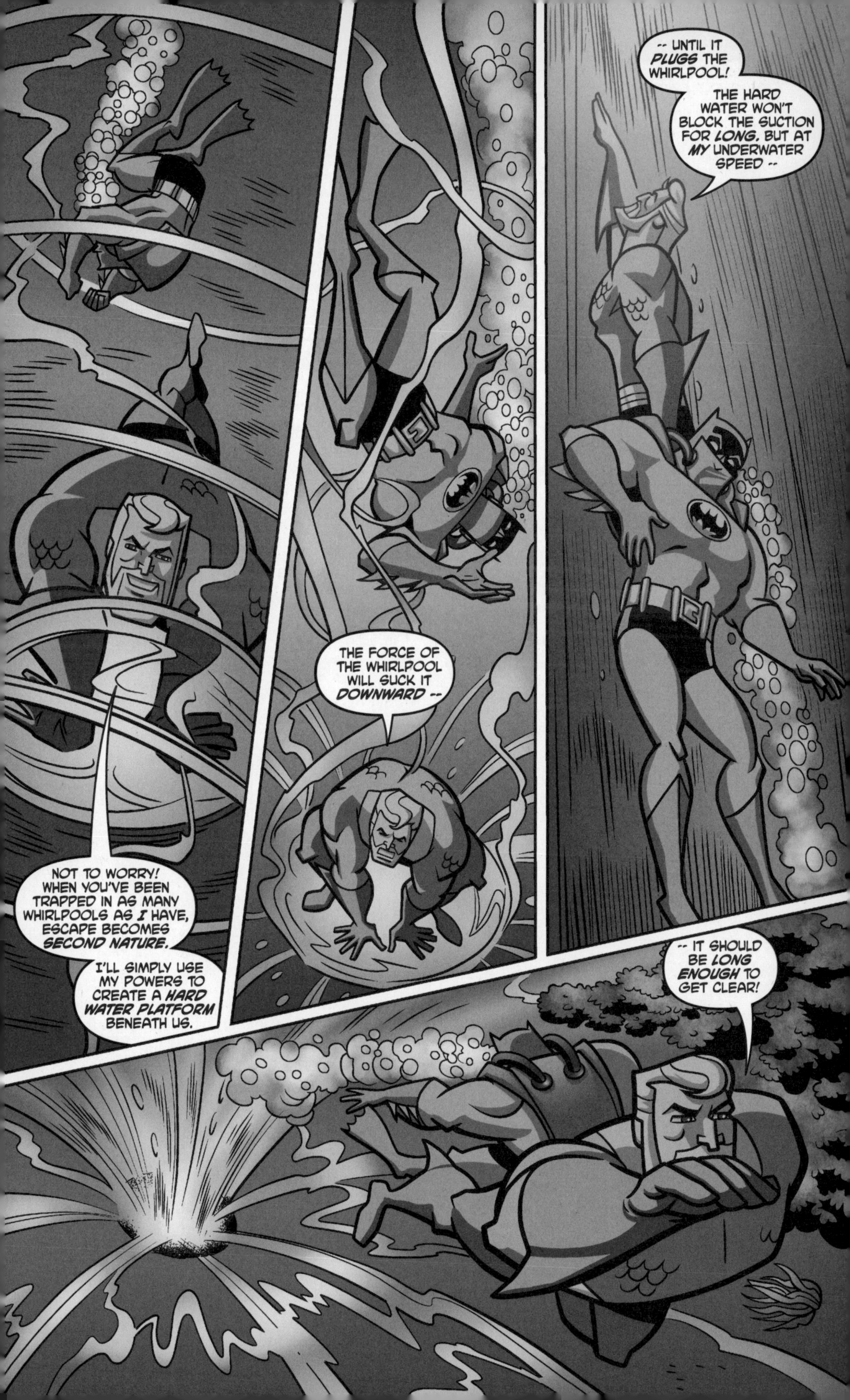
NOT TO WORRY! WHEN YOU'VE BEEN TRAPPED IN AS MANY WHIRLPOOLS AS I HAVE, ESCAPE BECOMES SECOND NATURE.
I'LL SIMPLY USE MY POWERS TO CREATE A HARD WATER PLATFORM BENEATH US.
THE FORCE OF THE WHIRLPOOL WILL SUCK IT DOWNWARD --
-- UNTIL IT PLUGS THE WHIRLPOOL!
THE HARD WATER WON'T BLOCK THE SUCTION FOR LONG. BUT AT MY UNDERWATER SPEED --
-- IT SHOULD BE LONG ENOUGH TO GET CLEAR!

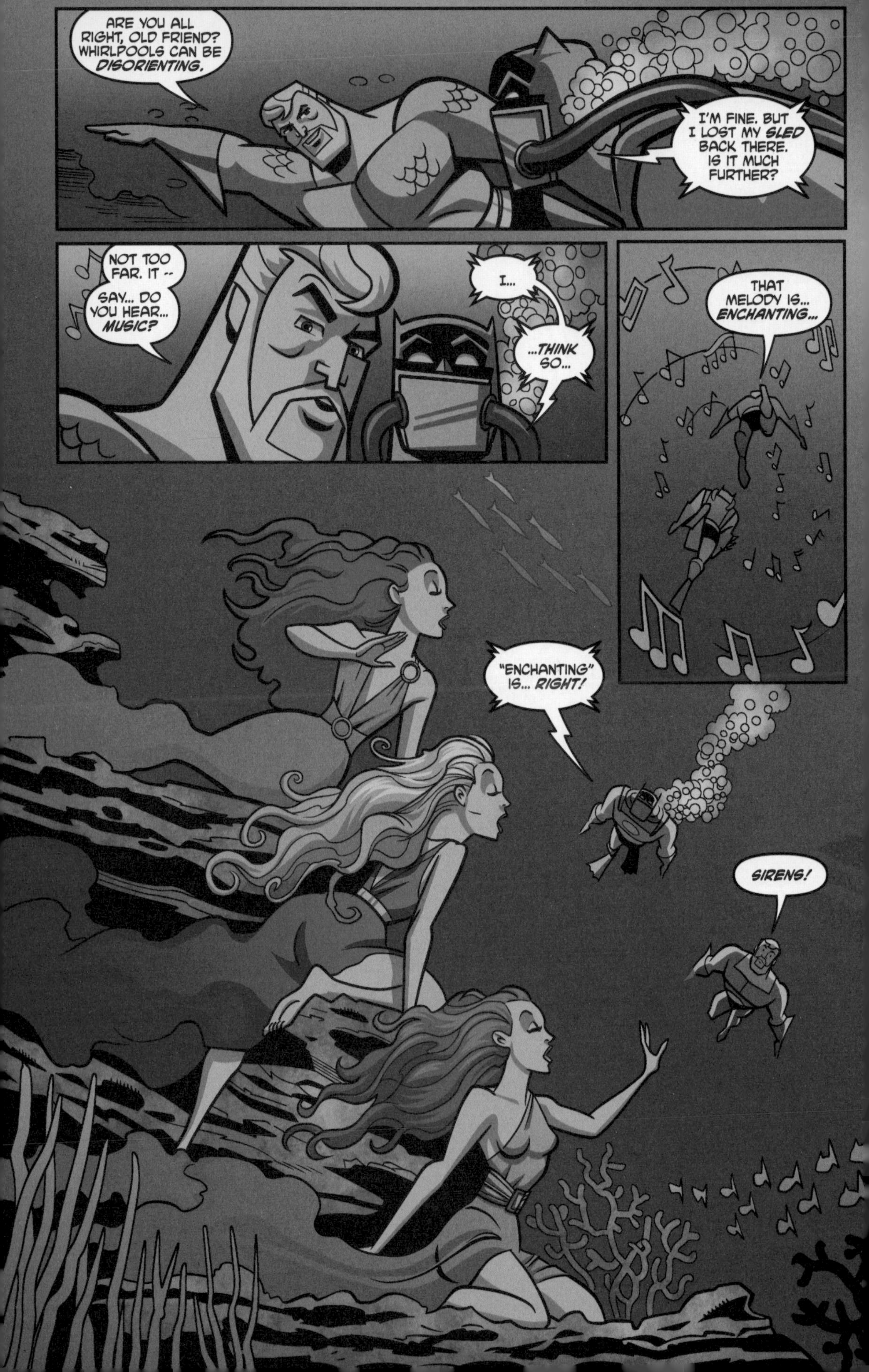
ARE YOU ALL RIGHT, OLD FRIEND? WHIRLPOOLS CAN BE DISORIENTING.
I'M FINE. BUT I LOST MY SLED BACK THERE. IS IT MUCH FURTHER?
NOT TOO FAR. IT --
SAY... DO YOU HEAR... MUSIC?
I...
...THINK SO...
THAT MELODY IS... ENCHANTING...
"ENCHANTING" IS... RIGHT!
SIRENS!

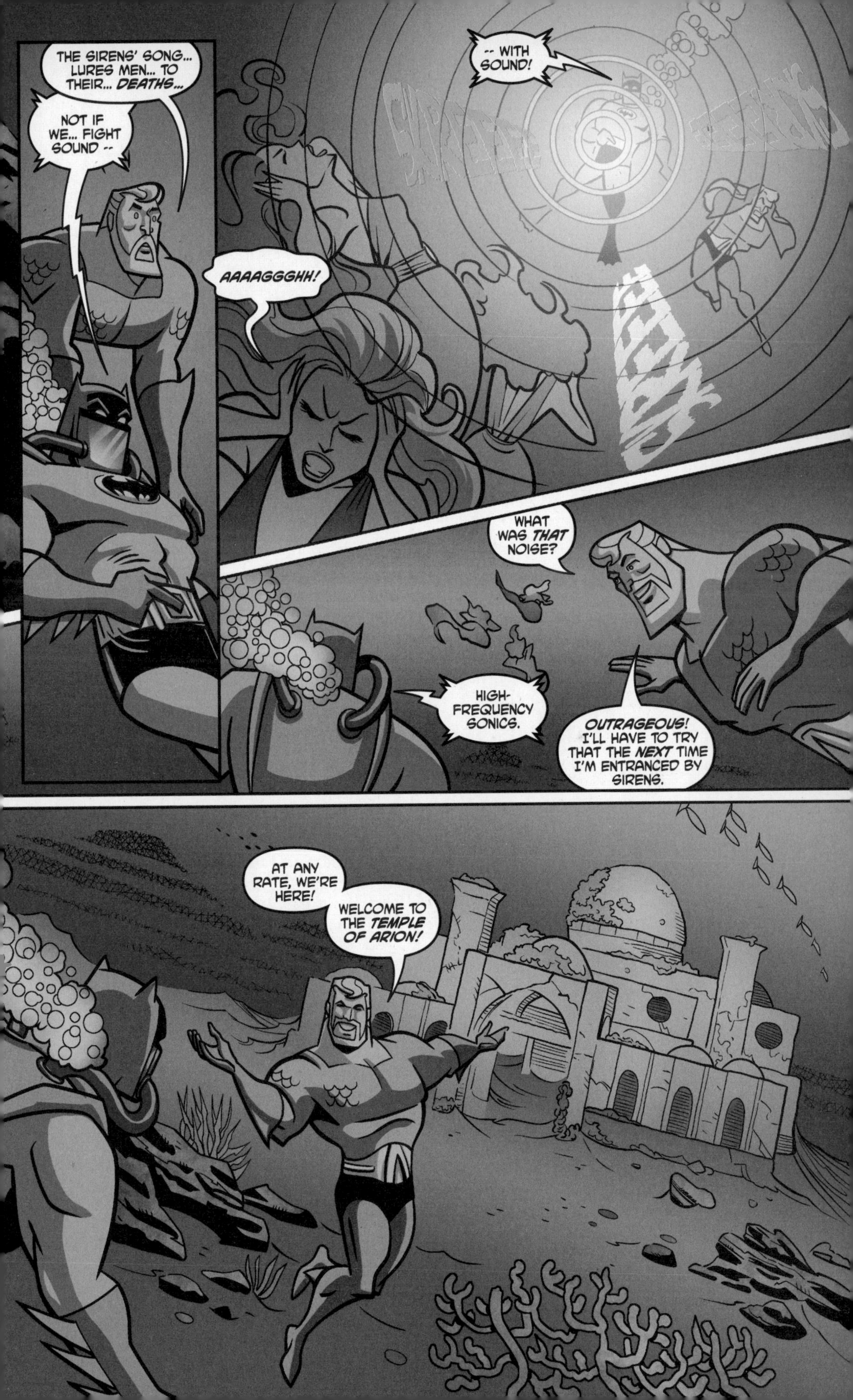
THE SIRENS' SONG... LURES MEN... TO THEIR... DEATHS...
NOT IF WE... FIGHT SOUND --
-- WITH SOUND!
AAAAGGGHH!
WHAT WAS THAT NOISE?
HIGH-FREQUENCY SONICS.
OUTRAGEOUS! I'LL HAVE TO TRY THAT THE NEXT TIME I'M ENTRANCED BY SIRENS.
AT ANY RATE, WE'RE HERE!
WELCOME TO THE TEMPLE OF ARION!

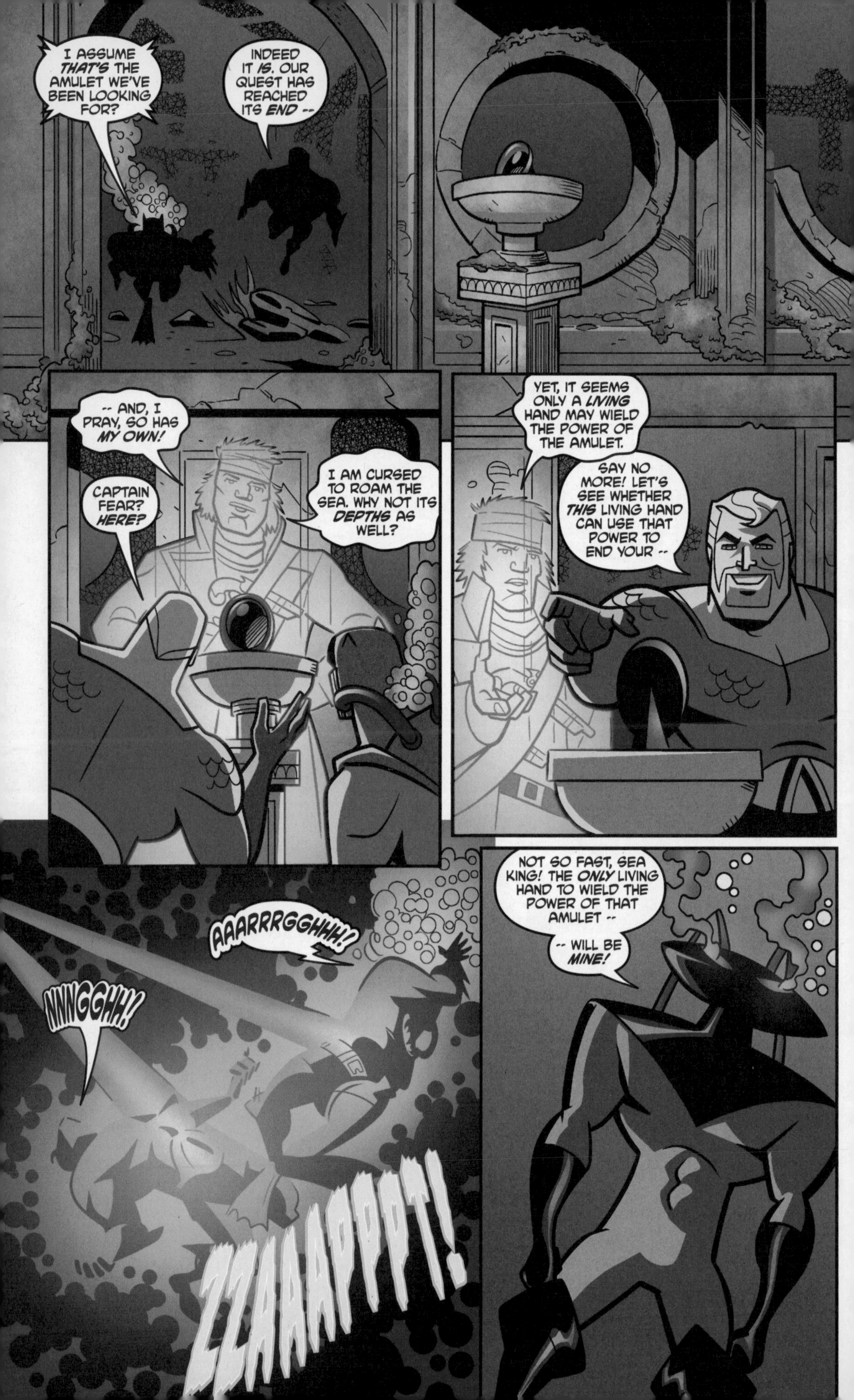
I ASSUME THAT'S THE AMULET WE'VE BEEN LOOKING FOR?
INDEED IT IS. OUR QUEST HAS REACHED ITS END --
-- AND, I PRAY, SO HAS MY OWN!
CAPTAIN FEAR? HERE?
I AM CURSED TO ROAM THE SEA. WHY NOT ITS DEPTHS AS WELL?
YET, IT SEEMS ONLY A LIVING HAND MAY WIELD THE POWER OF THE AMULET.
SAY NO MORE! LET'S SEE WHETHER THIS LIVING HAND CAN USE THAT POWER TO END YOUR --
AAARRRGGHHH!
NNNGGHH!
ZZAAAPPPT!
NOT SO FAST, SEA KING! THE ONLY LIVING HAND TO WIELD THE POWER OF THAT AMULET --
-- WILL BE MINE!

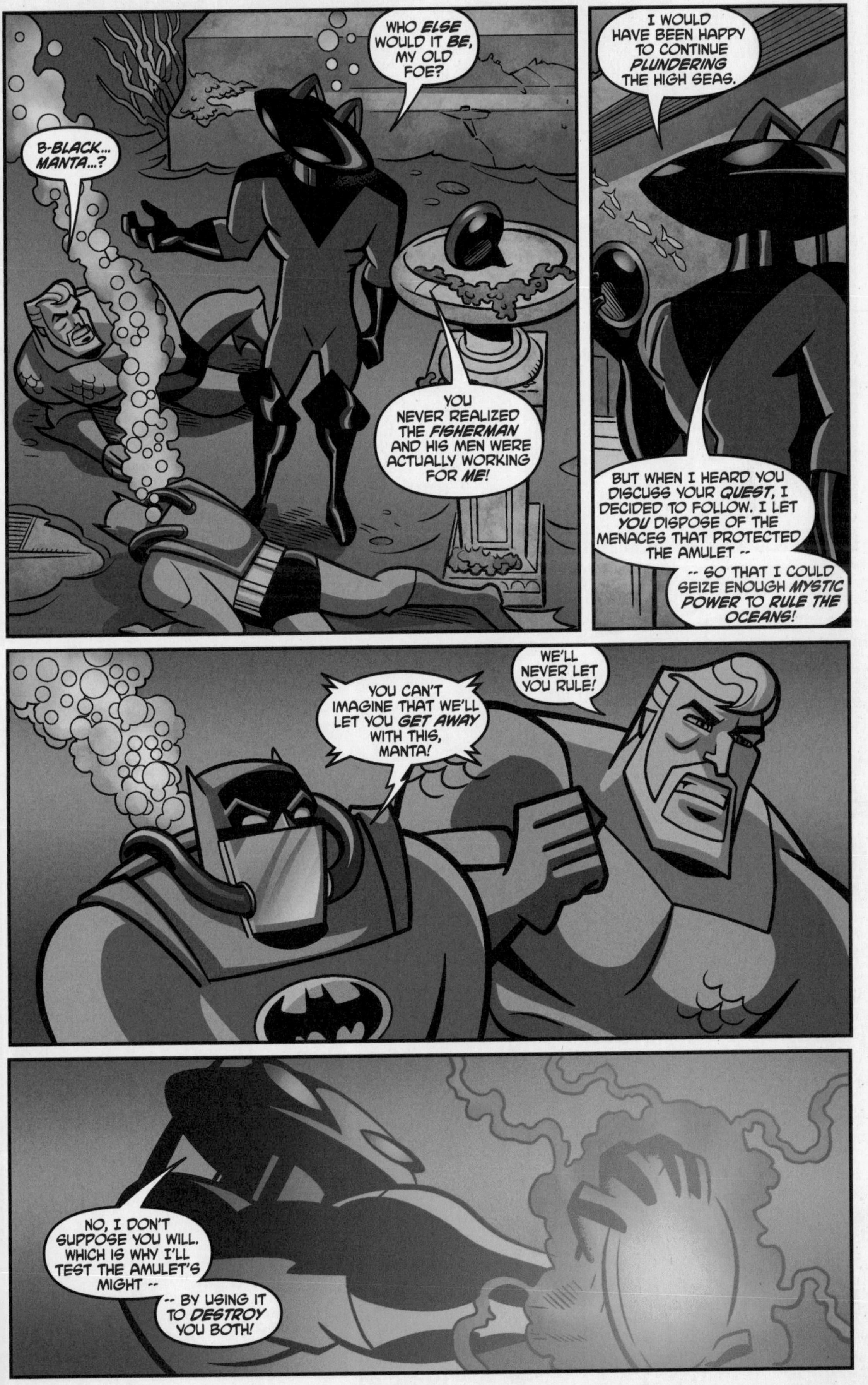

B-BLACK... MANTA...?
WHO ELSE WOULD IT BE, MY OLD FOE?
YOU NEVER REALIZED THE FISHERMAN AND HIS MEN WERE ACTUALLY WORKING FOR ME!
I WOULD HAVE BEEN HAPPY TO CONTINUE PLUNDERING THE HIGH SEAS.
BUT WHEN I HEARD YOU DISCUSS YOUR QUEST, I DECIDED TO FOLLOW. I LET YOU DISPOSE OF THE MENACES THAT PROTECTED THE AMULET --
-- SO THAT I COULD SEIZE ENOUGH MYSTIC POWER TO RULE THE OCEANS!
YOU CAN'T IMAGINE THAT WE'LL LET YOU GET AWAY WITH THIS, MANTA!
WE'LL NEVER LET YOU RULE!
NO, I DON'T SUPPOSE YOU WILL. WHICH IS WHY I'LL TEST THE AMULET'S MIGHT --
-- BY USING IT TO DESTROY YOU BOTH!

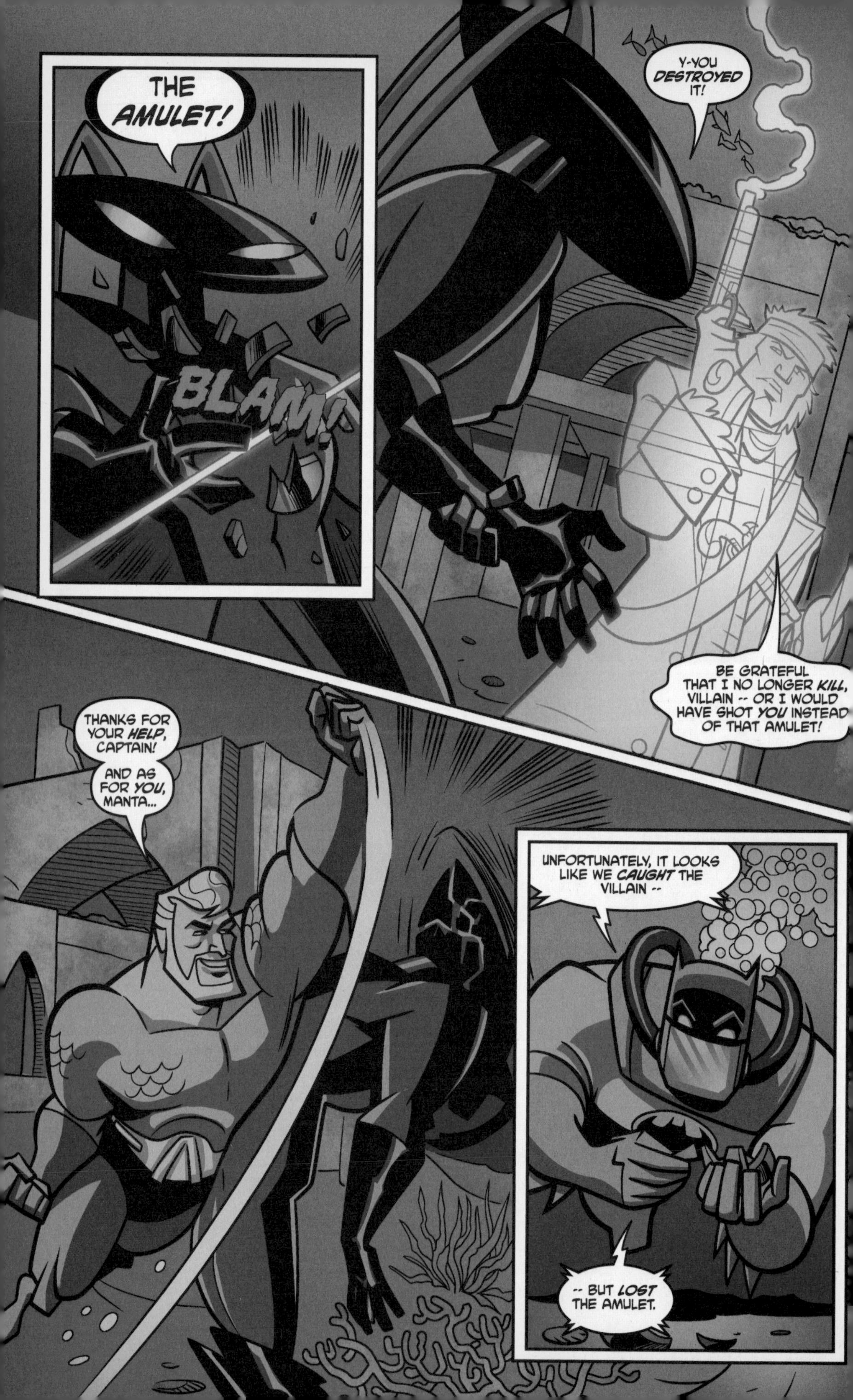
THE AMULET!
BLAM!
Y-YOU DESTROYED IT!
BE GRATEFUL THAT I NO LONGER KILL, VILLAIN -- OR I WOULD HAVE SHOT YOU INSTEAD OF THAT AMULET!
THANKS FOR YOUR HELP, CAPTAIN!
AND AS FOR YOU, MANTA...
UNFORTUNATELY, IT LOOKS LIKE WE CAUGHT THE VILLAIN --
-- BUT LOST THE AMULET.

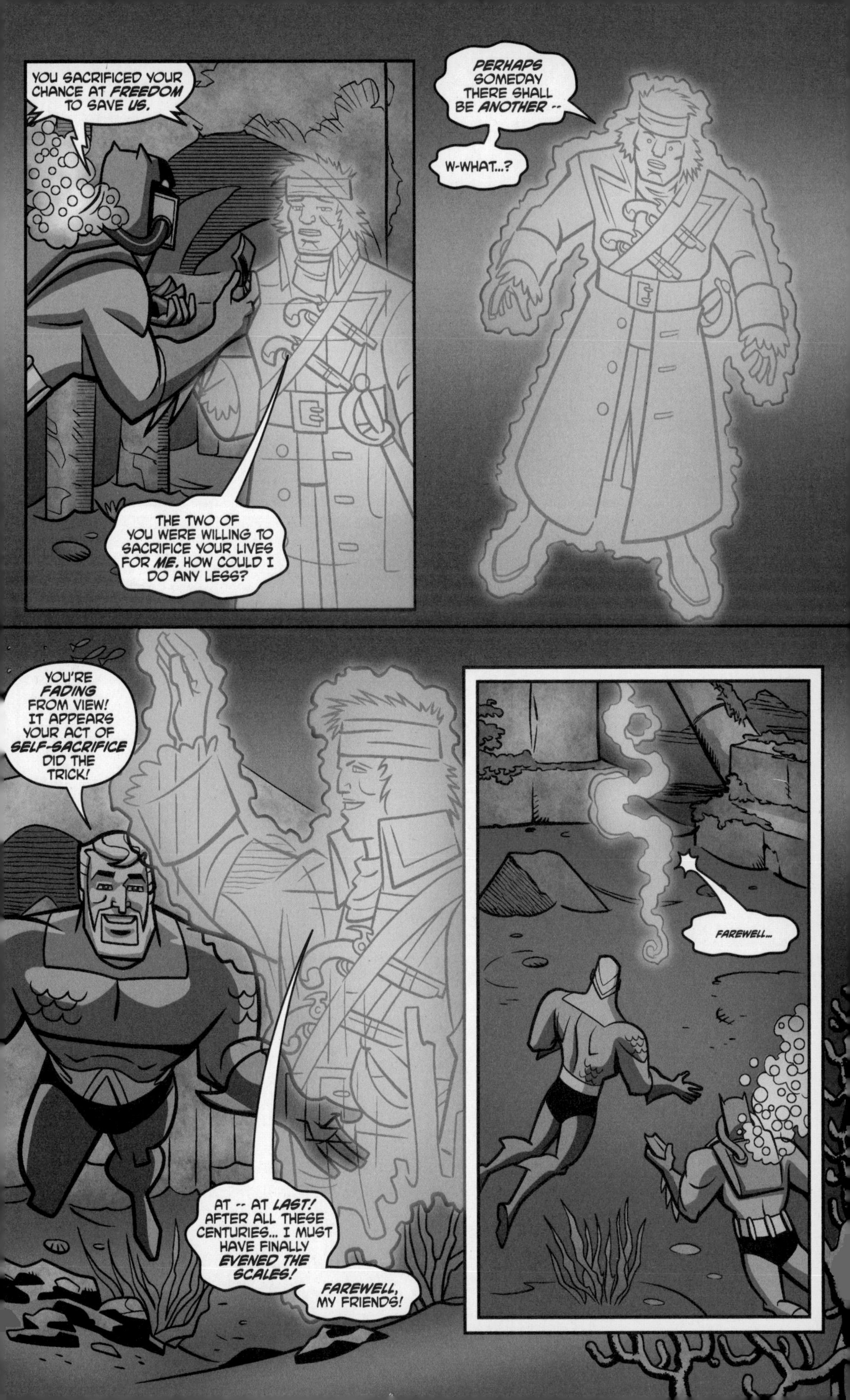
YOU SACRIFICED YOUR CHANCE AT *FREEDOM* TO SAVE *US*.
THE TWO OF YOU WERE WILLING TO SACRIFICE YOUR LIVES FOR *ME*. HOW COULD I DO ANY LESS?
PERHAPS SOMEDAY THERE SHALL BE *ANOTHER* --
W-WHAT...?
YOU'RE *FADING* FROM VIEW! IT APPEARS YOUR ACT OF *SELF-SACRIFICE* DID THE TRICK!
AT -- AT *LAST!* AFTER ALL THESE CENTURIES... I MUST HAVE FINALLY *EVENED THE SCALES!*
FAREWELL, MY FRIENDS!
FAREWELL...

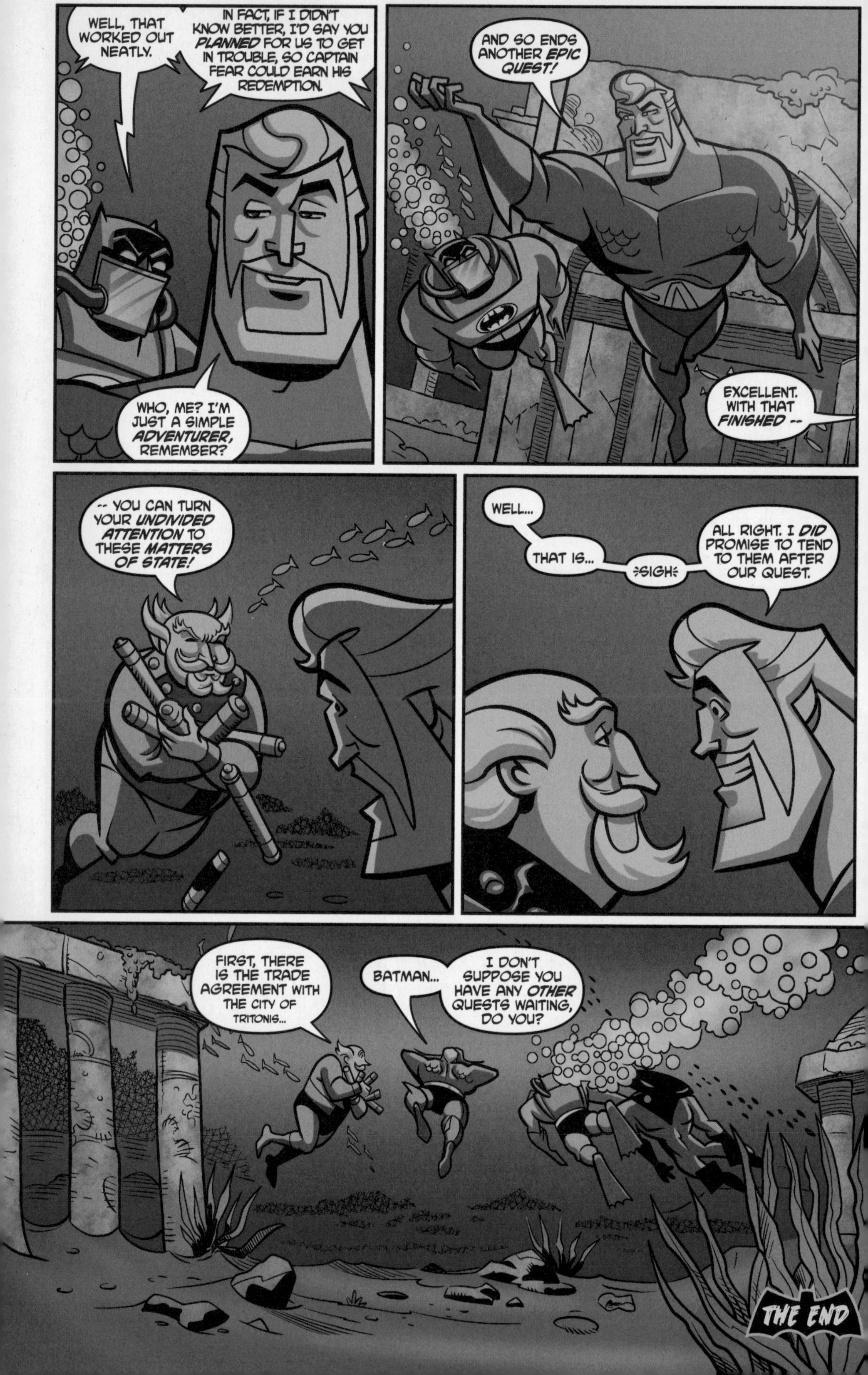
WELL, THAT WORKED OUT NEATLY.
IN FACT, IF I DIDN'T KNOW BETTER, I'D SAY YOU *PLANNED* FOR US TO GET IN TROUBLE, SO CAPTAIN FEAR COULD EARN HIS REDEMPTION.
WHO, ME? I'M JUST A SIMPLE *ADVENTURER*, REMEMBER?
AND SO ENDS ANOTHER *EPIC QUEST!*
EXCELLENT. WITH THAT *FINISHED* --
-- YOU CAN TURN YOUR *UNDIVIDED ATTENTION* TO THESE *MATTERS OF STATE!*
WELL...
THAT IS...
SIGH
ALL RIGHT. I *DID* PROMISE TO TEND TO THEM AFTER OUR QUEST.
FIRST, THERE IS THE TRADE AGREEMENT WITH THE CITY OF TRITONIS...
BATMAN...
I DON'T SUPPOSE YOU HAVE ANY *OTHER* QUESTS WAITING, DO YOU?
THE END

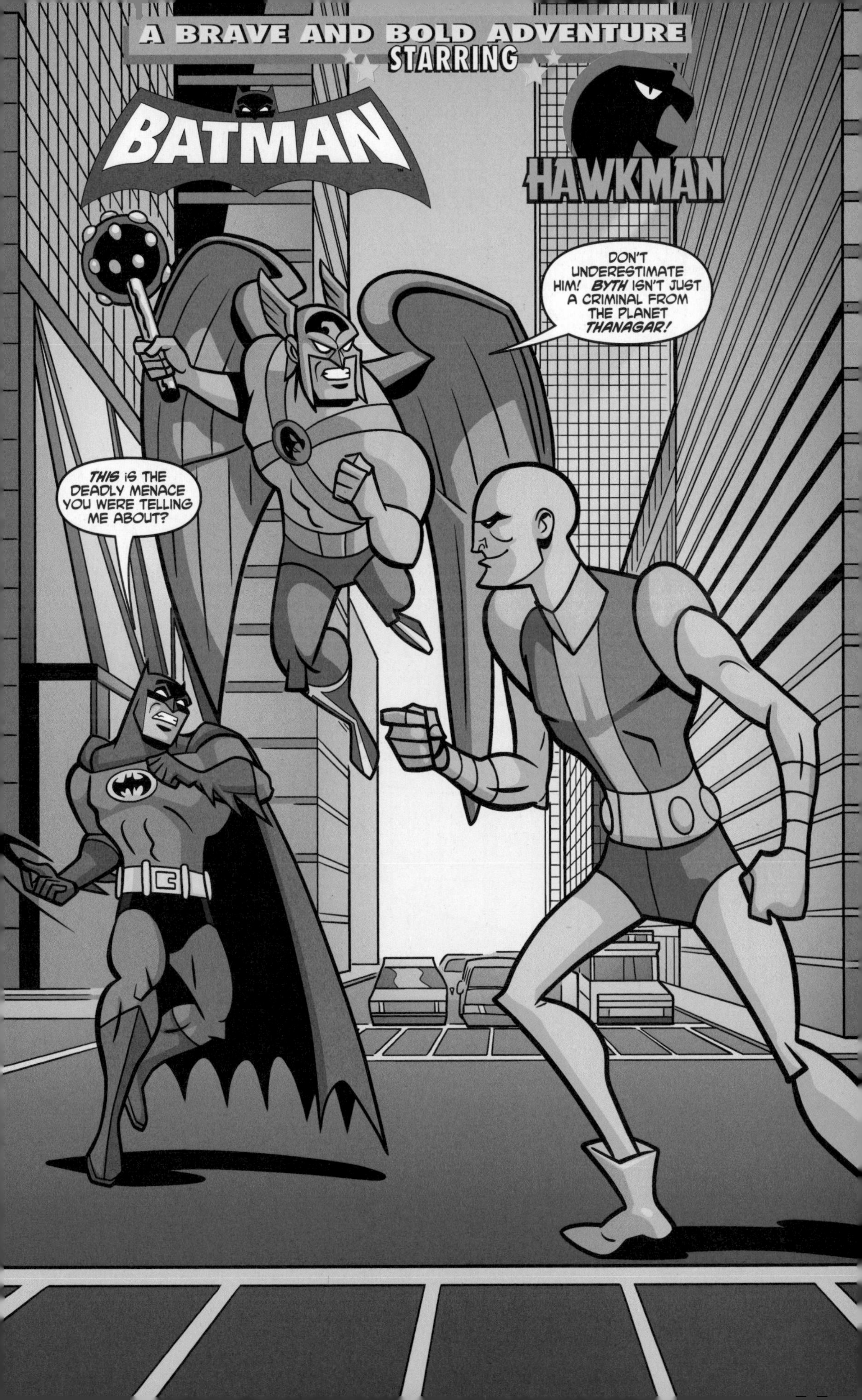
A BRAVE AND BOLD ADVENTURE
STARRING
BATMAN
HAWKMAN
DON'T UNDERESTIMATE HIM! BYTH ISN'T JUST A CRIMINAL FROM THE PLANET THANAGAR!
THIS IS THE DEADLY MENACE YOU WERE TELLING ME ABOUT?

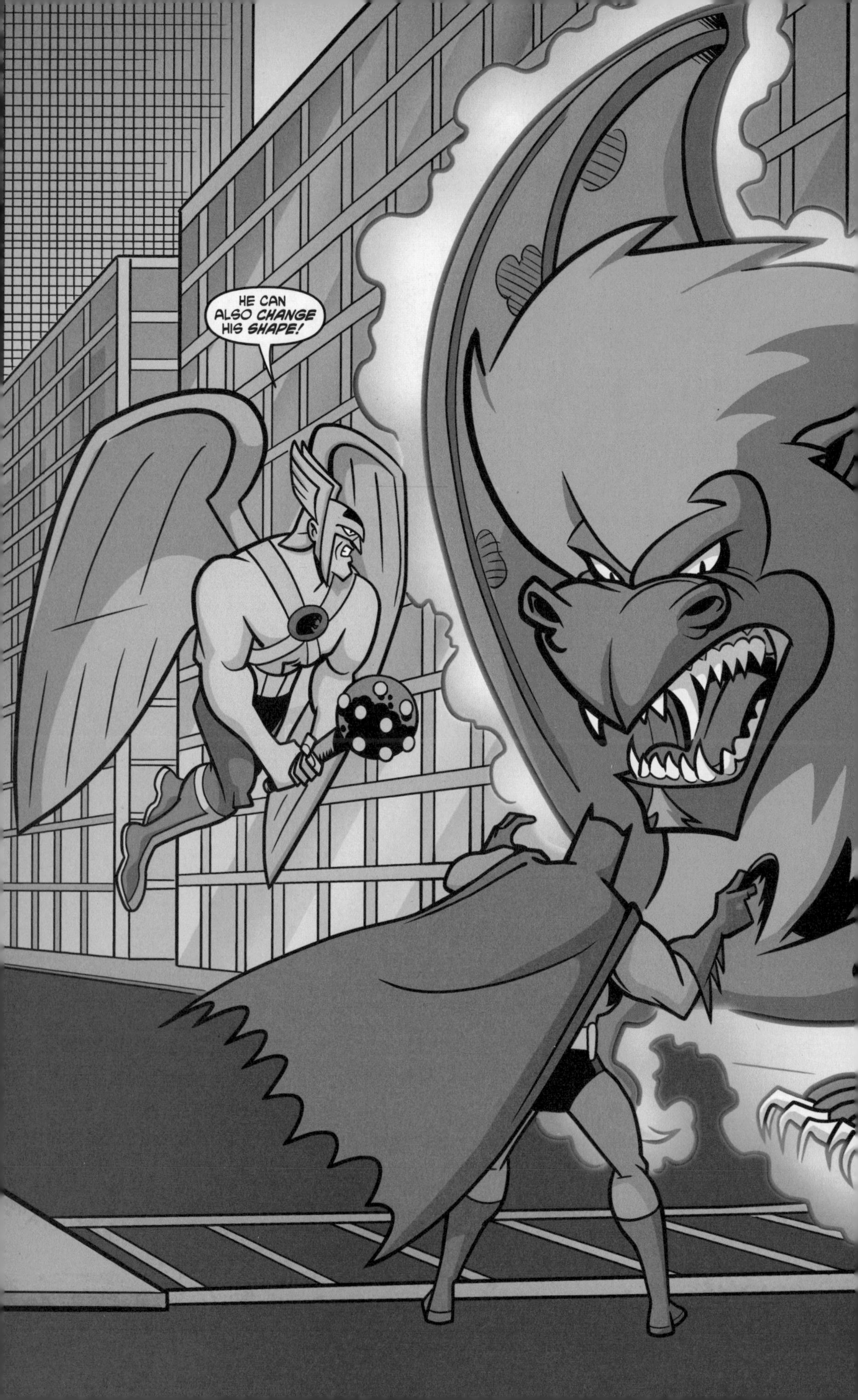
HE CAN ALSO *CHANGE* HIS *SHAPE!*

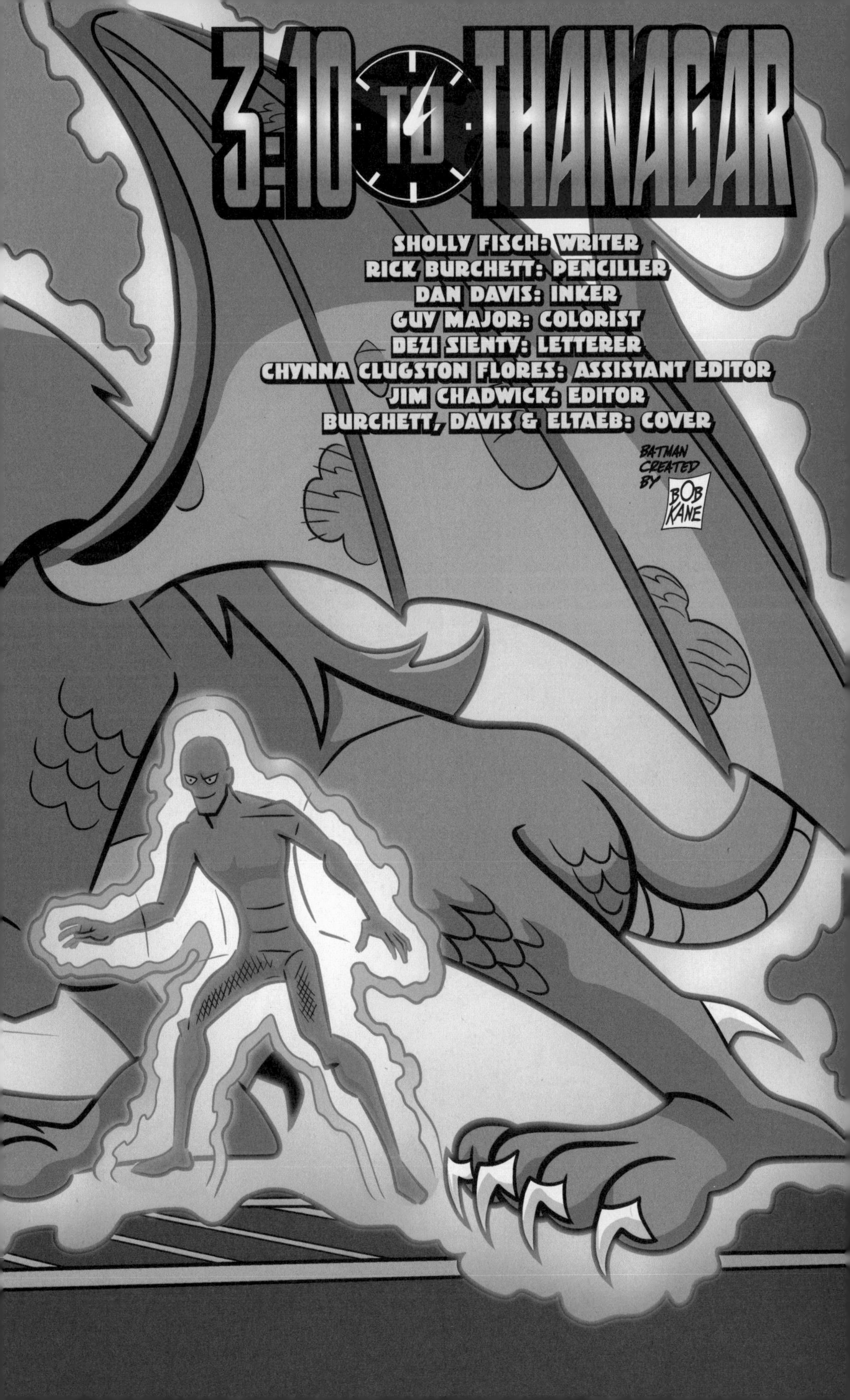
3:10 TO THANAGAR
SHOLLY FISCH: WRITER
RICK BURCHETT: PENCILLER
DAN DAVIS: INKER
GUY MAJOR: COLORIST
DEZI SIENTY: LETTERER
CHYNNA CLUGSTON FLORES: ASSISTANT EDITOR
JIM CHADWICK: EDITOR
BURCHETT, DAVIS & ELTAEB: COVER
BATMAN CREATED BY BOB KANE

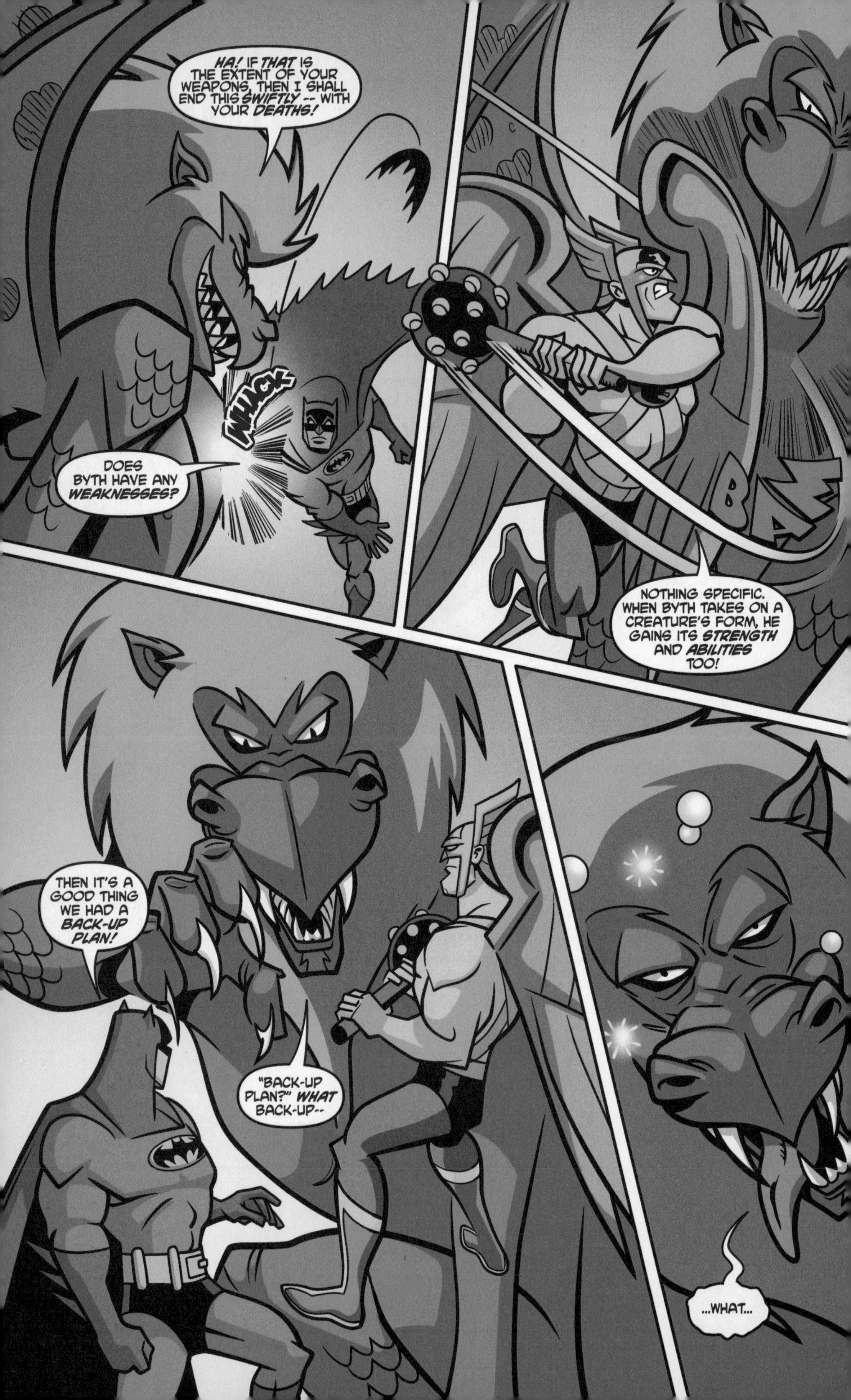

HA! IF THAT IS THE EXTENT OF YOUR WEAPONS, THEN I SHALL END THIS SWIFTLY -- WITH YOUR DEATHS!
WHACK
DOES BYTH HAVE ANY WEAKNESSES?
BAM
NOTHING SPECIFIC. WHEN BYTH TAKES ON A CREATURE'S FORM, HE GAINS ITS STRENGTH AND ABILITIES TOO!
THEN IT'S A GOOD THING WE HAD A BACK-UP PLAN!
"BACK-UP PLAN?" WHAT BACK-UP--
...WHAT...

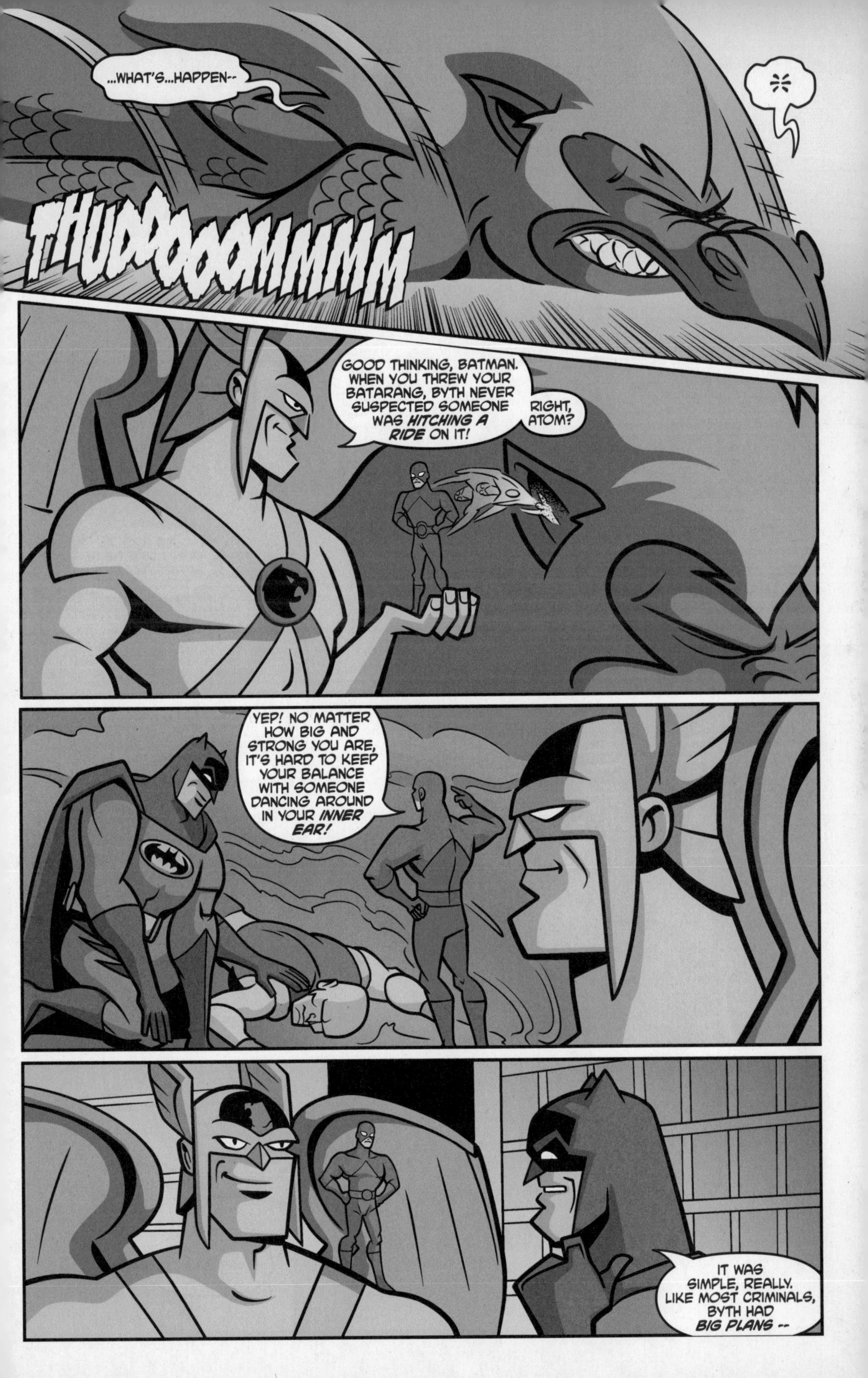
...WHAT'S...HAPPEN--
THUDOOOMMMMM
GOOD THINKING, BATMAN. WHEN YOU THREW YOUR BATARANG, BYTH NEVER SUSPECTED SOMEONE WAS *HITCHING A RIDE* ON IT!
RIGHT, ATOM?
YEP! NO MATTER HOW BIG AND STRONG YOU ARE, IT'S HARD TO KEEP YOUR BALANCE WITH SOMEONE DANCING AROUND IN YOUR *INNER EAR!*
IT WAS SIMPLE, REALLY. LIKE MOST CRIMINALS, BYTH HAD *BIG PLANS* --

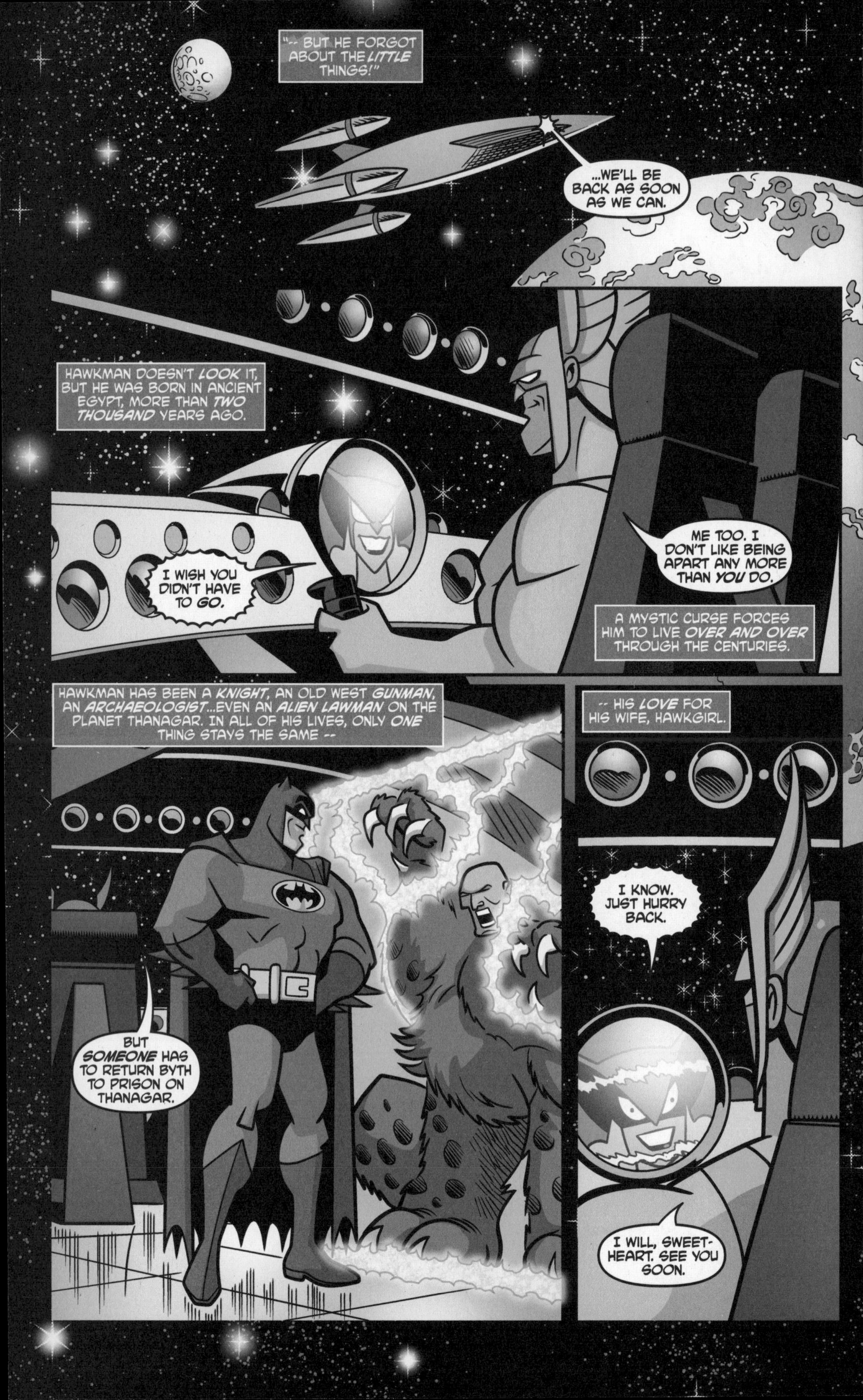
"-- BUT HE FORGOT ABOUT THE *LITTLE* THINGS!"
...WE'LL BE BACK AS SOON AS WE CAN.
HAWKMAN DOESN'T *LOOK* IT, BUT HE WAS BORN IN ANCIENT EGYPT, MORE THAN *TWO THOUSAND* YEARS AGO.
I WISH YOU DIDN'T HAVE TO *GO*.
ME TOO. I DON'T LIKE BEING APART ANY MORE THAN *YOU* DO.
A MYSTIC CURSE FORCES HIM TO LIVE *OVER AND OVER* THROUGH THE CENTURIES.
HAWKMAN HAS BEEN A *KNIGHT*, AN OLD WEST *GUNMAN*, AN *ARCHAEOLOGIST*...EVEN AN *ALIEN LAWMAN* ON THE PLANET THANAGAR. IN ALL OF HIS LIVES, ONLY *ONE* THING STAYS THE SAME --
BUT *SOMEONE* HAS TO RETURN BYTH TO PRISON ON THANAGAR.
-- HIS *LOVE* FOR HIS WIFE, HAWKGIRL.
I KNOW. JUST HURRY BACK.
I WILL, SWEET-HEART. SEE YOU SOON.

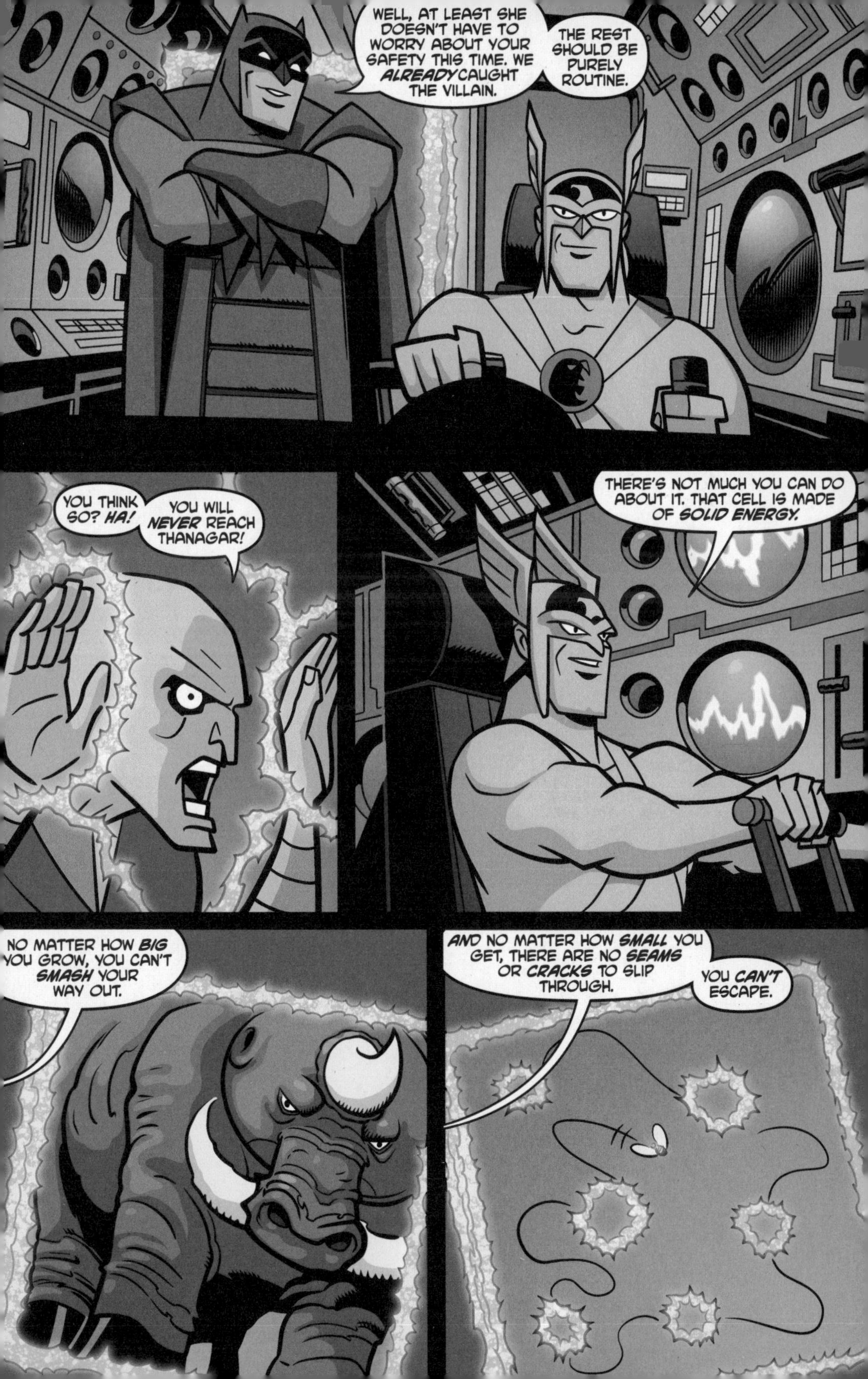
WELL, AT LEAST SHE DOESN'T HAVE TO WORRY ABOUT YOUR SAFETY THIS TIME. WE ALREADY CAUGHT THE VILLAIN.
THE REST SHOULD BE PURELY ROUTINE.
YOU THINK SO? HA!
YOU WILL NEVER REACH THANAGAR!
THERE'S NOT MUCH YOU CAN DO ABOUT IT. THAT CELL IS MADE OF SOLID ENERGY.
NO MATTER HOW BIG YOU GROW, YOU CAN'T SMASH YOUR WAY OUT.
AND NO MATTER HOW SMALL YOU GET, THERE ARE NO SEAMS OR CRACKS TO SLIP THROUGH.
YOU CAN'T ESCAPE.

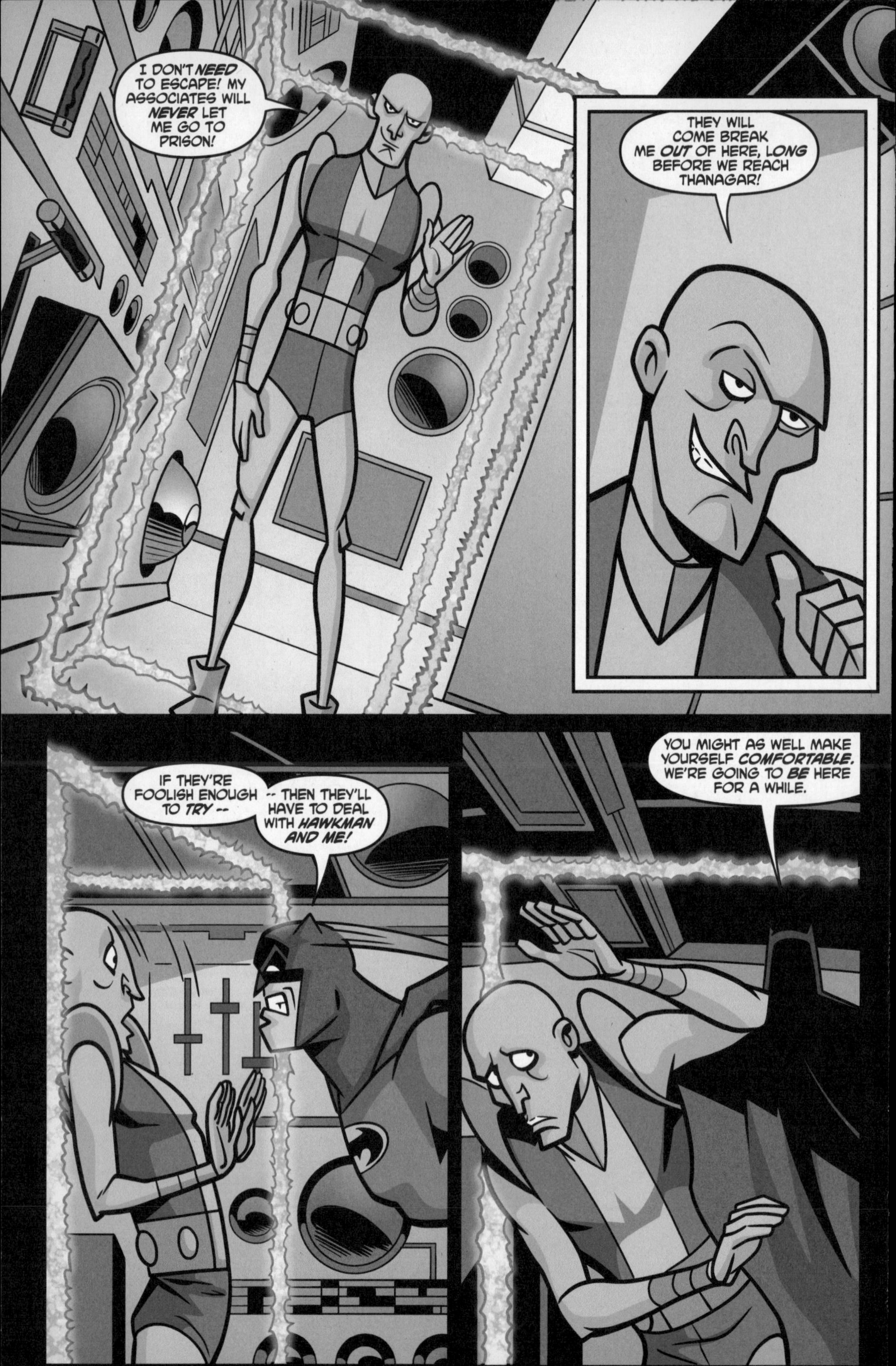
I DON'T NEED TO ESCAPE! MY ASSOCIATES WILL NEVER LET ME GO TO PRISON!
THEY WILL COME BREAK ME OUT OF HERE, LONG BEFORE WE REACH THANAGAR!
IF THEY'RE FOOLISH ENOUGH TO TRY --
-- THEN THEY'LL HAVE TO DEAL WITH HAWKMAN AND ME!
YOU MIGHT AS WELL MAKE YOURSELF COMFORTABLE. WE'RE GOING TO BE HERE FOR A WHILE.

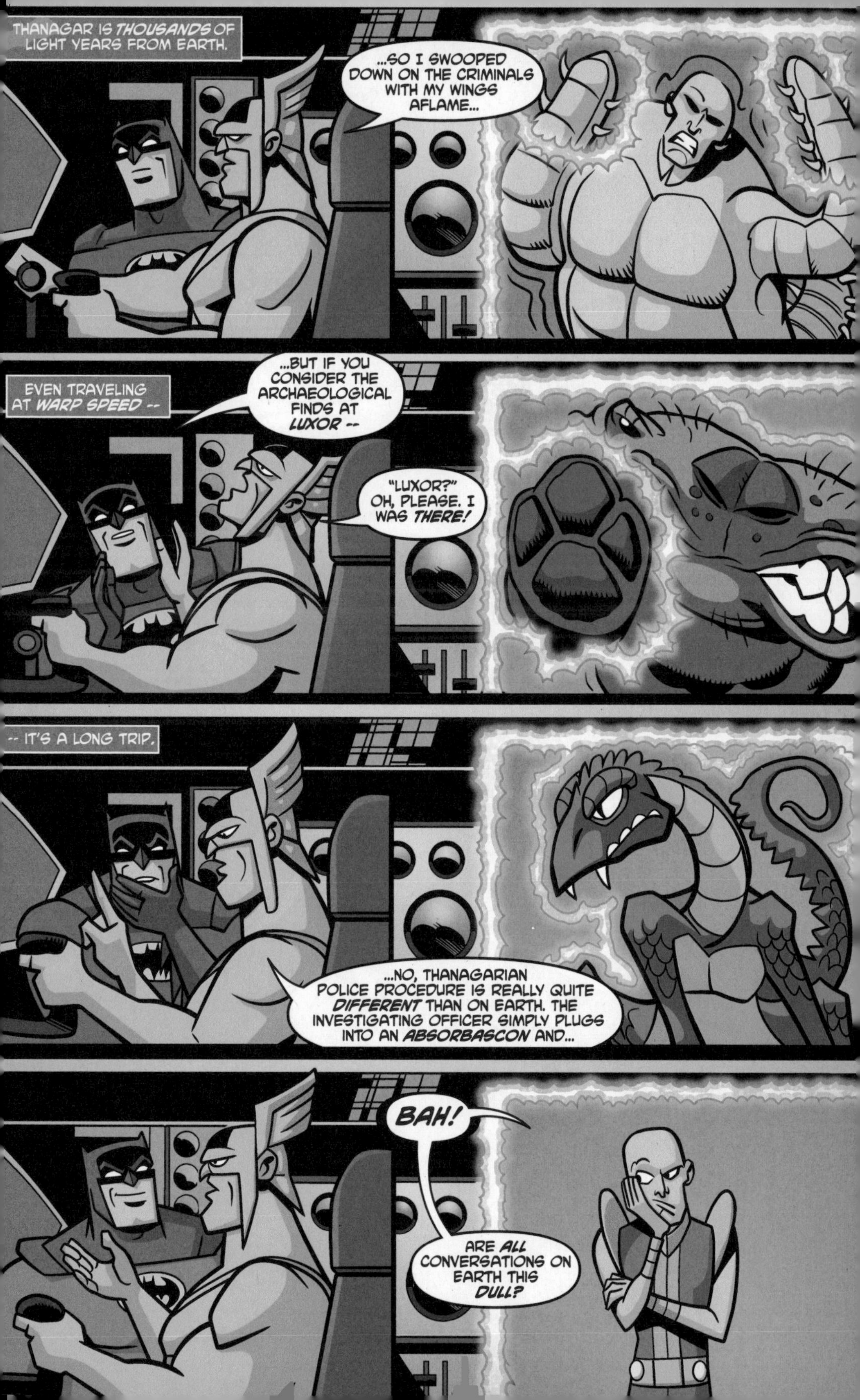
THANAGAR IS THOUSANDS OF LIGHT YEARS FROM EARTH.
...SO I SWOOPED DOWN ON THE CRIMINALS WITH MY WINGS AFLAME...
EVEN TRAVELING AT WARP SPEED --
...BUT IF YOU CONSIDER THE ARCHAEOLOGICAL FINDS AT LUXOR --
"LUXOR?" OH, PLEASE. I WAS THERE!
-- IT'S A LONG TRIP.
...NO, THANAGARIAN POLICE PROCEDURE IS REALLY QUITE DIFFERENT THAN ON EARTH. THE INVESTIGATING OFFICER SIMPLY PLUGS INTO AN ABSORBASCON AND...
BAH!
ARE ALL CONVERSATIONS ON EARTH THIS DULL?

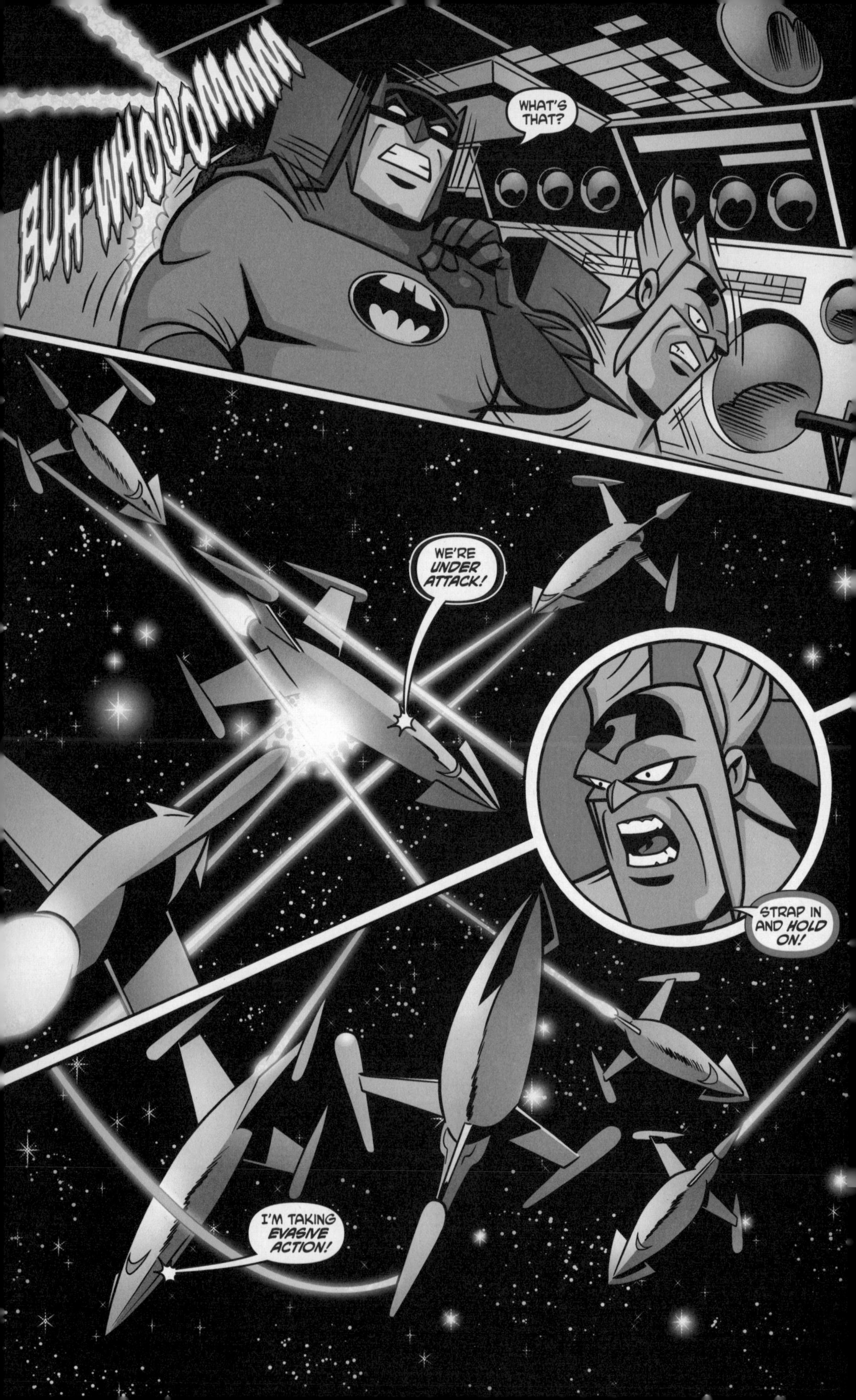
BUH-WHOOOMMM
WHAT'S THAT?
WE'RE UNDER ATTACK!
STRAP IN AND HOLD ON!
I'M TAKING EVASIVE ACTION!

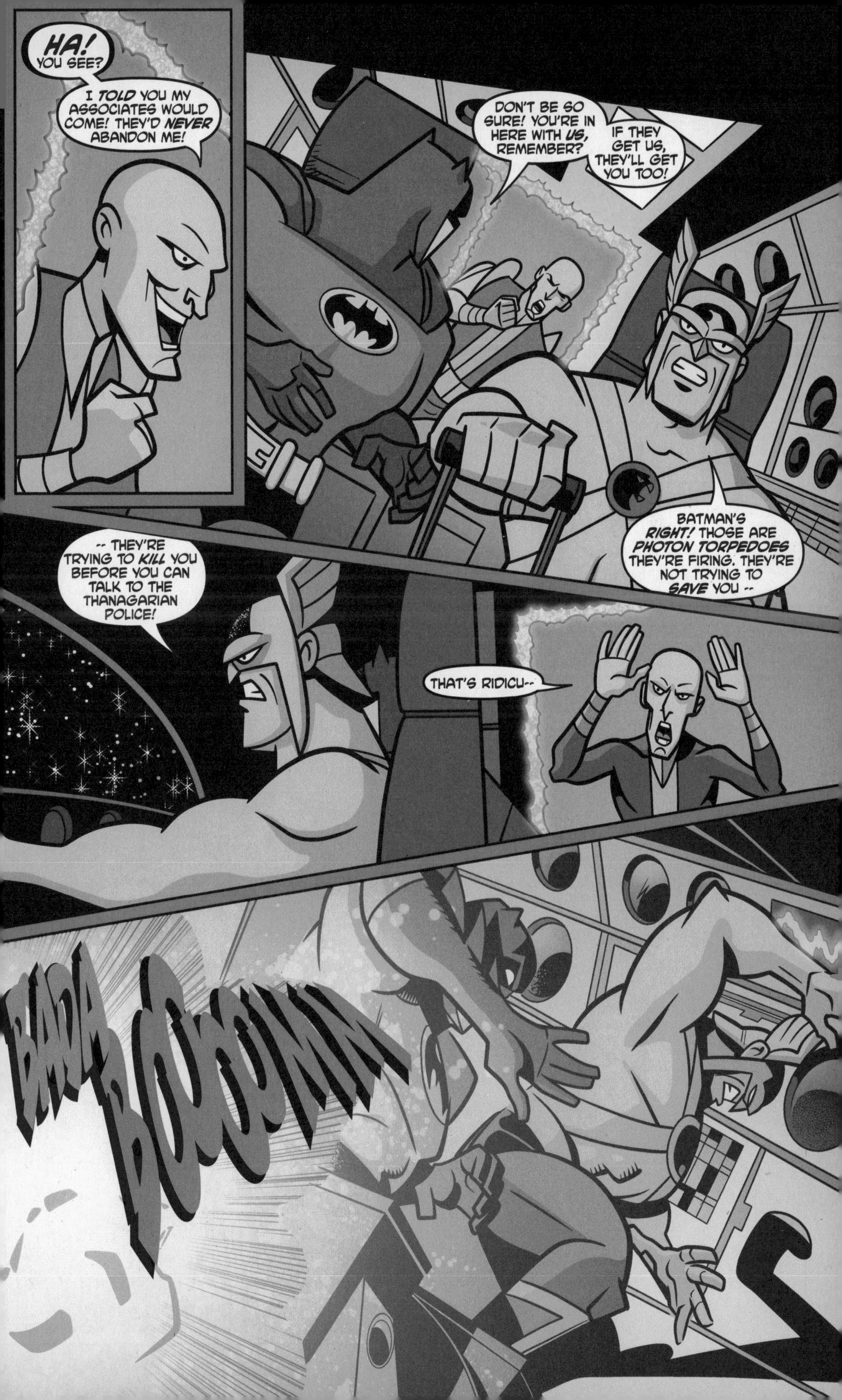

HA! YOU SEE?
I TOLD YOU MY ASSOCIATES WOULD COME! THEY'D NEVER ABANDON ME!
DON'T BE SO SURE! YOU'RE IN HERE WITH US, REMEMBER?
IF THEY GET US, THEY'LL GET YOU TOO!
BATMAN'S RIGHT! THOSE ARE PHOTON TORPEDOES THEY'RE FIRING. THEY'RE NOT TRYING TO SAVE YOU --
-- THEY'RE TRYING TO KILL YOU BEFORE YOU CAN TALK TO THE THANAGARIAN POLICE!
THAT'S RIDICU--
BADA BOOOMM

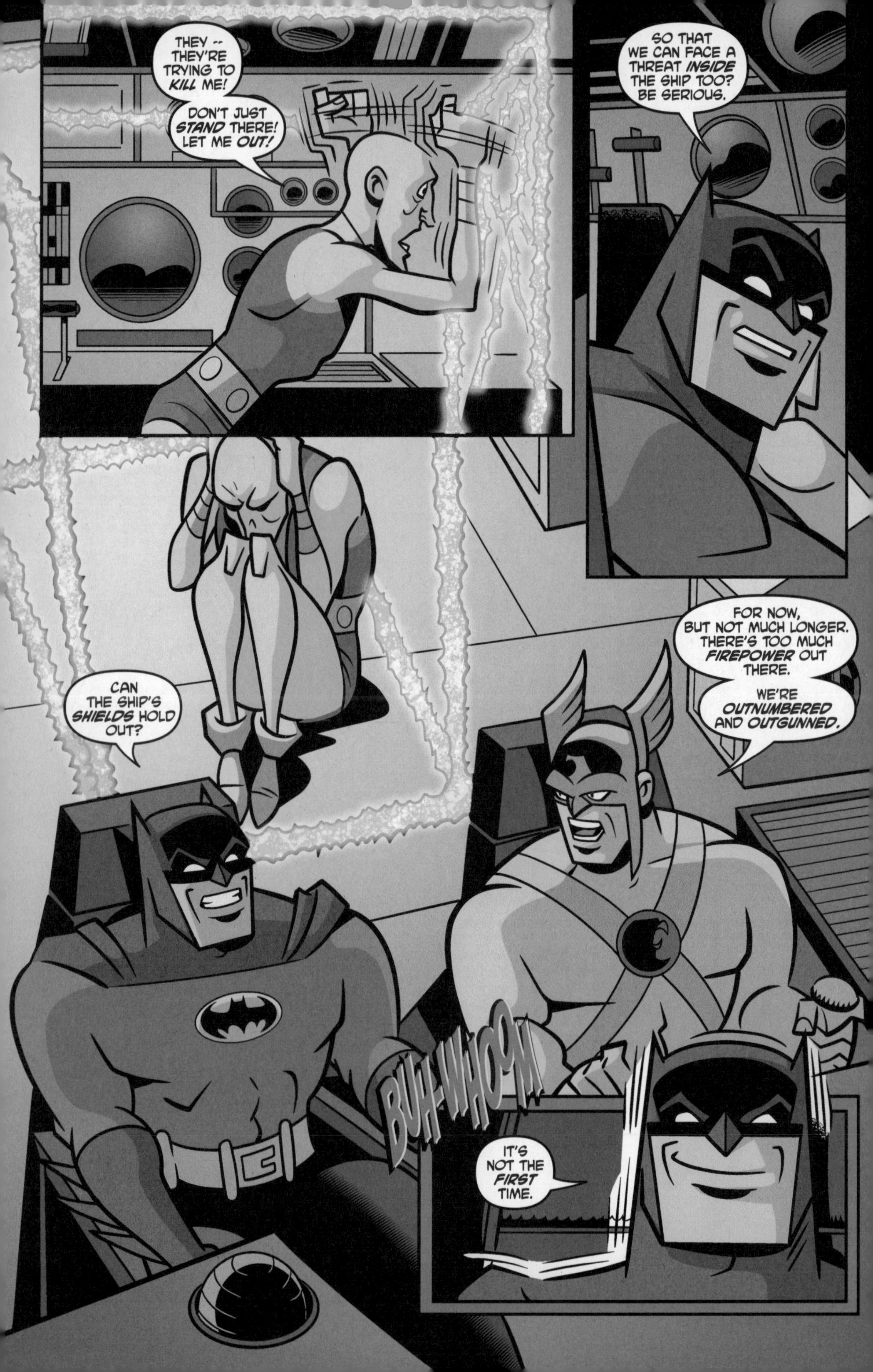
THEY -- THEY'RE TRYING TO KILL ME!
DON'T JUST STAND THERE! LET ME OUT!
SO THAT WE CAN FACE A THREAT INSIDE THE SHIP TOO? BE SERIOUS.
CAN THE SHIP'S SHIELDS HOLD OUT?
FOR NOW, BUT NOT MUCH LONGER. THERE'S TOO MUCH FIREPOWER OUT THERE.
WE'RE OUTNUMBERED AND OUTGUNNED.
BUH-WHOOM
IT'S NOT THE FIRST TIME.

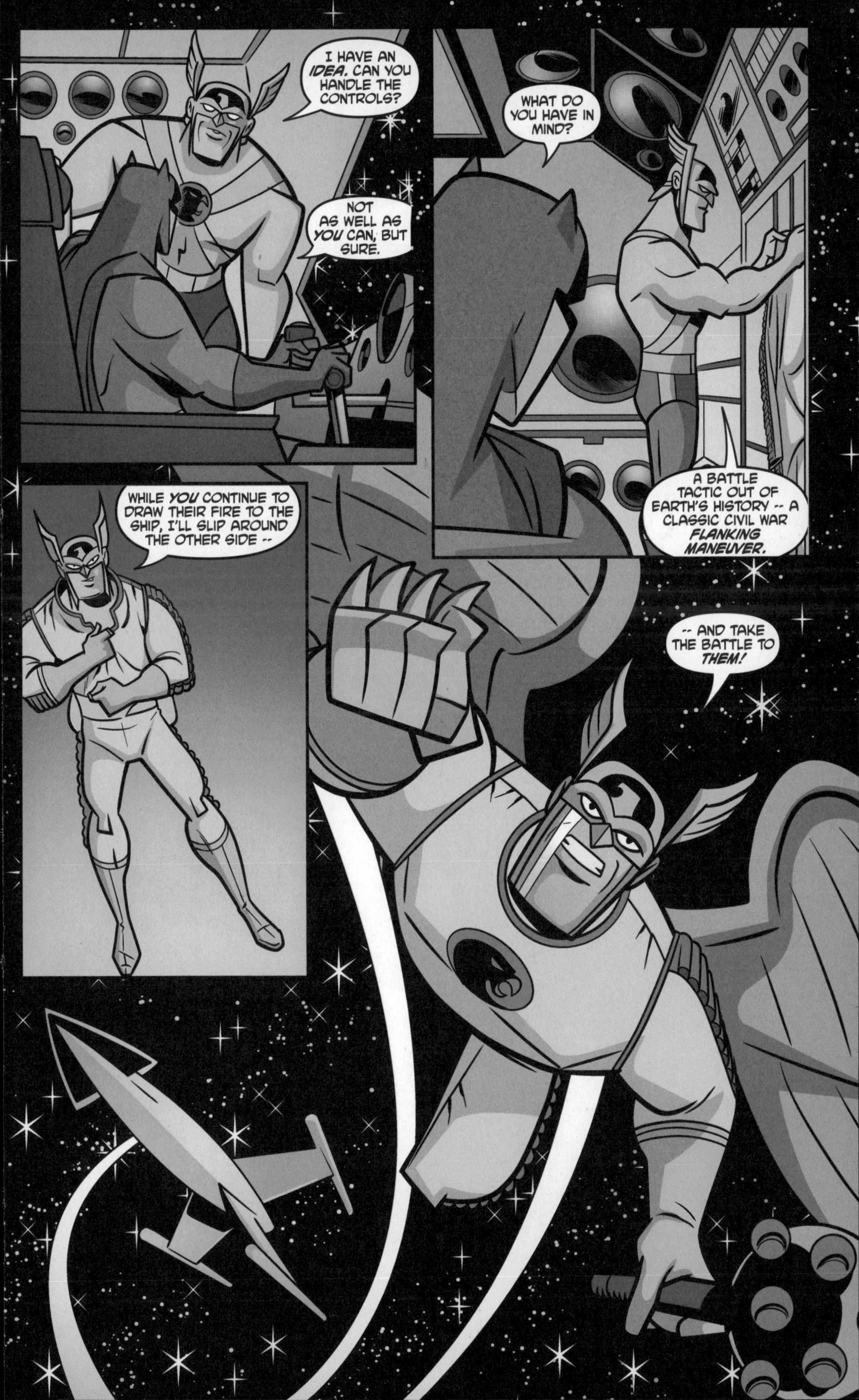

I HAVE AN IDEA. CAN YOU HANDLE THE CONTROLS?
NOT AS WELL AS YOU CAN, BUT SURE.
WHAT DO YOU HAVE IN MIND?
A BATTLE TACTIC OUT OF EARTH'S HISTORY -- A CLASSIC CIVIL WAR FLANKING MANEUVER.
WHILE YOU CONTINUE TO DRAW THEIR FIRE TO THE SHIP, I'LL SLIP AROUND THE OTHER SIDE --
-- AND TAKE THE BATTLE TO THEM!

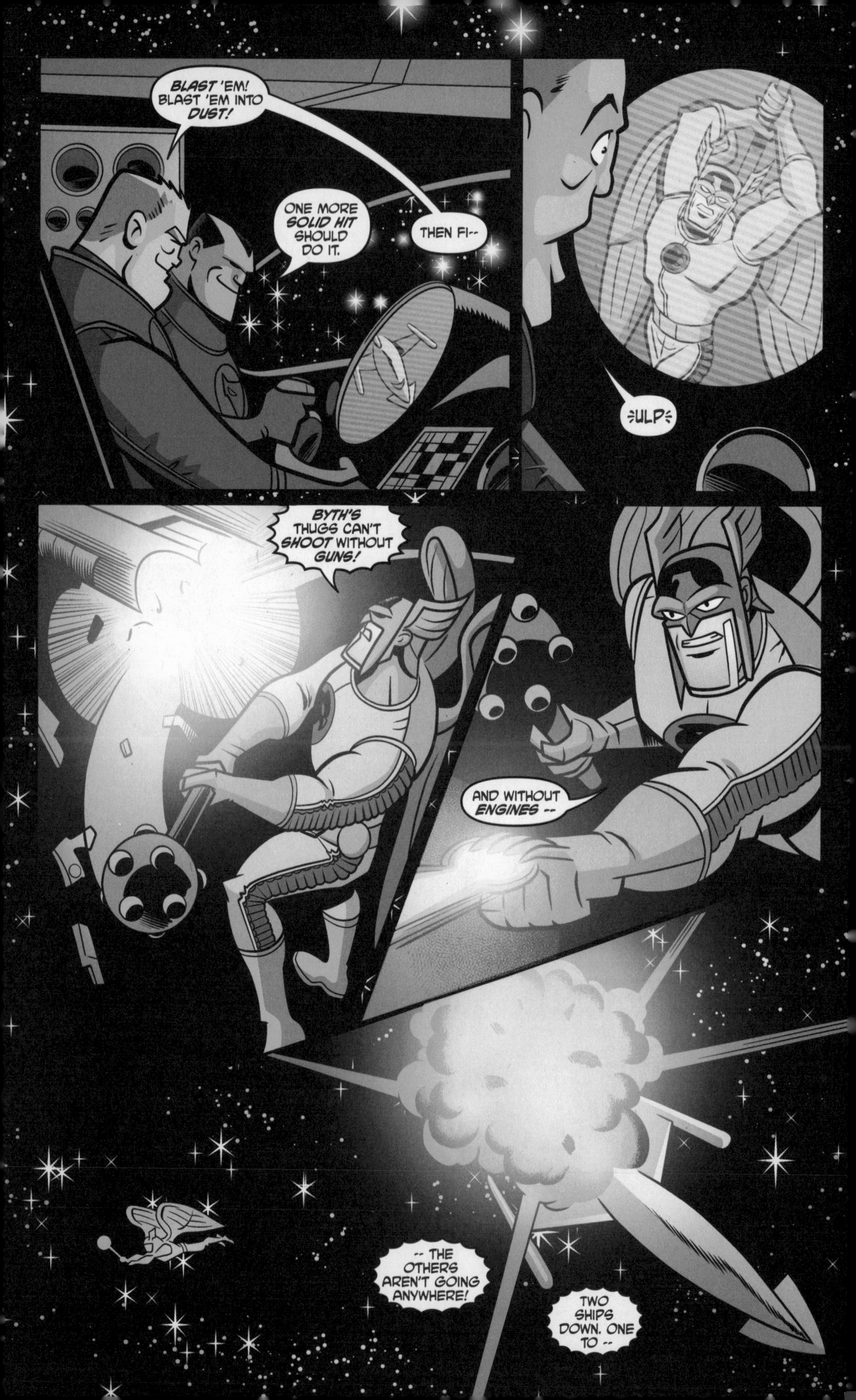
BLAST 'EM! BLAST 'EM INTO DUST!
ONE MORE SOLID HIT SHOULD DO IT.
THEN FI--
ULP
BYTH'S THUGS CAN'T SHOOT WITHOUT GUNS!
AND WITHOUT ENGINES --
-- THE OTHERS AREN'T GOING ANYWHERE!
TWO SHIPS DOWN. ONE TO --

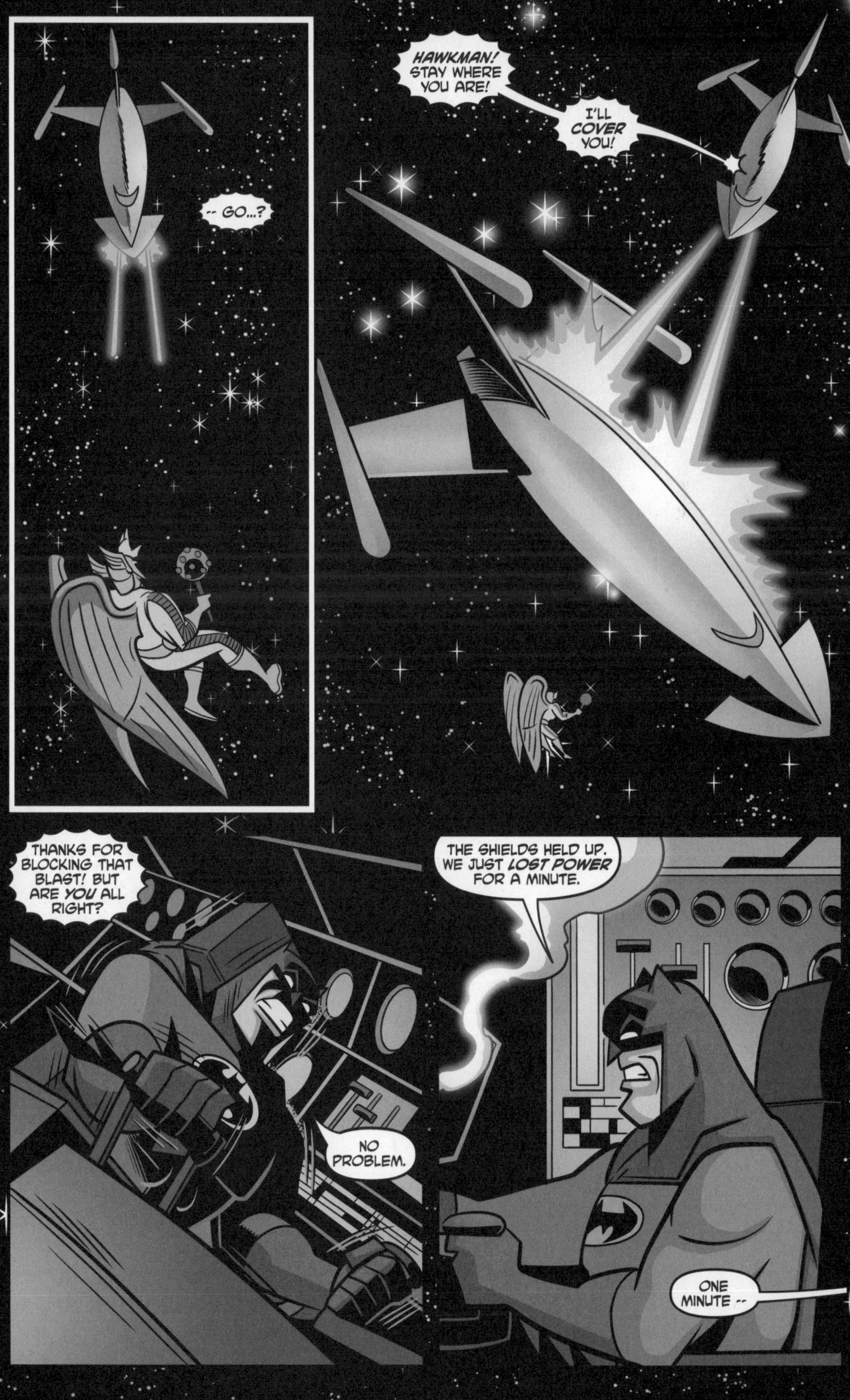
-- GO...?
HAWKMAN! STAY WHERE YOU ARE!
I'LL COVER YOU!
THANKS FOR BLOCKING THAT BLAST! BUT ARE YOU ALL RIGHT?
NO PROBLEM.
THE SHIELDS HELD UP. WE JUST LOST POWER FOR A MINUTE.
ONE MINUTE --

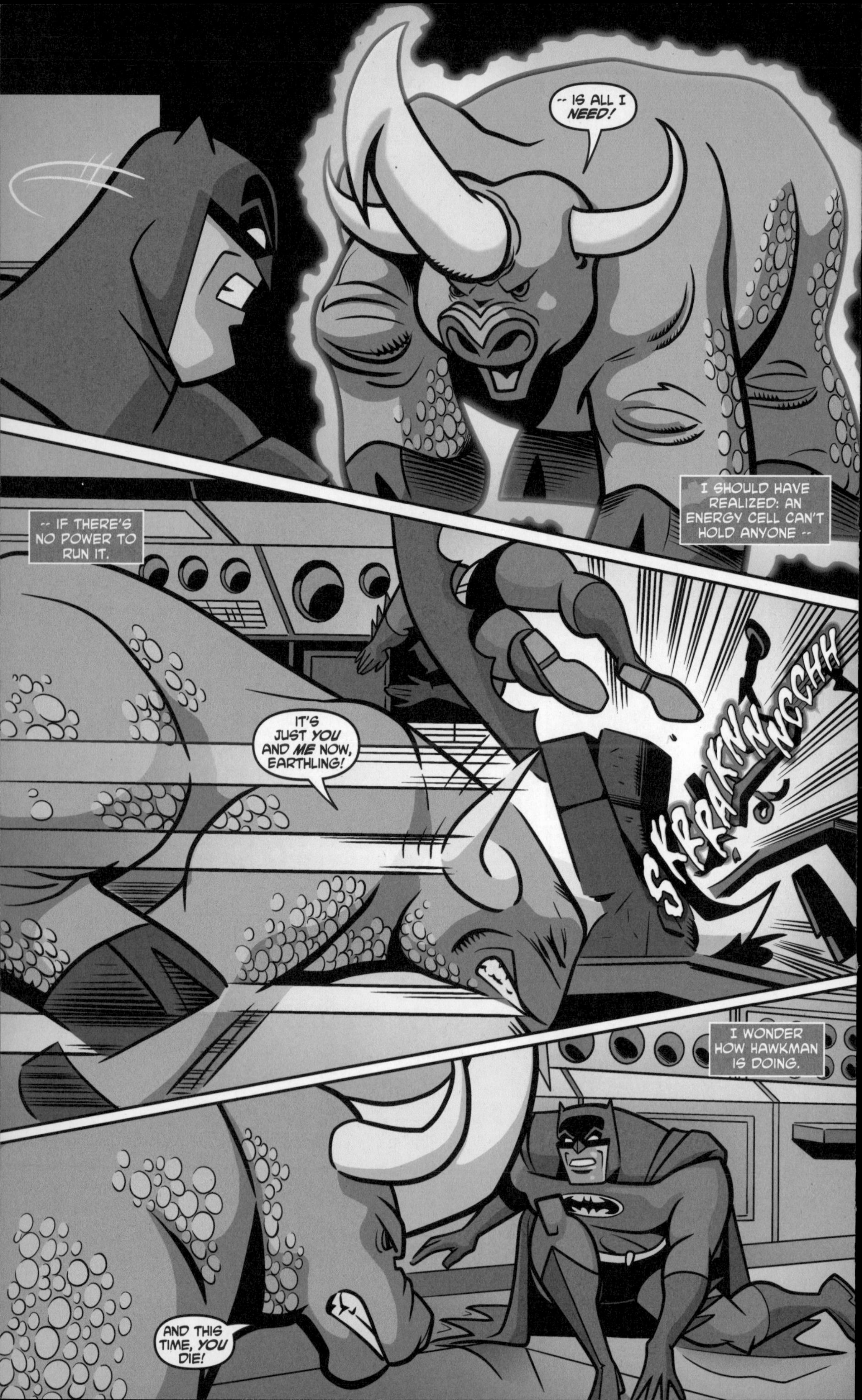
-- IS ALL I NEED!
I SHOULD HAVE REALIZED: AN ENERGY CELL CAN'T HOLD ANYONE --
-- IF THERE'S NO POWER TO RUN IT.
IT'S JUST YOU AND ME NOW, EARTHLING!
SKRAKNNGCHH
I WONDER HOW HAWKMAN IS DOING.
AND THIS TIME, YOU DIE!

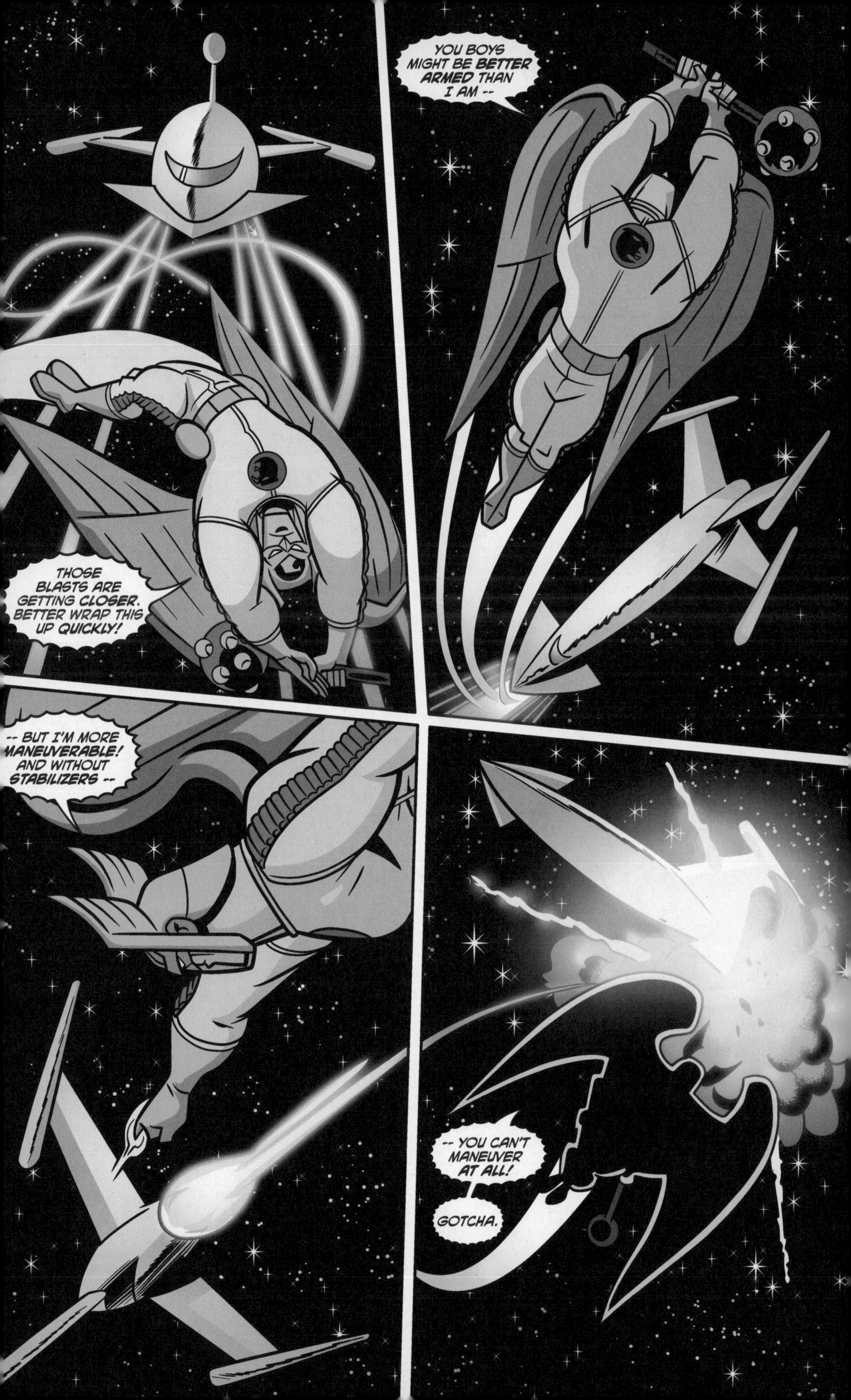
THOSE BLASTS ARE GETTING CLOSER. BETTER WRAP THIS UP QUICKLY!
YOU BOYS MIGHT BE BETTER ARMED THAN I AM --
-- BUT I'M MORE MANEUVERABLE! AND WITHOUT STABILIZERS --
-- YOU CAN'T MANEUVER AT ALL!
GOTCHA.

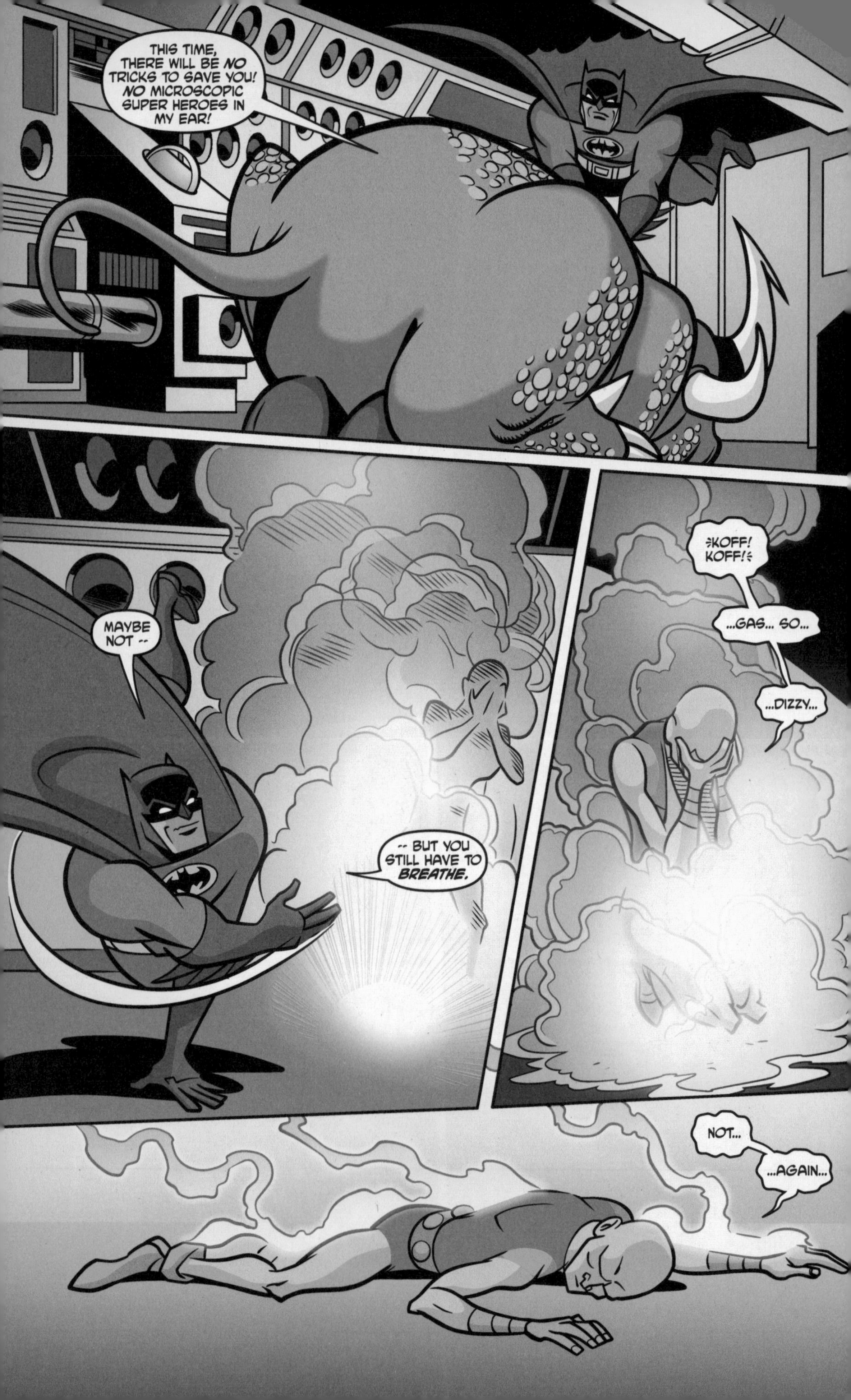
THIS TIME, THERE WILL BE *NO* TRICKS TO SAVE YOU! *NO* MICROSCOPIC SUPER HEROES IN MY EAR!
MAYBE NOT --
-- BUT YOU STILL HAVE TO *BREATHE.*
KOFF! KOFF!
...GAS... SO...
...DIZZY...
NOT...
...AGAIN...

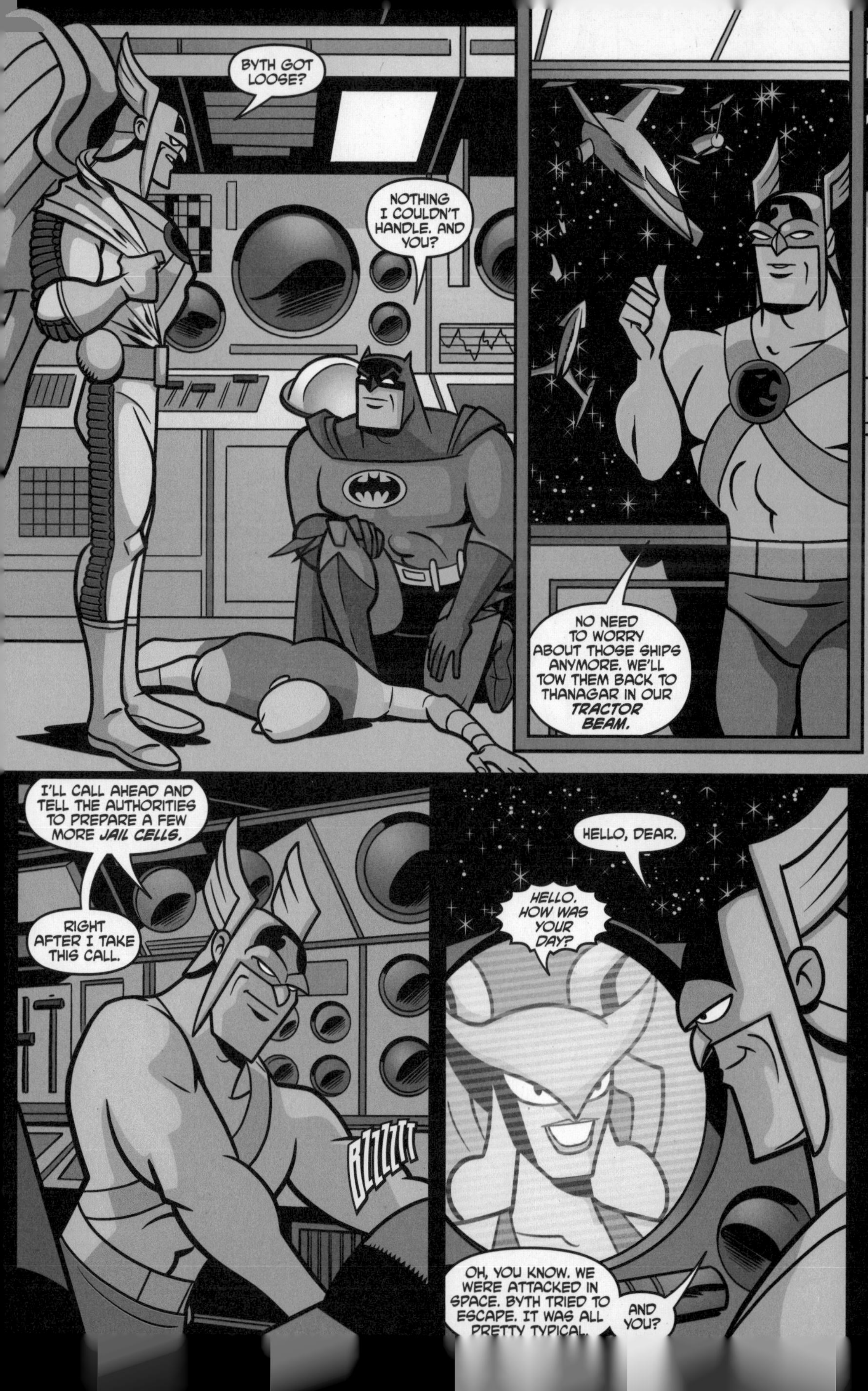
BYTH GOT LOOSE?
NOTHING I COULDN'T HANDLE. AND YOU?
NO NEED TO WORRY ABOUT THOSE SHIPS ANYMORE. WE'LL TOW THEM BACK TO THANAGAR IN OUR *TRACTOR BEAM.*
I'LL CALL AHEAD AND TELL THE AUTHORITIES TO PREPARE A FEW MORE *JAIL CELLS.*
RIGHT AFTER I TAKE THIS CALL.
BZZZZT
HELLO, DEAR.
HELLO. HOW WAS YOUR DAY?
OH, YOU KNOW. WE WERE ATTACKED IN SPACE. BYTH TRIED TO ESCAPE. IT WAS ALL PRETTY TYPICAL.
AND YOU?

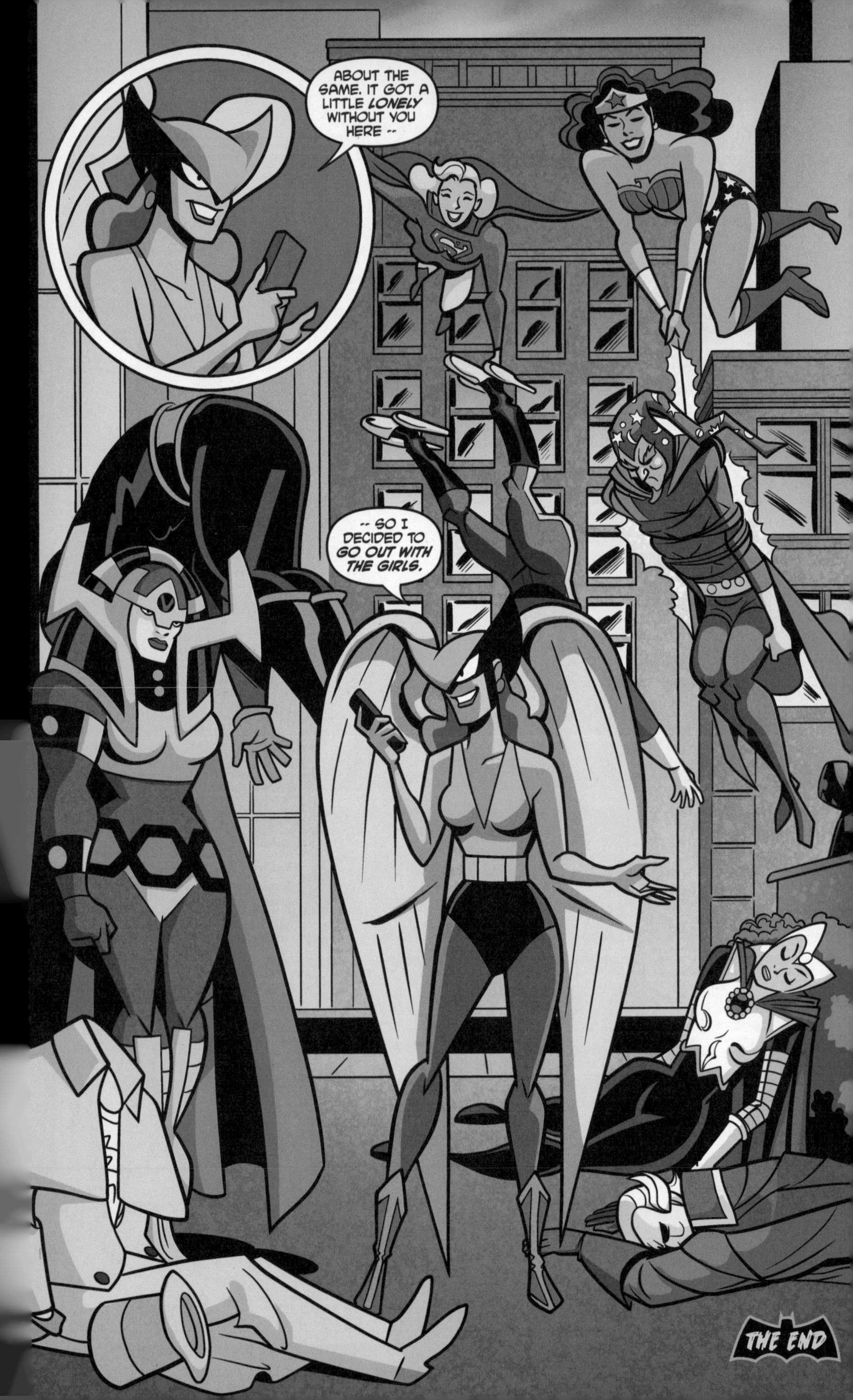
ABOUT THE SAME. IT GOT A LITTLE *LONELY* WITHOUT YOU HERE --
-- SO I DECIDED TO *GO OUT WITH THE GIRLS.*
THE END

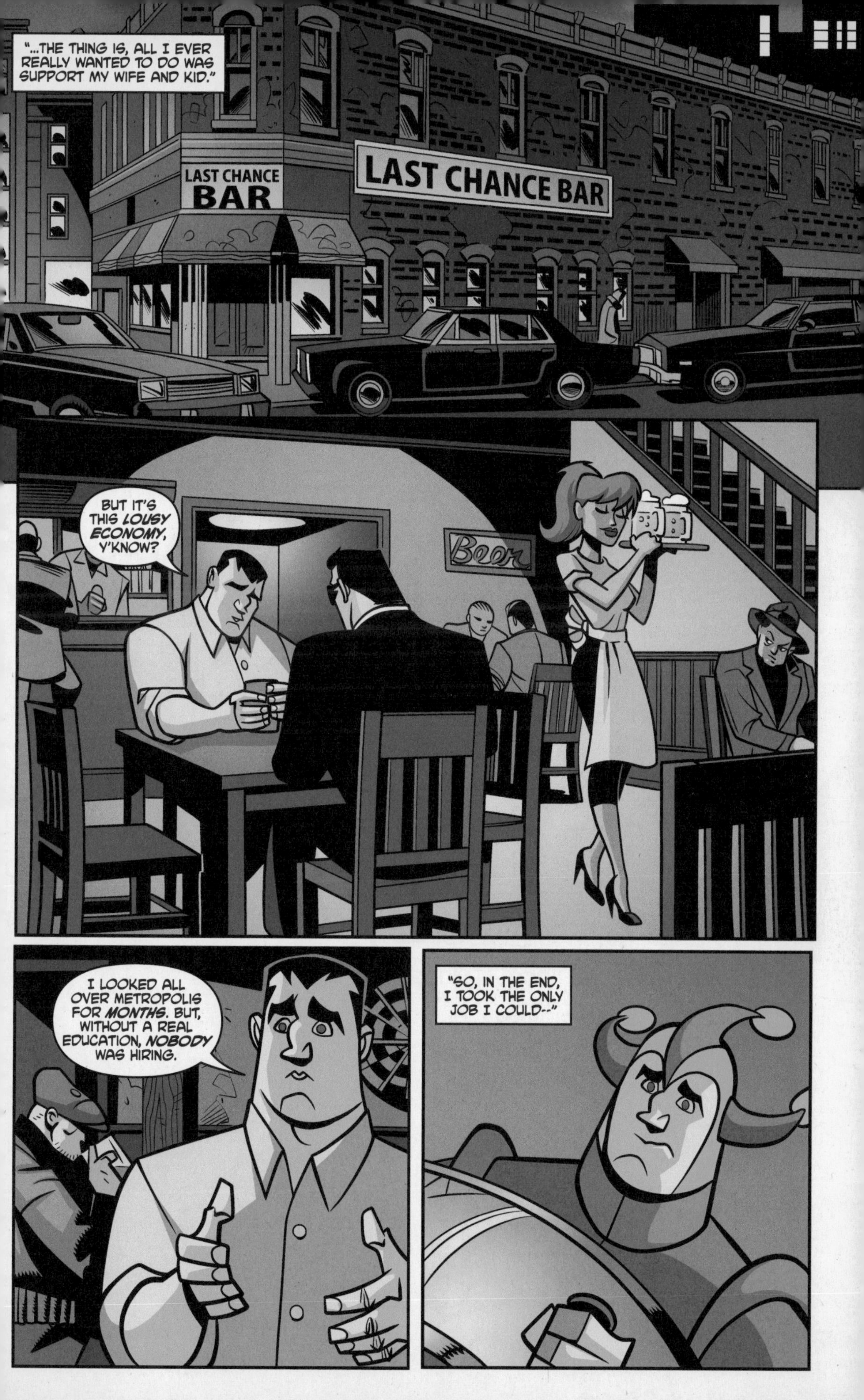
"...THE THING IS, ALL I EVER REALLY WANTED TO DO WAS SUPPORT MY WIFE AND KID."
LAST CHANCE BAR
LAST CHANCE BAR
BUT IT'S THIS *LOUSY ECONOMY*, Y'KNOW?
Beer
I LOOKED ALL OVER METROPOLIS FOR *MONTHS*. BUT, WITHOUT A REAL EDUCATION, *NOBODY* WAS HIRING.
"SO, IN THE END, I TOOK THE ONLY JOB I COULD--"

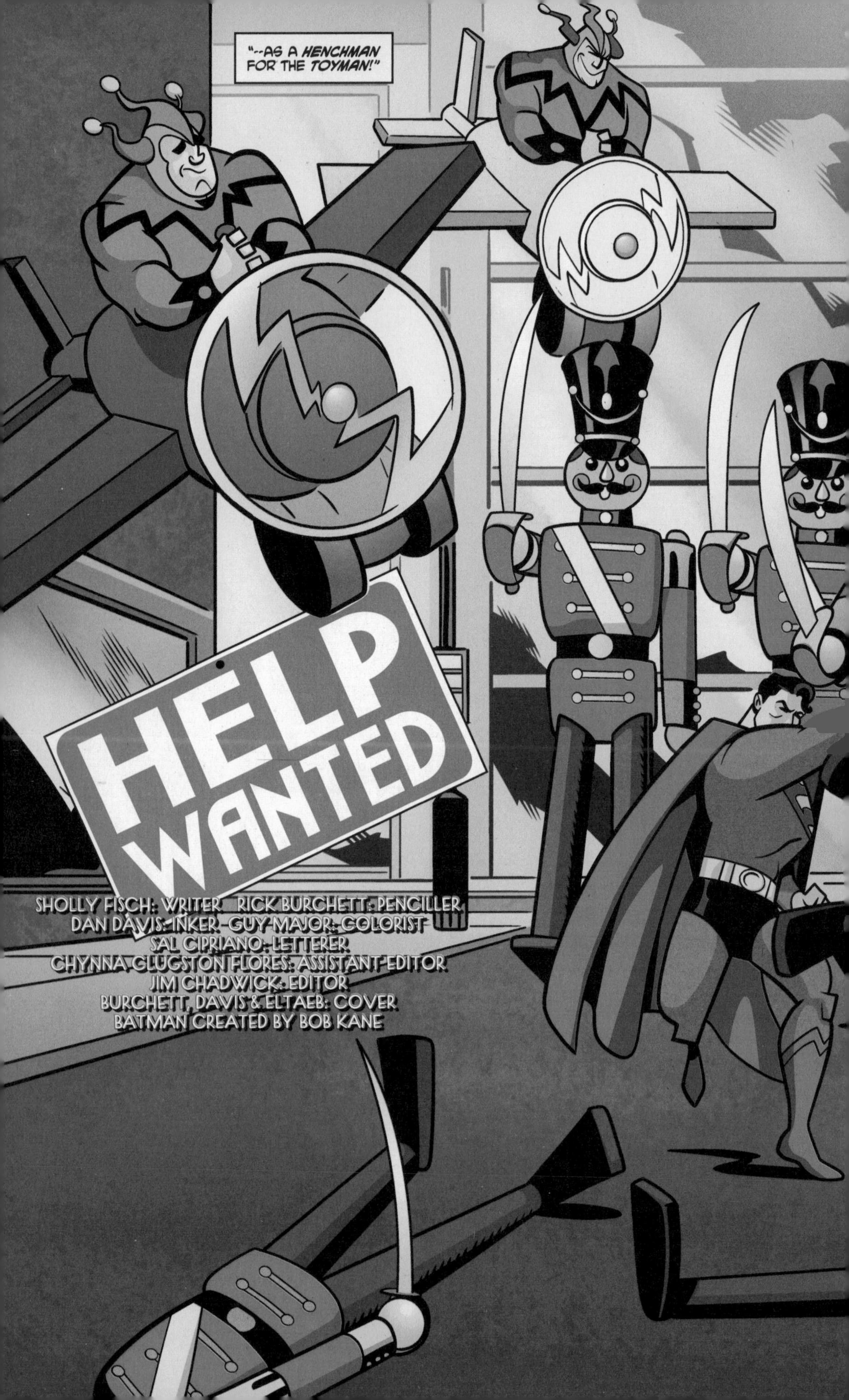
"--AS A HENCHMAN FOR THE TOYMAN!"
HELP WANTED
SHOLLY FISCH: WRITER RICK BURCHETT: PENCILLER
DAN DAVIS: INKER GUY MAJOR: COLORIST
SAL CIPRIANO: LETTERER
CHYNNA CLUGSTON FLORES: ASSISTANT EDITOR
JIM CHADWICK: EDITOR
BURCHETT, DAVIS & ELTAEB: COVER
BATMAN CREATED BY BOB KANE

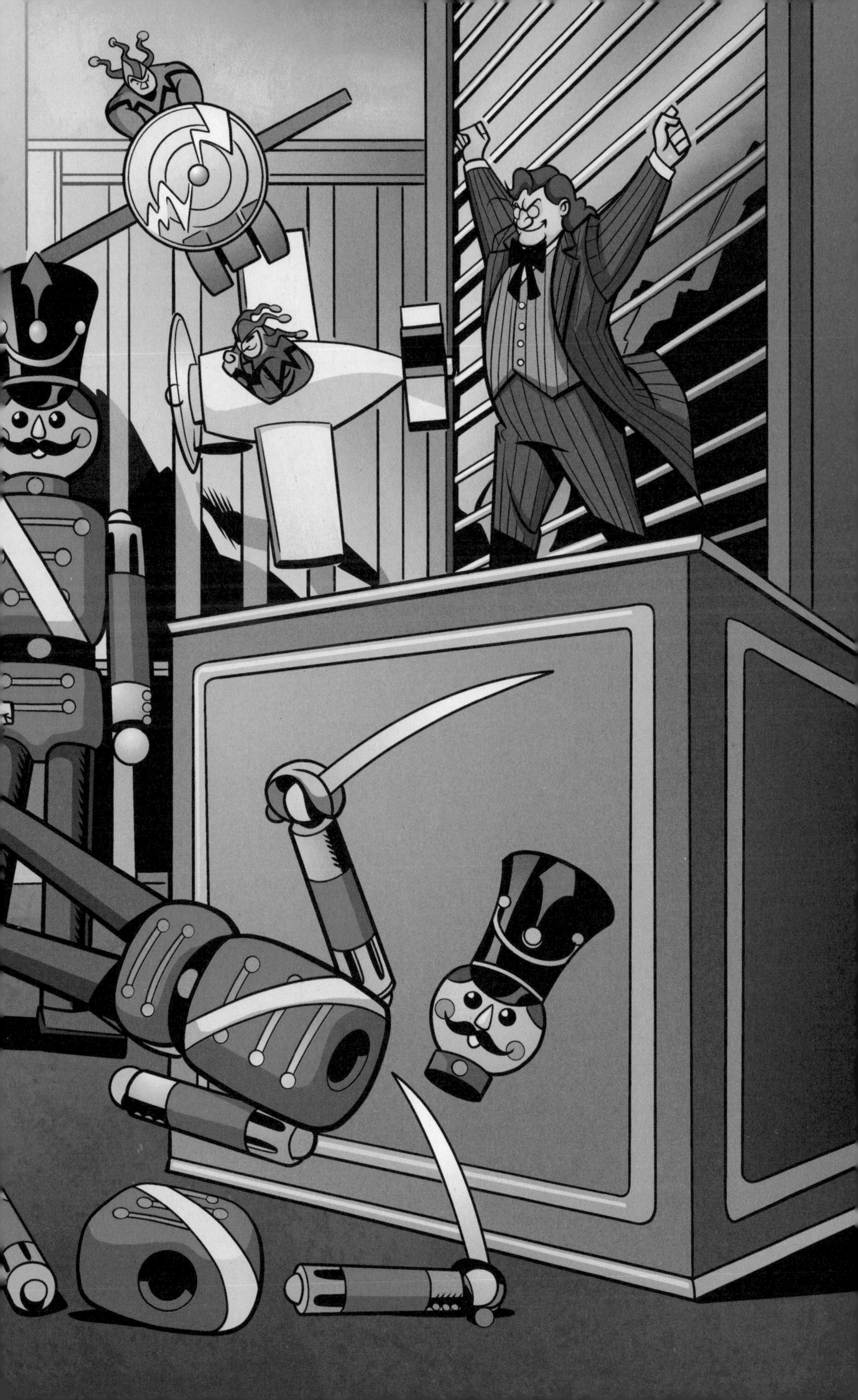

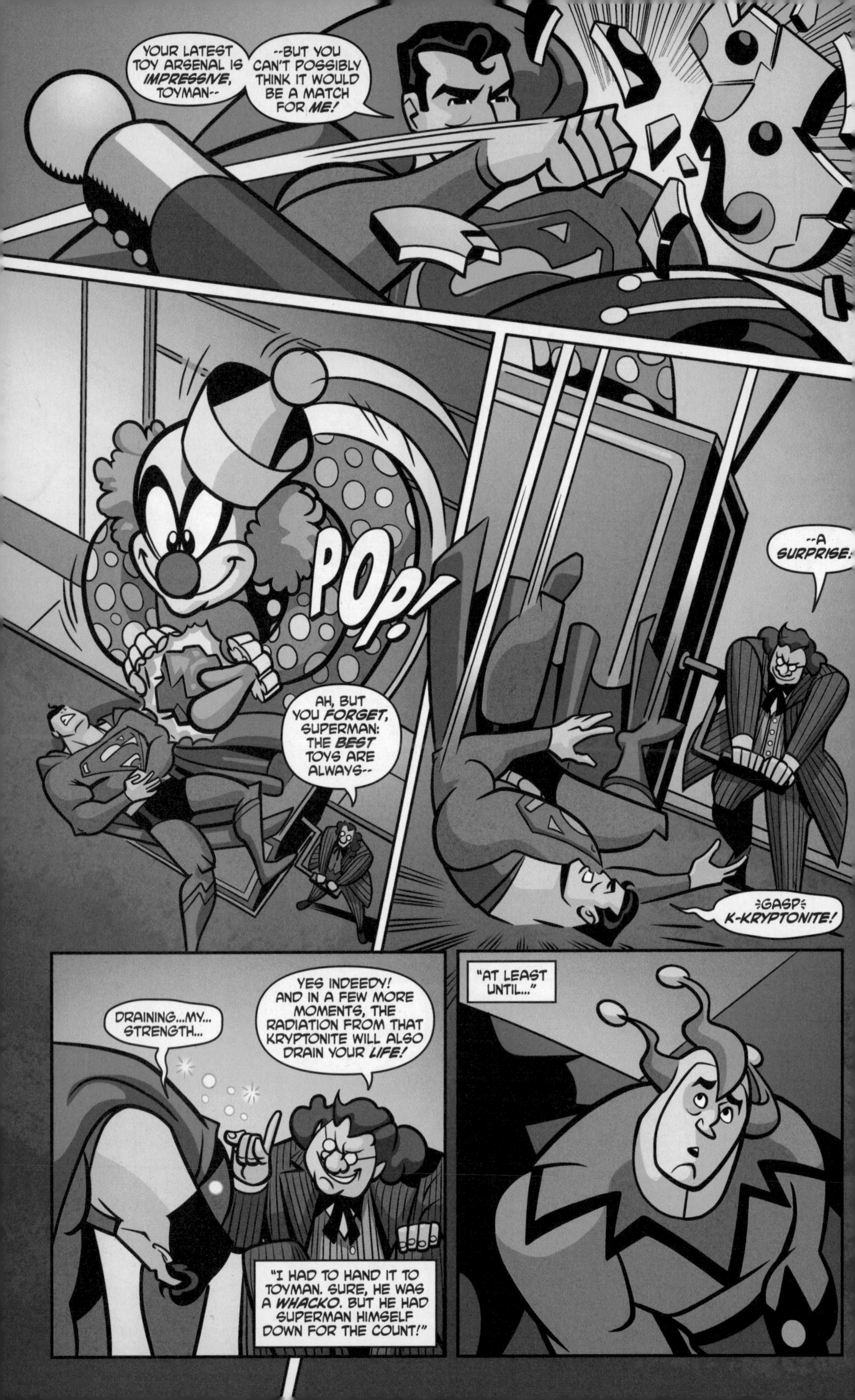
YOUR LATEST TOY ARSENAL IS *IMPRESSIVE*, TOYMAN--
--BUT YOU CAN'T POSSIBLY THINK IT WOULD BE A MATCH FOR *ME!*
POP!
AH, BUT YOU *FORGET*, SUPERMAN: THE *BEST* TOYS ARE ALWAYS--
--A *SURPRISE!*
GASP K-KRYPTONITE!
DRAINING...MY... STRENGTH...
YES INDEEDY! AND IN A FEW MORE MOMENTS, THE RADIATION FROM THAT KRYPTONITE WILL ALSO DRAIN YOUR *LIFE!*
"I HAD TO HAND IT TO TOYMAN. SURE, HE WAS A *WHACKO*. BUT HE HAD SUPERMAN HIMSELF DOWN FOR THE COUNT!"
"AT LEAST UNTIL..."

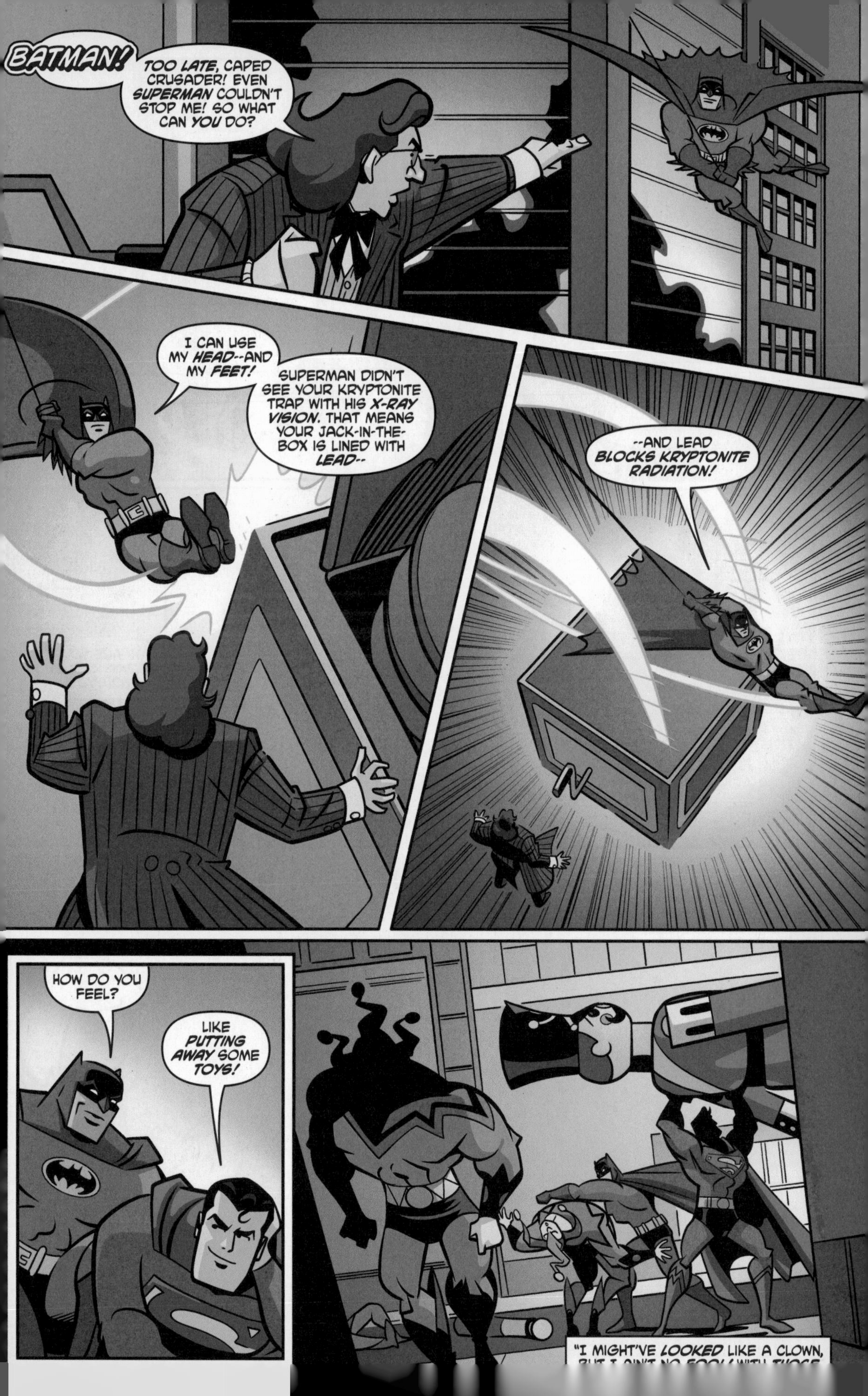
BATMAN!
TOO LATE, CAPED CRUSADER! EVEN SUPERMAN COULDN'T STOP ME! SO WHAT CAN YOU DO?
I CAN USE MY HEAD--AND MY FEET!
SUPERMAN DIDN'T SEE YOUR KRYPTONITE TRAP WITH HIS X-RAY VISION. THAT MEANS YOUR JACK-IN-THE-BOX IS LINED WITH LEAD--
--AND LEAD BLOCKS KRYPTONITE RADIATION!
HOW DO YOU FEEL?
LIKE PUTTING AWAY SOME TOYS!
"I MIGHT'VE LOOKED LIKE A CLOWN,

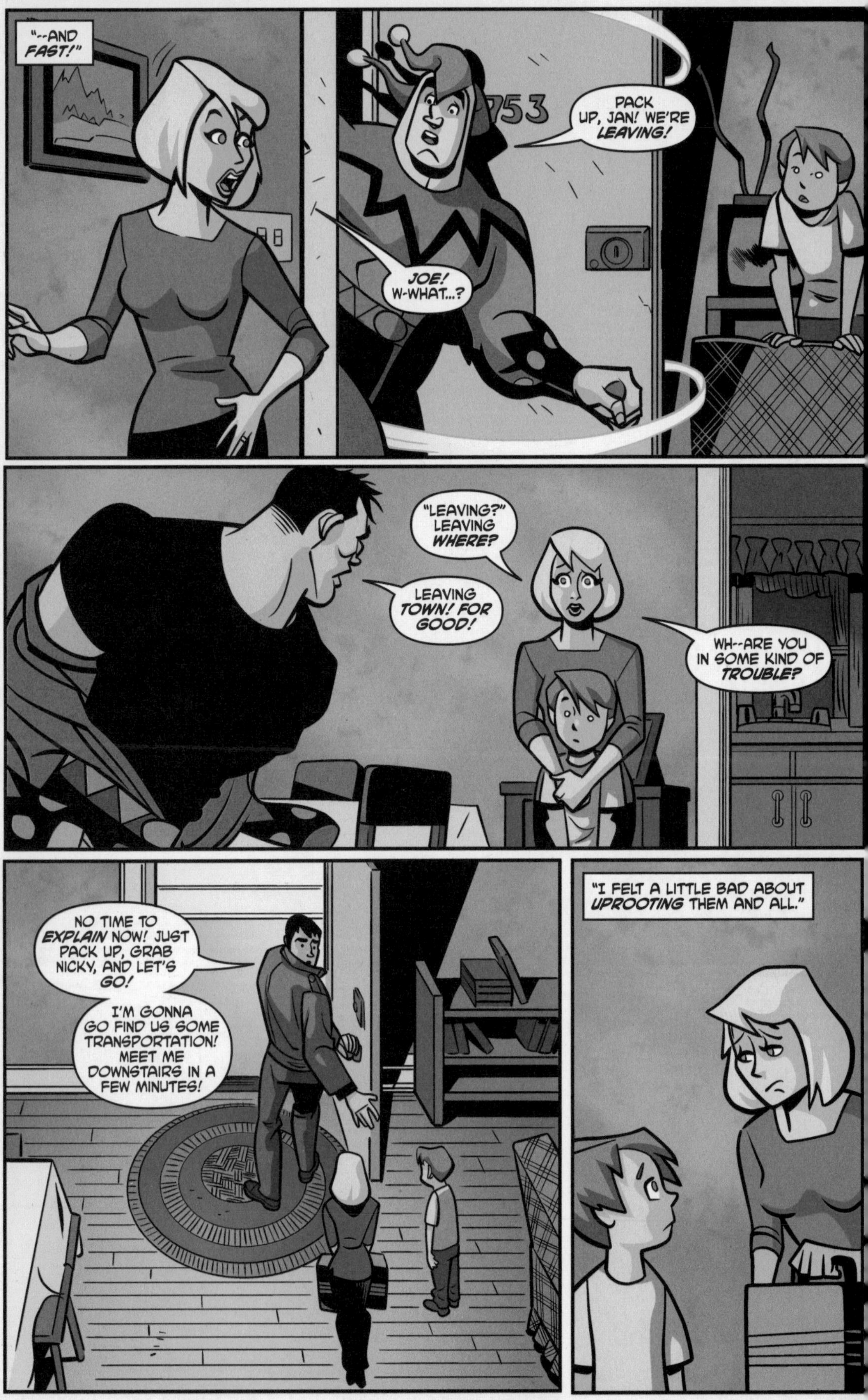
"--AND FAST!"
PACK UP, JAN! WE'RE LEAVING!
JOE! W-WHAT...?
"LEAVING?" LEAVING WHERE?
LEAVING TOWN! FOR GOOD!
WH--ARE YOU IN SOME KIND OF TROUBLE?
NO TIME TO EXPLAIN NOW! JUST PACK UP, GRAB NICKY, AND LET'S GO!
I'M GONNA GO FIND US SOME TRANSPORTATION! MEET ME DOWNSTAIRS IN A FEW MINUTES!
"I FELT A LITTLE BAD ABOUT UPROOTING THEM AND ALL."

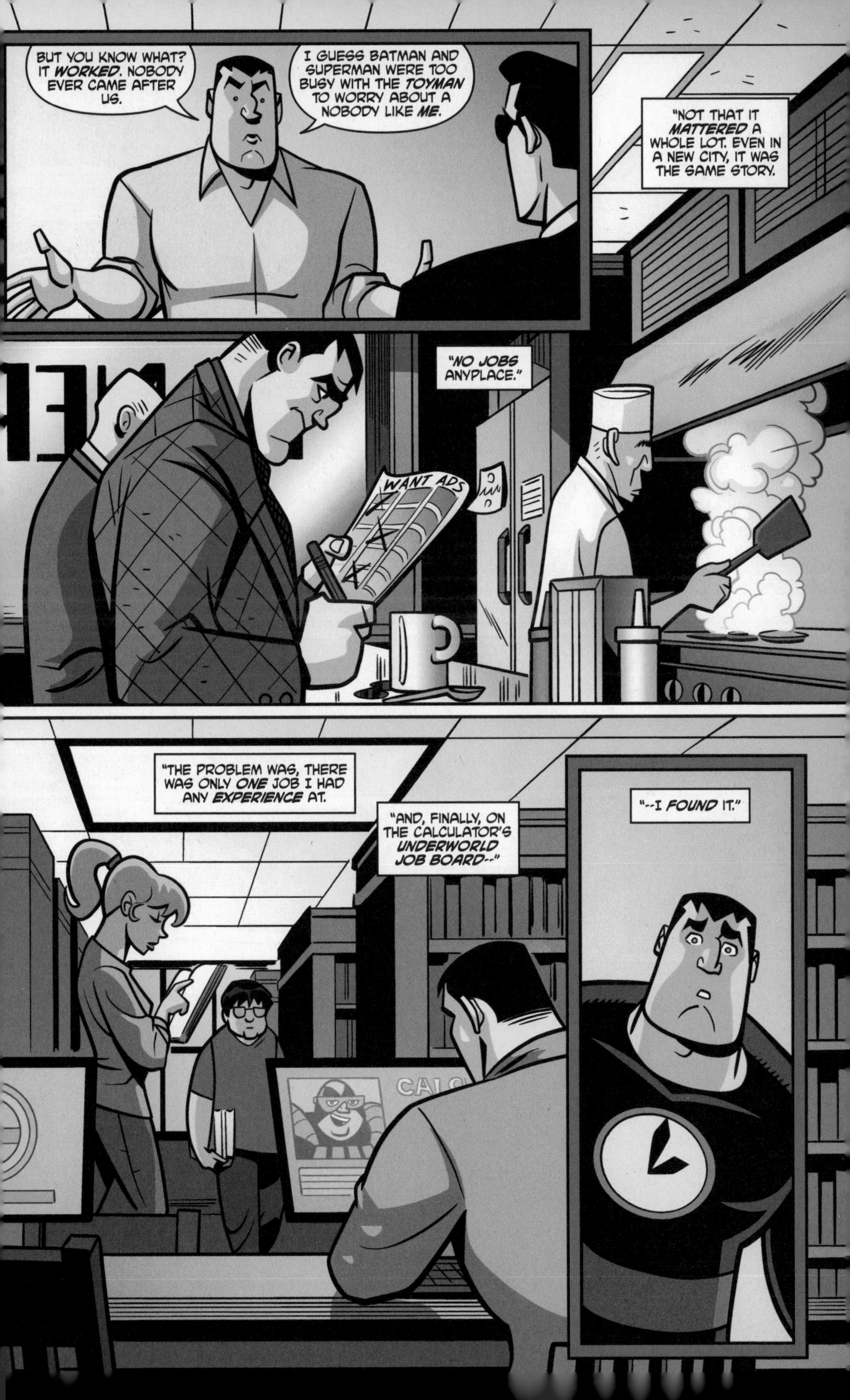
BUT YOU KNOW WHAT? IT WORKED. NOBODY EVER CAME AFTER US.
I GUESS BATMAN AND SUPERMAN WERE TOO BUSY WITH THE TOYMAN TO WORRY ABOUT A NOBODY LIKE ME.
"NOT THAT IT MATTERED A WHOLE LOT. EVEN IN A NEW CITY, IT WAS THE SAME STORY.
"NO JOBS ANYPLACE."
WANT ADS
"THE PROBLEM WAS, THERE WAS ONLY ONE JOB I HAD ANY EXPERIENCE AT.
"AND, FINALLY, ON THE CALCULATOR'S UNDERWORLD JOB BOARD--"
"--I FOUND IT."

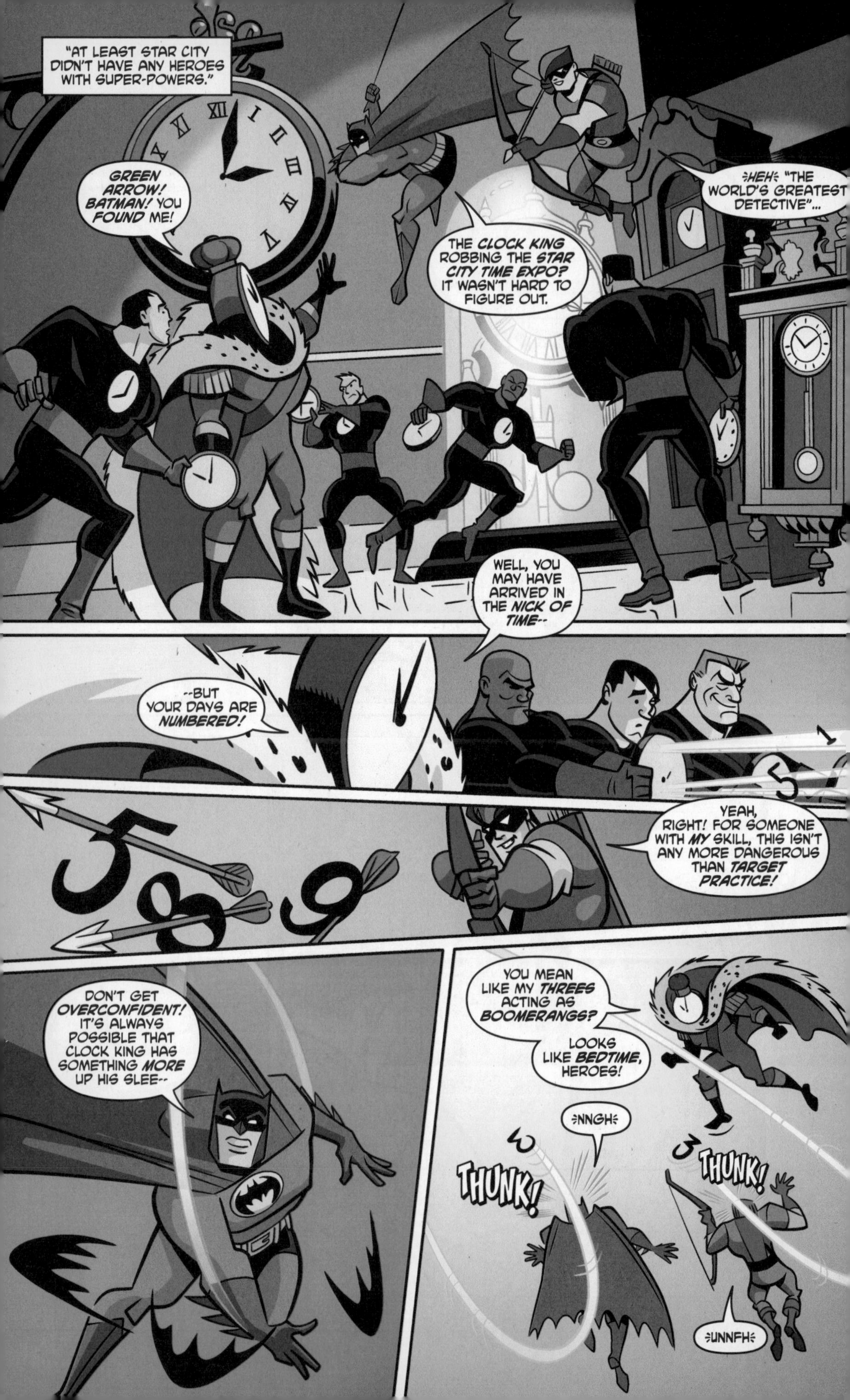
"AT LEAST STAR CITY DIDN'T HAVE ANY HEROES WITH SUPER-POWERS."
GREEN ARROW! BATMAN! YOU FOUND ME!
THE CLOCK KING ROBBING THE STAR CITY TIME EXPO? IT WASN'T HARD TO FIGURE OUT.
HEH "THE WORLD'S GREATEST DETECTIVE"...
WELL, YOU MAY HAVE ARRIVED IN THE NICK OF TIME--
--BUT YOUR DAYS ARE NUMBERED!
YEAH, RIGHT! FOR SOMEONE WITH MY SKILL, THIS ISN'T ANY MORE DANGEROUS THAN TARGET PRACTICE!
DON'T GET OVERCONFIDENT! IT'S ALWAYS POSSIBLE THAT CLOCK KING HAS SOMETHING MORE UP HIS SLEE--
YOU MEAN LIKE MY THREES ACTING AS BOOMERANGS?
LOOKS LIKE BEDTIME, HEROES!
NNGH
THUNK!
THUNK!
UNNFH

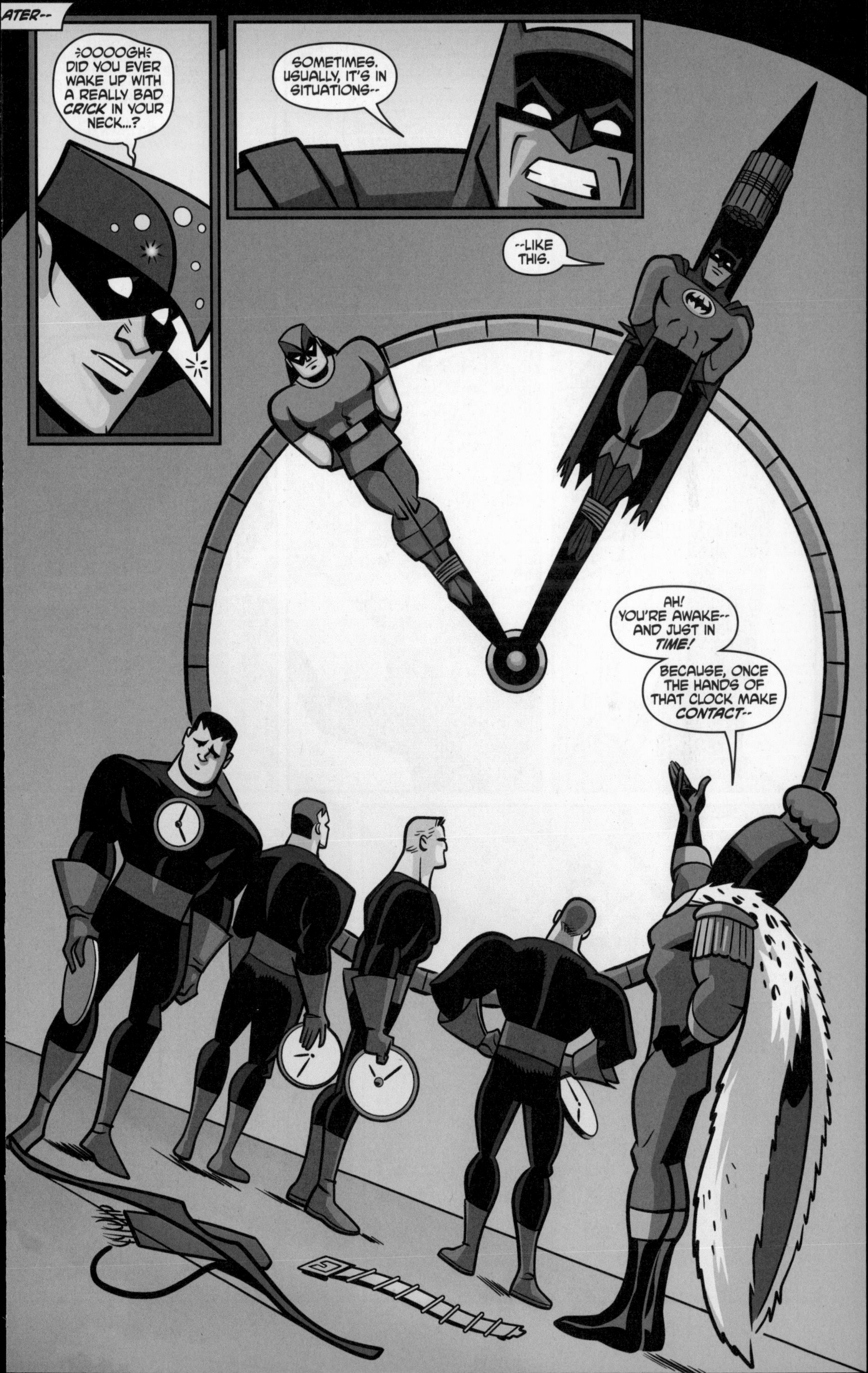

LATER--
OOOOGH! DID YOU EVER WAKE UP WITH A REALLY BAD CRICK IN YOUR NECK...?
SOMETIMES. USUALLY, IT'S IN SITUATIONS--
--LIKE THIS.
AH! YOU'RE AWAKE-- AND JUST IN TIME!
BECAUSE, ONCE THE HANDS OF THAT CLOCK MAKE CONTACT--

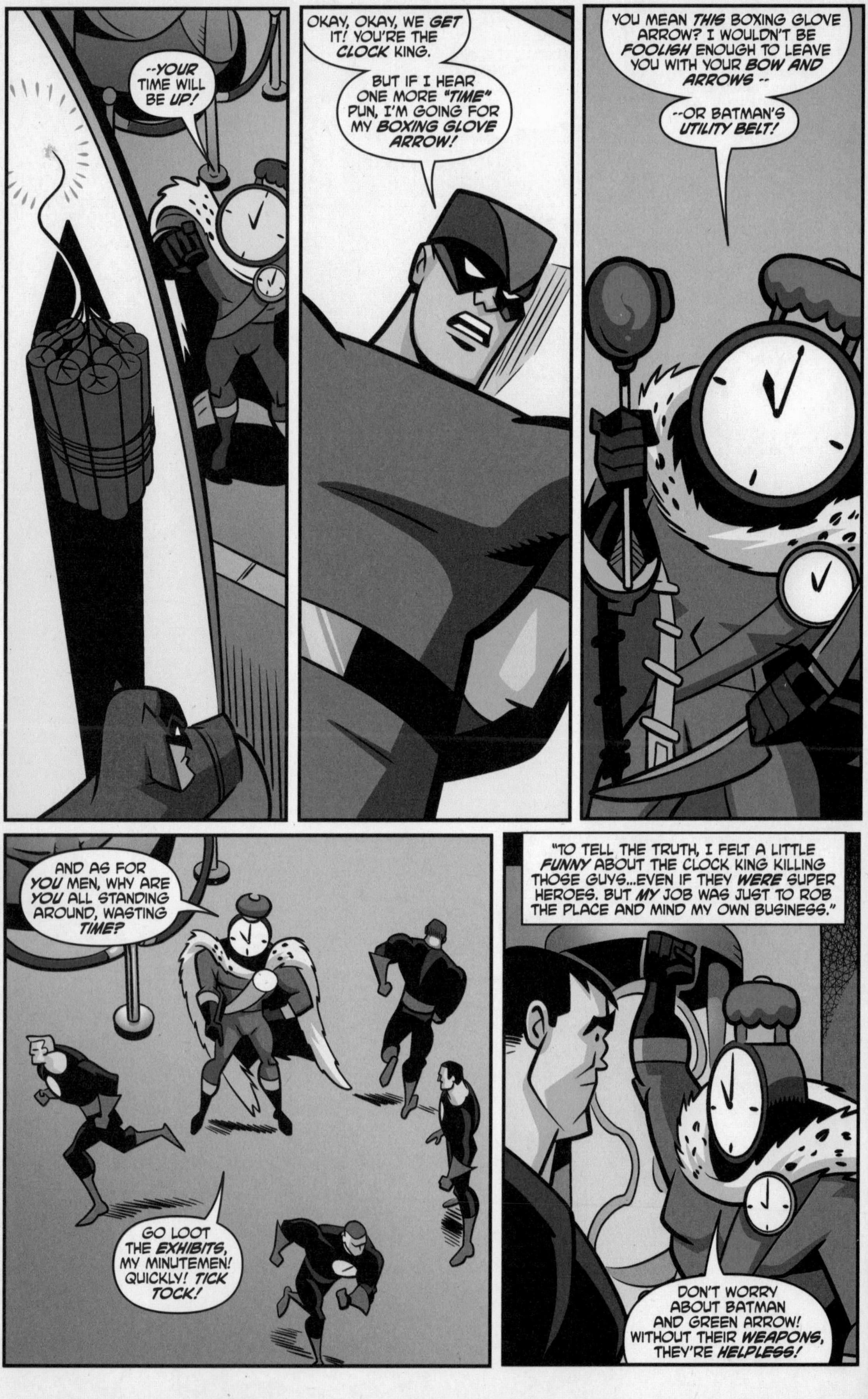
--YOUR TIME WILL BE UP!
OKAY, OKAY, WE GET IT! YOU'RE THE CLOCK KING.
BUT IF I HEAR ONE MORE "TIME" PUN, I'M GOING FOR MY BOXING GLOVE ARROW!
YOU MEAN THIS BOXING GLOVE ARROW? I WOULDN'T BE FOOLISH ENOUGH TO LEAVE YOU WITH YOUR BOW AND ARROWS --
--OR BATMAN'S UTILITY BELT!
AND AS FOR YOU MEN, WHY ARE YOU ALL STANDING AROUND, WASTING TIME?
GO LOOT THE EXHIBITS, MY MINUTEMEN! QUICKLY! TICK TOCK!
"TO TELL THE TRUTH, I FELT A LITTLE FUNNY ABOUT THE CLOCK KING KILLING THOSE GUYS...EVEN IF THEY WERE SUPER HEROES. BUT MY JOB WAS JUST TO ROB THE PLACE AND MIND MY OWN BUSINESS."
DON'T WORRY ABOUT BATMAN AND GREEN ARROW! WITHOUT THEIR WEAPONS, THEY'RE HELPLESS!

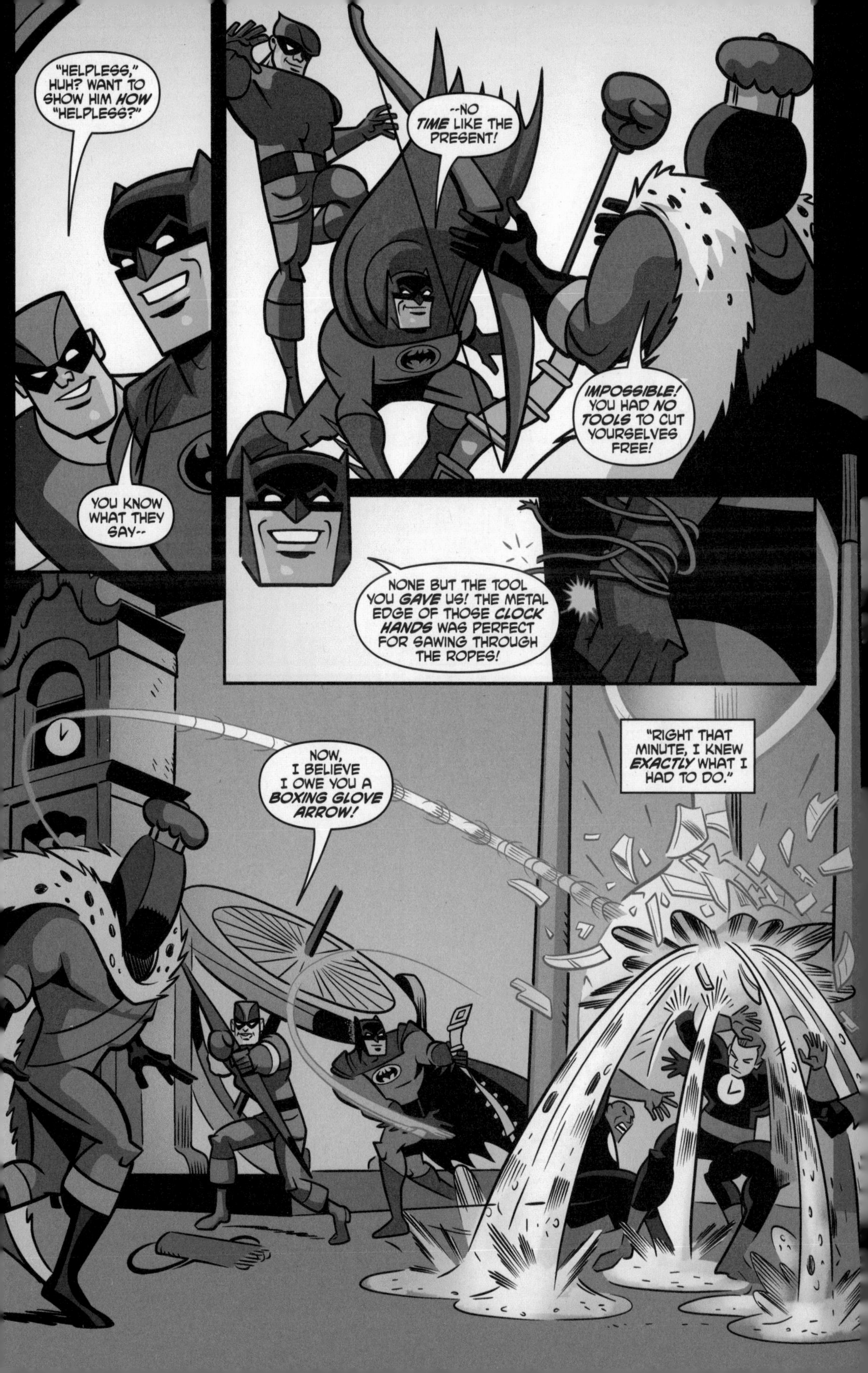
"HELPLESS," HUH? WANT TO SHOW HIM HOW "HELPLESS?"
YOU KNOW WHAT THEY SAY--
--NO TIME LIKE THE PRESENT!
IMPOSSIBLE! YOU HAD NO TOOLS TO CUT YOURSELVES FREE!
NONE BUT THE TOOL YOU GAVE US! THE METAL EDGE OF THOSE CLOCK HANDS WAS PERFECT FOR SAWING THROUGH THE ROPES!
NOW, I BELIEVE I OWE YOU A BOXING GLOVE ARROW!
"RIGHT THAT MINUTE, I KNEW EXACTLY WHAT I HAD TO DO."

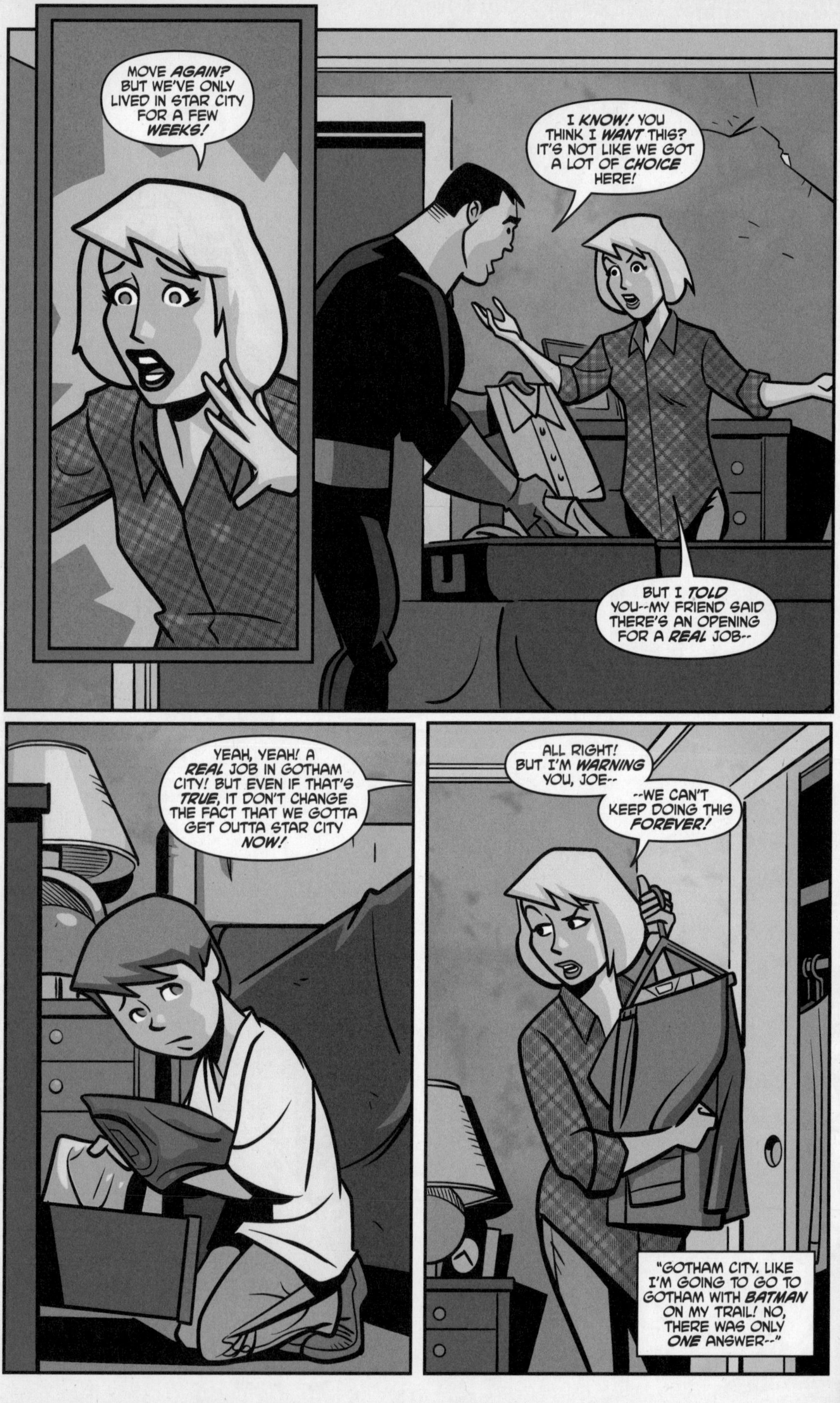
MOVE AGAIN? BUT WE'VE ONLY LIVED IN STAR CITY FOR A FEW WEEKS!
I KNOW! YOU THINK I WANT THIS? IT'S NOT LIKE WE GOT A LOT OF CHOICE HERE!
BUT I TOLD YOU--MY FRIEND SAID THERE'S AN OPENING FOR A REAL JOB--
YEAH, YEAH! A REAL JOB IN GOTHAM CITY! BUT EVEN IF THAT'S TRUE, IT DON'T CHANGE THE FACT THAT WE GOTTA GET OUTTA STAR CITY NOW!
ALL RIGHT! BUT I'M WARNING YOU, JOE--
--WE CAN'T KEEP DOING THIS FOREVER!
"GOTHAM CITY. LIKE I'M GOING TO GO TO GOTHAM WITH BATMAN ON MY TRAIL! NO, THERE WAS ONLY ONE ANSWER--"

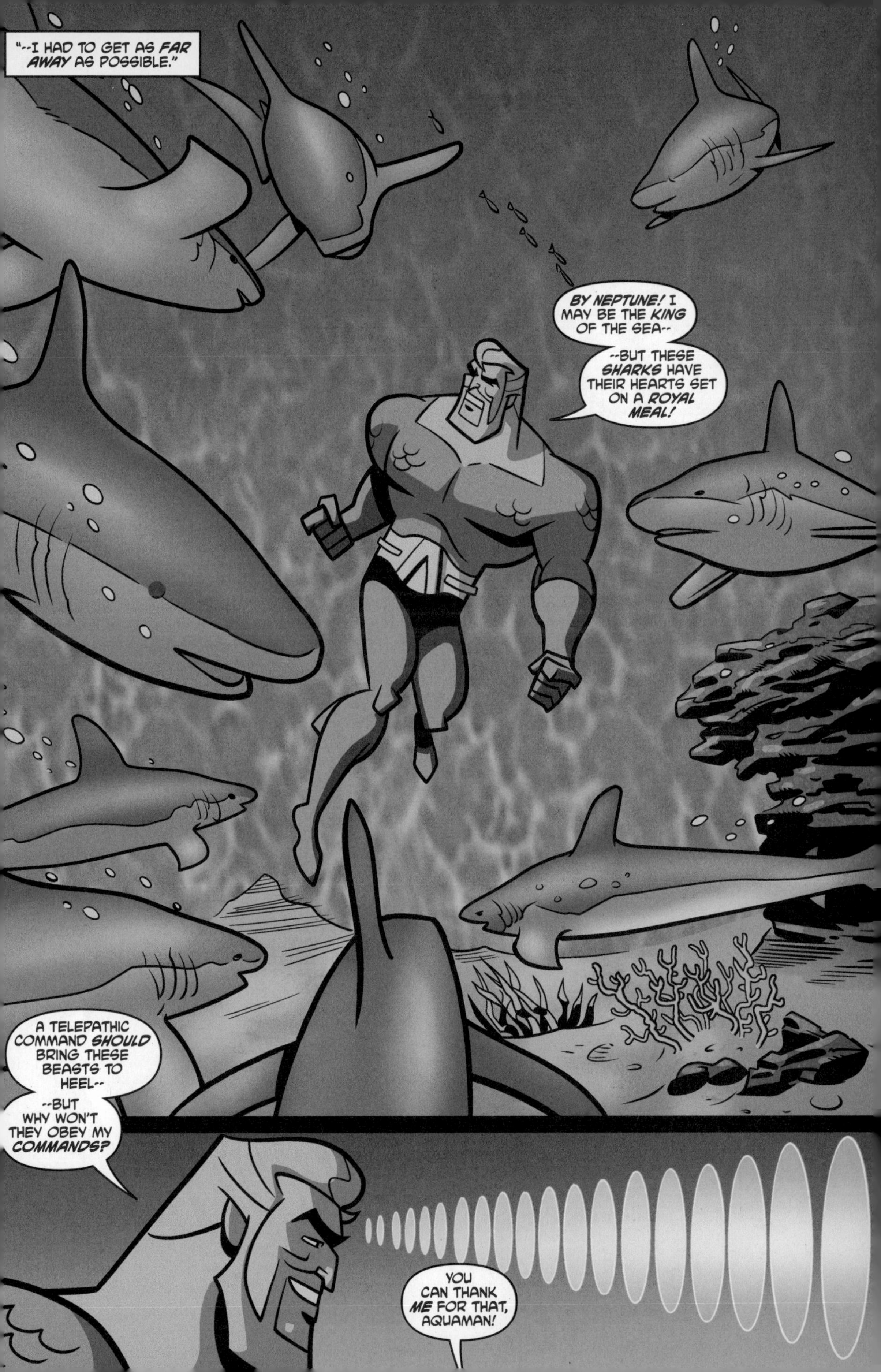
"--I HAD TO GET AS FAR AWAY AS POSSIBLE."
BY NEPTUNE! I MAY BE THE KING OF THE SEA--
--BUT THESE SHARKS HAVE THEIR HEARTS SET ON A ROYAL MEAL!
A TELEPATHIC COMMAND SHOULD BRING THESE BEASTS TO HEEL--
--BUT WHY WON'T THEY OBEY MY COMMANDS?
YOU CAN THANK ME FOR THAT, AQUAMAN!

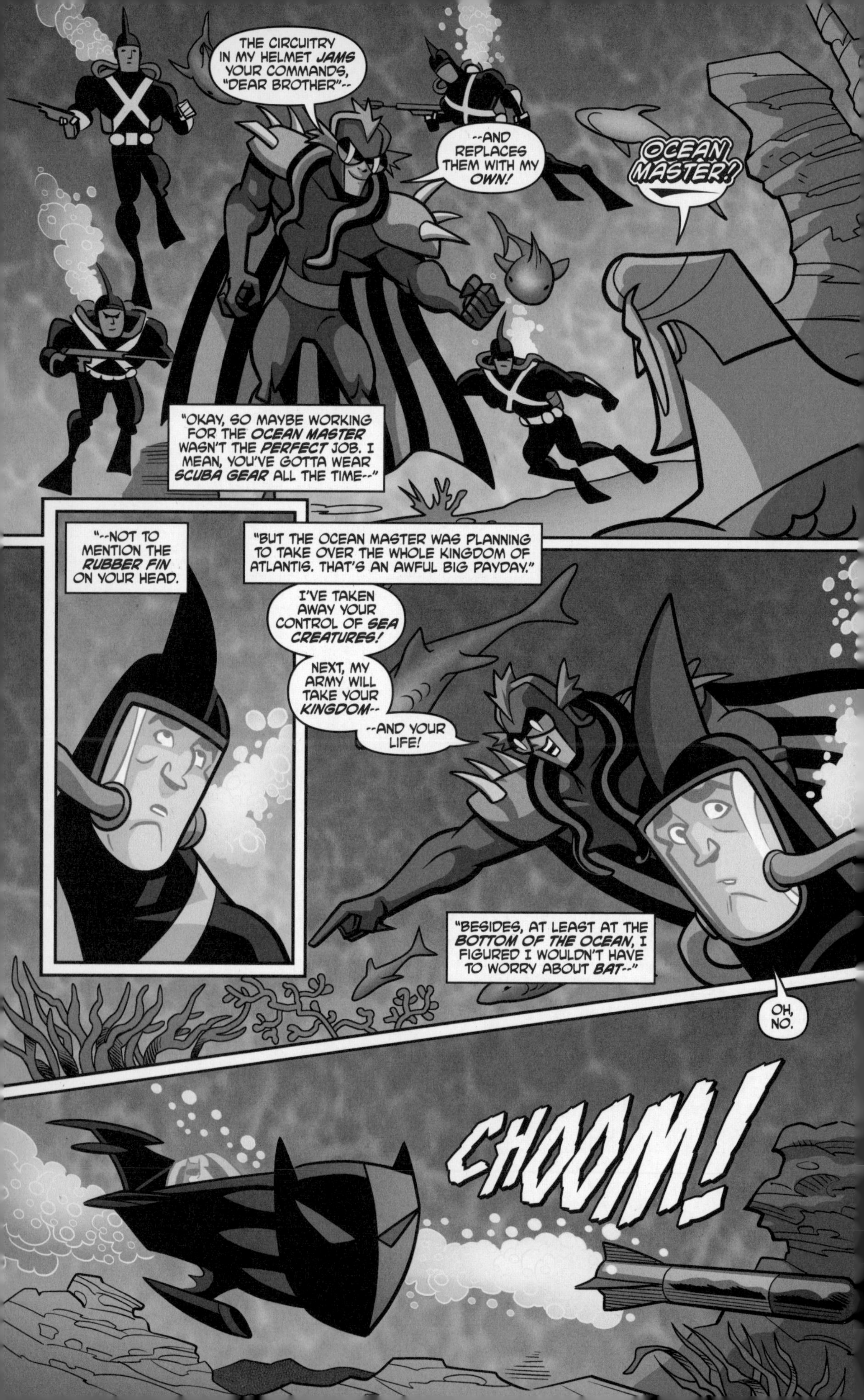

THE CIRCUITRY IN MY HELMET JAMS YOUR COMMANDS, "DEAR BROTHER"--
--AND REPLACES THEM WITH MY OWN!
OCEAN MASTER!
"OKAY, SO MAYBE WORKING FOR THE OCEAN MASTER WASN'T THE PERFECT JOB. I MEAN, YOU'VE GOTTA WEAR SCUBA GEAR ALL THE TIME--"
"--NOT TO MENTION THE RUBBER FIN ON YOUR HEAD.
"BUT THE OCEAN MASTER WAS PLANNING TO TAKE OVER THE WHOLE KINGDOM OF ATLANTIS. THAT'S AN AWFUL BIG PAYDAY."
I'VE TAKEN AWAY YOUR CONTROL OF SEA CREATURES!
NEXT, MY ARMY WILL TAKE YOUR KINGDOM--
--AND YOUR LIFE!
"BESIDES, AT LEAST AT THE BOTTOM OF THE OCEAN, I FIGURED I WOULDN'T HAVE TO WORRY ABOUT BAT--"
OH, NO.
CHOOM!

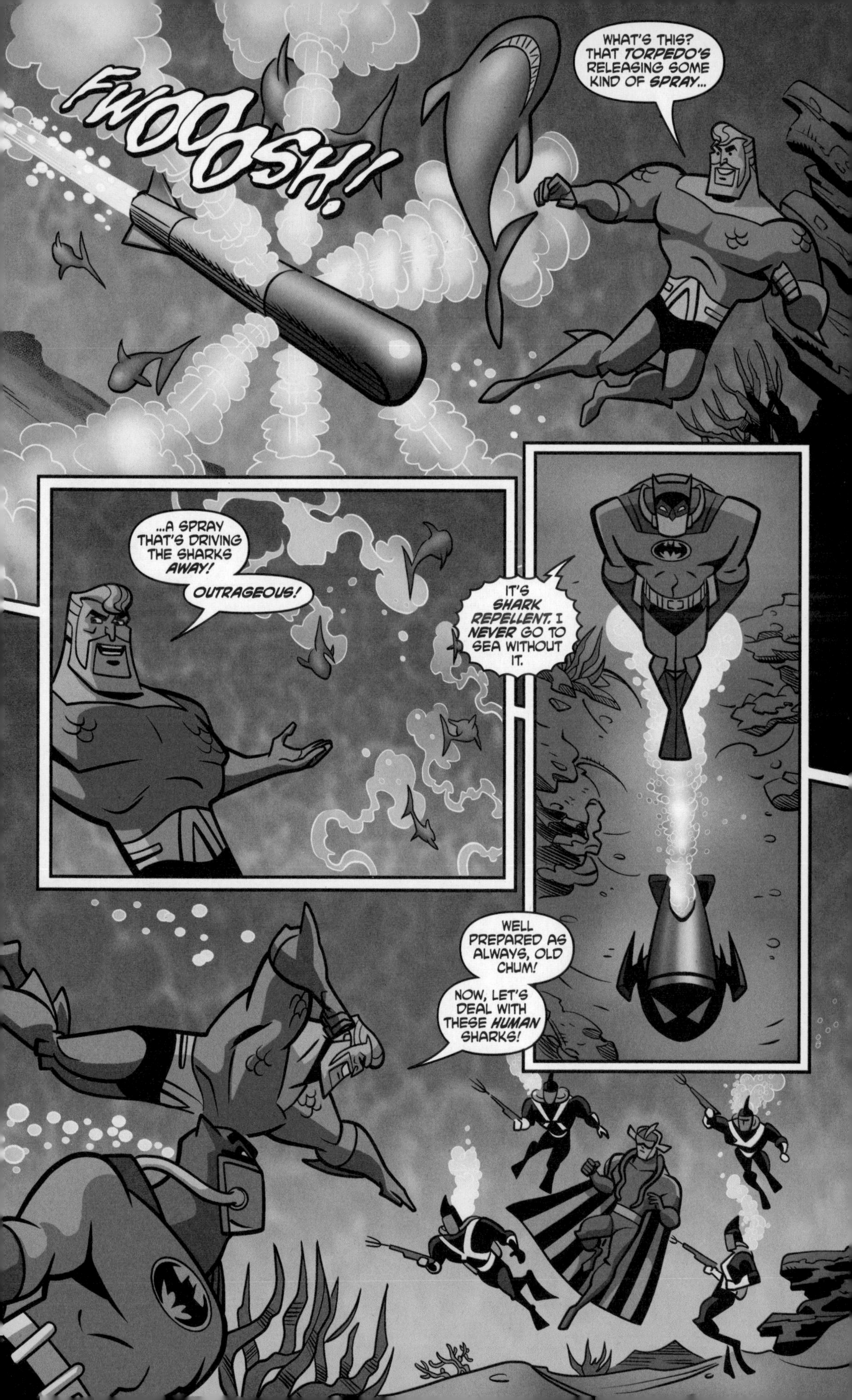
FWOOOSH!!
WHAT'S THIS? THAT TORPEDO'S RELEASING SOME KIND OF SPRAY...
...A SPRAY THAT'S DRIVING THE SHARKS AWAY!
OUTRAGEOUS!
IT'S SHARK REPELLENT. I NEVER GO TO SEA WITHOUT IT.
WELL PREPARED AS ALWAYS, OLD CHUM!
NOW, LET'S DEAL WITH THESE HUMAN SHARKS!

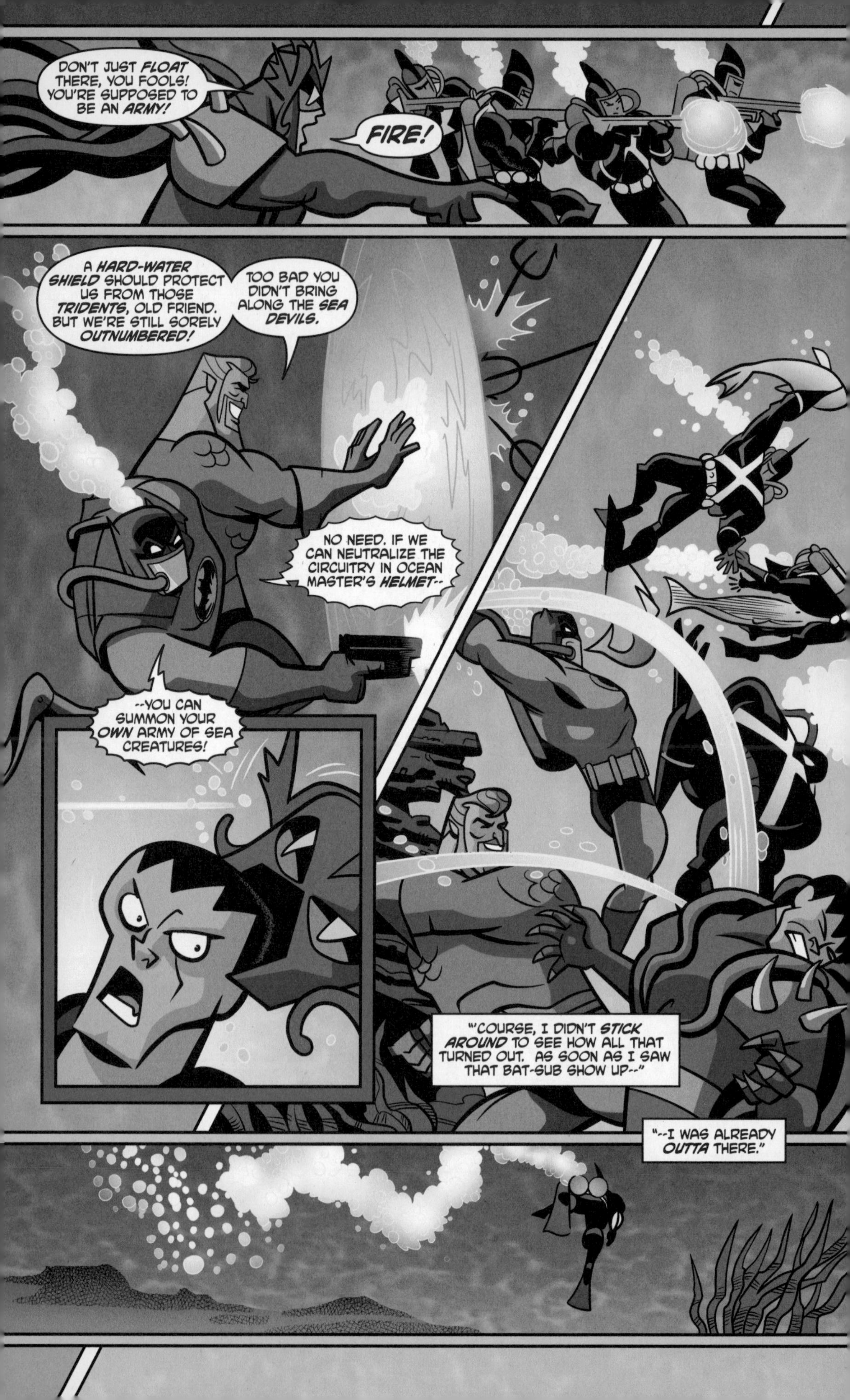

DON'T JUST FLOAT THERE, YOU FOOLS! YOU'RE SUPPOSED TO BE AN ARMY!
FIRE!
A HARD-WATER SHIELD SHOULD PROTECT US FROM THOSE TRIDENTS, OLD FRIEND. BUT WE'RE STILL SORELY OUTNUMBERED!
TOO BAD YOU DIDN'T BRING ALONG THE SEA DEVILS.
NO NEED. IF WE CAN NEUTRALIZE THE CIRCUITRY IN OCEAN MASTER'S HELMET--
--YOU CAN SUMMON YOUR OWN ARMY OF SEA CREATURES!
"'COURSE, I DIDN'T STICK AROUND TO SEE HOW ALL THAT TURNED OUT. AS SOON AS I SAW THAT BAT-SUB SHOW UP--"
"--I WAS ALREADY OUTTA THERE."

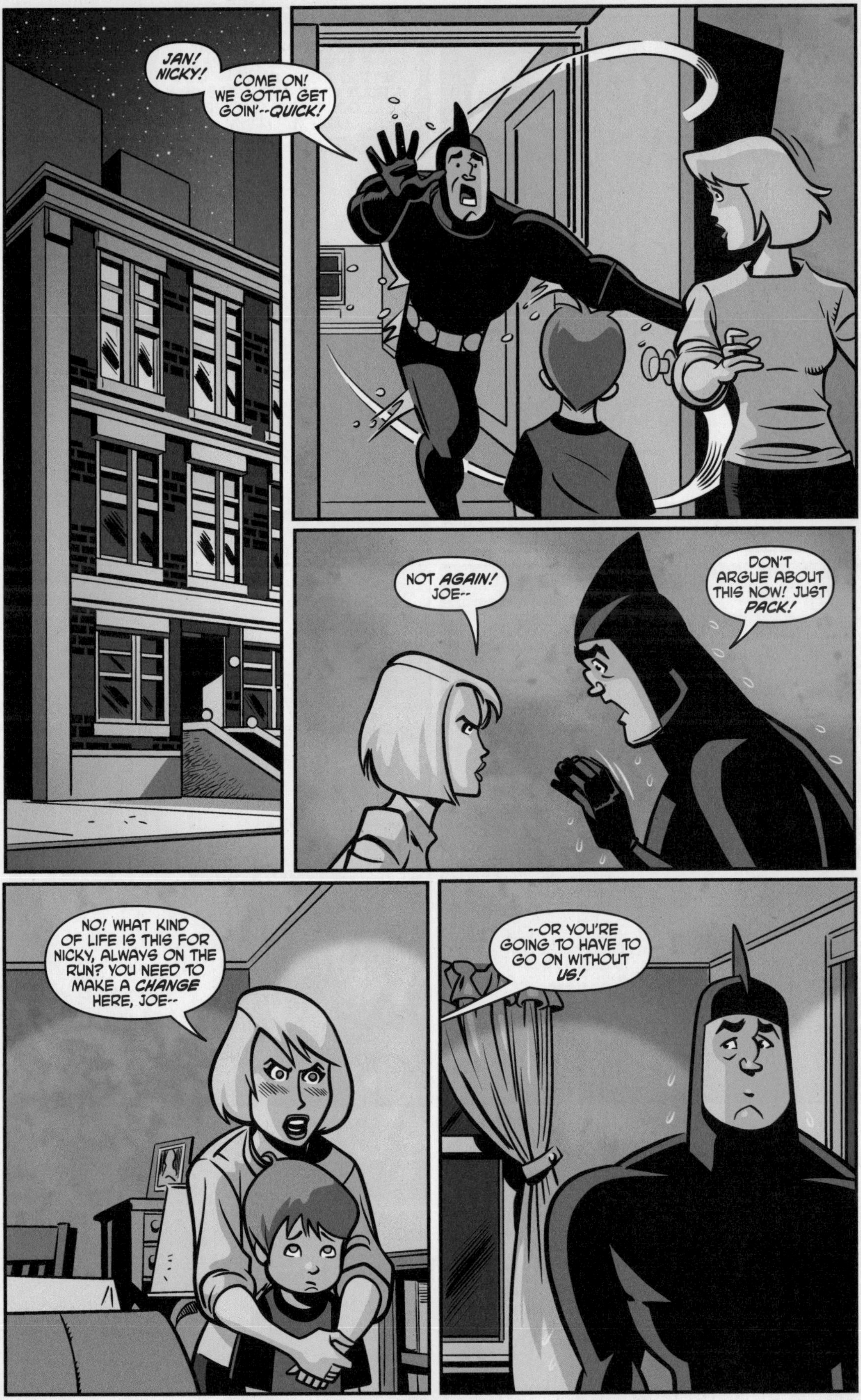
JAN! NICKY!
COME ON! WE GOTTA GET GOIN'--QUICK!
NOT AGAIN! JOE--
DON'T ARGUE ABOUT THIS NOW! JUST PACK!
NO! WHAT KIND OF LIFE IS THIS FOR NICKY, ALWAYS ON THE RUN? YOU NEED TO MAKE A CHANGE HERE, JOE--
--OR YOU'RE GOING TO HAVE TO GO ON WITHOUT US!

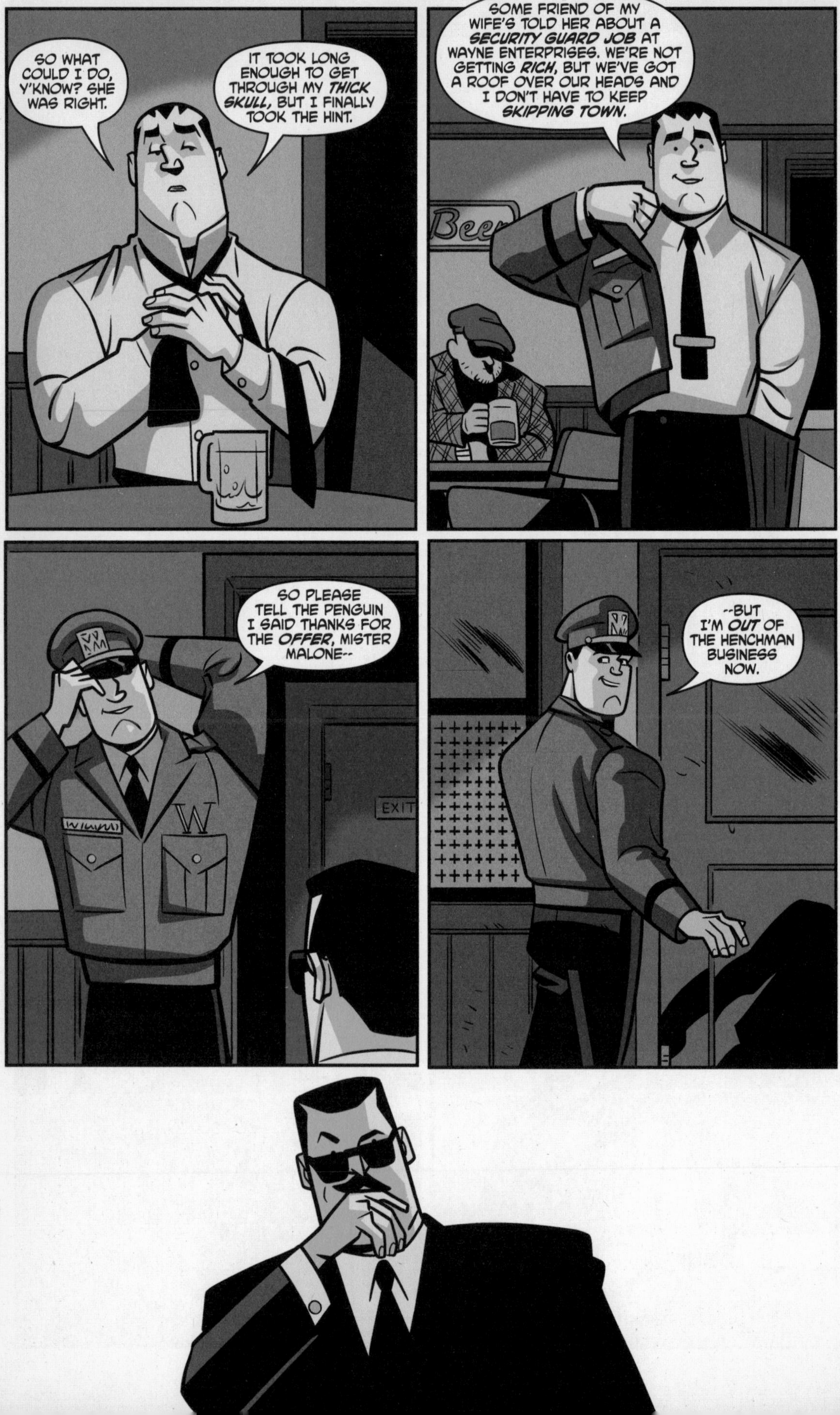
SO WHAT COULD I DO, Y'KNOW? SHE WAS RIGHT.
IT TOOK LONG ENOUGH TO GET THROUGH MY THICK SKULL, BUT I FINALLY TOOK THE HINT.
SOME FRIEND OF MY WIFE'S TOLD HER ABOUT A SECURITY GUARD JOB AT WAYNE ENTERPRISES. WE'RE NOT GETTING RICH, BUT WE'VE GOT A ROOF OVER OUR HEADS AND I DON'T HAVE TO KEEP SKIPPING TOWN.
SO PLEASE TELL THE PENGUIN I SAID THANKS FOR THE OFFER, MISTER MALONE--
EXIT
--BUT I'M OUT OF THE HENCHMAN BUSINESS NOW.

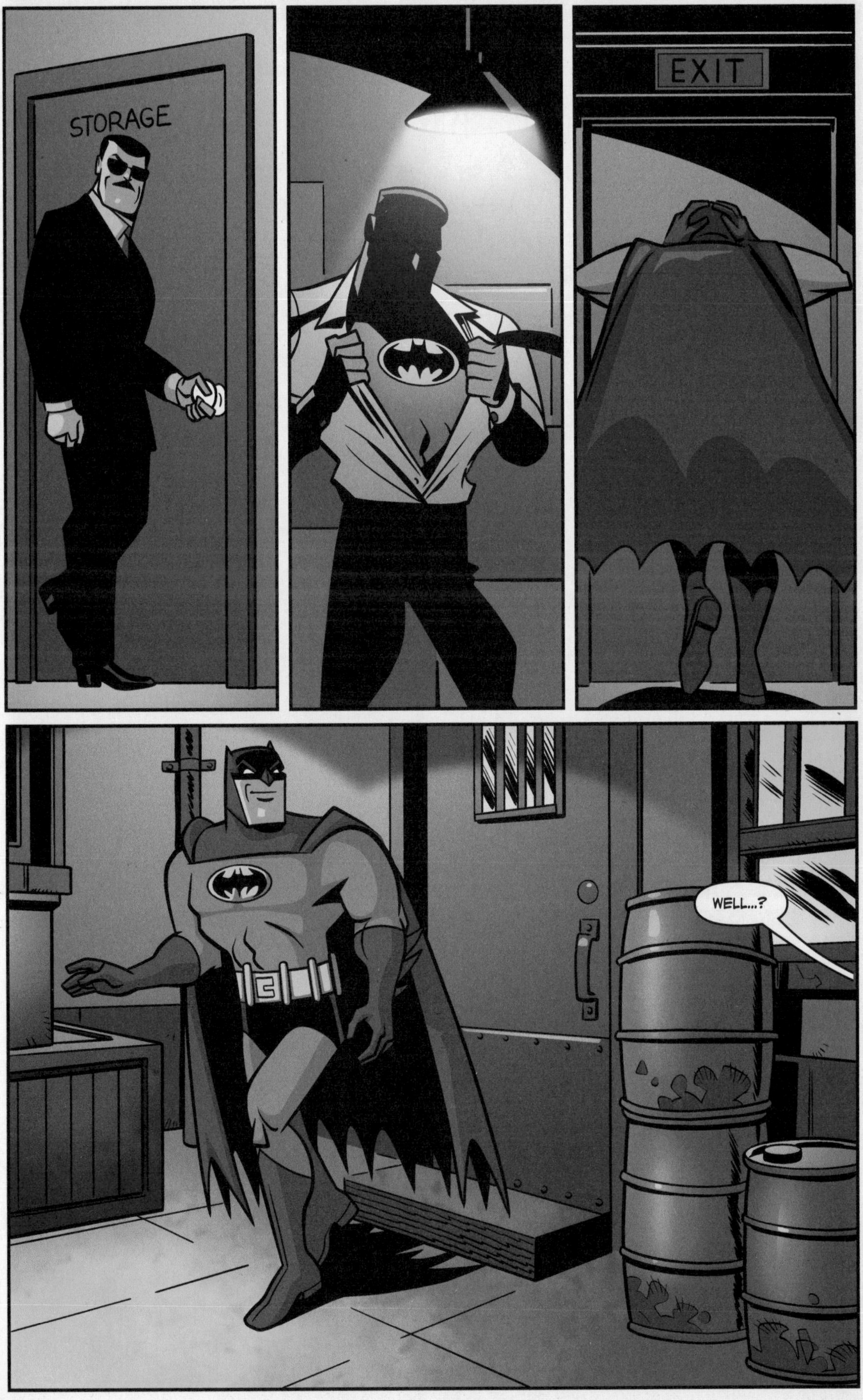
STORAGE
EXIT
WELL...?

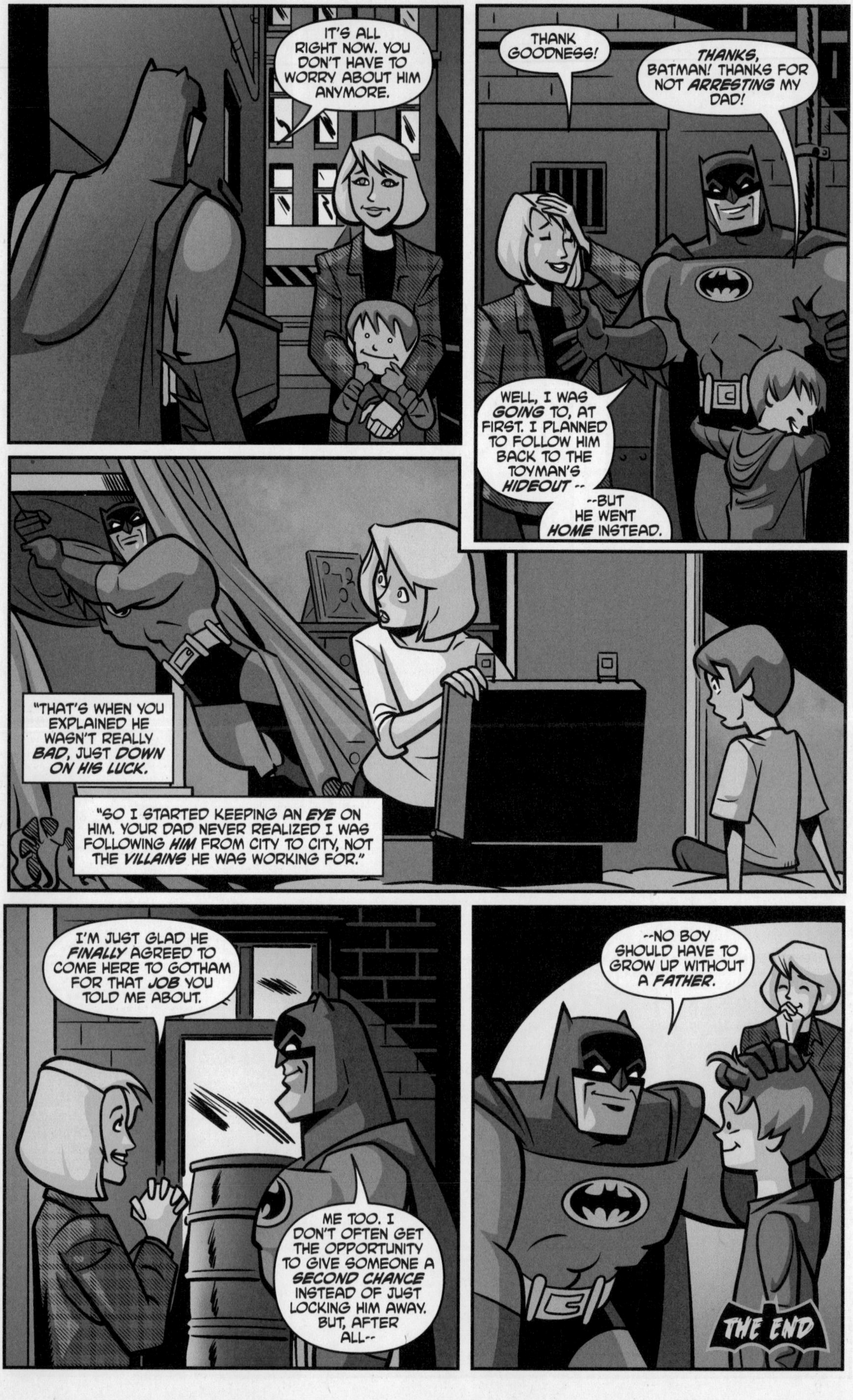
IT'S ALL RIGHT NOW. YOU DON'T HAVE TO WORRY ABOUT HIM ANYMORE.
THANK GOODNESS!
THANKS, BATMAN! THANKS FOR NOT ARRESTING MY DAD!
WELL, I WAS GOING TO, AT FIRST. I PLANNED TO FOLLOW HIM BACK TO THE TOYMAN'S HIDEOUT --
--BUT HE WENT HOME INSTEAD.
"THAT'S WHEN YOU EXPLAINED HE WASN'T REALLY BAD, JUST DOWN ON HIS LUCK.
"SO I STARTED KEEPING AN EYE ON HIM. YOUR DAD NEVER REALIZED I WAS FOLLOWING HIM FROM CITY TO CITY, NOT THE VILLAINS HE WAS WORKING FOR."
I'M JUST GLAD HE FINALLY AGREED TO COME HERE TO GOTHAM FOR THAT JOB YOU TOLD ME ABOUT.
ME TOO. I DON'T OFTEN GET THE OPPORTUNITY TO GIVE SOMEONE A SECOND CHANCE INSTEAD OF JUST LOCKING HIM AWAY. BUT, AFTER ALL--
--NO BOY SHOULD HAVE TO GROW UP WITHOUT A FATHER.
THE END

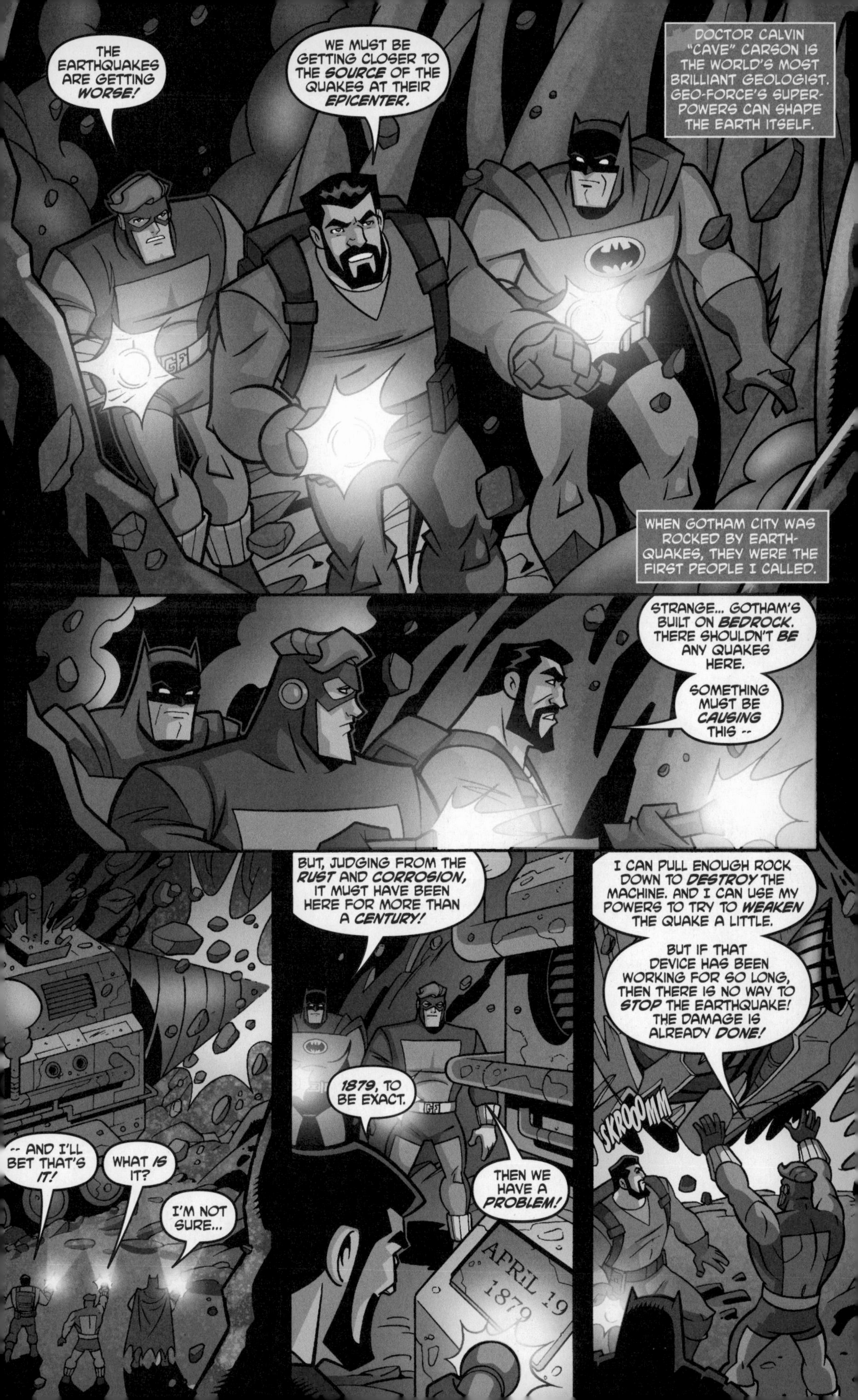
DOCTOR CALVIN "CAVE" CARSON IS THE WORLD'S MOST BRILLIANT GEOLOGIST. GEO-FORCE'S SUPER-POWERS CAN SHAPE THE EARTH ITSELF.
THE EARTHQUAKES ARE GETTING *WORSE!*
WE MUST BE GETTING CLOSER TO THE *SOURCE* OF THE QUAKES AT THEIR *EPICENTER.*
WHEN GOTHAM CITY WAS ROCKED BY EARTH-QUAKES, THEY WERE THE FIRST PEOPLE I CALLED.
STRANGE... GOTHAM'S BUILT ON *BEDROCK.* THERE SHOULDN'T *BE* ANY QUAKES HERE.
SOMETHING MUST BE *CAUSING* THIS --
-- AND I'LL BET THAT'S *IT!*
WHAT *IS* IT?
I'M NOT SURE...
BUT, JUDGING FROM THE *RUST* AND *CORROSION,* IT MUST HAVE BEEN HERE FOR MORE THAN A *CENTURY!*
1879, TO BE EXACT.
THEN WE HAVE A *PROBLEM!*
APRIL 19 1879
I CAN PULL ENOUGH ROCK DOWN TO *DESTROY* THE MACHINE. AND I CAN USE MY POWERS TO TRY TO *WEAKEN* THE QUAKE A LITTLE.
BUT IF THAT DEVICE HAS BEEN WORKING FOR SO LONG, THEN THERE IS NO WAY TO *STOP* THE EARTHQUAKE! THE DAMAGE IS ALREADY *DONE!*
SKROOOMM

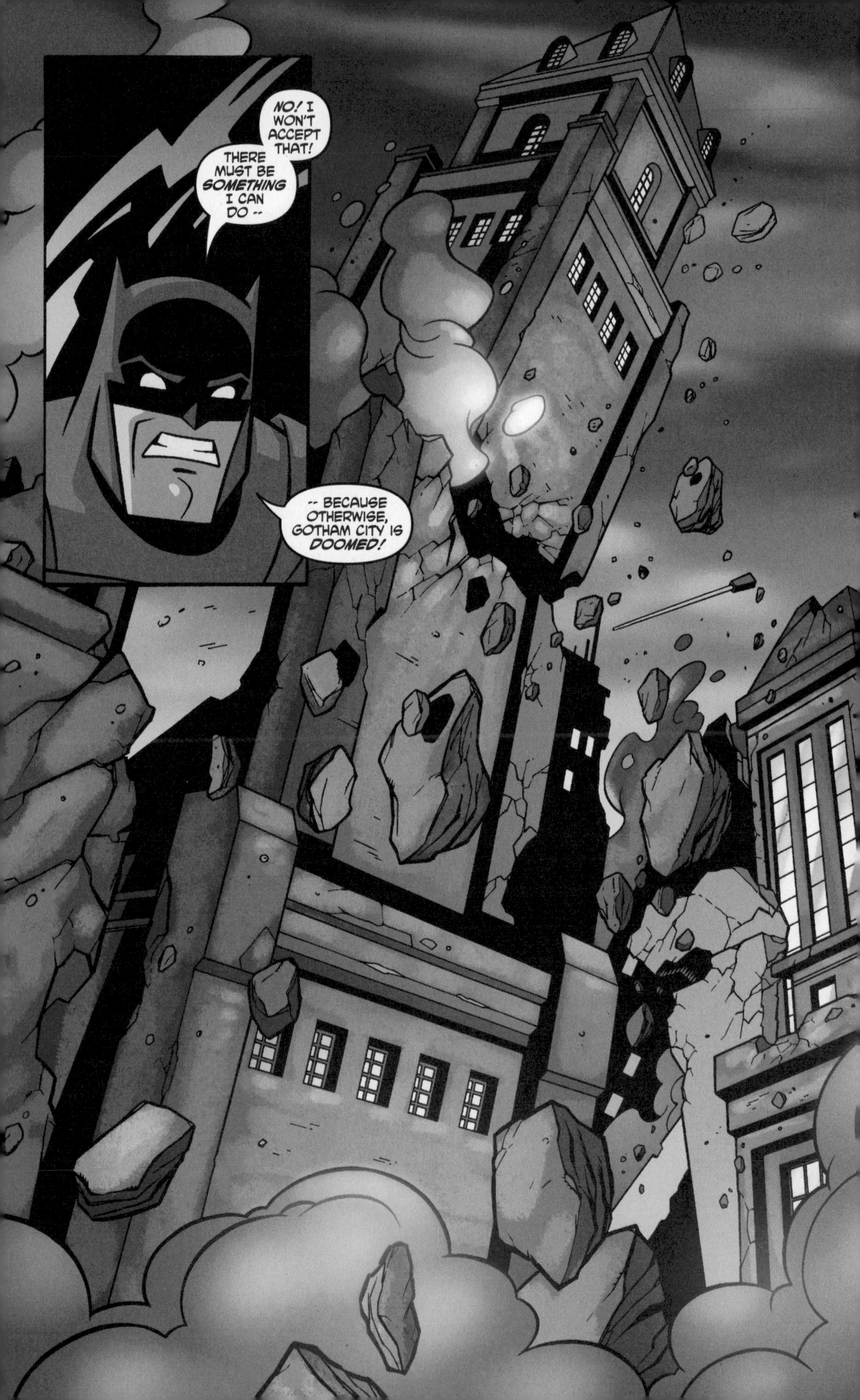
NO! I WON'T ACCEPT THAT!
THERE MUST BE SOMETHING I CAN DO --
-- BECAUSE OTHERWISE, GOTHAM CITY IS DOOMED!

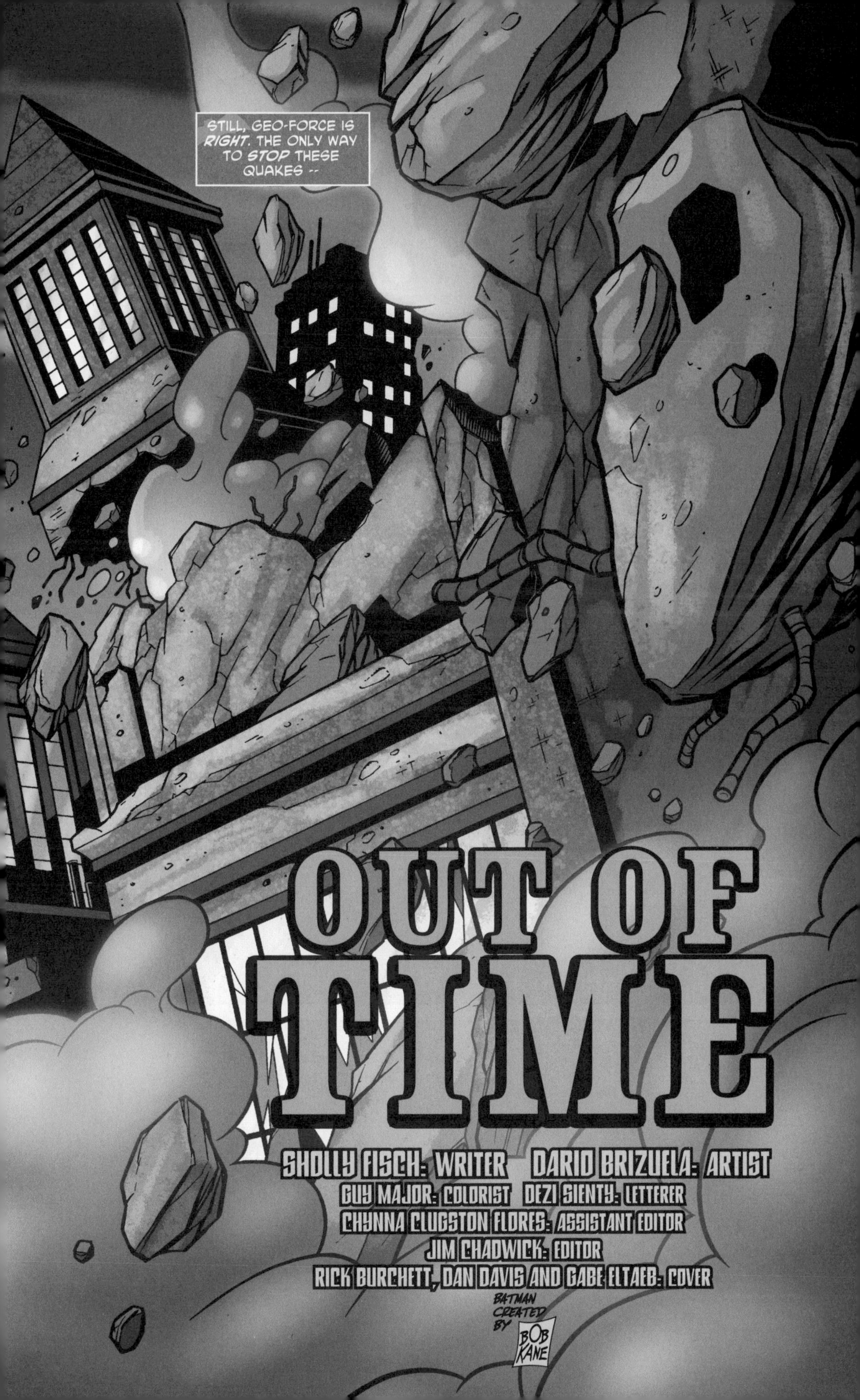
STILL, GEO-FORCE IS RIGHT. THE ONLY WAY TO STOP THESE QUAKES --
OUT OF TIME
SHOLLY FISCH: WRITER DARIO BRIZUELA: ARTIST
GUY MAJOR: COLORIST DEZI SIENTY: LETTERER
CHYNNA CLUGSTON FLORES: ASSISTANT EDITOR
JIM CHADWICK: EDITOR
RICK BURCHETT, DAN DAVIS AND GABE ELTAEB: COVER
BATMAN CREATED BY BOB KANE

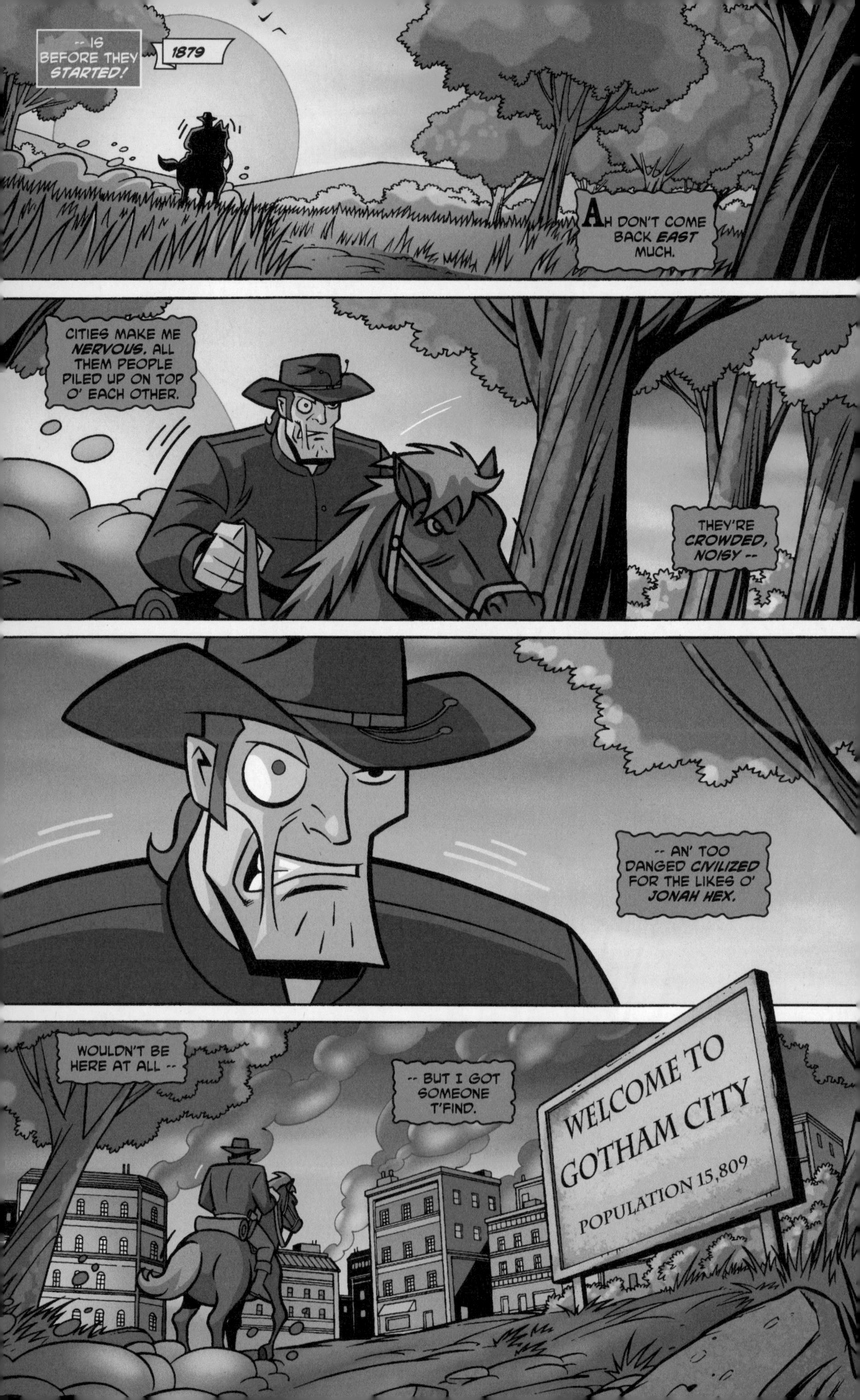
-- IS BEFORE THEY *STARTED!*
1879
AH DON'T COME BACK *EAST* MUCH.
CITIES MAKE ME *NERVOUS.* ALL THEM PEOPLE PILED UP ON TOP O' EACH OTHER.
THEY'RE *CROWDED, NOISY* --
-- AN' TOO DANGED *CIVILIZED* FOR THE LIKES O' *JONAH HEX.*
WOULDN'T BE HERE AT ALL --
-- BUT I GOT SOMEONE T'FIND.
WELCOME TO GOTHAM CITY
POPULATION 15,809

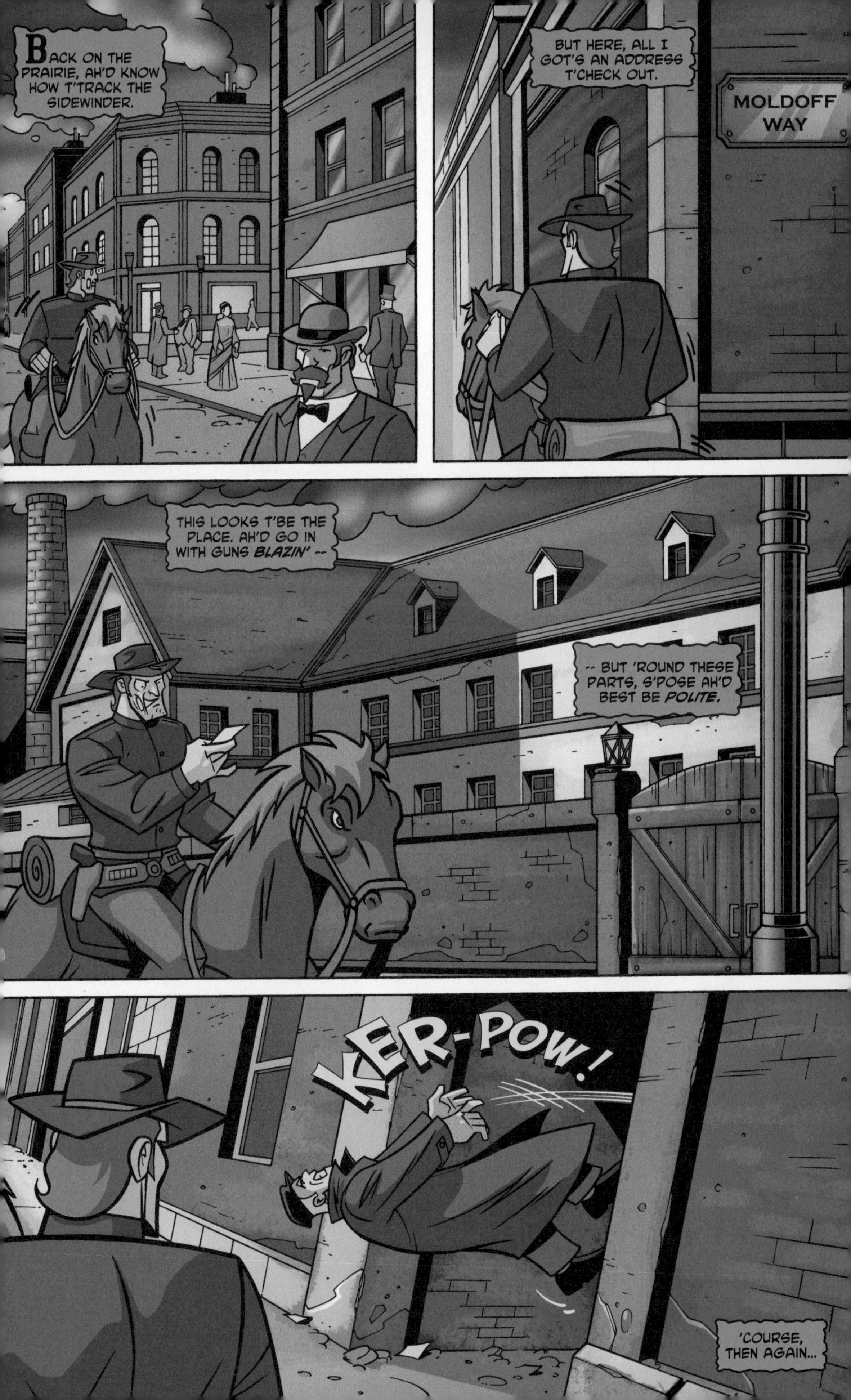
BACK ON THE PRAIRIE, AH'D KNOW HOW T'TRACK THE SIDEWINDER.
BUT HERE, ALL I GOT'S AN ADDRESS T'CHECK OUT.
MOLDOFF WAY
THIS LOOKS T'BE THE PLACE. AH'D GO IN WITH GUNS BLAZIN' --
-- BUT 'ROUND THESE PARTS, S'POSE AH'D BEST BE POLITE.
KER-POW!
'COURSE, THEN AGAIN...

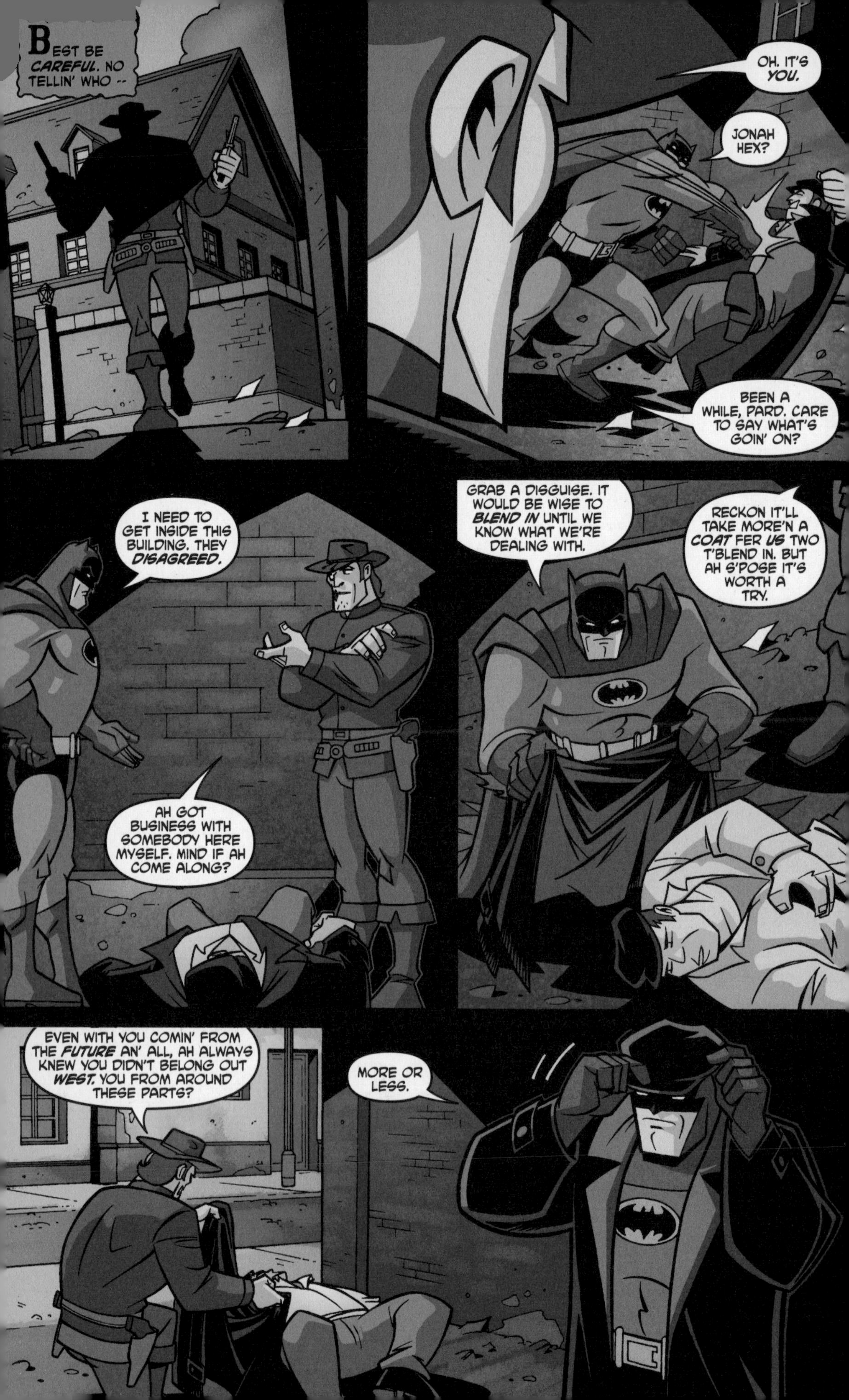
BEST BE CAREFUL. NO TELLIN' WHO --
OH. IT'S YOU.
JONAH HEX?
BEEN A WHILE, PARD. CARE TO SAY WHAT'S GOIN' ON?
I NEED TO GET INSIDE THIS BUILDING. THEY DISAGREED.
AH GOT BUSINESS WITH SOMEBODY HERE MYSELF. MIND IF AH COME ALONG?
GRAB A DISGUISE. IT WOULD BE WISE TO BLEND IN UNTIL WE KNOW WHAT WE'RE DEALING WITH.
RECKON IT'LL TAKE MORE'N A COAT FER US TWO T'BLEND IN. BUT AH S'POSE IT'S WORTH A TRY.
EVEN WITH YOU COMIN' FROM THE FUTURE AN' ALL, AH ALWAYS KNEW YOU DIDN'T BELONG OUT WEST. YOU FROM AROUND THESE PARTS?
MORE OR LESS.

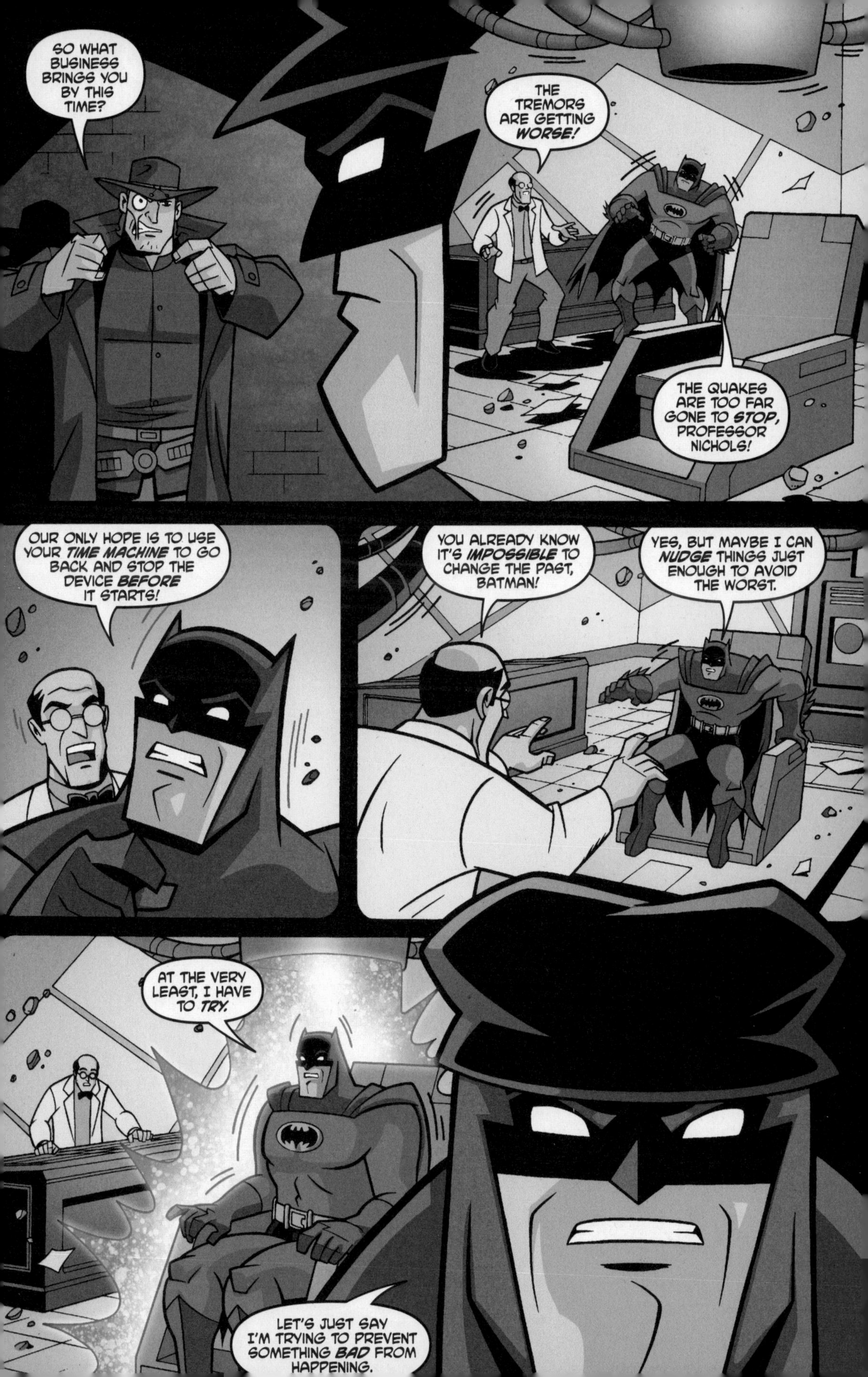
SO WHAT BUSINESS BRINGS YOU BY THIS TIME?
THE TREMORS ARE GETTING WORSE!
THE QUAKES ARE TOO FAR GONE TO STOP, PROFESSOR NICHOLS!
OUR ONLY HOPE IS TO USE YOUR TIME MACHINE TO GO BACK AND STOP THE DEVICE BEFORE IT STARTS!
YOU ALREADY KNOW IT'S IMPOSSIBLE TO CHANGE THE PAST, BATMAN!
YES, BUT MAYBE I CAN NUDGE THINGS JUST ENOUGH TO AVOID THE WORST.
AT THE VERY LEAST, I HAVE TO TRY.
LET'S JUST SAY I'M TRYING TO PREVENT SOMETHING BAD FROM HAPPENING.

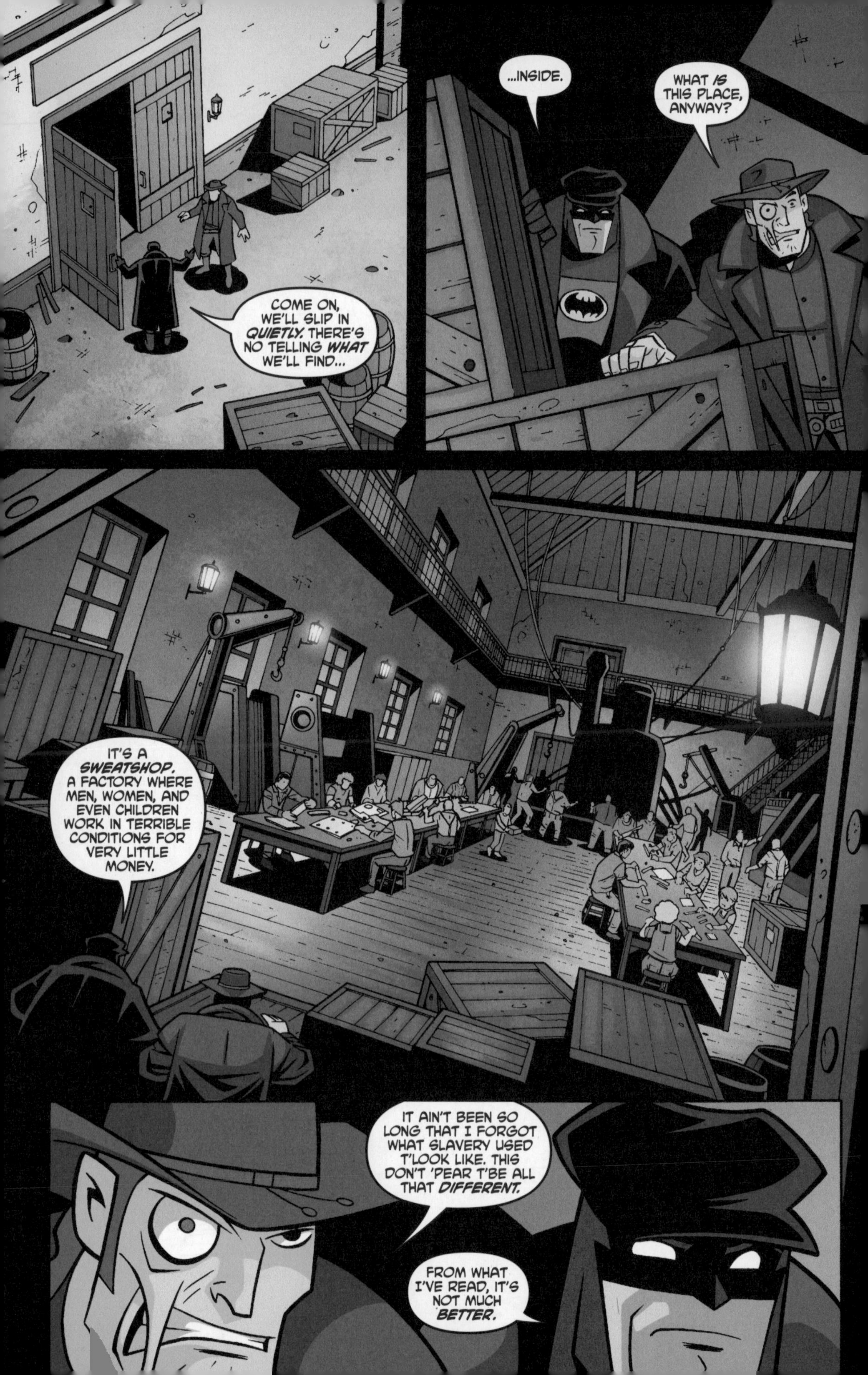
COME ON, WE'LL SLIP IN QUIETLY. THERE'S NO TELLING WHAT WE'LL FIND...
...INSIDE.
WHAT IS THIS PLACE, ANYWAY?
IT'S A SWEATSHOP. A FACTORY WHERE MEN, WOMEN, AND EVEN CHILDREN WORK IN TERRIBLE CONDITIONS FOR VERY LITTLE MONEY.
IT AIN'T BEEN SO LONG THAT I FORGOT WHAT SLAVERY USED T'LOOK LIKE. THIS DON'T 'PEAR T'BE ALL THAT DIFFERENT.
FROM WHAT I'VE READ, IT'S NOT MUCH BETTER.

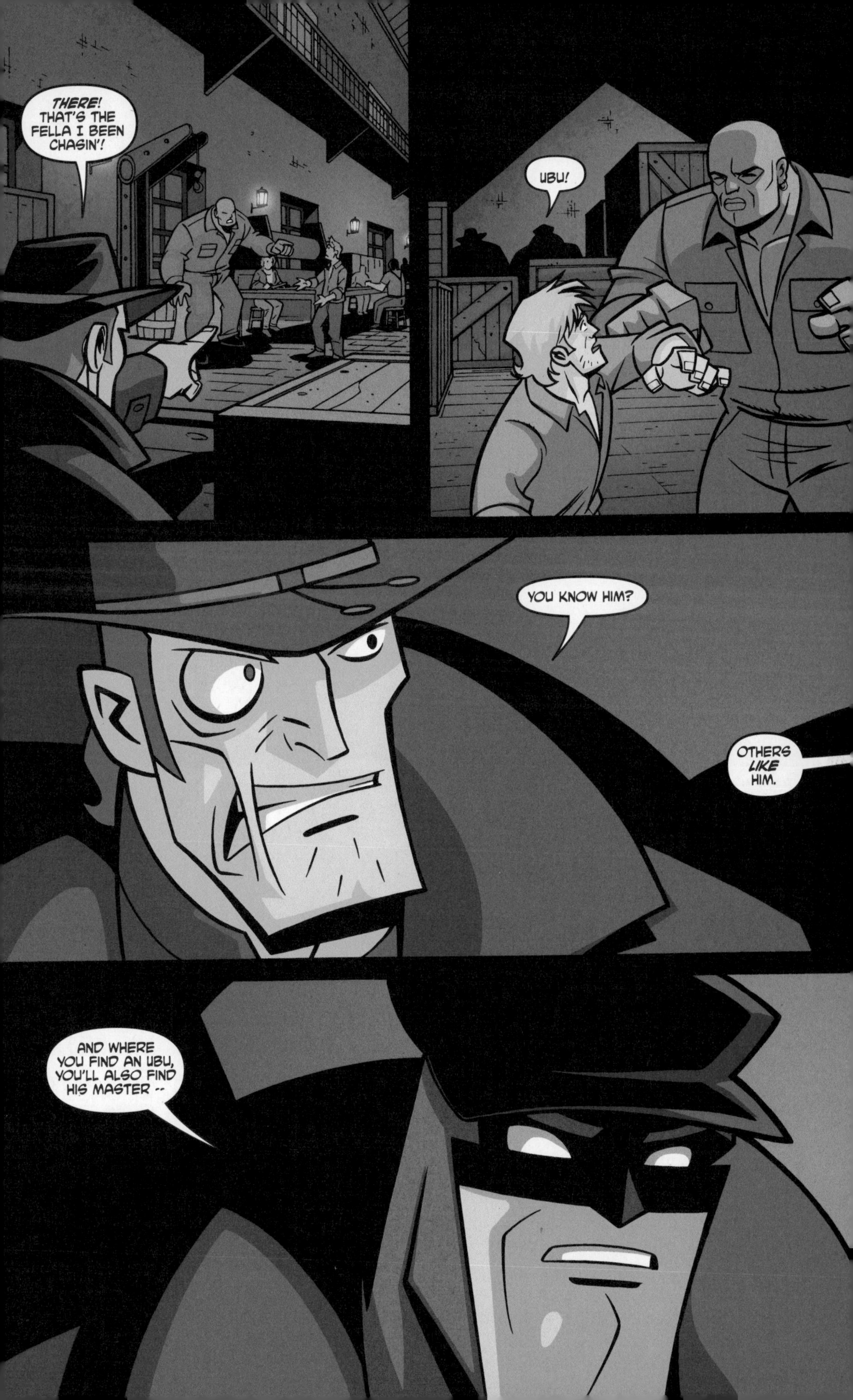
THERE! THAT'S THE FELLA I BEEN CHASIN'!
UBU!
YOU KNOW HIM?
OTHERS LIKE HIM.
AND WHERE YOU FIND AN UBU, YOU'LL ALSO FIND HIS MASTER --

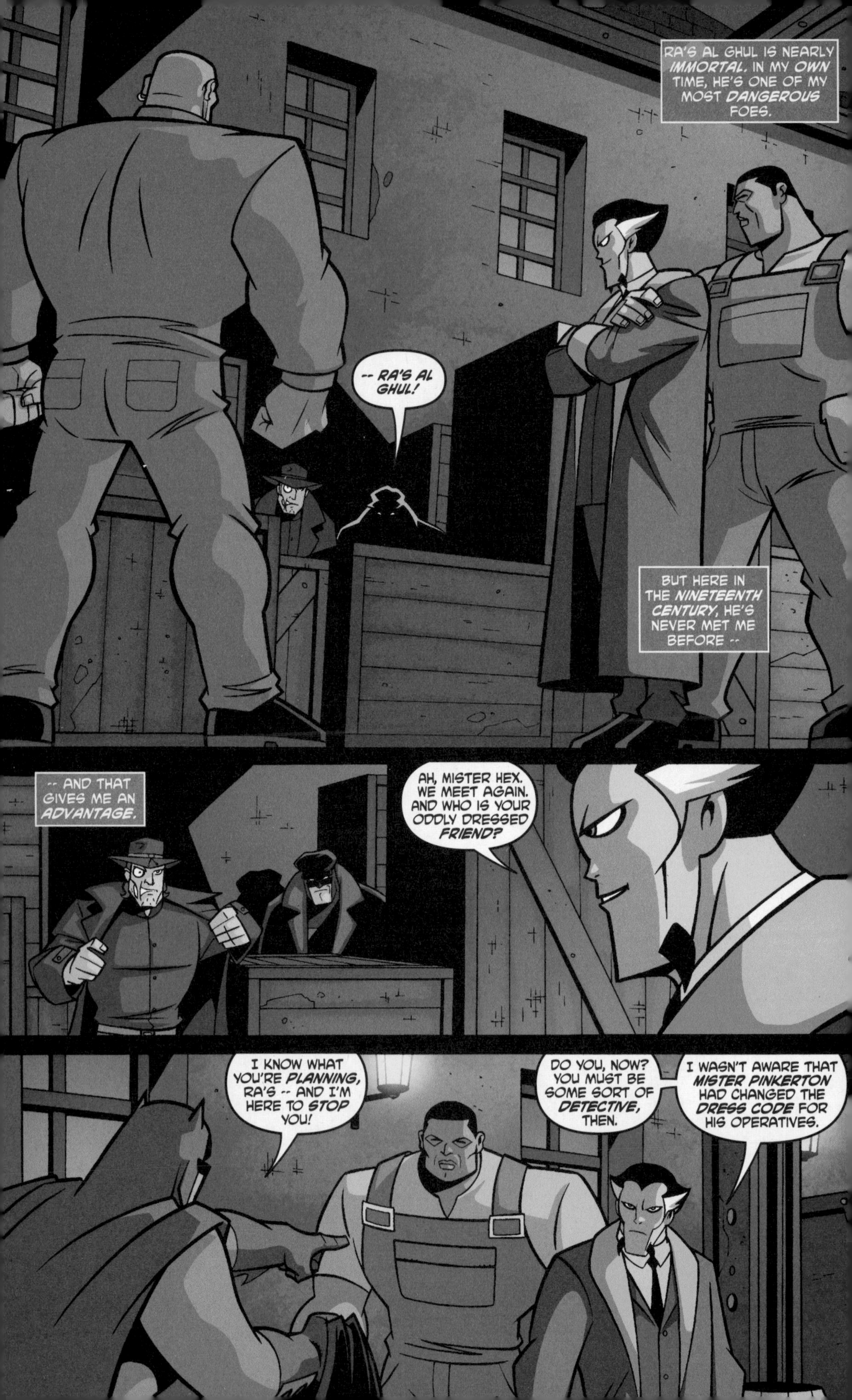
RA'S AL GHUL IS NEARLY IMMORTAL. IN MY OWN TIME, HE'S ONE OF MY MOST DANGEROUS FOES.
-- RA'S AL GHUL!
BUT HERE IN THE NINETEENTH CENTURY, HE'S NEVER MET ME BEFORE --
-- AND THAT GIVES ME AN ADVANTAGE.
AH, MISTER HEX. WE MEET AGAIN. AND WHO IS YOUR ODDLY DRESSED FRIEND?
I KNOW WHAT YOU'RE PLANNING, RA'S -- AND I'M HERE TO STOP YOU!
DO YOU, NOW? YOU MUST BE SOME SORT OF DETECTIVE, THEN.
I WASN'T AWARE THAT MISTER PINKERTON HAD CHANGED THE DRESS CODE FOR HIS OPERATIVES.

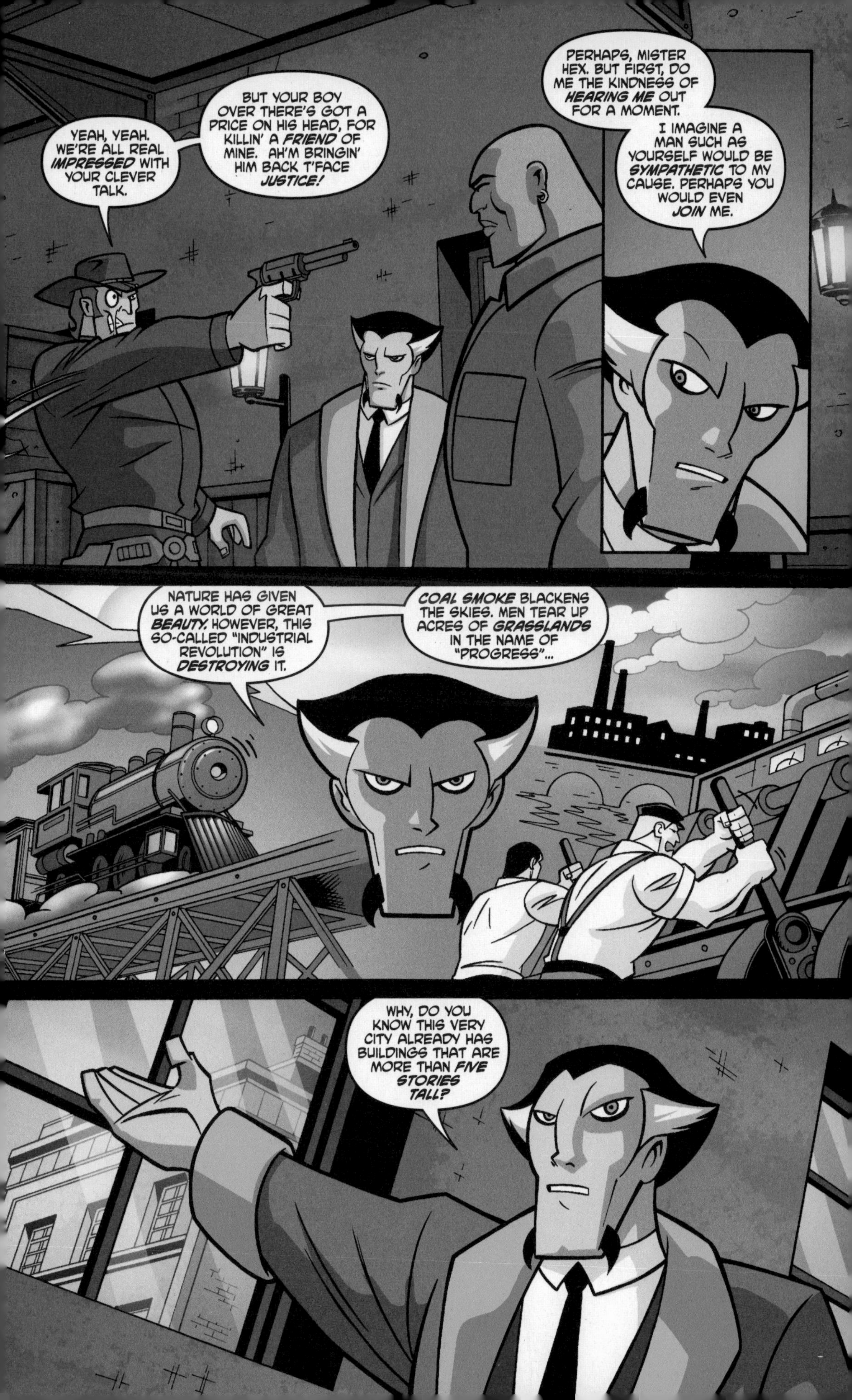
YEAH, YEAH. WE'RE ALL REAL IMPRESSED WITH YOUR CLEVER TALK.
BUT YOUR BOY OVER THERE'S GOT A PRICE ON HIS HEAD, FOR KILLIN' A FRIEND OF MINE. AH'M BRINGIN' HIM BACK T'FACE JUSTICE!
PERHAPS, MISTER HEX. BUT FIRST, DO ME THE KINDNESS OF HEARING ME OUT FOR A MOMENT.
I IMAGINE A MAN SUCH AS YOURSELF WOULD BE SYMPATHETIC TO MY CAUSE. PERHAPS YOU WOULD EVEN JOIN ME.
NATURE HAS GIVEN US A WORLD OF GREAT BEAUTY. HOWEVER, THIS SO-CALLED "INDUSTRIAL REVOLUTION" IS DESTROYING IT.
COAL SMOKE BLACKENS THE SKIES. MEN TEAR UP ACRES OF GRASSLANDS IN THE NAME OF "PROGRESS"...
WHY, DO YOU KNOW THIS VERY CITY ALREADY HAS BUILDINGS THAT ARE MORE THAN FIVE STORIES TALL?

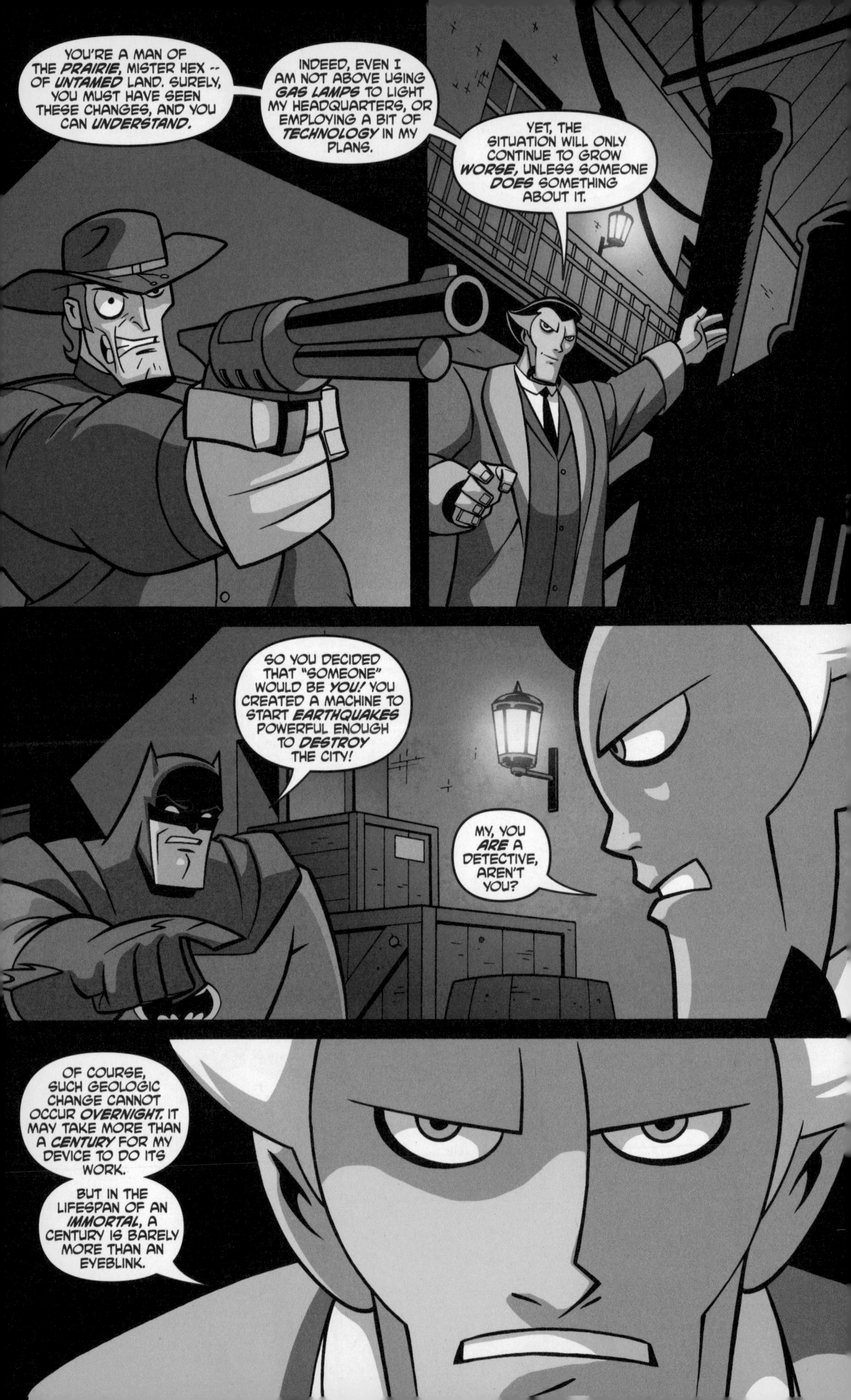

YOU'RE A MAN OF THE PRAIRIE, MISTER HEX -- OF UNTAMED LAND. SURELY, YOU MUST HAVE SEEN THESE CHANGES, AND YOU CAN UNDERSTAND.
INDEED, EVEN I AM NOT ABOVE USING GAS LAMPS TO LIGHT MY HEADQUARTERS, OR EMPLOYING A BIT OF TECHNOLOGY IN MY PLANS.
YET, THE SITUATION WILL ONLY CONTINUE TO GROW WORSE, UNLESS SOMEONE DOES SOMETHING ABOUT IT.
SO YOU DECIDED THAT "SOMEONE" WOULD BE YOU! YOU CREATED A MACHINE TO START EARTHQUAKES POWERFUL ENOUGH TO DESTROY THE CITY!
MY, YOU ARE A DETECTIVE, AREN'T YOU?
OF COURSE, SUCH GEOLOGIC CHANGE CANNOT OCCUR OVERNIGHT. IT MAY TAKE MORE THAN A CENTURY FOR MY DEVICE TO DO ITS WORK.
BUT IN THE LIFESPAN OF AN IMMORTAL, A CENTURY IS BARELY MORE THAN AN EYEBLINK.

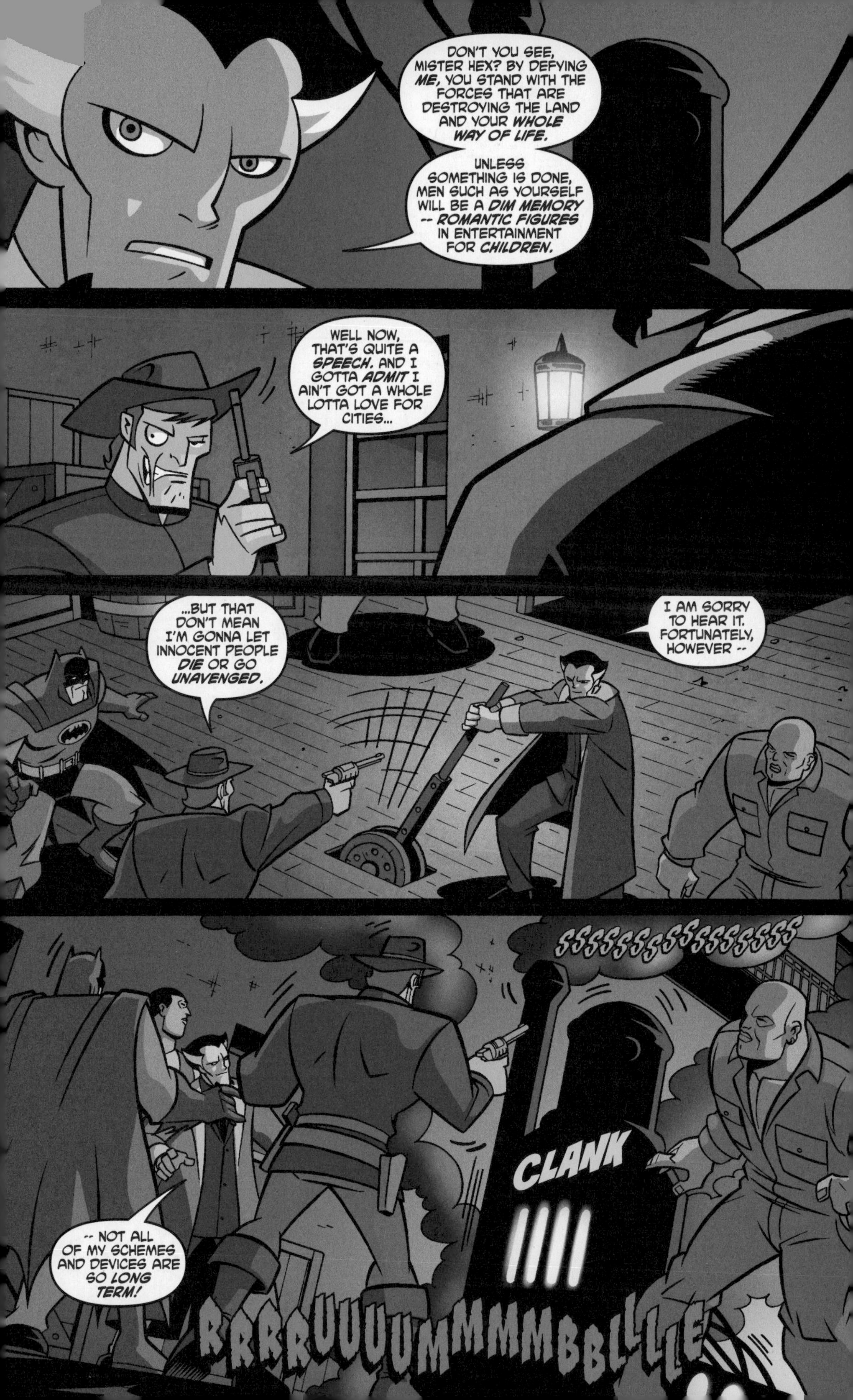
DON'T YOU SEE, MISTER HEX? BY DEFYING ME, YOU STAND WITH THE FORCES THAT ARE DESTROYING THE LAND AND YOUR WHOLE WAY OF LIFE.
UNLESS SOMETHING IS DONE, MEN SUCH AS YOURSELF WILL BE A DIM MEMORY -- ROMANTIC FIGURES IN ENTERTAINMENT FOR CHILDREN.
WELL NOW, THAT'S QUITE A SPEECH. AND I GOTTA ADMIT I AIN'T GOT A WHOLE LOTTA LOVE FOR CITIES...
...BUT THAT DON'T MEAN I'M GONNA LET INNOCENT PEOPLE DIE OR GO UNAVENGED.
I AM SORRY TO HEAR IT. FORTUNATELY, HOWEVER --
SSSSSSSSSSSSSSSSS
CLANK
-- NOT ALL OF MY SCHEMES AND DEVICES ARE SO LONG TERM!
RRRRUUUUUMMMMMBBLLLLE

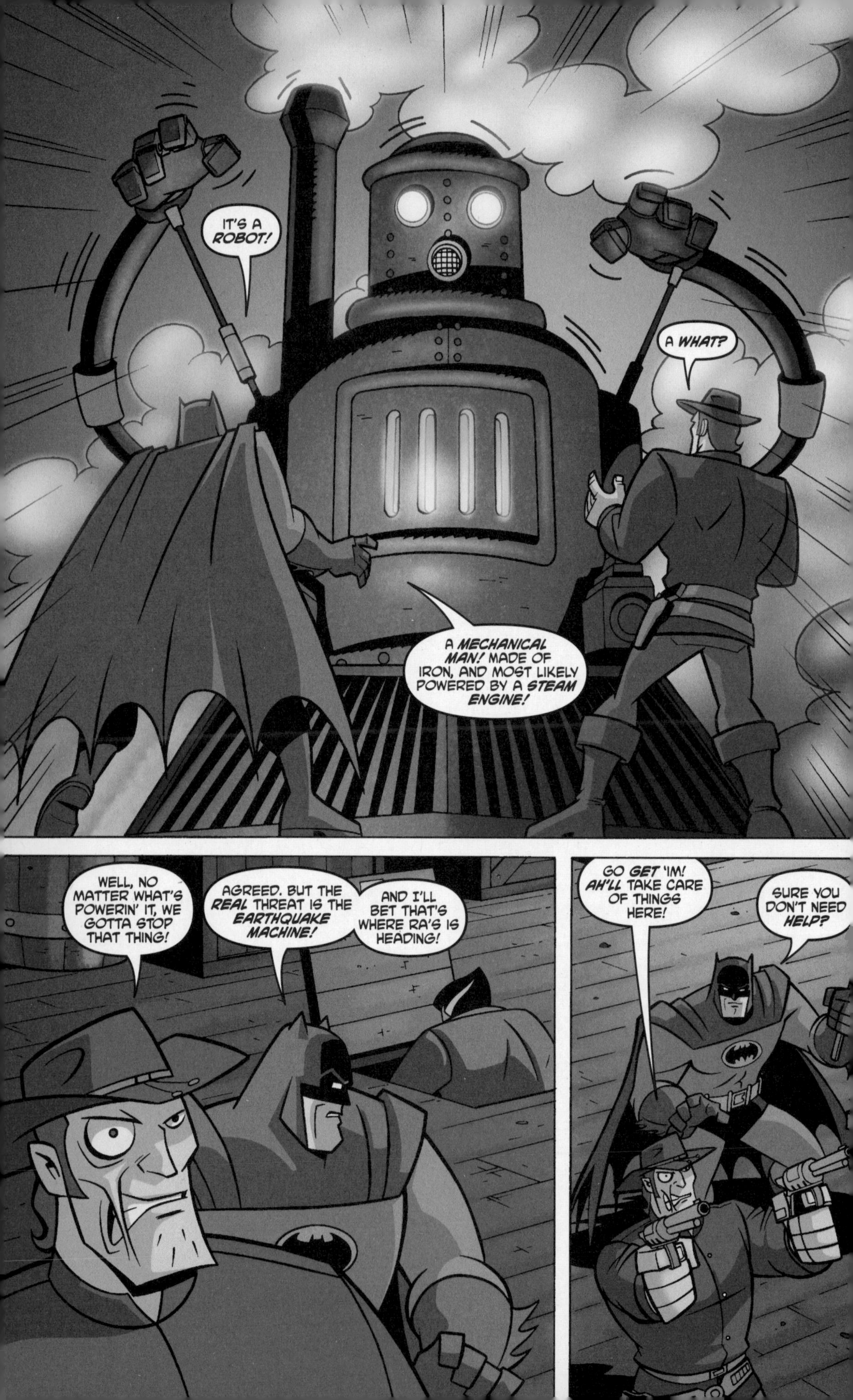
IT'S A ROBOT!
A WHAT?
A MECHANICAL MAN! MADE OF IRON, AND MOST LIKELY POWERED BY A STEAM ENGINE!
WELL, NO MATTER WHAT'S POWERIN' IT, WE GOTTA STOP THAT THING!
AGREED. BUT THE REAL THREAT IS THE EARTHQUAKE MACHINE!
AND I'LL BET THAT'S WHERE RA'S IS HEADING!
GO GET 'IM! AH'LL TAKE CARE OF THINGS HERE!
SURE YOU DON'T NEED HELP?

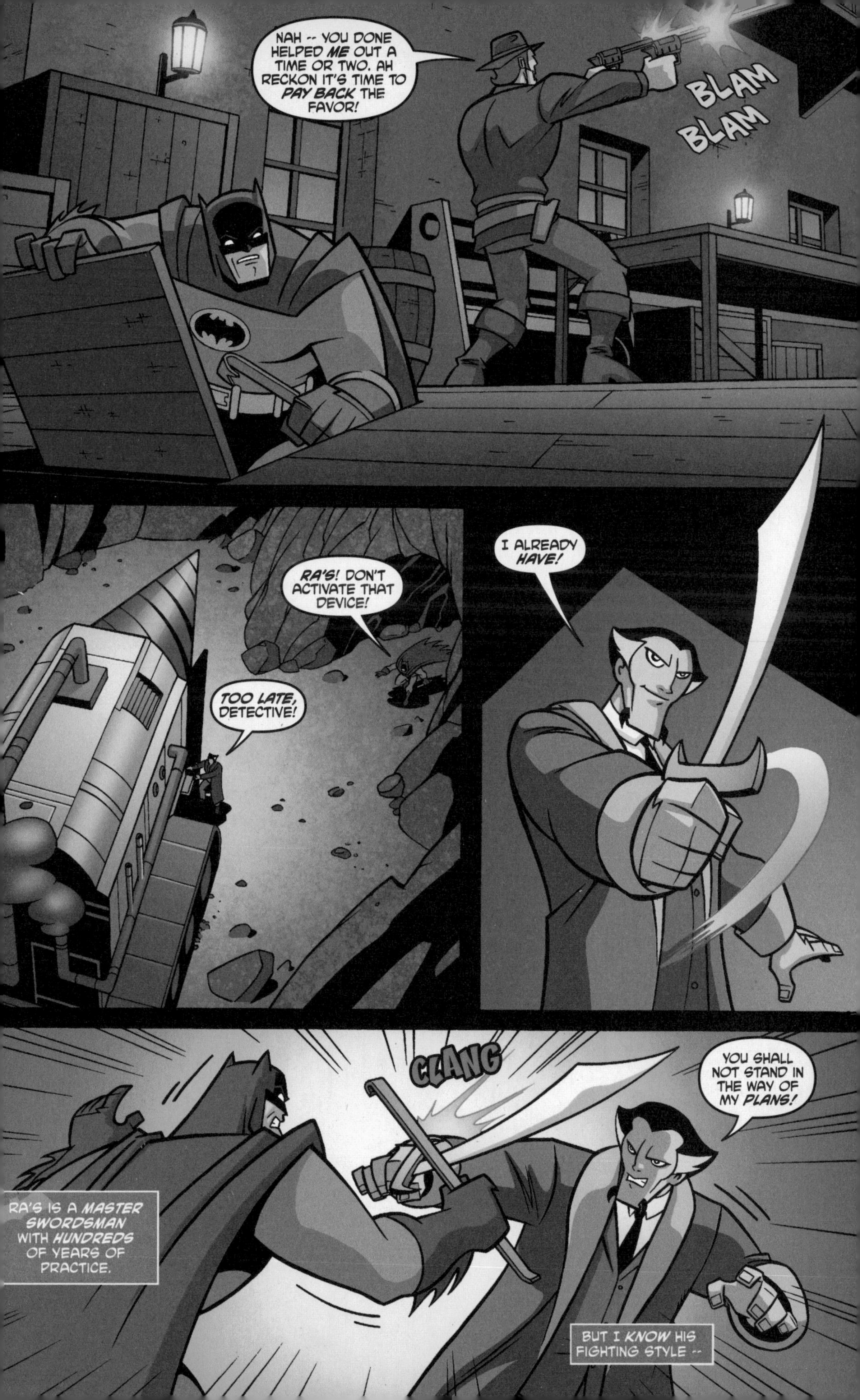
NAH -- YOU DONE HELPED ME OUT A TIME OR TWO. AH RECKON IT'S TIME TO PAY BACK THE FAVOR!
BLAM BLAM
RA'S! DON'T ACTIVATE THAT DEVICE!
TOO LATE, DETECTIVE!
I ALREADY HAVE!
CLANG
YOU SHALL NOT STAND IN THE WAY OF MY PLANS!
RA'S IS A MASTER SWORDSMAN WITH HUNDREDS OF YEARS OF PRACTICE.
BUT I KNOW HIS FIGHTING STYLE --

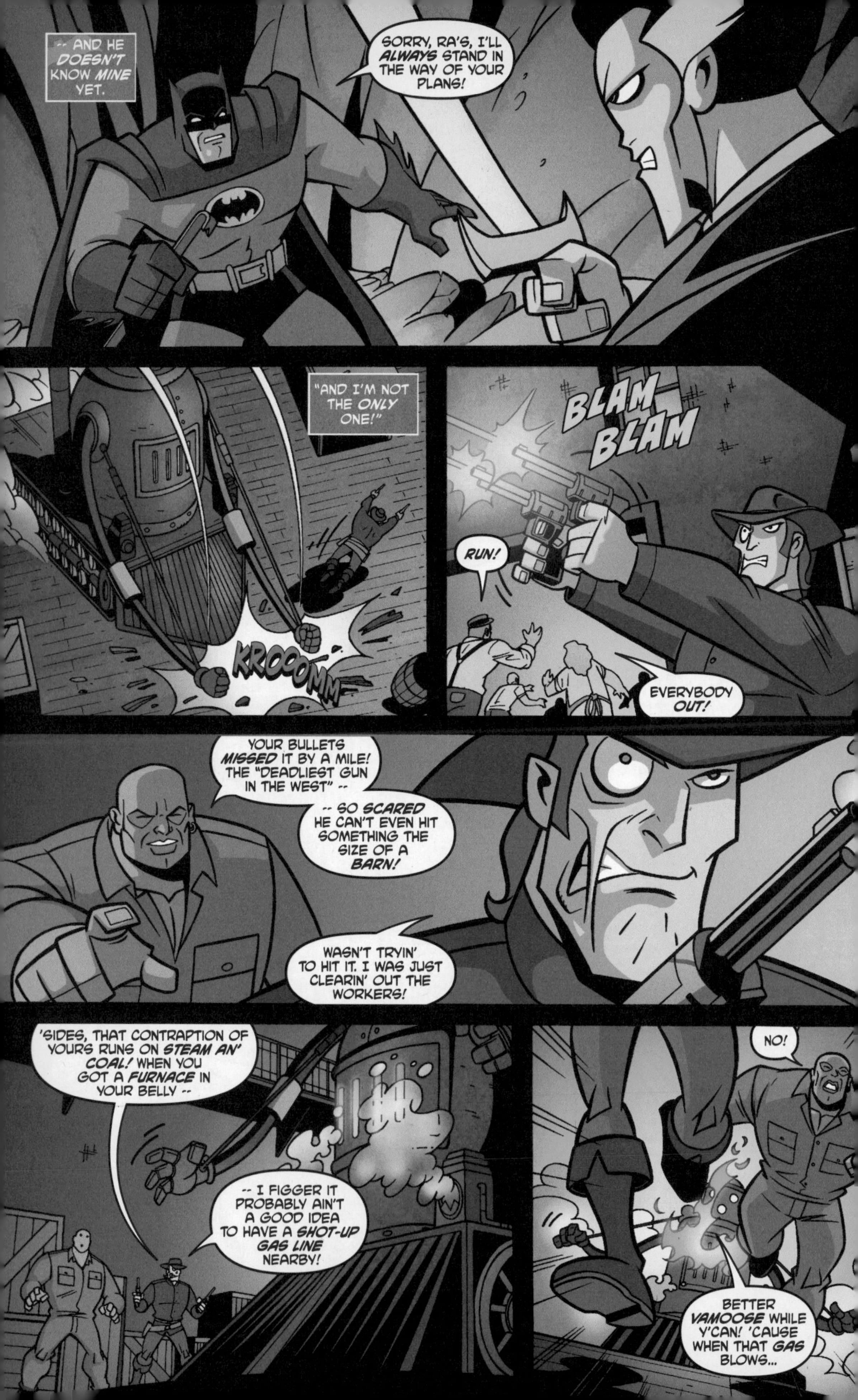
-- AND HE DOESN'T KNOW MINE YET.
SORRY, RA'S, I'LL ALWAYS STAND IN THE WAY OF YOUR PLANS!
"AND I'M NOT THE ONLY ONE!"
KROOOMM
BLAM BLAM
RUN!
EVERYBODY OUT!
YOUR BULLETS MISSED IT BY A MILE! THE "DEADLIEST GUN IN THE WEST" --
-- SO SCARED HE CAN'T EVEN HIT SOMETHING THE SIZE OF A BARN!
WASN'T TRYIN' TO HIT IT. I WAS JUST CLEARIN' OUT THE WORKERS!
'SIDES, THAT CONTRAPTION OF YOURS RUNS ON STEAM AN' COAL! WHEN YOU GOT A FURNACE IN YOUR BELLY --
-- I FIGGER IT PROBABLY AIN'T A GOOD IDEA TO HAVE A SHOT-UP GAS LINE NEARBY!
NO!
BETTER VAMOOSE WHILE Y'CAN! 'CAUSE WHEN THAT GAS BLOWS...

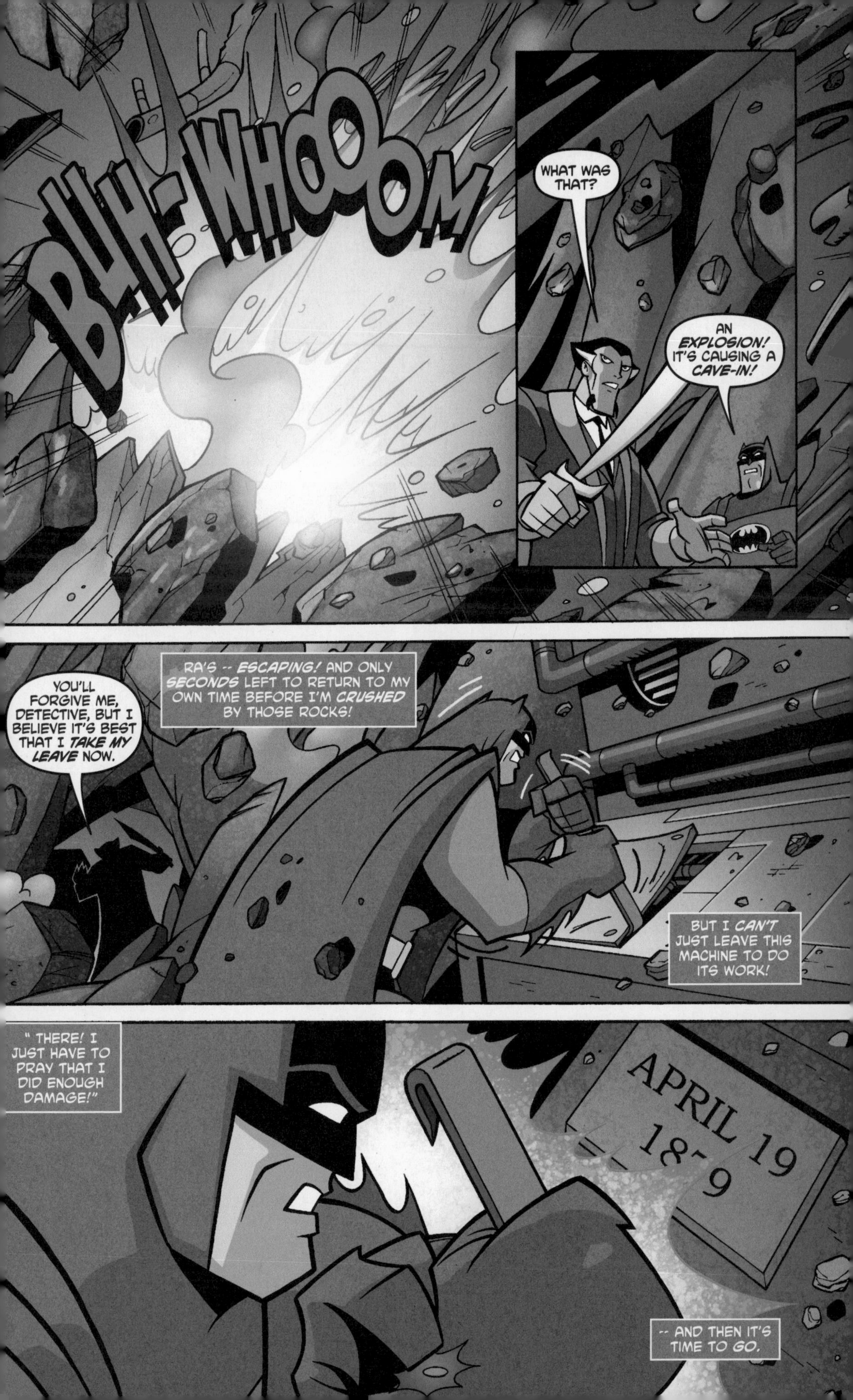
BUH-WHOOOOM
WHAT WAS THAT?
AN EXPLOSION! IT'S CAUSING A CAVE-IN!
YOU'LL FORGIVE ME, DETECTIVE, BUT I BELIEVE IT'S BEST THAT I TAKE MY LEAVE NOW.
RA'S -- ESCAPING! AND ONLY SECONDS LEFT TO RETURN TO MY OWN TIME BEFORE I'M CRUSHED BY THOSE ROCKS!
BUT I CAN'T JUST LEAVE THIS MACHINE TO DO ITS WORK!
" THERE! I JUST HAVE TO PRAY THAT I DID ENOUGH DAMAGE!"
APRIL 19
18-9
-- AND THEN IT'S TIME TO GO.

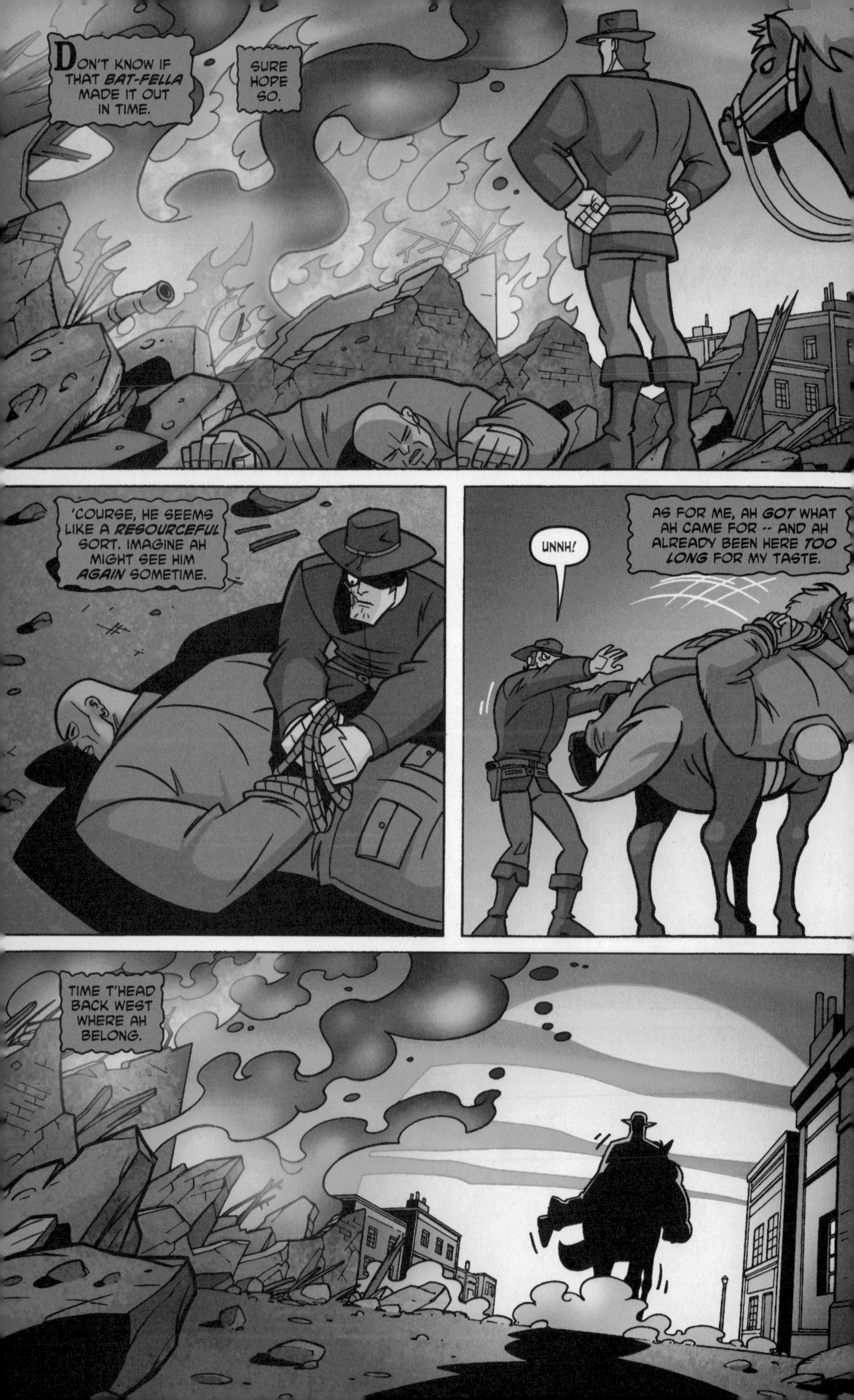
DON'T KNOW IF THAT BAT-FELLA MADE IT OUT IN TIME.
SURE HOPE SO.
'COURSE, HE SEEMS LIKE A RESOURCEFUL SORT. IMAGINE AH MIGHT SEE HIM AGAIN SOMETIME.
UNNH!
AS FOR ME, AH GOT WHAT AH CAME FOR -- AND AH ALREADY BEEN HERE TOO LONG FOR MY TASTE.
TIME T'HEAD BACK WEST WHERE AH BELONG.

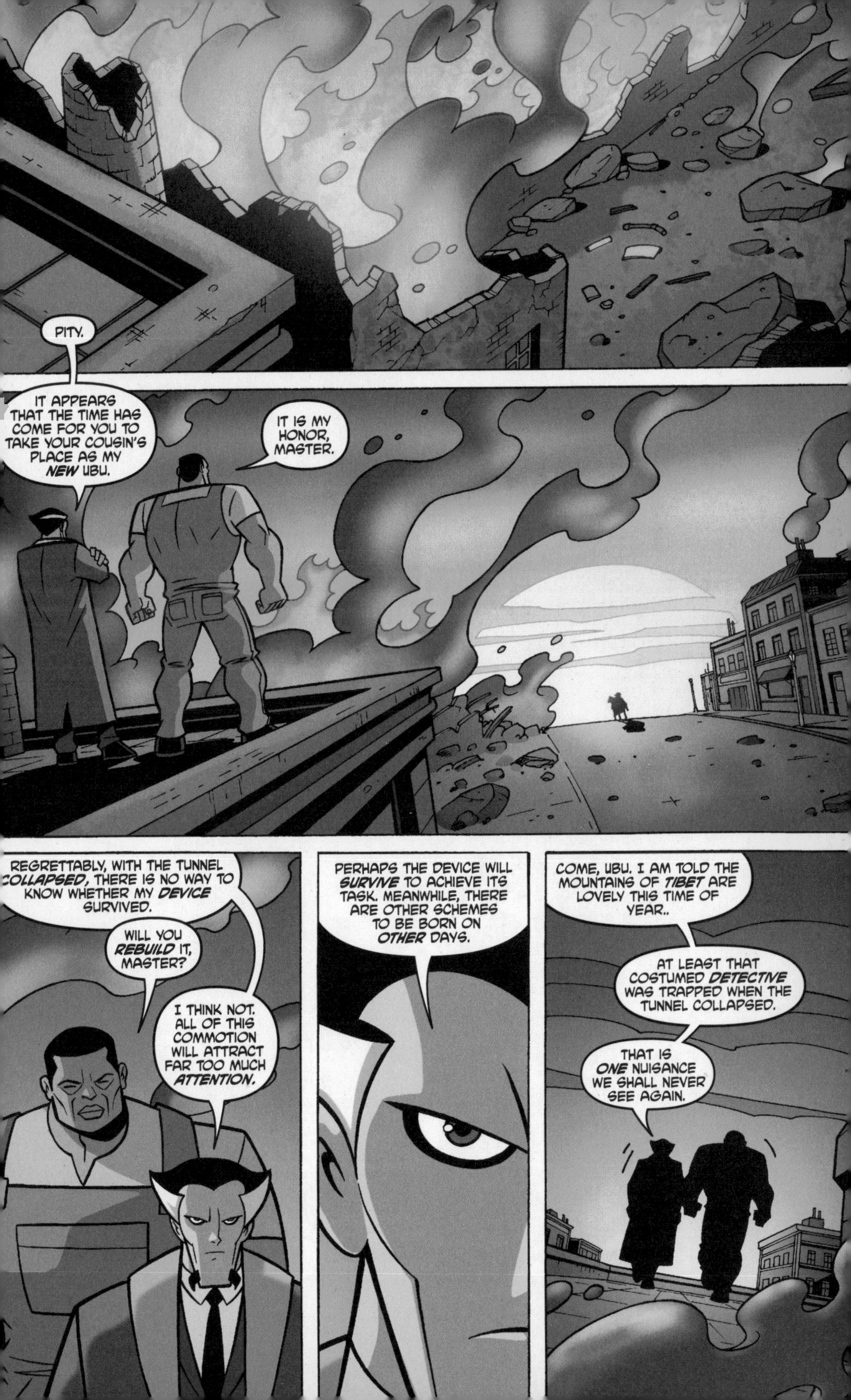
PITY.
IT APPEARS THAT THE TIME HAS COME FOR YOU TO TAKE YOUR COUSIN'S PLACE AS MY *NEW* UBU.
IT IS MY HONOR, MASTER.
REGRETTABLY, WITH THE TUNNEL *COLLAPSED*, THERE IS NO WAY TO KNOW WHETHER MY *DEVICE* SURVIVED.
WILL YOU *REBUILD* IT, MASTER?
I THINK NOT. ALL OF THIS COMMOTION WILL ATTRACT FAR TOO MUCH *ATTENTION*.
PERHAPS THE DEVICE WILL *SURVIVE* TO ACHIEVE ITS TASK. MEANWHILE, THERE ARE OTHER SCHEMES TO BE BORN ON *OTHER* DAYS.
COME, UBU. I AM TOLD THE MOUNTAINS OF *TIBET* ARE LOVELY THIS TIME OF YEAR..
AT LEAST THAT COSTUMED *DETECTIVE* WAS TRAPPED WHEN THE TUNNEL COLLAPSED.
THAT IS *ONE* NUISANCE WE SHALL NEVER SEE AGAIN.

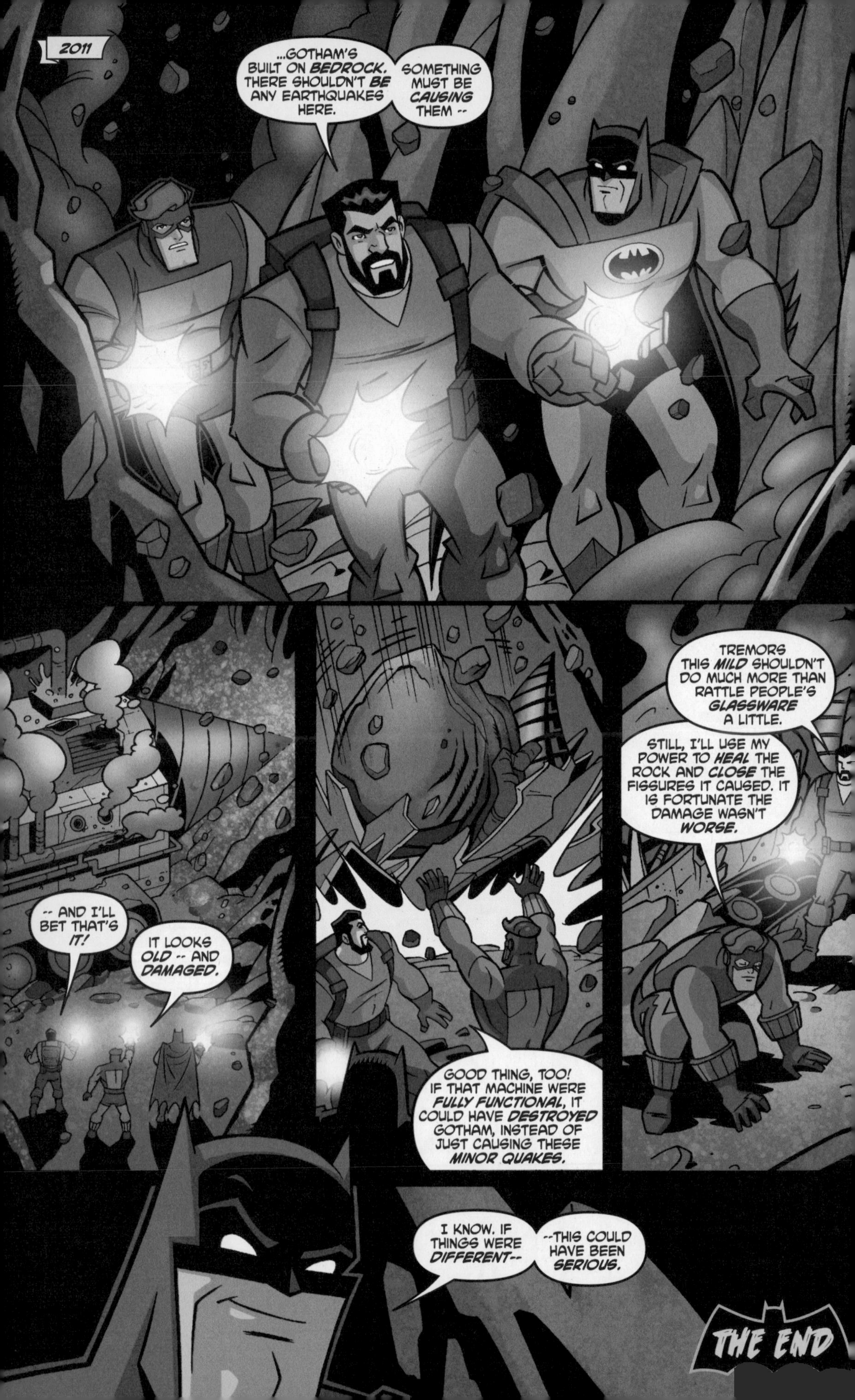
2011
...GOTHAM'S BUILT ON BEDROCK. THERE SHOULDN'T BE ANY EARTHQUAKES HERE.
SOMETHING MUST BE CAUSING THEM --
-- AND I'LL BET THAT'S IT!
IT LOOKS OLD -- AND DAMAGED.
GOOD THING, TOO! IF THAT MACHINE WERE FULLY FUNCTIONAL, IT COULD HAVE DESTROYED GOTHAM, INSTEAD OF JUST CAUSING THESE MINOR QUAKES.
TREMORS THIS MILD SHOULDN'T DO MUCH MORE THAN RATTLE PEOPLE'S GLASSWARE A LITTLE.
STILL, I'LL USE MY POWER TO HEAL THE ROCK AND CLOSE THE FISSURES IT CAUSED. IT IS FORTUNATE THE DAMAGE WASN'T WORSE.
I KNOW. IF THINGS WERE DIFFERENT--
--THIS COULD HAVE BEEN SERIOUS.
THE END

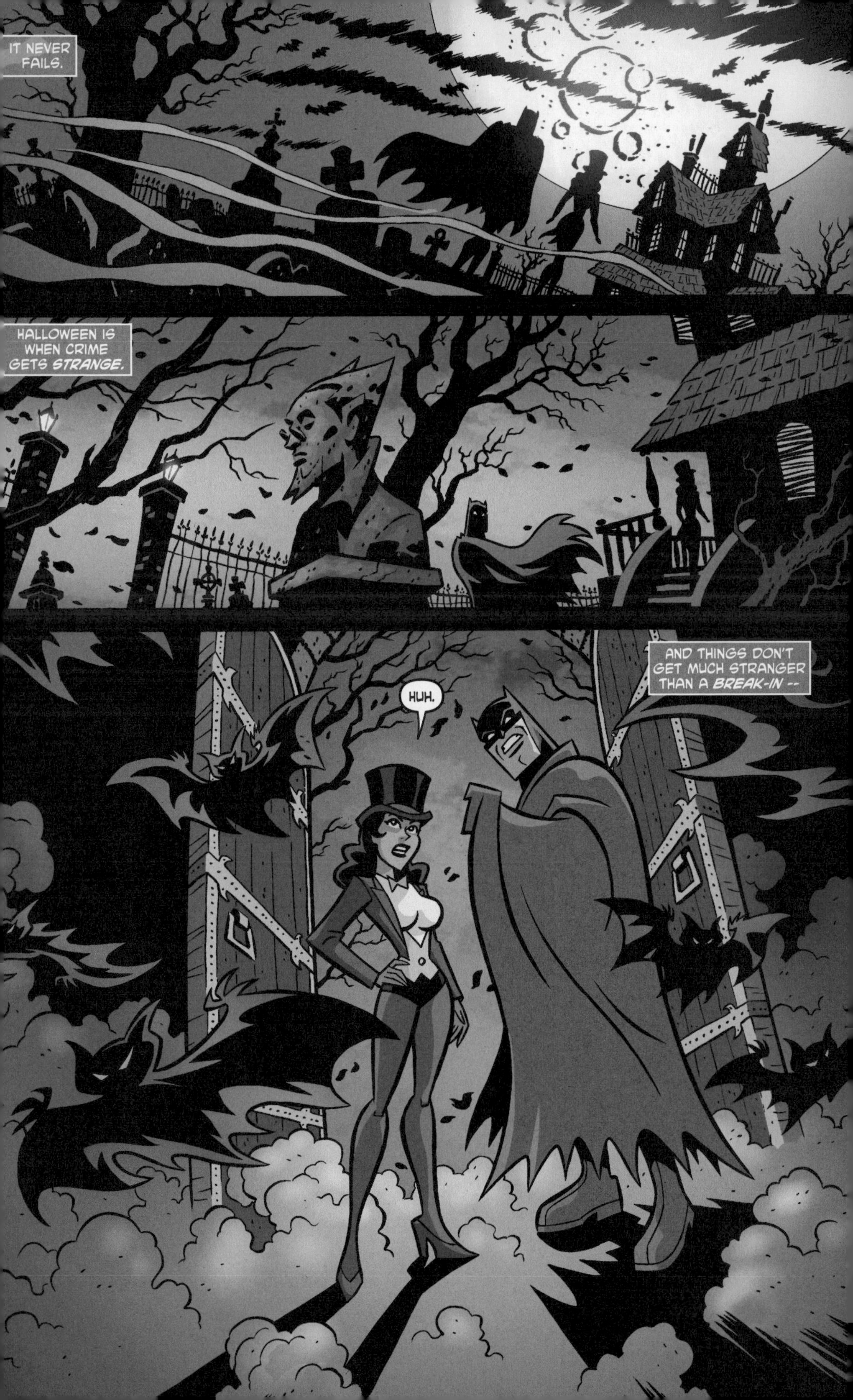
IT NEVER FAILS.
HALLOWEEN IS WHEN CRIME GETS *STRANGE.*
AND THINGS DON'T GET MUCH STRANGER THAN A *BREAK-IN* --
HUH.

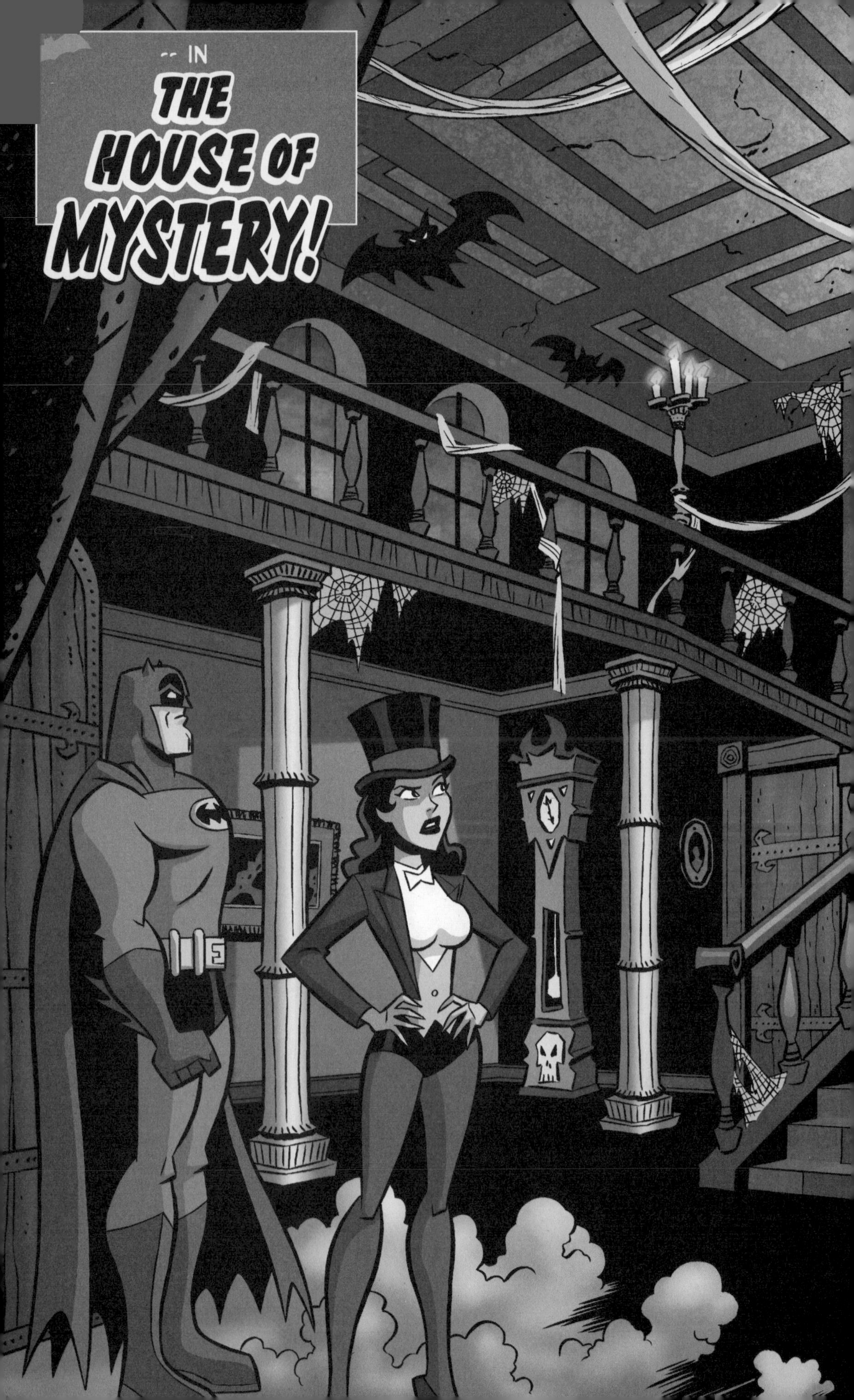
-- IN
THE HOUSE OF MYSTERY!

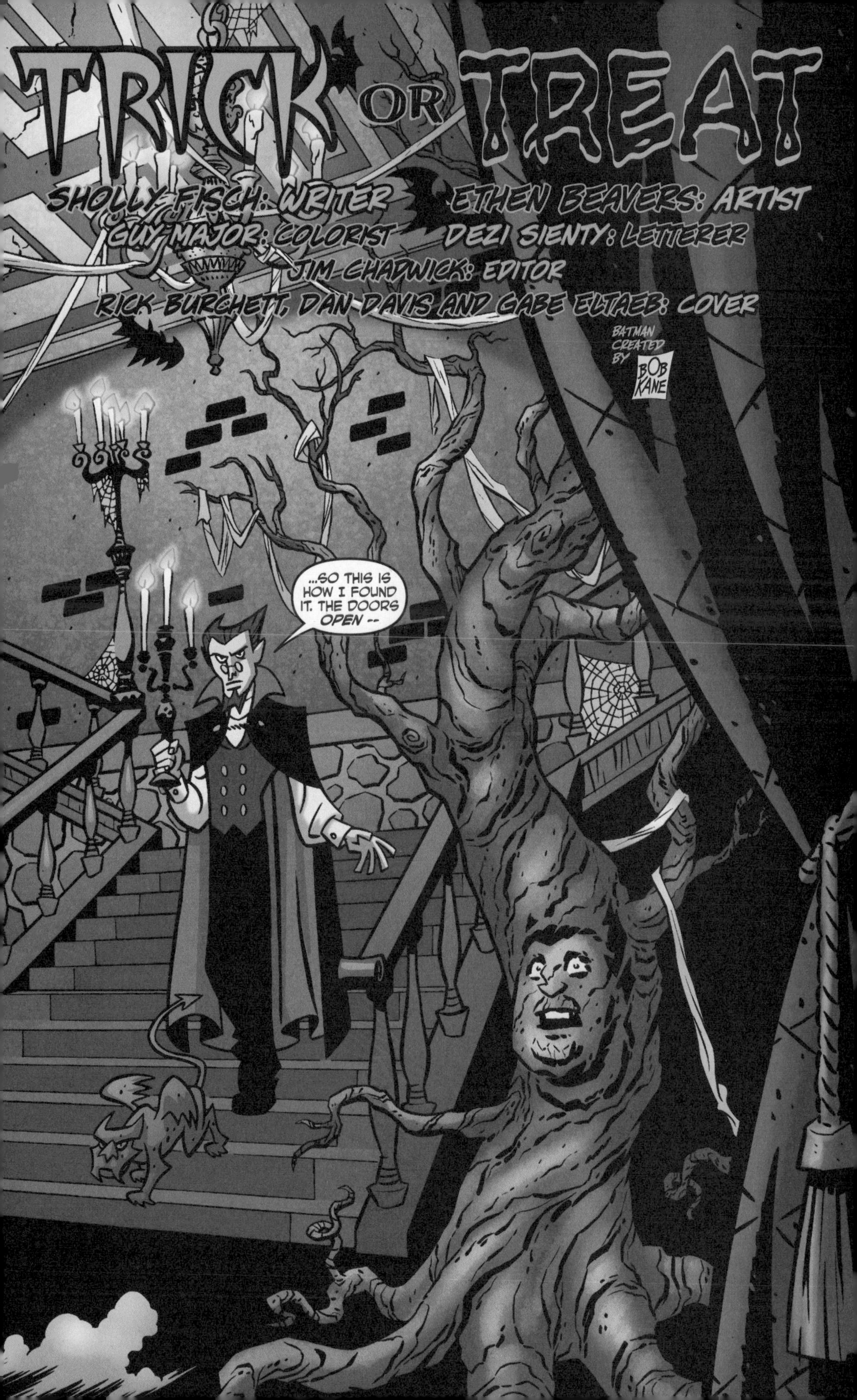
TRICK OR TREAT
SHOLLY FISCH: WRITER
ETHEN BEAVERS: ARTIST
GUY MAJOR: COLORIST
DEZI SIENTY: LETTERER
JIM CHADWICK: EDITOR
RICK BURCHETT, DAN DAVIS AND GABE ELTAEB: COVER
BATMAN CREATED BY BOB KANE
...SO THIS IS HOW I FOUND IT. THE DOORS OPEN --

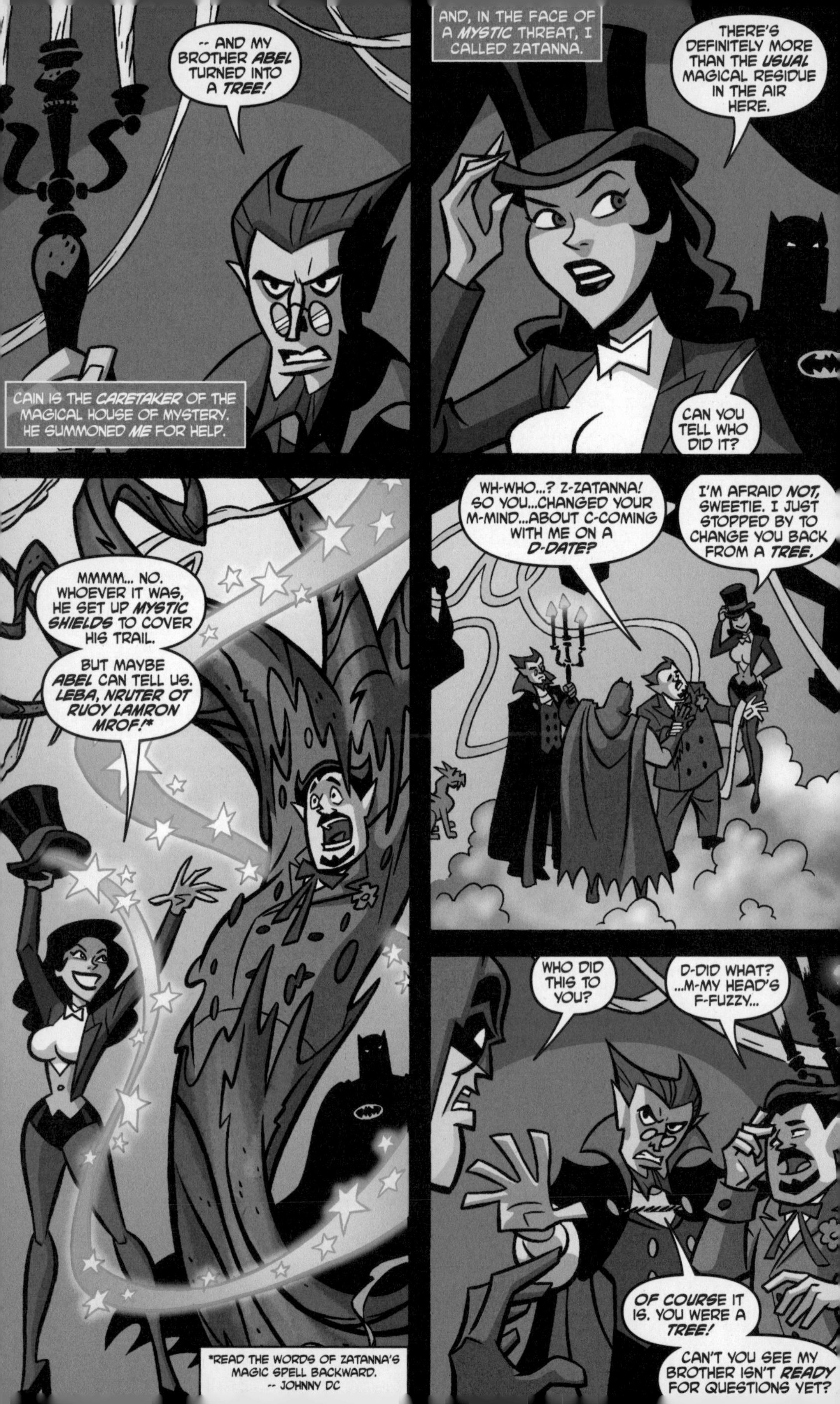
-- AND MY BROTHER ABEL TURNED INTO A TREE!
CAIN IS THE CARETAKER OF THE MAGICAL HOUSE OF MYSTERY. HE SUMMONED ME FOR HELP.
AND, IN THE FACE OF A MYSTIC THREAT, I CALLED ZATANNA.
THERE'S DEFINITELY MORE THAN THE USUAL MAGICAL RESIDUE IN THE AIR HERE.
CAN YOU TELL WHO DID IT?
MMMM... NO. WHOEVER IT WAS, HE SET UP MYSTIC SHIELDS TO COVER HIS TRAIL.
BUT MAYBE ABEL CAN TELL US. LEBA, NRUTER OT RUOY LAMRON MROF!*
*READ THE WORDS OF ZATANNA'S MAGIC SPELL BACKWARD. -- JOHNNY DC
WH-WHO...? Z-ZATANNA! SO YOU...CHANGED YOUR M-MIND...ABOUT C-COMING WITH ME ON A D-DATE?
I'M AFRAID NOT, SWEETIE. I JUST STOPPED BY TO CHANGE YOU BACK FROM A TREE.
WHO DID THIS TO YOU?
D-DID WHAT? ...M-MY HEAD'S F-FUZZY...
OF COURSE IT IS. YOU WERE A TREE!
CAN'T YOU SEE MY BROTHER ISN'T READY FOR QUESTIONS YET?

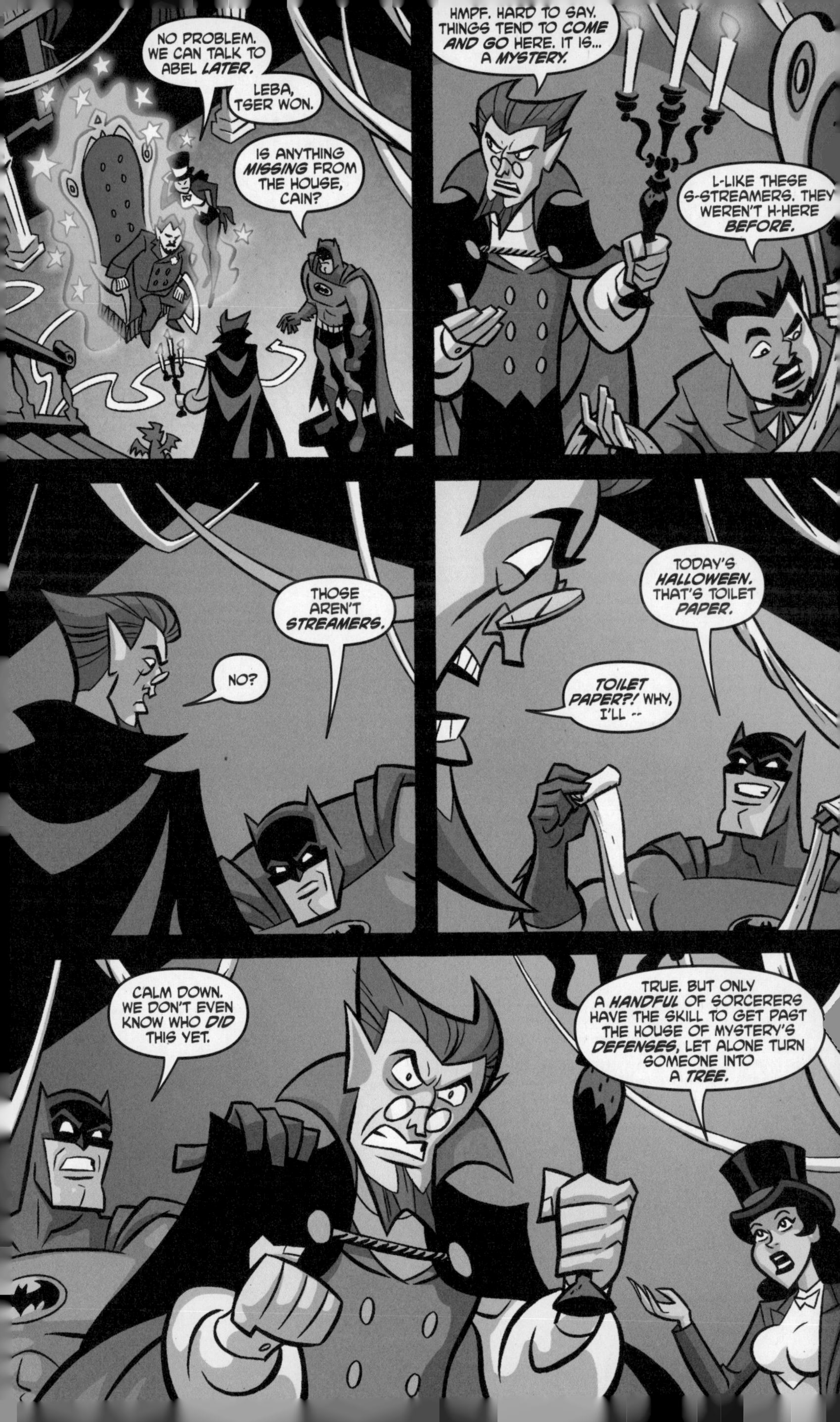
NO PROBLEM. WE CAN TALK TO ABEL LATER.
LEBA, TSER WON.
IS ANYTHING MISSING FROM THE HOUSE, CAIN?
HMPF. HARD TO SAY. THINGS TEND TO COME AND GO HERE. IT IS... A MYSTERY.
L-LIKE THESE S-STREAMERS. THEY WEREN'T H-HERE BEFORE.
THOSE AREN'T STREAMERS.
NO?
TODAY'S HALLOWEEN. THAT'S TOILET PAPER.
TOILET PAPER?! WHY, I'LL --
CALM DOWN. WE DON'T EVEN KNOW WHO DID THIS YET.
TRUE. BUT ONLY A HANDFUL OF SORCERERS HAVE THE SKILL TO GET PAST THE HOUSE OF MYSTERY'S DEFENSES, LET ALONE TURN SOMEONE INTO A TREE.

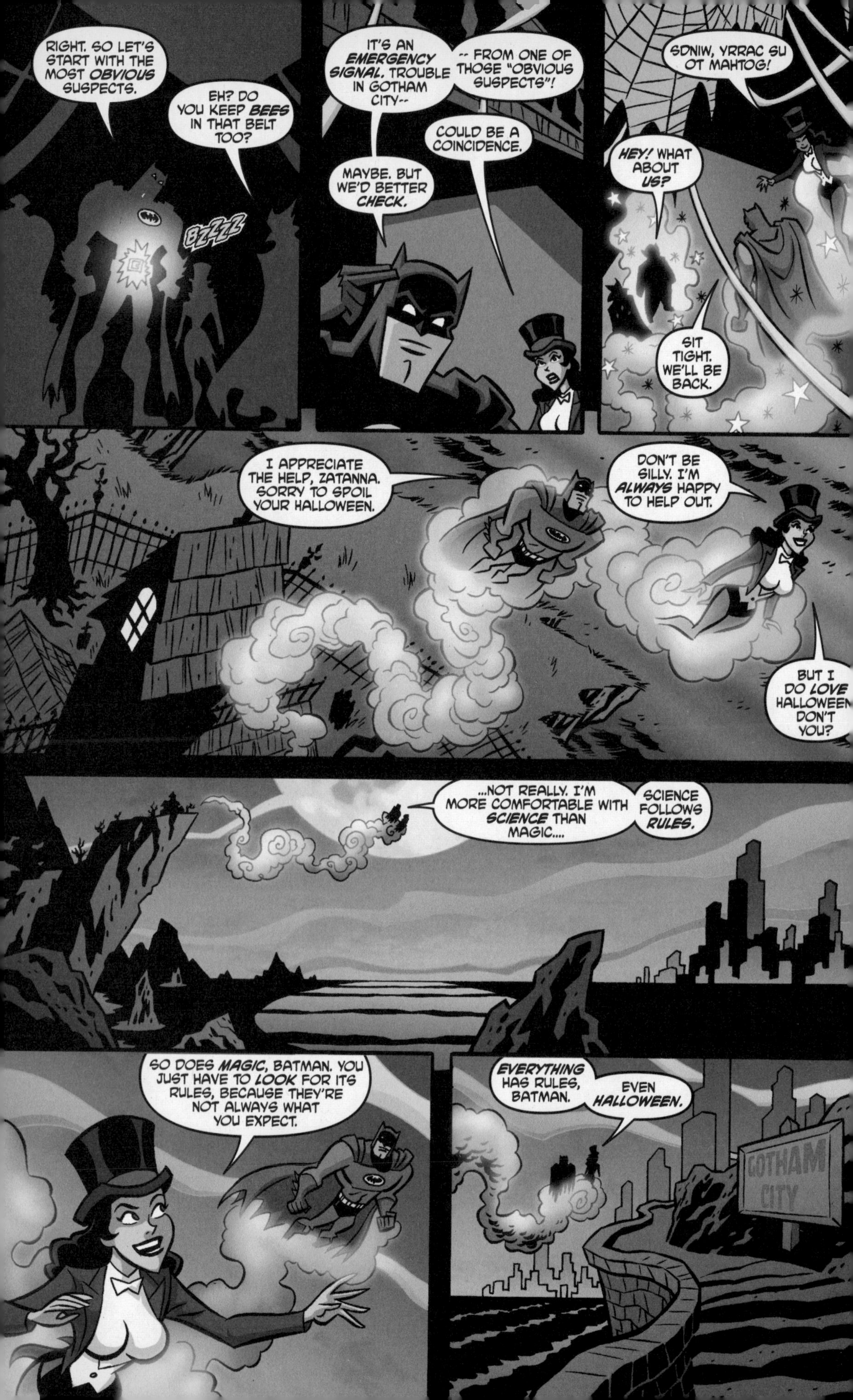
RIGHT. SO LET'S START WITH THE MOST OBVIOUS SUSPECTS.
EH? DO YOU KEEP BEES IN THAT BELT TOO?
BZZZZ
IT'S AN EMERGENCY SIGNAL. TROUBLE IN GOTHAM CITY--
-- FROM ONE OF THOSE "OBVIOUS SUSPECTS"!
COULD BE A COINCIDENCE.
MAYBE. BUT WE'D BETTER CHECK.
SDNIW, YRRAC SU OT MAHTOG!
HEY! WHAT ABOUT US?
SIT TIGHT. WE'LL BE BACK.
I APPRECIATE THE HELP, ZATANNA. SORRY TO SPOIL YOUR HALLOWEEN.
DON'T BE SILLY. I'M ALWAYS HAPPY TO HELP OUT.
BUT I DO LOVE HALLOWEEN DON'T YOU?
...NOT REALLY. I'M MORE COMFORTABLE WITH SCIENCE THAN MAGIC....
SCIENCE FOLLOWS RULES.
SO DOES MAGIC, BATMAN. YOU JUST HAVE TO LOOK FOR ITS RULES, BECAUSE THEY'RE NOT ALWAYS WHAT YOU EXPECT.
EVERYTHING HAS RULES, BATMAN.
EVEN HALLOWEEN.
GOTHAM CITY

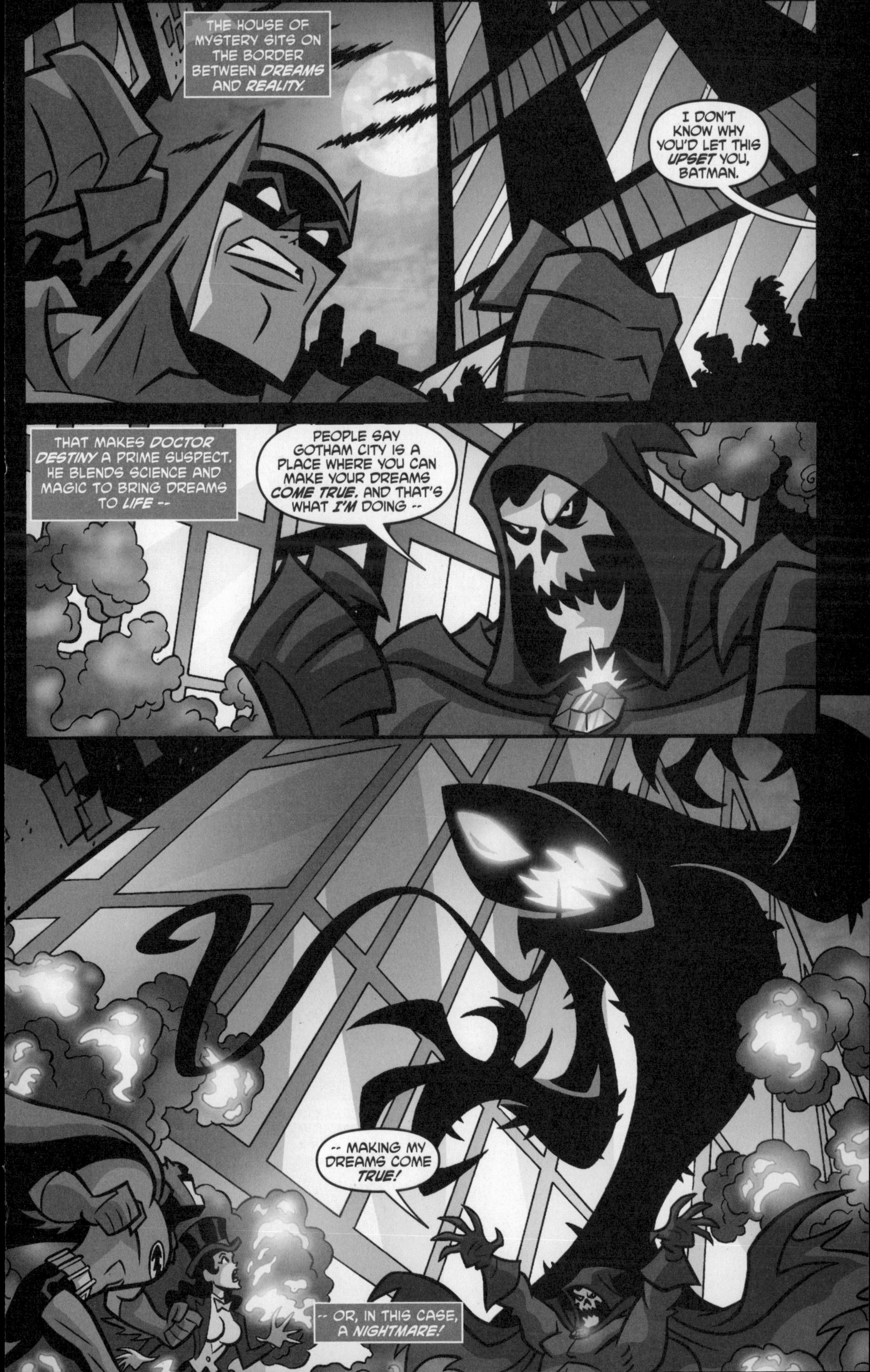
THE HOUSE OF MYSTERY SITS ON THE BORDER BETWEEN *DREAMS* AND *REALITY*.
I DON'T KNOW WHY YOU'D LET THIS *UPSET* YOU, BATMAN.
THAT MAKES *DOCTOR DESTINY* A PRIME SUSPECT. HE BLENDS SCIENCE AND MAGIC TO BRING DREAMS TO *LIFE* --
PEOPLE SAY GOTHAM CITY IS A PLACE WHERE YOU CAN MAKE YOUR DREAMS *COME TRUE*. AND THAT'S WHAT *I'M* DOING --
-- MAKING MY DREAMS COME *TRUE*!
-- OR, IN THIS CASE, A *NIGHTMARE*!

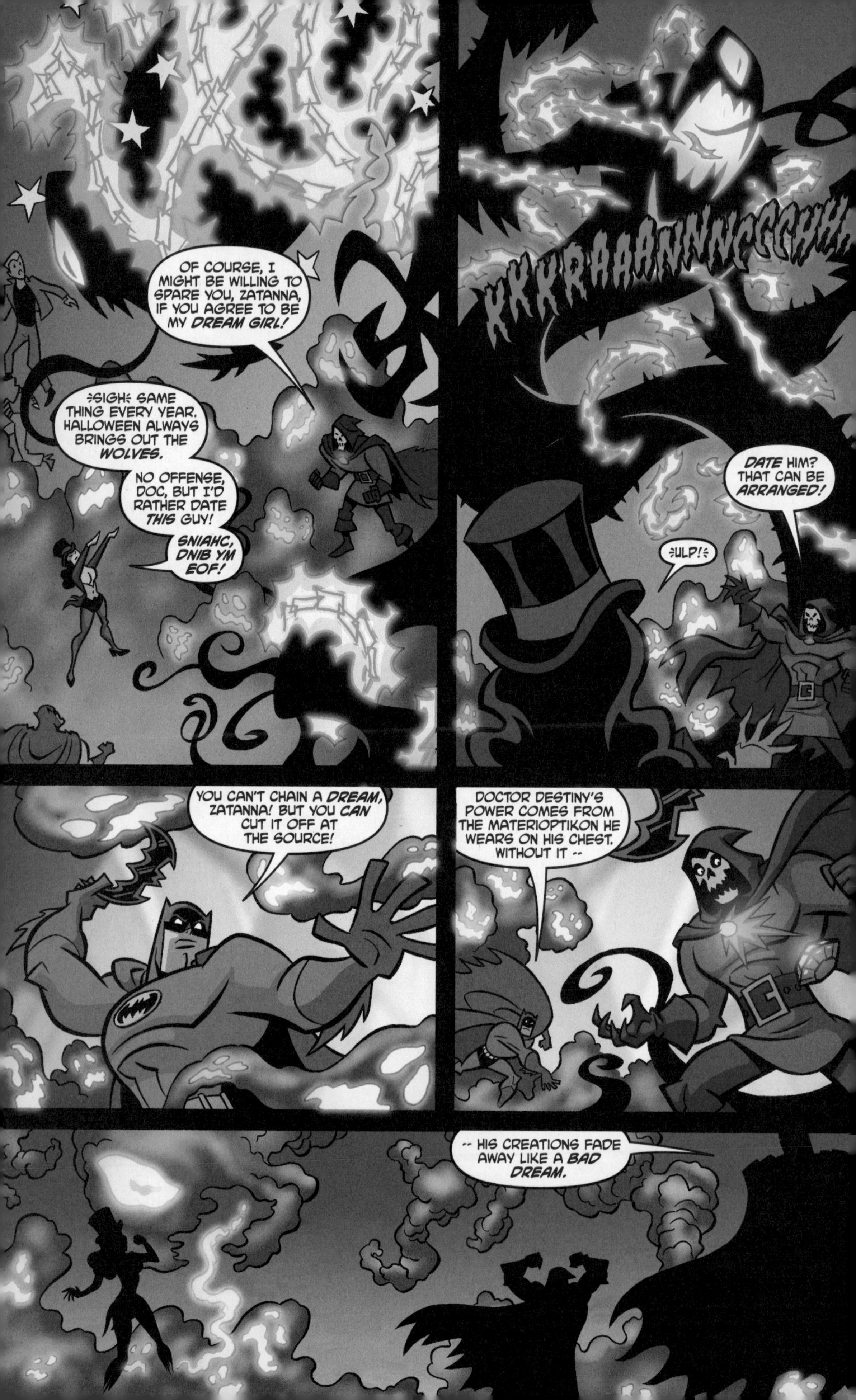

OF COURSE, I MIGHT BE WILLING TO SPARE YOU, ZATANNA, IF YOU AGREE TO BE MY DREAM GIRL!
⁂SIGH⁂ SAME THING EVERY YEAR. HALLOWEEN ALWAYS BRINGS OUT THE WOLVES.
NO OFFENSE, DOC, BUT I'D RATHER DATE THIS GUY!
SNIAHC, DNIB YM EOF!
KKKRAAANNNCCCHH
DATE HIM? THAT CAN BE ARRANGED!
⁂ULP!⁂
YOU CAN'T CHAIN A DREAM, ZATANNA! BUT YOU CAN CUT IT OFF AT THE SOURCE!
DOCTOR DESTINY'S POWER COMES FROM THE MATERIOPTIKON HE WEARS ON HIS CHEST. WITHOUT IT --
-- HIS CREATIONS FADE AWAY LIKE A BAD DREAM.

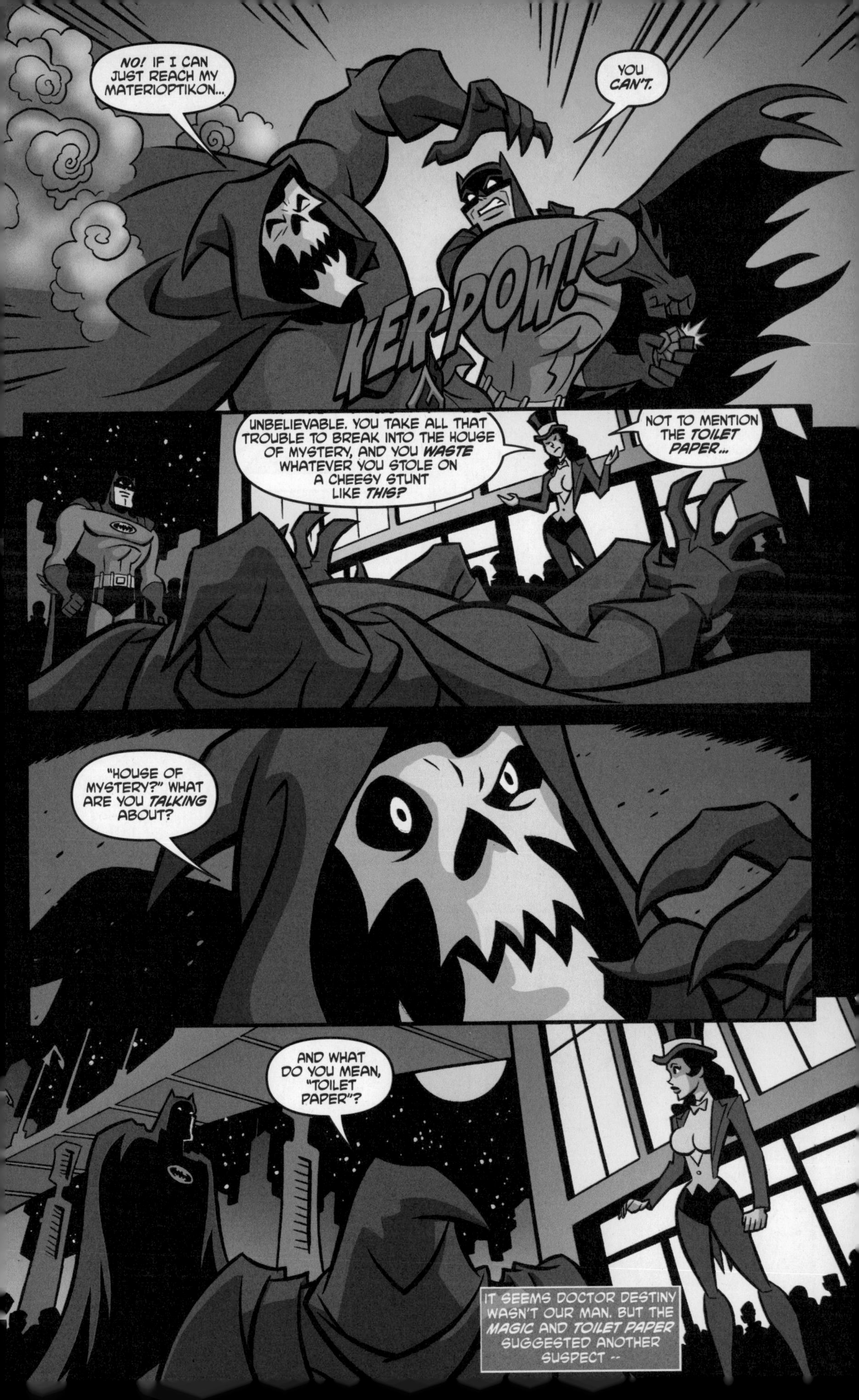
NO! IF I CAN JUST REACH MY MATERIOPTIKON...
YOU CAN'T.
KER-POW!
UNBELIEVABLE. YOU TAKE ALL THAT TROUBLE TO BREAK INTO THE HOUSE OF MYSTERY, AND YOU WASTE WHATEVER YOU STOLE ON A CHEESY STUNT LIKE THIS?
NOT TO MENTION THE TOILET PAPER...
"HOUSE OF MYSTERY?" WHAT ARE YOU TALKING ABOUT?
AND WHAT DO YOU MEAN, "TOILET PAPER"?
IT SEEMS DOCTOR DESTINY WASN'T OUR MAN. BUT THE MAGIC AND TOILET PAPER SUGGESTED ANOTHER SUSPECT --

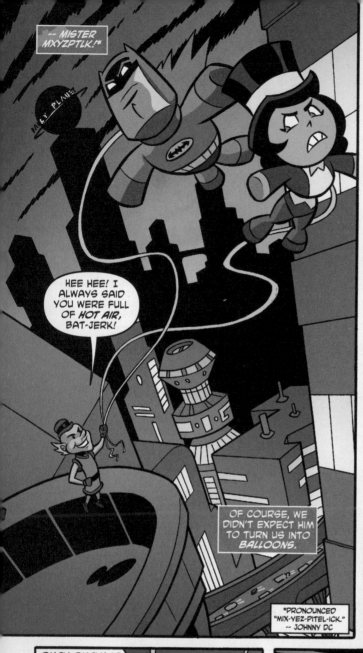

-- MISTER MXYZPTLK!*

HEE HEE! I ALWAYS SAID YOU WERE FULL OF *HOT AIR*, BAT-JERK!

OF COURSE, WE DIDN'T EXPECT HIM TO TURN US INTO *BALLOONS*.

*PRONOUNCED "MIX-YEZ-PITEL-ICK."
-- JOHNNY DC.

AS A *MAGICAL IMP*, MXYZPTLK'S POWER RIVALS ZATANNA'S. BUT WITH HER MOUTH *PAINTED ON*, ZATANNA CAN'T *SPEAK* TO BREAK HIS SPELL.

WHAT TO DO *NOW*, I WONDER? SHOULD I JUST LET YOU BOTH *FLOAT AWAY*? OR MAYBE I SHOULD INTRODUCE YOU TO MY "*POP!*"

THAT MEANS IT'S UP TO *ME*.

WHAT IN THE--? HEY! WATCH IT WITH THE STRING!

OKAY, OKAY! NO NEED TO GO ALL *SCARY EYES*. I GET IT.

I'LL TURN YOU BACK TO NORMAL.

YEESH, AT LEAST *SUPERMAN* CAN TAKE A *JOKE*.

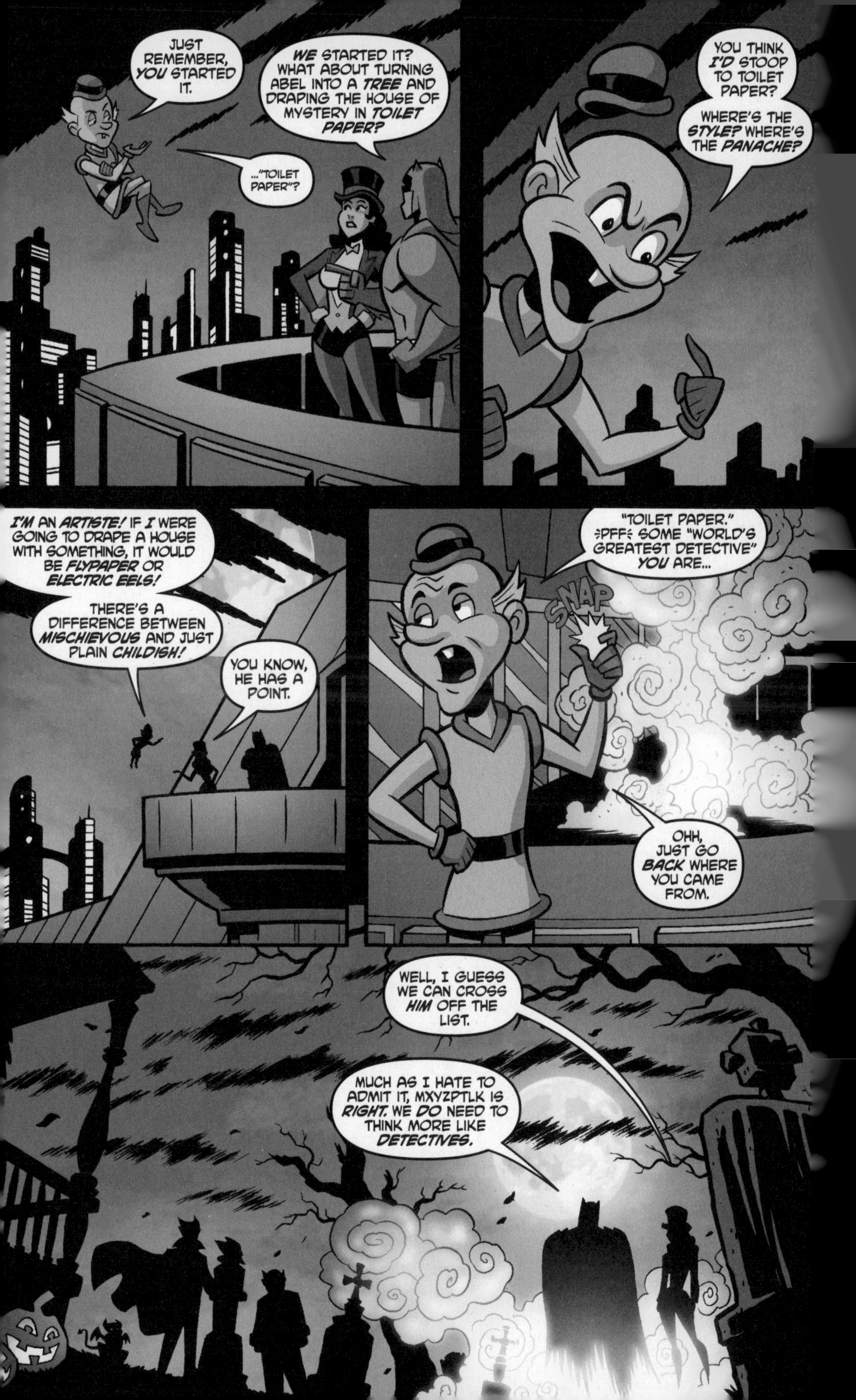
JUST REMEMBER, *YOU* STARTED IT.
WE STARTED IT? WHAT ABOUT TURNING ABEL INTO A *TREE* AND DRAPING THE HOUSE OF MYSTERY IN *TOILET PAPER?*
..."TOILET PAPER"?
YOU THINK *I'D* STOOP TO TOILET PAPER?
WHERE'S THE *STYLE?* WHERE'S THE *PANACHE?*
I'M AN *ARTISTE!* IF *I* WERE GOING TO DRAPE A HOUSE WITH SOMETHING, IT WOULD BE *FLYPAPER* OR *ELECTRIC EELS!*
THERE'S A DIFFERENCE BETWEEN *MISCHIEVOUS* AND JUST PLAIN *CHILDISH!*
YOU KNOW, HE HAS A POINT.
"TOILET PAPER." PFF SOME "WORLD'S GREATEST DETECTIVE" *YOU* ARE...
SNAP
OHH, JUST GO *BACK* WHERE YOU CAME FROM.
WELL, I GUESS WE CAN CROSS *HIM* OFF THE LIST.
MUCH AS I HATE TO ADMIT IT, MXYZPTLK IS *RIGHT.* WE *DO* NEED TO THINK MORE LIKE *DETECTIVES.*

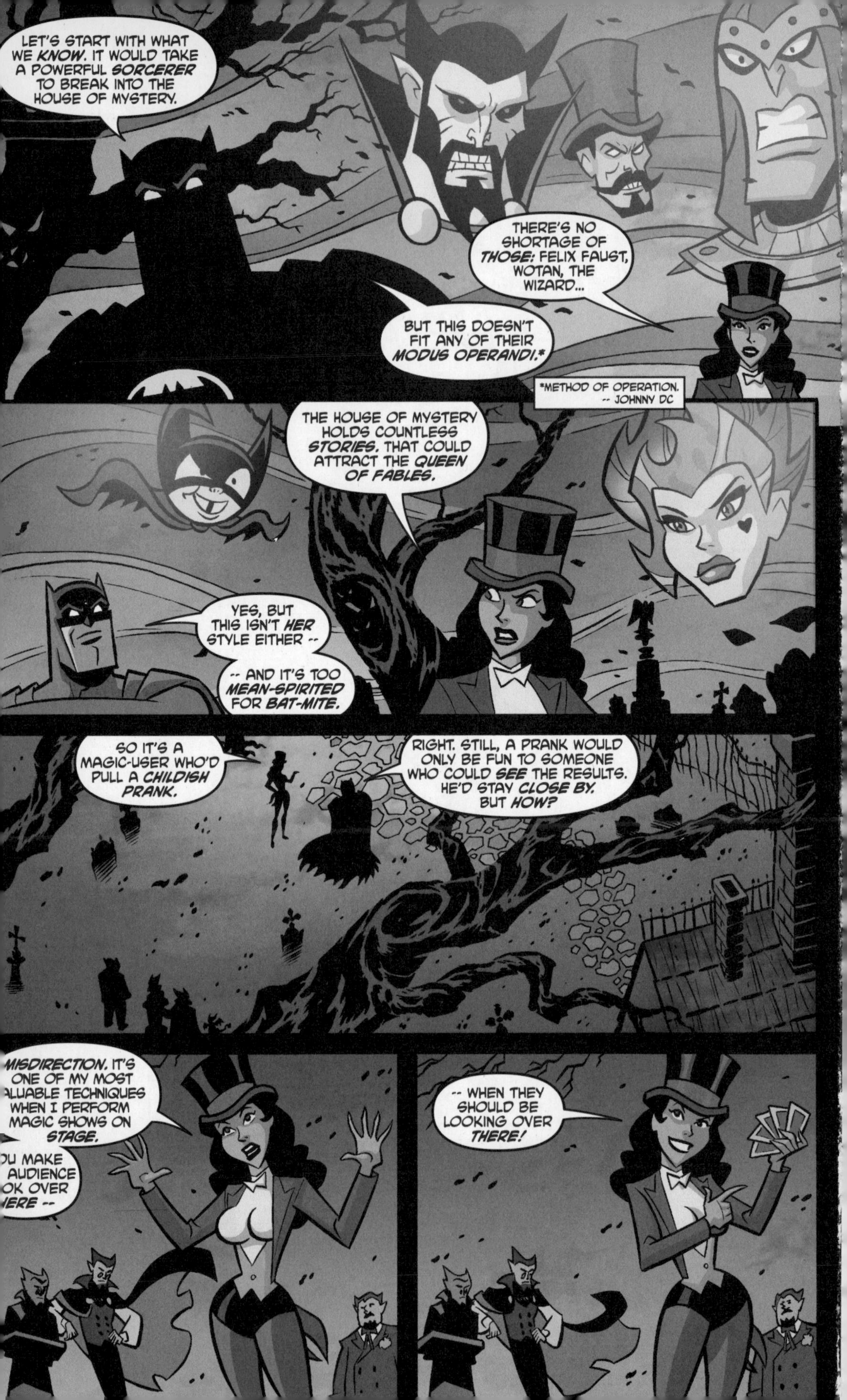
LET'S START WITH WHAT WE KNOW. IT WOULD TAKE A POWERFUL SORCERER TO BREAK INTO THE HOUSE OF MYSTERY.
THERE'S NO SHORTAGE OF THOSE: FELIX FAUST, WOTAN, THE WIZARD...
BUT THIS DOESN'T FIT ANY OF THEIR MODUS OPERANDI.*
*METHOD OF OPERATION. -- JOHNNY DC
THE HOUSE OF MYSTERY HOLDS COUNTLESS STORIES. THAT COULD ATTRACT THE QUEEN OF FABLES.
YES, BUT THIS ISN'T HER STYLE EITHER --
-- AND IT'S TOO MEAN-SPIRITED FOR BAT-MITE.
SO IT'S A MAGIC-USER WHO'D PULL A CHILDISH PRANK.
RIGHT. STILL, A PRANK WOULD ONLY BE FUN TO SOMEONE WHO COULD SEE THE RESULTS. HE'D STAY CLOSE BY. BUT HOW?
MISDIRECTION. IT'S ONE OF MY MOST VALUABLE TECHNIQUES WHEN I PERFORM MAGIC SHOWS ON STAGE.
OU MAKE AUDIENCE OK OVER ERE --
-- WHEN THEY SHOULD BE LOOKING OVER THERE!

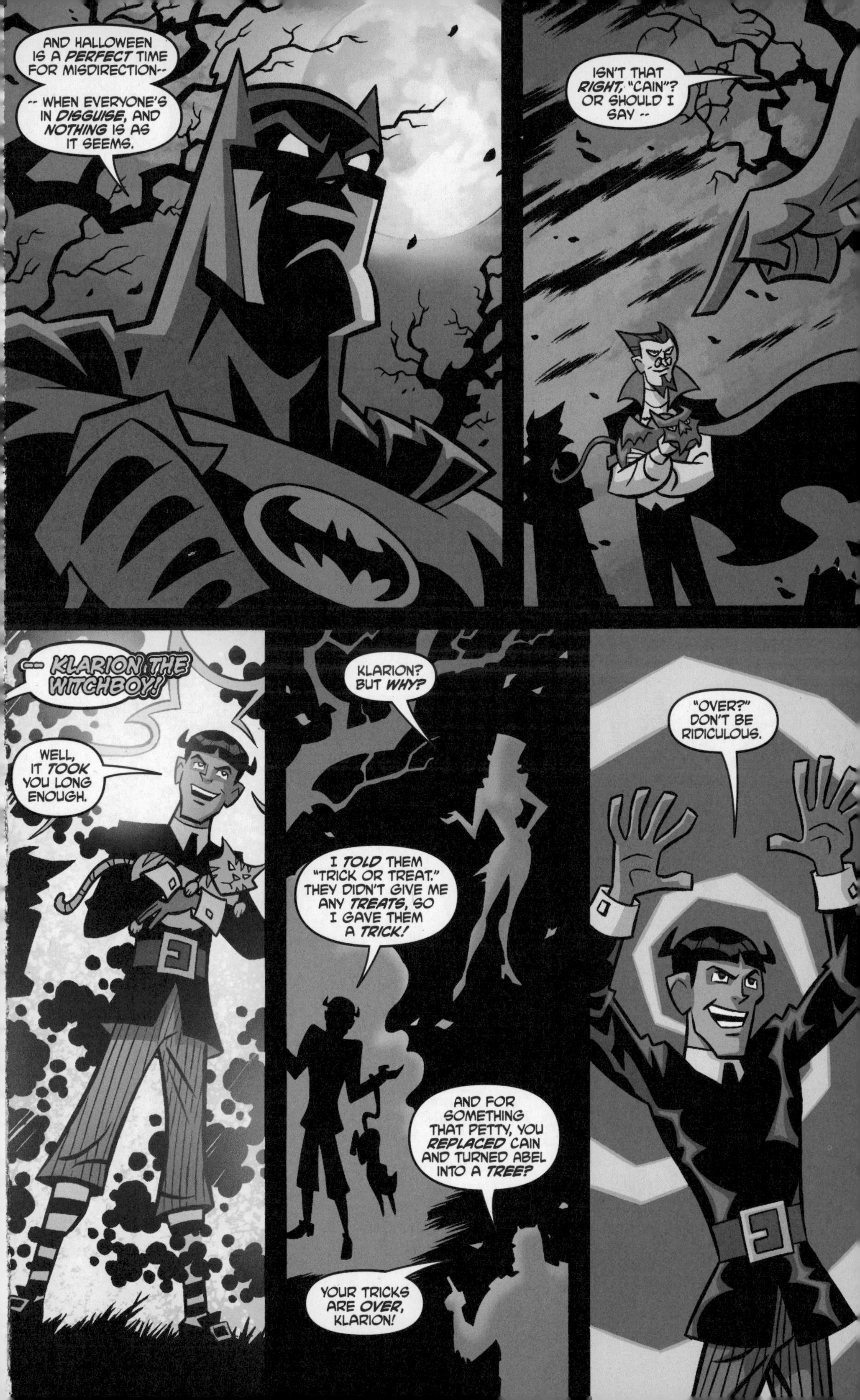
AND HALLOWEEN IS A *PERFECT* TIME FOR MISDIRECTION--
-- WHEN EVERYONE'S IN *DISGUISE*, AND *NOTHING* IS AS IT SEEMS.
ISN'T THAT *RIGHT*, "CAIN"? OR SHOULD I SAY --
-- KLARION THE WITCHBOY!
WELL, IT *TOOK* YOU LONG ENOUGH.
KLARION? BUT *WHY?*
I *TOLD* THEM "TRICK OR TREAT." THEY DIDN'T GIVE ME ANY *TREATS*, SO I GAVE THEM A *TRICK!*
AND FOR SOMETHING THAT PETTY, YOU *REPLACED* CAIN AND TURNED ABEL INTO A *TREE?*
YOUR TRICKS ARE *OVER*, KLARION!
"OVER?" DON'T BE RIDICULOUS.

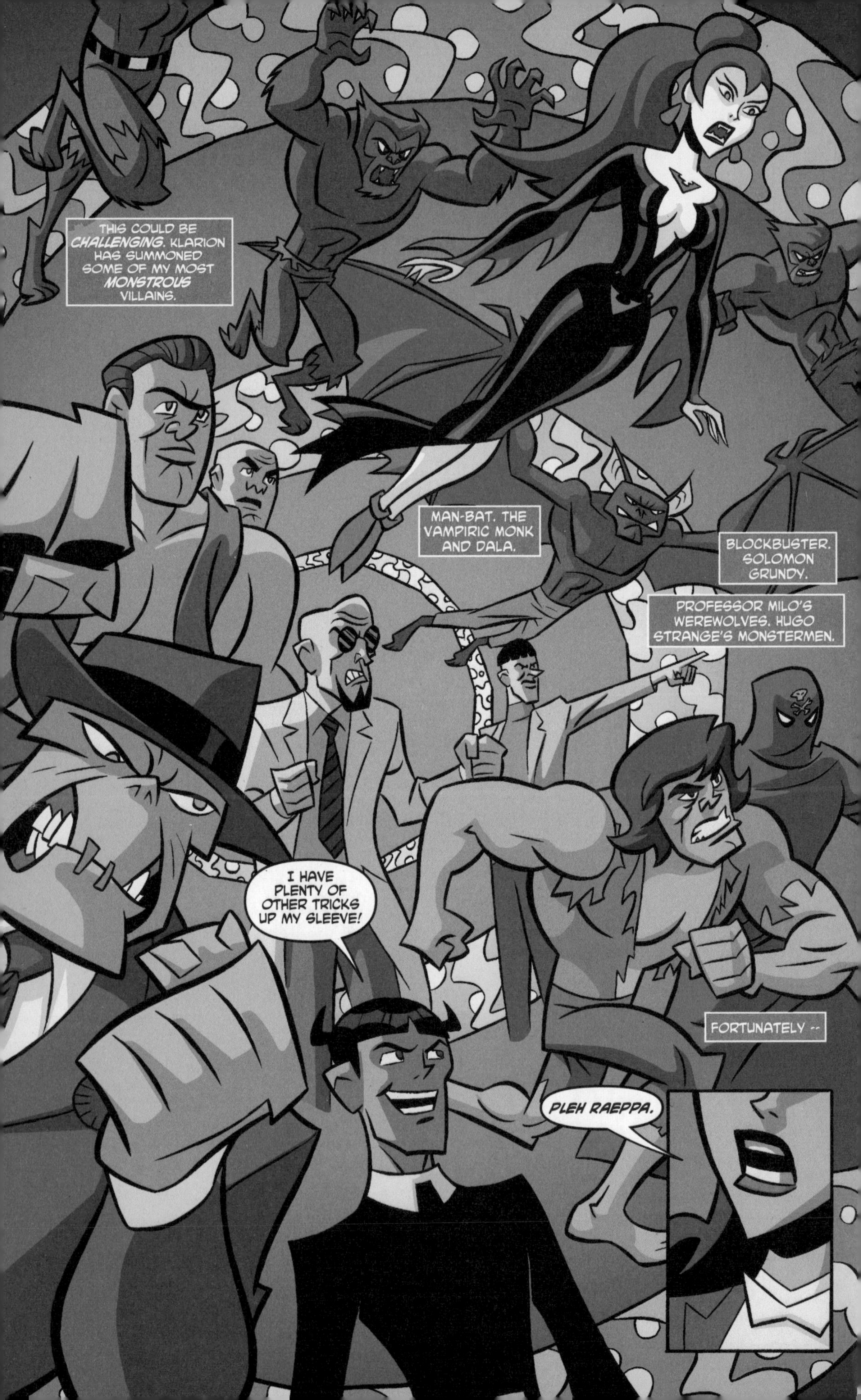
THIS COULD BE *CHALLENGING*. KLARION HAS SUMMONED SOME OF MY MOST *MONSTROUS* VILLAINS.
MAN-BAT. THE VAMPIRIC MONK AND DALA.
BLOCKBUSTER. SOLOMON GRUNDY.
PROFESSOR MILO'S WEREWOLVES. HUGO STRANGE'S MONSTERMEN.
I HAVE PLENTY OF OTHER TRICKS UP MY SLEEVE!
FORTUNATELY --
PLEH RAEPPA.

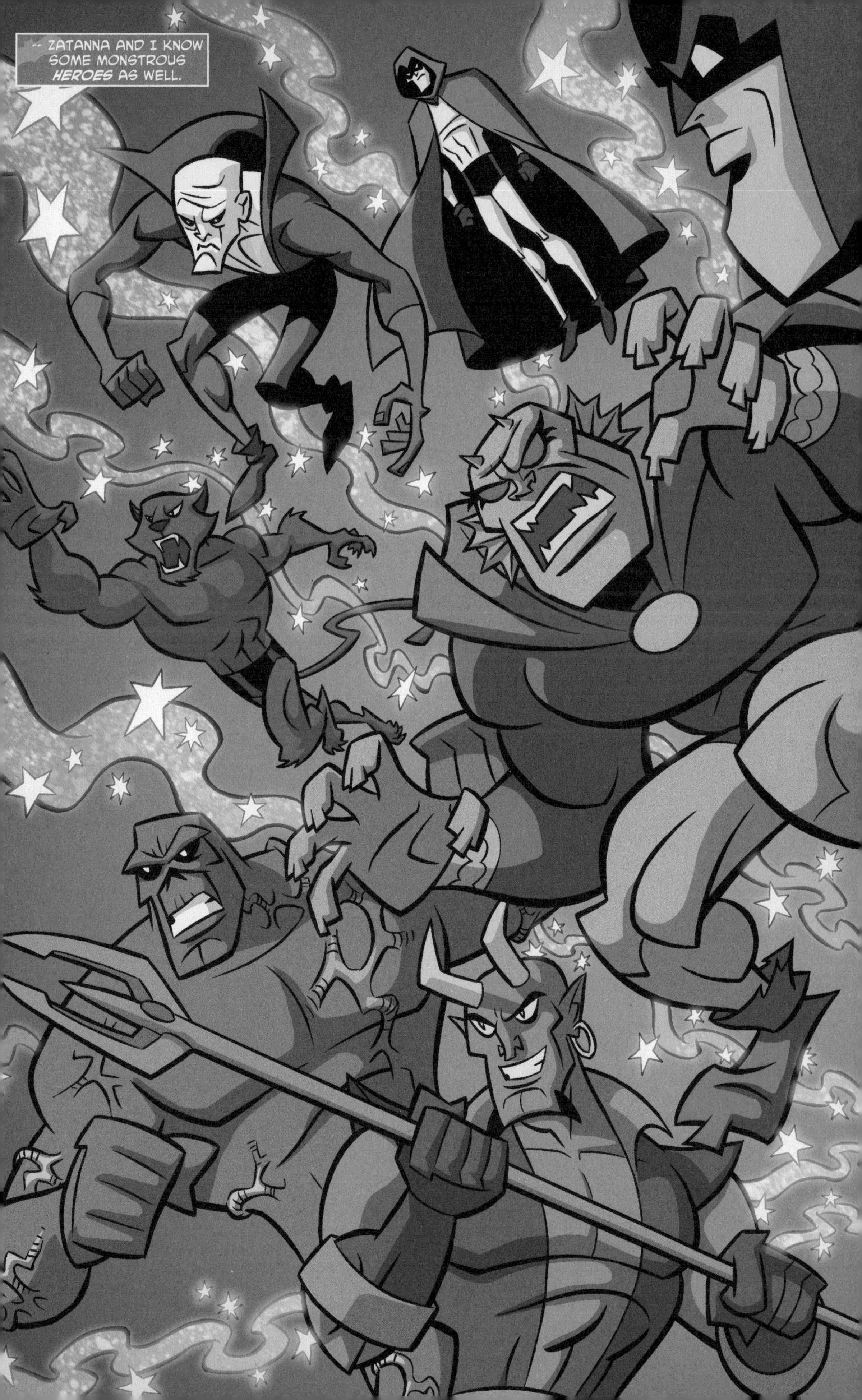
-- ZATANNA AND I KNOW SOME MONSTROUS *HEROES* AS WELL.

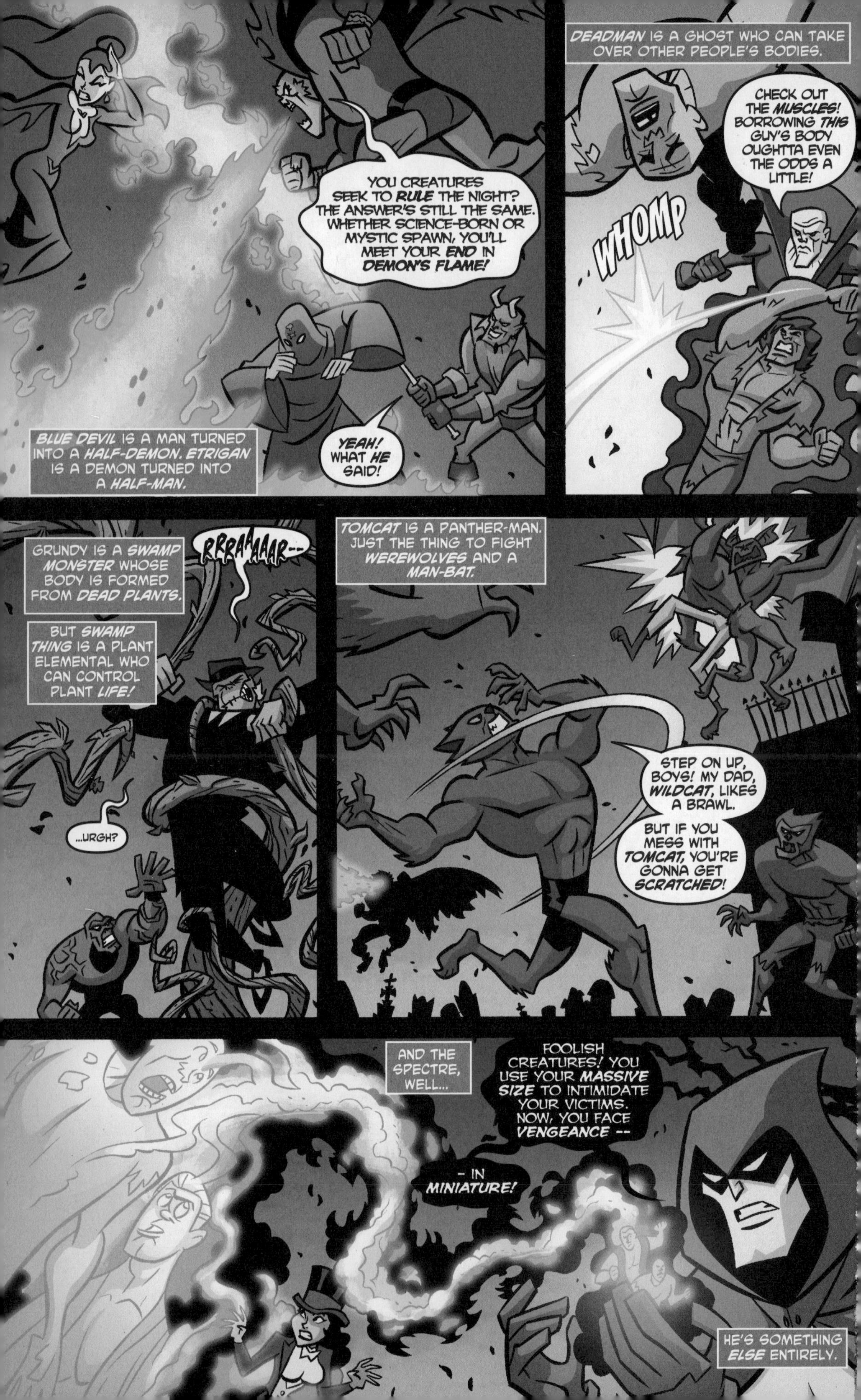
YOU CREATURES SEEK TO RULE THE NIGHT? THE ANSWER'S STILL THE SAME. WHETHER SCIENCE-BORN OR MYSTIC SPAWN, YOU'LL MEET YOUR END IN DEMON'S FLAME!
BLUE DEVIL IS A MAN TURNED INTO A HALF-DEMON. ETRIGAN IS A DEMON TURNED INTO A HALF-MAN.
YEAH! WHAT HE SAID!
DEADMAN IS A GHOST WHO CAN TAKE OVER OTHER PEOPLE'S BODIES.
CHECK OUT THE MUSCLES! BORROWING THIS GUY'S BODY OUGHTTA EVEN THE ODDS A LITTLE!
WHOMP
GRUNDY IS A SWAMP MONSTER WHOSE BODY IS FORMED FROM DEAD PLANTS.
BUT SWAMP THING IS A PLANT ELEMENTAL WHO CAN CONTROL PLANT LIFE!
RRRAAAAAR--
...URGH?
TOMCAT IS A PANTHER-MAN. JUST THE THING TO FIGHT WEREWOLVES AND A MAN-BAT.
STEP ON UP, BOYS! MY DAD, WILDCAT, LIKES A BRAWL.
BUT IF YOU MESS WITH TOMCAT, YOU'RE GONNA GET SCRATCHED!
AND THE SPECTRE, WELL...
FOOLISH CREATURES! YOU USE YOUR MASSIVE SIZE TO INTIMIDATE YOUR VICTIMS. NOW, YOU FACE VENGEANCE --
- IN MINIATURE!
HE'S SOMETHING ELSE ENTIRELY.

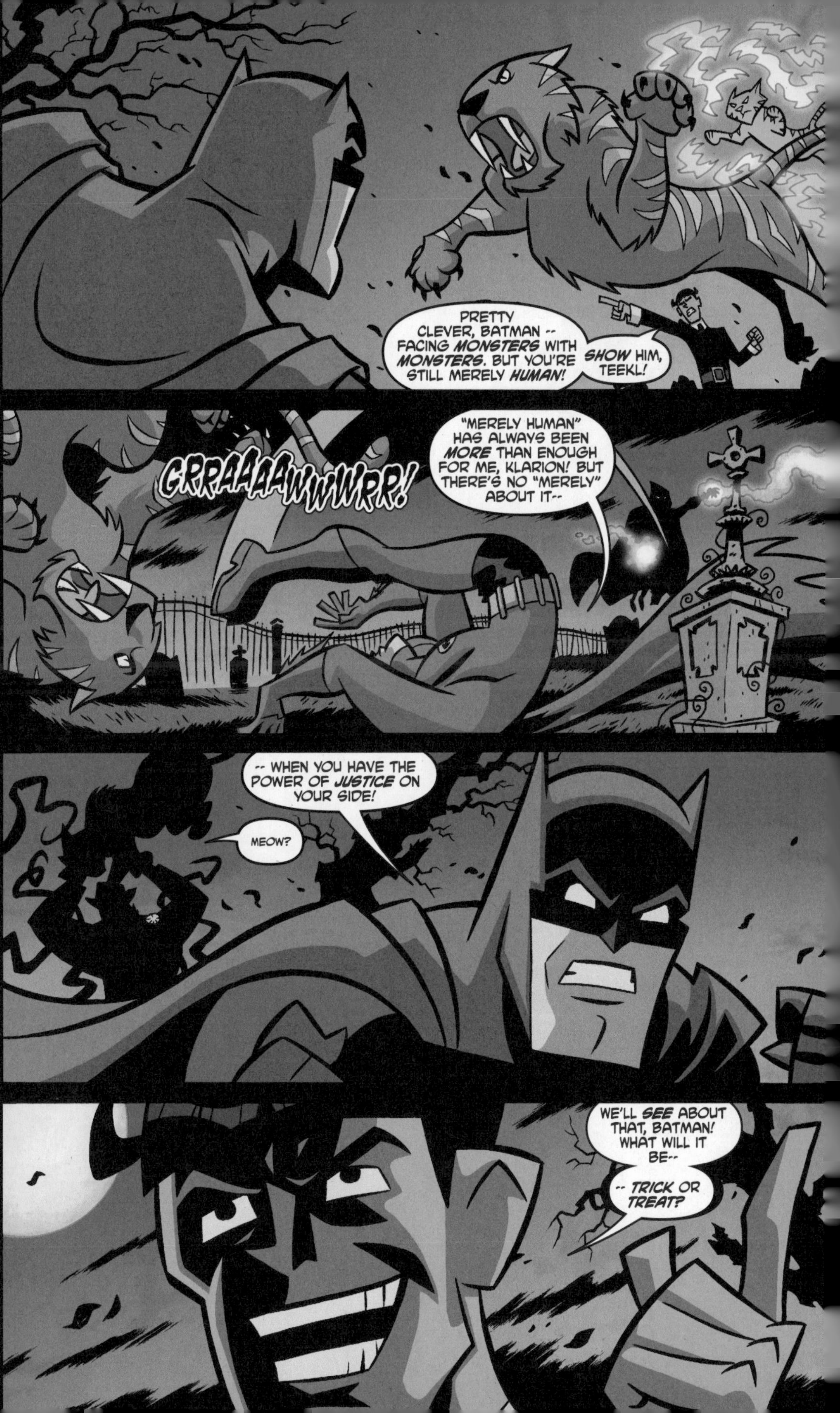
PRETTY CLEVER, BATMAN -- FACING MONSTERS WITH MONSTERS. BUT YOU'RE STILL MERELY HUMAN!
SHOW HIM, TEEKL!
GRRAAAAWWWRR!
"MERELY HUMAN" HAS ALWAYS BEEN MORE THAN ENOUGH FOR ME, KLARION! BUT THERE'S NO "MERELY" ABOUT IT--
-- WHEN YOU HAVE THE POWER OF JUSTICE ON YOUR SIDE!
MEOW?
WE'LL SEE ABOUT THAT, BATMAN! WHAT WILL IT BE--
-- TRICK OR TREAT?

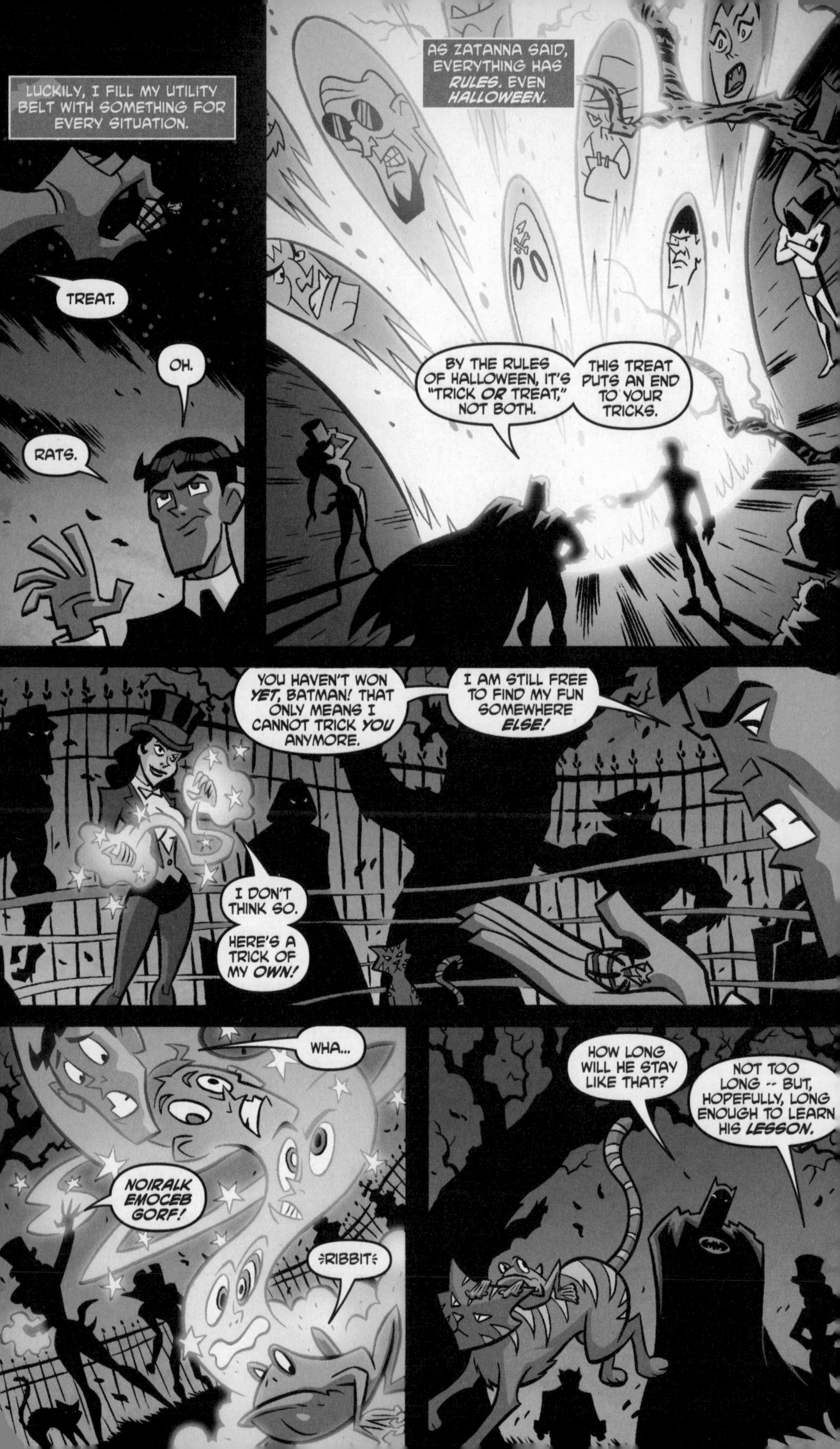
LUCKILY, I FILL MY UTILITY BELT WITH SOMETHING FOR EVERY SITUATION.
TREAT.
OH.
RATS.
AS ZATANNA SAID, EVERYTHING HAS RULES. EVEN HALLOWEEN.
BY THE RULES OF HALLOWEEN, IT'S "TRICK OR TREAT," NOT BOTH.
THIS TREAT PUTS AN END TO YOUR TRICKS.
YOU HAVEN'T WON YET, BATMAN! THAT ONLY MEANS I CANNOT TRICK YOU ANYMORE.
I AM STILL FREE TO FIND MY FUN SOMEWHERE ELSE!
I DON'T THINK SO.
HERE'S A TRICK OF MY OWN!
WHA...
NOIRALK EMOCEB GORF!
RIBBIT
HOW LONG WILL HE STAY LIKE THAT?
NOT TOO LONG -- BUT, HOPEFULLY, LONG ENOUGH TO LEARN HIS LESSON.

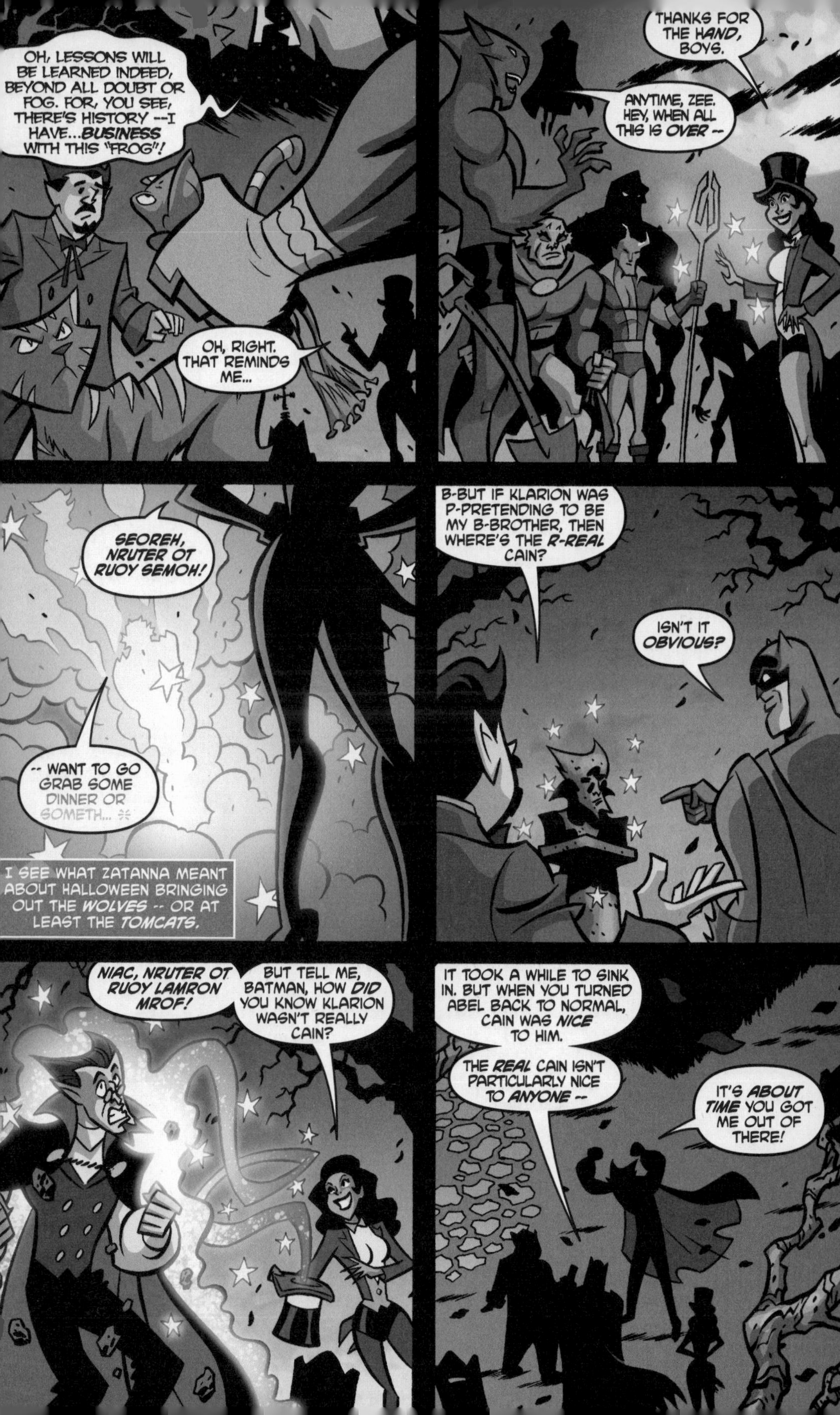
OH, LESSONS WILL BE LEARNED INDEED, BEYOND ALL DOUBT OR FOG. FOR, YOU SEE, THERE'S HISTORY --I HAVE...BUSINESS WITH THIS "FROG"!
OH, RIGHT. THAT REMINDS ME...
THANKS FOR THE HAND, BOYS.
ANYTIME, ZEE. HEY, WHEN ALL THIS IS OVER --
SEOREH, NRUTER OT RUOY SEMOH!
-- WANT TO GO GRAB SOME DINNER OR SOMETH...
I SEE WHAT ZATANNA MEANT ABOUT HALLOWEEN BRINGING OUT THE WOLVES -- OR AT LEAST THE TOMCATS.
B-BUT IF KLARION WAS P-PRETENDING TO BE MY B-BROTHER, THEN WHERE'S THE R-REAL CAIN?
ISN'T IT OBVIOUS?
NIAC, NRUTER OT RUOY LAMRON MROF!
BUT TELL ME, BATMAN, HOW DID YOU KNOW KLARION WASN'T REALLY CAIN?
IT TOOK A WHILE TO SINK IN. BUT WHEN YOU TURNED ABEL BACK TO NORMAL, CAIN WAS NICE TO HIM.
THE REAL CAIN ISN'T PARTICULARLY NICE TO ANYONE --
IT'S ABOUT TIME YOU GOT ME OUT OF THERE!

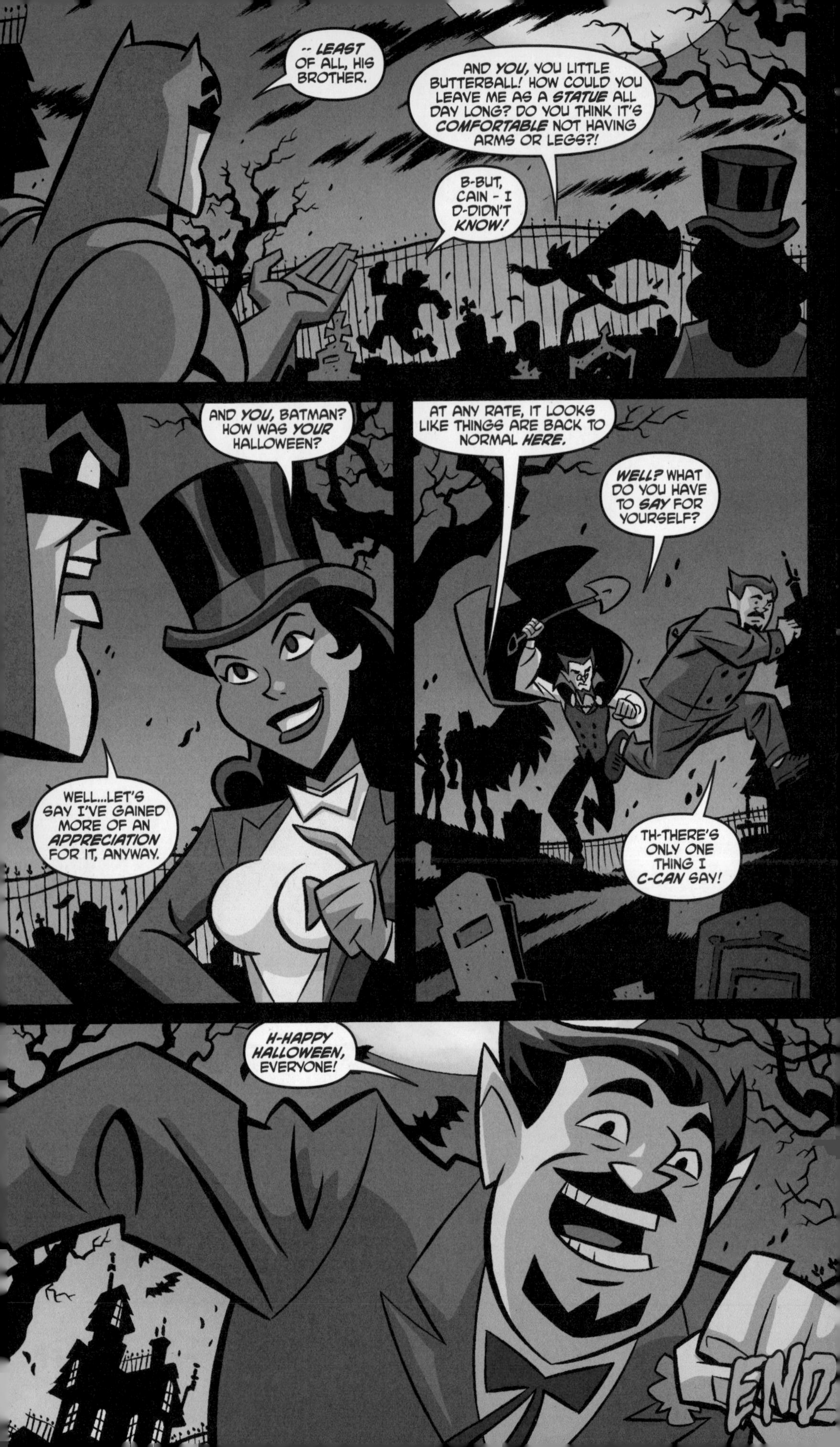
-- LEAST OF ALL, HIS BROTHER.
AND YOU, YOU LITTLE BUTTERBALL! HOW COULD YOU LEAVE ME AS A STATUE ALL DAY LONG? DO YOU THINK IT'S COMFORTABLE NOT HAVING ARMS OR LEGS?!
B-BUT, CAIN - I D-DIDN'T KNOW!
AND YOU, BATMAN? HOW WAS YOUR HALLOWEEN?
WELL...LET'S SAY I'VE GAINED MORE OF AN APPRECIATION FOR IT, ANYWAY.
AT ANY RATE, IT LOOKS LIKE THINGS ARE BACK TO NORMAL HERE.
WELL? WHAT DO YOU HAVE TO SAY FOR YOURSELF?
TH-THERE'S ONLY ONE THING I C-CAN SAY!
H-HAPPY HALLOWEEN, EVERYONE!
END

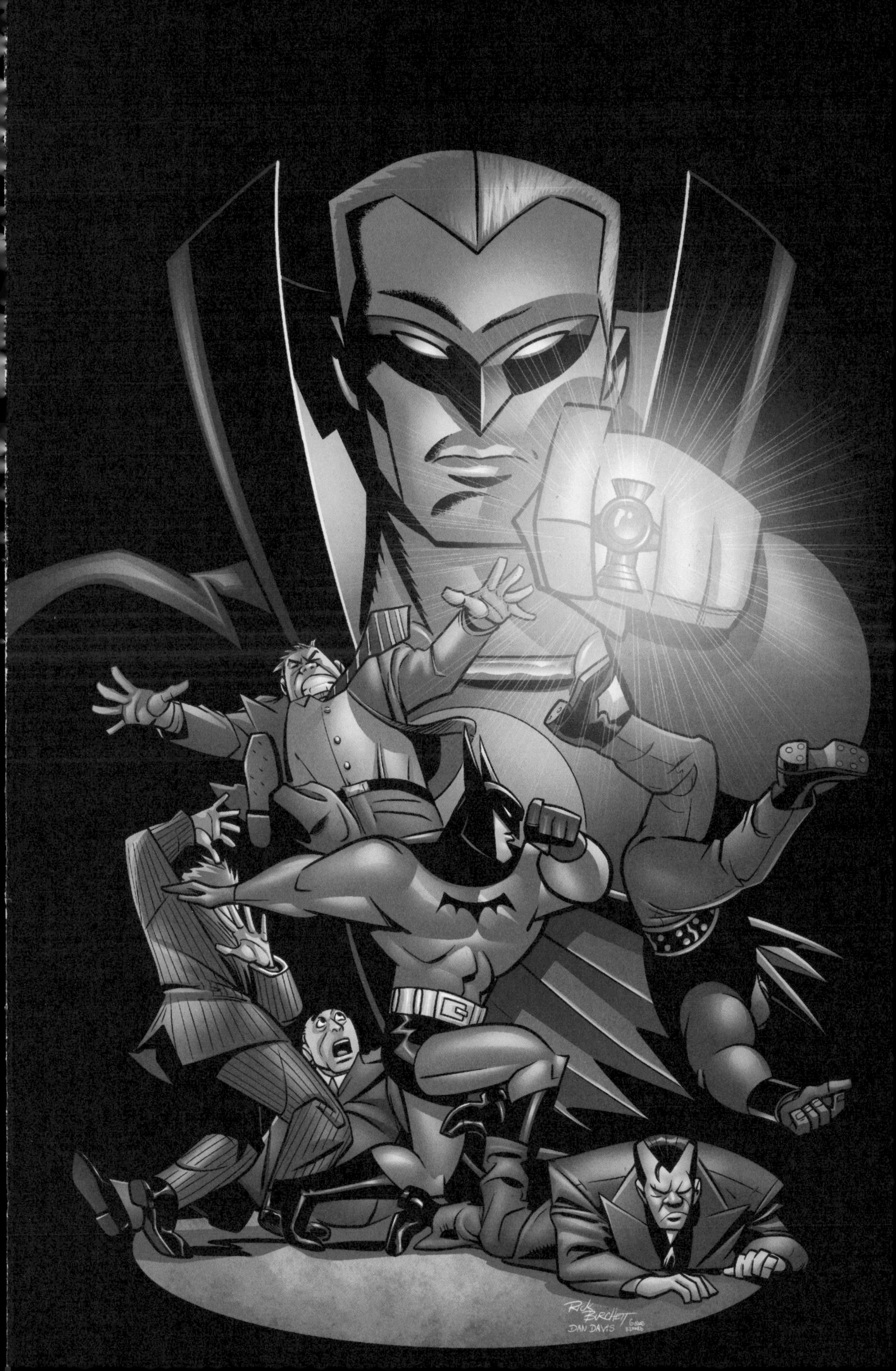
RICK BURCHETT
DAN DAVIS

THE ALL-NEW BATMAN: THE BRAVE AND THE BOLD #8

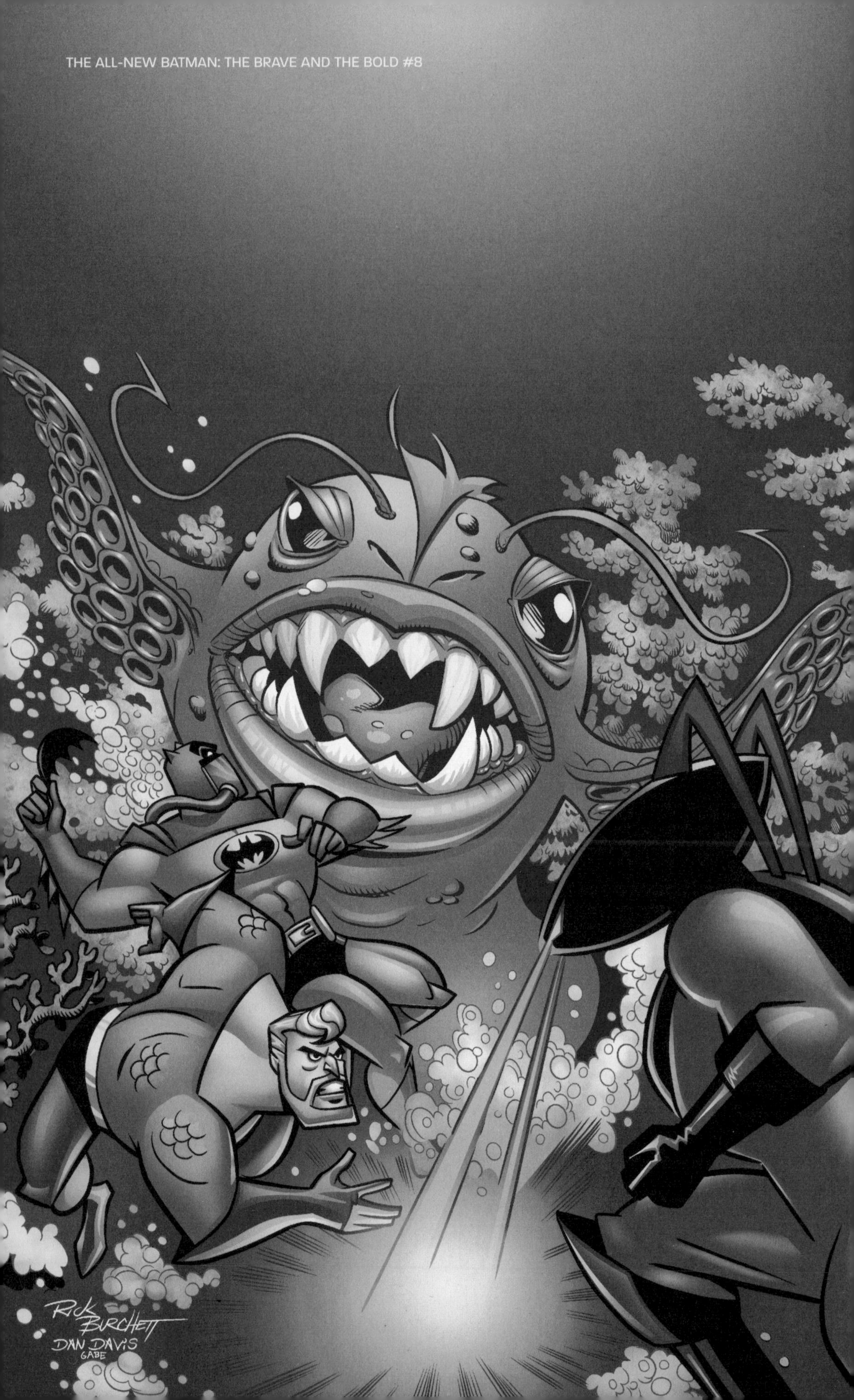
RICK BURCHETT
DAN DAVIS
GABE

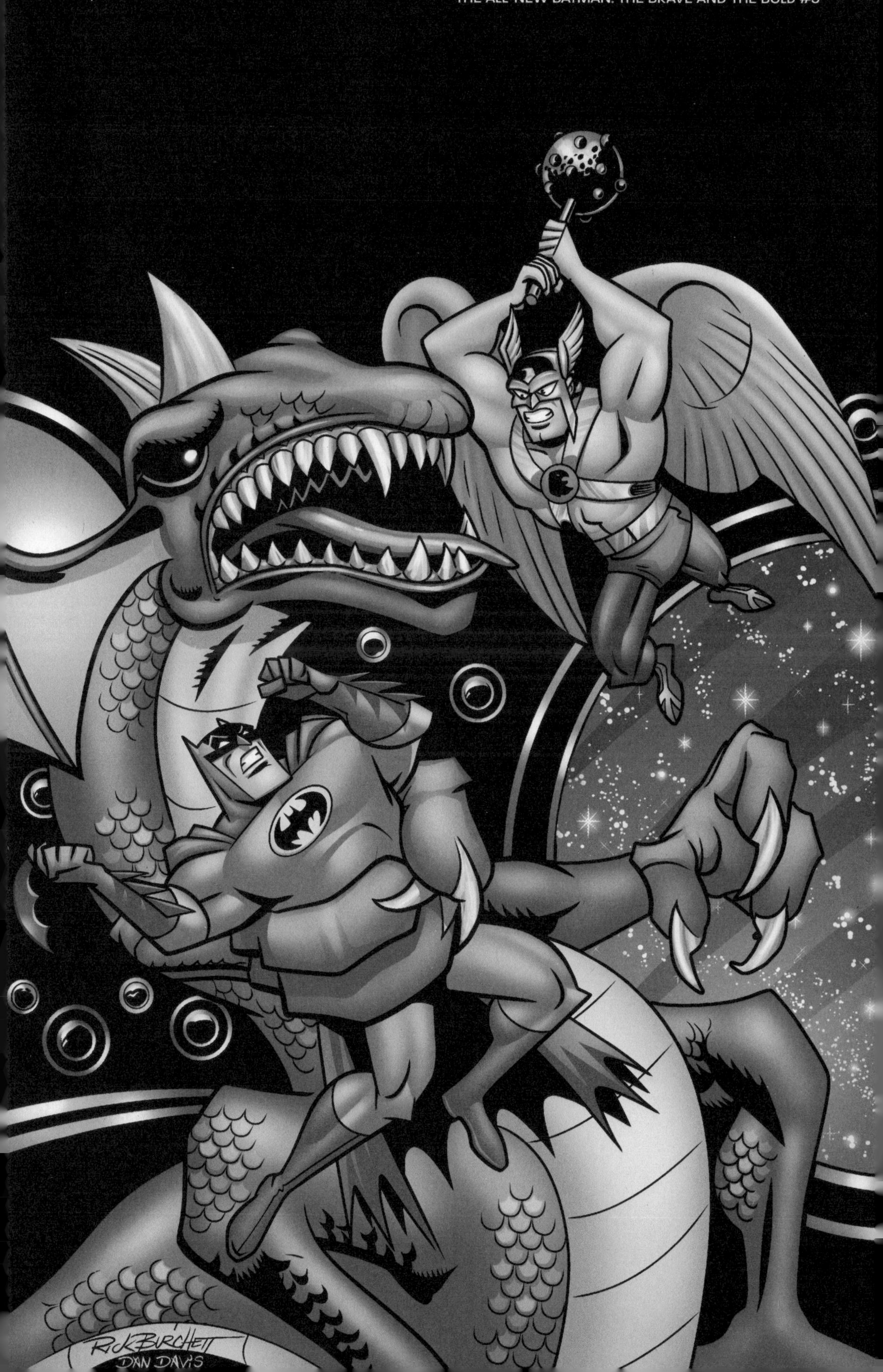
RICK BURCHETT
DAN DAVIS

THE ALL-NEW BATMAN: THE BRAVE AND THE BOLD #10

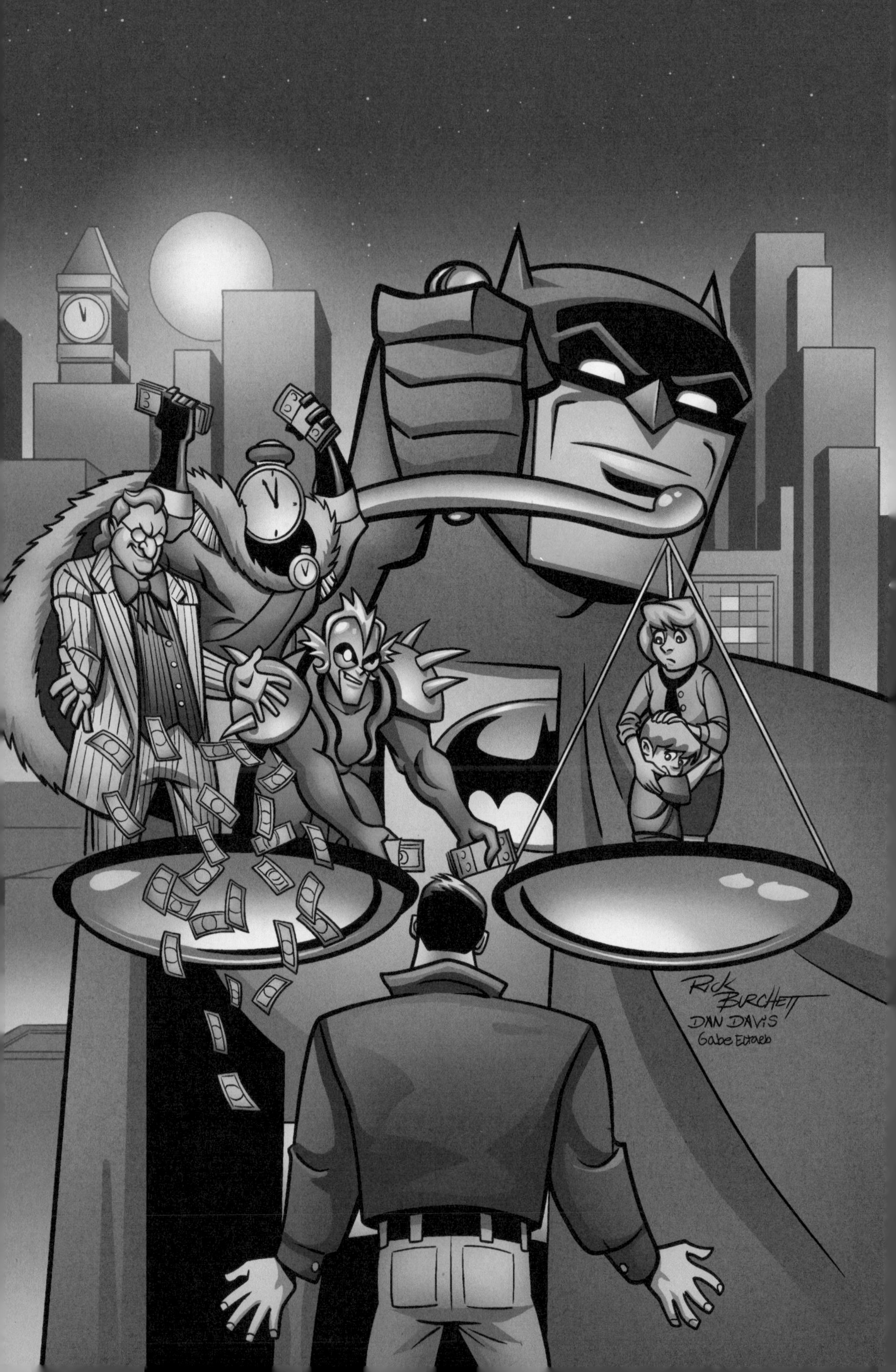
RICK BURCHETT
DAN DAVIS
Gabe Eltaeb

THE ALL-NEW BATMAN: THE BRAVE AND THE BOLD #11

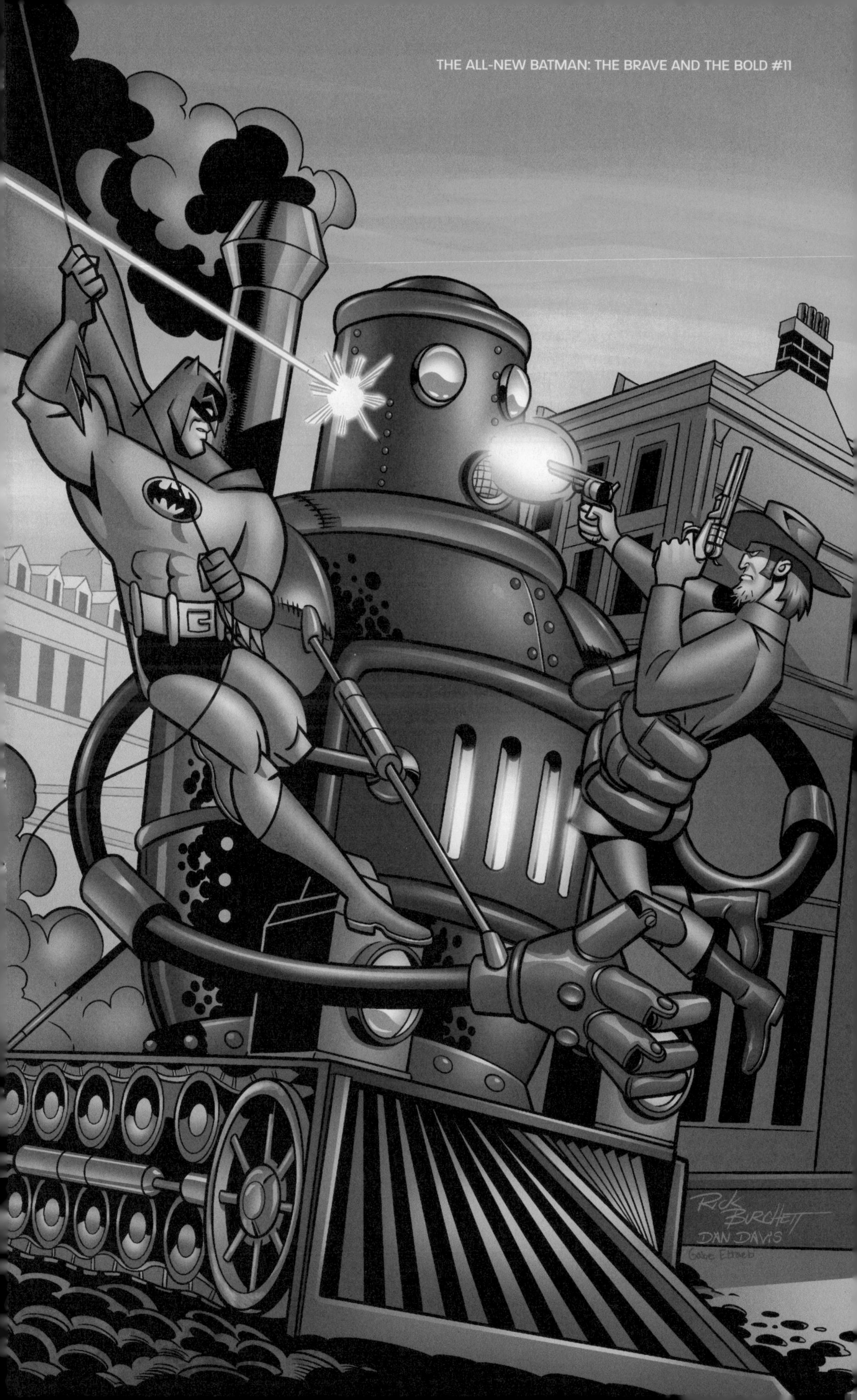
RICK BURCHETT
DAN DAVIS

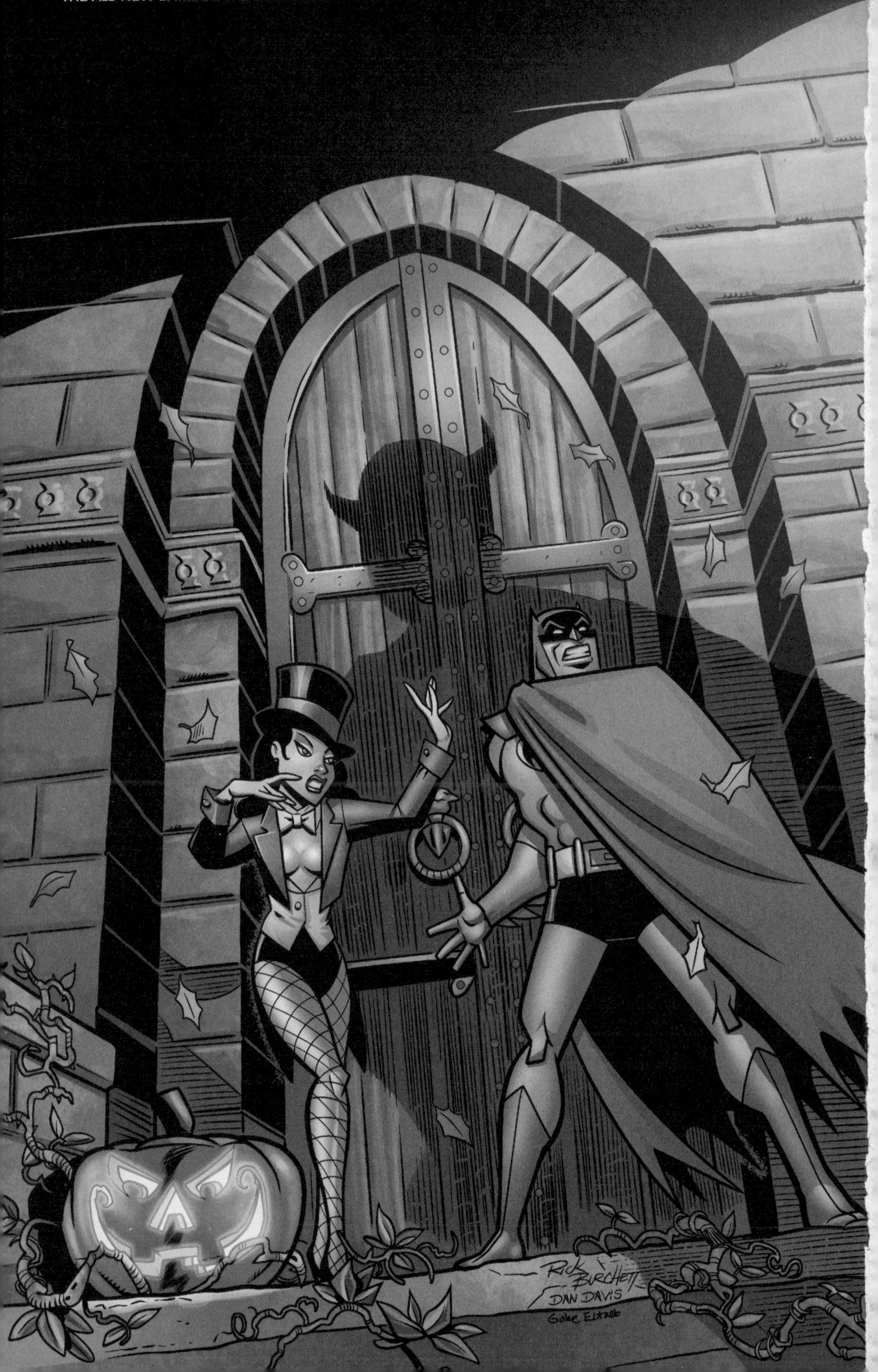
RICK BURCHETT
DAN DAVIS